Murder On Main Street

Mysterious Island or Haunted Place?

HUNTER LAROCHE

authorHOUSE®

AuthorHouse™
1663 Liberty Drive
Bloomington, IN 47403
www.authorhouse.com
Phone: 833-262-8899

Published by AuthorHouse 06/23/2022

ISBN: 978-1-6655-6355-0 (sc)
ISBN: 978-1-6655-6354-3 (e)

Print information available on the last page.

This book is printed on acid-free paper.

DEDICATION

This book is dedicated to Sandal Cate, my editor, for all her hard work to make this book become a reality.

MONHEGAN PLANTATION IN MAINE, UNITED STATES

Monhegan /mɒnˈhiːgən/ is a plantation in Lincoln County, Maine, United States, about 12 nautical miles (22 km) off the mainland. The population was 69 at the 2010 census The island has a tragic story associated with it and a famous personality. (From the New England Historical Society)

In the summer of 1953, Sally Maynard Moran visited Monhegan. She stayed at one of the cottages the artist (Rockwell Kent) still owned, joined by his daughter, Mrs. Kathleen Finney, and her children. One day she announced she was going to take a walk. She was never seen again alive. Three weeks after she disappeared, her body was discovered floating in the ocean off Portland Light. "Mrs. Sally Maynard Moran, 49, New York society figure whose disappearance from the artists' colony was a sensation last July, was murdered and thrown into the sea on the Maine coast, officials announced today," reported the **Chicago Tribune** on Oct. 4, 1953. Pathologists had determined she died of blunt force trauma to the head. They said she couldn't have fallen from Monhegan's 100-foot cliffs, because her body would have had multiple bruises and fractures. The only other injury Sally Moran suffered was a broken arm. Investigators learned two strange men were seen walking near the Kent cottage on the night of her death. An islander heard a voice shout, "Get your hands off me." Did Rockwell Kent have something to do with the murder of Sally Maynard? The rumor dogged him for years. The theory about the Monhegan murder had several flaws. One was that Kent was in New York at the time of Sally Maynard's death. Another was that she wasn't murdered – at least according to her grandniece, **Martha Wolfe of Winchester, Va.** The Kennebec County *attorney general gave Wolfe copies of the cold case file in 2006. Wolfe then pored over the files and concluded her great-aunt's death was an accident. Kent and his wife believed she committed suicide because she couldn't face leaving the island. They had gotten her a job as a secretary because her ex-husband's business reverses lowered her alimony. Sally Maynard Moran had fallen into despair and uncertainty, her psychiatrist told the Kents.*

September, 1972

Ricky Blair was strolling up Main Street on Nantucket Island with his golden retriever, Madaket, who was walking a few paces behind him. It was seven-thirty in the morning and what seemed to him to be starting off to be a wonderful day. The skies were clear, the sun was shining and there was a light breeze which made a perfect recipe for a September morning. Rick, in his patrolman's outfit, was now in his sixth year of working with the Nantucket Police Department. He had several jobs going at once. He did pet sitting for a few island families who visited every summer season. Additionally, for three or four days a week he would host the 'Sconset Whisperer walking tour several times a day. He enjoyed the island and all it had to offer to someone like him.

On this particular morning, as he was walking past Bob Tonkin's car which was parked in front of Tonkin's Antiques store on Main Street. Madaket stopped and started looking directly at the old Jeep Wagoneer that Mr. Tonkins owned. When Rick looked back, he gave a short little whistle to Madaket, but the dog was fixated on the automobile and did not move. Rick whistled again, but still Madaket would not move.

Rick knew one thing about Madaket - when that dog's mind was made up about something Rick could never dissuade it to leave something alone. Madaket silently implored Rick to look into whatever the dog was watching.

Rick walked back to where Madaket was sitting and asked, "So, Madaket, what's on your mind?"

Madaket looked up at Rick and then back to the car.

Rick said, "OK, Madaket, let me look inside and check it out."

He went to the driver's side window which was lowered about a quarter of the way as were all the others. First, he peered into the back seat. Then he went to the rear window and looked in the cargo area. Nothing seemed out of place. He observed that the car did not have any flat tires. It just looked like a normal car parked on Main Street.

Rick went back to the sidewalk to where Madaket was waiting and said, "OK, everything is fine here, pup. Let's get going." But Madaket would not move. He would not take his eyes off the car. Rick was perplexed as he knew that Madaket had very strong instincts and had proven it many times in the past.

Rick bent down, rubbed the dog behind his ears but Madaket was not moving, not an inch. Rick thought to himself, knowing the dog's keen sense, there had to be something bothering him about the car. So he went to the passenger's side front door and opened it up only to see, all curled up and tangled up in her leash, Bob Tonkin's King Charles Spaniel puppy, Daisy, tucked halfway under the front seat. Rick quickly untangled Daisy and picked her up. She was panting heavily and seemed a little shaken.

Rick thought that Mr. Tonkin must have arrived at his shop early and left Daisy in the car so he could grab a quick breakfast following which he would then return and take Daisy into his office.

Rick knocked on the door of Tonkin's Antiques. He looked inside through the front door window panes. The door was locked so he could not enter. He tied Daisy to the bench in front of the pharmacy which was just a few doors up from the store. He went inside to get her a small cup of water. Daisy just about inhaled every drop. Madaket stood right beside Daisy the entire time, not moving from her side.

Rita Mignosa was walking down the street when she saw Daisy and Rick Blair. She stopped to pet Daisy and started up a conversation with Rick. As she was petting Daisy, she asked Rick, "Where is Bob? Enjoying breakfast at one of the morning restaurants?"

Rick said, "Well, Rita, oddly enough Madaket and I were walking up the street when Madaket did an abrupt halt in front of Bob's car and would not budge. I found Daisy all tangled up on the floor of the passenger's seat. Poor puppy!"

Rita replied, "We all know Bob likes to arrive in town early, have breakfast somewhere and start his day. It's still quite cool so you can most likely just put Daisy back into the car. I can see the windows are down and I'm sure Bob will be back soon. I will keep an eye out for him from our store."

"Thanks, Rita, I need to get on with my morning patrol. I hope you have a good day's business ahead! Come on, Madaket, we have work to do!"

Rita gave Daisy a kiss on top of her head and continued onto her grocery market.

Rick put Daisy back into the front seat of Mr. Tonkin's Jeep, and he and Madaket were on their way. After walking about twenty feet Madaket stopped and turned back towards Bob's car. But this time the dog was looking more towards the antique shop. Rick looked at Madaket, and said with mild exasperation, "Now what?"

Madaket just turned around, walked to the entrance of Tonkin's Antiques and started scratching at the door. As Rick hustled to the door to get Madaket, Sylvia Lussier stopped to comment.

"My goodness, Rick," she exclaimed. "Al and I were walking by here late last night after dinner at the Boarding House, and Bob's car was parked right there. I tell you, he works some long hours. And here he's already back in the office, I guess. Good for him! You have got to make hay when the sun shines! It's a short season for sales as we all know."

Madaket started whining, and Sylvia chuckled. "It looks like he wants to get inside and buy an antique water bowl! Your dog has expensive taste!" She laughed and strolled away.

Rick focused on Madaket. "What is it, boy? What's got you spooked?"

Once again Rick peered into the storefront window. As he didn't see anything out of the ordinary, he reached into his satchel and pulled out Madaket's leash. He attached it to his collar and said, "OK, enough Madaket, let's move!"

Reluctantly Madaket walked away with Rick but not before looking back at the shop a couple of times.

Rick and Madaket returned to the station just a couple of blocks away from the antique shop. Jimmy Jaksic was sitting at the dispatcher's desk reading a magazine. He looked up and queried with a smile, "Anything big happening in the metropolis of Nantucket?"

Rick told him, "Morning, Jimmy. Nah, no big news. We just noticed that Bob Tonkin's dog, Daisy, was all tangled up in her leash on the passenger seat of his Wagoneer. He must be having breakfast somewhere. Other than that, all is fine and dandy in Nantucket proper."

Back on Main Street, Rita and Don were sitting out front on the bench of Mignosa's Market when Rita said worriedly, "You know, something's not right."

Don asked, "What do you mean, my dear?"

Rita explained the story about Daisy being all tangled up in the front seat of Bob's car, and how Rick Blair got the dog untangled and gave it some water. She ended saying, "So Rick put Daisy back into the car figuring Bob would return any time now. I promised I would keep an eye out for Bob. I'm going to walk up there and check on Daisy. Bob should have been back by now. He's always open for business by eight a.m."

Don volunteered, "Why don't I walk up there with you? We've got enough early coverage in the store."

When they got up to the car, Daisy was still sitting on the front seat. Then it struck Rita who informed Don, "Hey, Don, I just realized that when I left the store last night, Bob's car was in the exact same spot as it was now. That seems a bit strange."

Don did not pay much attention to her comment but did offer, "Hold on. Let me get a small bowl of water, the dog might still be thirsty. Maybe Bob got sidetracked talking with a client."

When Don offered a small bowl Daisy inhaled it.

Rita then said, "Let me take her for a quick walk. She's been here for a bit of time now."

"OK, Rita. I'll head back to the store. See you soon," replied Don.

Daisy definitely needed to go, and Rita sensed it. Why would the dog need to go so urgently if Bob had walked her prior to going to his office? Even the amount of water that Rick had given her should not have had such an urgent effect on her. It was now eight-thirty, and this she knew was not like Bob at all as he was a very punctual person.

Rita then took Daisy to the market. She noticed Mark and Carol McGarvey sitting in a booth at Les' Lunch Box. She stopped over to say hello. Daisy started wagging her tail and nudging Carol's leg. Carol was Bob Tonkin's landscaper. She also dog sat Daisy wen Bob had to go off island. It was often hard for Carol to give Daisy back to Bob as they had a lot of fun together. Carol really adored Daisy!

Carol asked, "So, Rita, why are you walking Daisy?"

Rita quickly explained that perhaps Bob had a longer meeting with a client over breakfast, and she noticed Daisy still in the car when typically, both the dog and her owner would be in the shop by this hour. So she had decided to take her for a short walk and then to the market. She had left a note to that effect on Bob's windshield.

Carol reached down to pet Daisy and said, "That was thoughtful. Hopefully her 'daddy' will be along to pick her up soon! So good to see you, Rita!"

Rita walked into the back of the market and placed a beach towel on the floor of her office, and Daisy quickly made it into her new bed. She curled up and watched Rita's every move. Rita then called the police station and asked to speak with Constable Kosmo. She was told that he would not be in until eleven as he had a meeting with the town council. She asked if he could please call her as soon as he returned to the station.

Rita then told Don, "Something's not right. I could swear I remember Bob's car being parked right where it is now when I walked home last night. The chance of that is pretty slim, wouldn't you say?"

Don replied, "Well, you know he always arrives early and there are hardly any cars parked on Main Street early in the morning. Maybe it's just a coincidence. And we both know he would never leave Daisy alone in the car for any stretch of time." Don reached down and patted Daisy on the head.

"I know, but something doesn't feel right," Rita repeated. As she worked around the store she kept looking over to Tonkin's Antiques. She could still see the yellow note paper under Bob's windshield wiper that she had left for him so he wouldn't think Daisy has been kidnapped.

Shortly, Bob Molder entered Mignosa's Market and saw Rita. He greeted her, "Hello, I see old Bob is back at it bright and early today! He was at our place last night for a Scotch and a glass of wine. He ordered his usual steak frites. When he finished, he headed right out."

"Oh, really?" commented Rita, picturing the scene. "I know he stops off to see you often. What time did he leave last night?"

Bob answered, "It must have been around eight or so as it was starting to get dark."

Rita continued, "Was Daisy with him?"

"No, he said Daisy was curled up in the car, sleeping soundly! He said he had a very good day, sold a very nice painting that a lady had stopped by numerous times to view. And she finally made the purchase. He also mentioned that he had been up to Boston last week with an extremely rare object. He told me it was brought to him last month by someone here on the island. Bob said he took it to Boston and spent two days with a very well-informed man on the subject of the item. Both of them wanted to research the item in more depth. Then he brought it back with him. Furthermore, he said that if it turns out to be what this Harvard antiques expert thinks it is, and if it genuine, then it would make the news big time. The expert believes it might be a real find as he specializes in extremely rare artifacts, but at this point both of the men believe it is just a copycat piece, a counterfeit, or a knock off."

Bob took a breath, held a finger up to his lips indicating a possible secret, and continued. "As of now he has not told his clients anything about the findings as to whether it might be genuine or a fake. He is just on hold awaiting more information from the historian guy in Boston. Then he just paid his check, said he was going to pick up some catalogs at the office and then head home."

Rita then related the story to Bob about Rick Blair finding Daisy all tangled up in the front seat of Bob's car, and how she thought the car had been parked at the same spot the night before, and also stated that Bob is always open by eight a.m. and it was now going on close to nine.

Bob Molder thought that was strange as well, as everyone knew how fond of animals Bob was, and he would never leave a pet in a car for a long period of time.

Rita added that Daisy was extremely thirsty when Rick Blair gave her some water and also when Don did as well. She said she was surprised by the fact Daisy needed to relieve herself almost right away when Rita took her for a walk, figuring if Bob had taken her out prior to arriving in town then she would not have been so desperate to go for a walk. She ended saying things did not add up in Rita's mind as to where Bob Tonkin was at the moment.

Bob Molder said, "Beats me. I came in to get a few things for the restaurant, so I'd better get on with it. Let me know if anything surfaces or if I can help in any way. How's your stock of Romaine lettuce?"

Rita gave Bob a thumbs up and he headed to the produce section of the store. "See ya soon, and thanks."

Back in the office, Rita looked at Daisy who was sleeping soundly. Rita called the police station again and gave a message to Jim Jaksic for Kosmo to call her as soon as possible. Then she asked if Kosmo might have his radio with him.

Jimmy said, "Hold for a moment. Let me try him."

Fifteen minutes later Kosmo walked into Mignosa's Market. Rita once again retold the story from start to finish about Daisy, Rick Blair, and how the car seemed to be in the same spot as the night before, saying things just did not add up to her.

Kosmo called into the station from his walkie-talkie, and asked if Deputy Donato had arrived yet?

Right then Mark Donato entered the station. Jimmy Jaksic pointed to the microphone and Mark jumped right over to it. Constable Kosmo asked him to go and look in the box with the spare keys of all the downtown stores and find the one for Tonkins Antiques. Then Mark should bring it and meet him there.

Mark replied excitedly, "What's up? Break in? Shooting? What gives?"

Kosmo rolled his eyes and reassured him, "No, nothing like that, Deputy. It's just I need to check something out. I will see you in a few minutes. Thanks."

Mark arrived all out of breath as he half walked and half ran to the Main Street store. Rita was there waiting with Kosmo who said to Rita, "Just wait out here for a moment, Rita, while we check things out inside the shop."

The deputy unlocked the front door, and even though there was some very good sunlight coming in through the front windows, they turned on the inside lights. They cautiously entered and at first glance everything looked normal. Then they noticed that off to one side a mirror had fallen and shattered onto the floor.

Mark, thinking it slipped off the dresser it was sitting on, said, "Well, that's going to take a couple sweepings to clean up, all that shattered glass on the floor. I hope it was not an expensive piece."

Kosmo thought differently but said nothing.

Mark informed his boss, "I'll head back to his office to make sure the back door is secure."

One thing that Kosmo had noticed was that the front door had an automatic lock closure on it. Therefore, if it was in locked mode, once someone shut the door it remained closed until a person used a key to unlock it. He left the door slightly open.

Kosmo said to Mark, "Let's do this together and slowly. There is no rush. Let's just see what plays out here. For all we know Mr. Tonkin will walk through the front door any moment now."

As they made their way towards the back of the store Kosmo and Mark also noticed some things that seemed to have been knocked over lying on the floor. Kosmo now knew that something was not right. He told Mark, "Let's take this very slowly. Something is wrong here. It almost appears like a burglary has taken place."

Mark, who was now all wide-eyed, had his hand on his pistol ready for action.

Several feet ahead of them Kosmo spotted two feet on the floor. The rest of the body was hidden by a large armoire. Mark almost jumped out of his skin! There lay Bob Tonkin in a pool of semi-dried blood from a large gash which most likely was in the back of his head.

"Oh, my gosh, Chief! What do we do now?" Mark had never seen an apparently dead body except at family funerals.

"Just hang on, Mark, and if you feel a little faint, go sit on that chair over there. I'll take it from here."

Kosmo radioed the station to get the paramedics from the fire station. He asked Jimmy Jaksic to send Rick Blair, minus his dog, with some crime scene tape right away to Tonkin's.

The next day, all the residents of the island were talking about Bob Tonkin's murder. Rita was working in the market, and Daisy was following her down all of the aisles of the store. Rita looked down at her and said, "What am I going to do with you, you cutie pie?"

Right then Carol McGarvey entered the store. Daisy saw her and ran right over to her, tail wagging nonstop. Over coffee in Les' Lunchbox, Carol and Rita discussed the horrible event that had been revealed the day before. Rita stroked Daisy, knowing she was now an orphan. Daisy jumped up on the table and wiggled her way into Carol's lap! They both realized that Carol was now going to be Daisy's new owner. At least one good thing resulted from the tragedy on the island.

MUSKEGET ISLAND, NANTUCKET

Muskeget Island is part of the terminal moraine marking the maximum extent of the last glacial ice sheet to reach the northeastern coast. It has an area of 292 acres (1.18 km²). The Muskeget Island group contains Dry Shoal, Skiff Island, Tombolo Point, and Adams Island. Much of Muskeget is owned by the town of Nantucket. There are currently two unoccupied shacks on the island, both of which are remnants of old structures. Muskeget has a high elevation of fourteen feet. Its northern shore is mostly sand dunes, while its southern shore is mainly marshes. A sandy point protects the lagoon.

April 1972

Six months prior…

Beth English was on duty at the police station. The phone rang. Beth answered, "Nantucket Police station, how may I direct your call?"

"This is Harbor Master Ted Hudgins. Put me through to the chief right away."

"OK, Ted, please hold. Let me patch you through."

Beth buzzed her boss. "Chief, Harbor Master Ted Hudgins is on line one requesting to be put through to you right away, as he stated."

"OK, Beth, patch him through. Thanks."

"Kosmo here. What's up, Ted?"

"With Malice Towards None," Ted said loudly.

"What?" Kosmo asked.

"Oh, it's just a quote I am working on, Chief. You see, I have to give a presentation for the Ladies Club luncheon and I thought I would open up with a powerful quote! It's an old Abe Lincoln quote, you see."

Kosmo cut him off saying, "Yes, Ted, I am aware of it. What is so important about this call?"

Ted replied, "Well, Chief, we are expecting a huge dense fog bank to hit Nantucket around four p.m., and I just want to let you know I'm prepared. I checked with Sheila Lucey at the Coast Guard as well, and told her I have people in place just in case a couple of boating mishaps occur."

"Well, that's just fine, Ted. You carry on. If anything else arises just give a call here to dispatch. But I believe between you and Sheila, you will have it under control."

"OK, Roger that, Chief." Then again in a loud voice Ted said, "There is no substitute for victory!'" As he was about to tell Kosmo, "That's a quote from General MacArthur," Kosmo hung up the phone.

Wendy Dow and Nancy Eblen were planning their upcoming summer travels. Both of them were secretaries for Aetna Life and Casualty in Hartford, Connecticut, and they had worked together for several years since graduating from the same high school. They were counting down the days. They had narrowed their trip plans and had reworked it several times in their travel journals. Their current plans were to head down to Mystic, stay with friends for two nights, then head on to Newport, Rhode Island, for two more evenings. After that they would drive Nancy's Rambler to the shores of Cape Cod. They would stay a night in Chatham at the Wequassett Inn and then take the ferry over to Nantucket. They had two weeks to enjoy time away from the office and to see some New England summer resort areas.

Their first few days were a glorious start to their vacation with time at the shore and a chance to tour one of the mansions in Newport. They finally arrived on Nantucket having come over from Chatham on an early ferry. They left their luggage at the Nesbitt Inn where they were booked for two nights. With recommendations from friends, they enjoyed a hearty breakfast at the Jared Coffin Hotel which was right up Broad Street from the ferry. Then they went to the Visitors Bureau and picked up a few brochures. They were told that Rob Coles offered a very nice island tour that was reasonably priced. They looked at each other and nodded as if to say that would be a good way to start their day.

They located Mr. Coles parked in front of the Nantucket Atheneum and explained to him that they would like to take a tour of the island and then find a very nice place for lunch. Mr. Coles asked a few particulars of what they were seeking- beaches, history, gardens? In unison they said they were avid flower lovers. Mr. Coles told them that 'Sconset would be the ideal place for them. He could take them for a short tour of the island and drop them in the quaint village of 'Sconset where they could enjoy a very nice but perhaps a bit pricey lunch at the Chanticleer. He explained as it looked like it was going to be a very nice day, weather-wise, that lunch might be served in the garden. He noted that as they both were wearing sweaters, they should be quite comfortable sitting outside.

They enjoyed the tour before arriving in 'Sconset. When they arrived in the village, they were both in flower box heaven! They absolutely loved the village lanes, the freshly planted window boxes and the walk along the 'Sconset bluffs.

After their leisurely stroll through 'Sconset they went to the Chanticleer Inn. Upon entering the fenced in yard, they thought they had just stepped into an English garden! The iconic carousel horse bedecked the center of the restaurant courtyard. The beautiful hanging fuchsia plants contrasted so nicely with the white building. They were warmly greeted by the hostess and quickly seated at a comfortable table under the morning glory-vined trellis.

They selected two glasses of Sancerre. They decided to share a plate of Nantucket Bay scallops quickly seared with garlic and herbs along with some fresh lightly wilted spinach with a good hint of garlic. They mopped their dishes clean and the shared plate as well.

The server asked, "Might you ladies like another glass of wine?"

Nancy inquired, "Would you have a nice bottle of Muscadet or something crisp to go with some fresh oysters on the half-shell?"

The wine arrived in a silver wine stand packed in ice. It was just what they were seeking. they then devoured a platter of a dozen nicely chilled oysters.

When the waiter stopped to remove the platter, Wendy asked, "Might we wait for a while before placing our order for the next course?" The waiter nodded.

They sipped the wine and put their heads together. Wendy whispered conspiratorially, "Could you imagine the both of us spending the entire summer out here?"

"That would be a dream come true," Nancy exclaimed.

Wendy nodded enthusiastically, "I would give anything not to have to go back to Aetna and sit at my desk typing every day!"

Nancy looked as if a lightbulb had just gone off in her head. "You know, Wendy, we could go into the window box business! Only if we could find a house with a small barn to serve as a working area. If these summer people can do it for their homes, we can match what they do or even better! Consider all the beautiful stuff we both grow at our parents' homes. Our gardens look just as nice as this one here," she indicated, pointing around the courtyard.

"We can dream, can't we?" Wendy added with a smile.

The waiter came by. They ordered a lobster salad, once again to share, and it turned out to be enough for both of them. They finished the wine, paid the bill and met Mr. Coles at the 'Sconset market at the pre- arranged time.

On the ride back to town they told Mr. Coles to drop them at the Nesbitt Inn as they were booked there for two nights. They declared were going to just be lazy for the next couple of days! They thanked him for the personalized tour, gave him a generous tip and stepped out at the front door of the old Victorian-styled inn.

Hunter Laroche

BONE CHURCH, KUTNA HORA SEDLEC OSSUARY PRAGUE, CZECH REPUBLIC

The chapel is decorated with the bones of somewhere between 40,000 and 70,000 human skeletons as a memento mori to those buried there, around 30,000 of which are estimated to have been plague victims. Although there have been bones in the church for hundreds of years, they didn't come into their current decorative form until 1870 when the Schwarzenberg family commissioned woodcarver FrantišekRint to decorate the chapel with the piles of bones that were harbored in the church's crypt.

The girls checked in, both of them selecting which room suited each. Nancy's room was finished in a nautical theme, while Wendy's was done in a light pink and lavender floral theme. Both of the rooms were facing Broad Street with lots of natural light.

After they unpacked, they conferred with Dolly and Nobby, the innkeepers. Wendy asked, "Where might you suggest we go for dinner?"

In unison the innkeepers said, "Cioppino's! It's a great place with a lovely warm feeling and reasonable prices. This evening the temperature is going to drop, so the restaurant right across the street is the best venue for a cool night! Oh, and there are extra blankets on the top shelf in each of your rooms."

The girls thanked them both and headed out to explore Nantucket Town. They took their time walking the cobblestone streets of Nantucket. Every area they explored was a relaxing delight for the both of them. But soon the sun started to set and the temperature dropped quite rapidly.

Nancy said, "I'm ready to grab a sweater, and we have enough time to freshen up before supper." Wendy nodded in agreement.

As they headed back to the Nesbitt Inn, they stopped at the window-front of Kendrick's Real Estate Office. They looked at the listings taped inside the front window. Both of them were quite taken aback at the prices for the properties advertised. They started giggling to each other and Wendy declared, "Well, we might have *some* money saved up between the both of us, but these prices are well out of our range!"

They turned to walk towards Federal Street when Tom Kendrick approached them and introduced himself. He handed them his card and said, "If you're looking for some real estate here, feel free to reach out to me. From week-to- week different properties at different price ranges often come on the market."

Nancy said, "It's very nice to meet you, Mr. Kendrick, and thanks for the information. However, we are only here for a couple of days. Our plans are to head back to Connecticut as it's the end of our vacation time. As much as we find Nantucket enchanting, it's not really in either of our future plans or in our budget range."

Tom nodded and said, "Well, one never knows. If some questions arise feel free to reach out and contact me with any questions you might have. Enjoy the rest of your stay here on the Grey Lady!"

Later on in the evening they were seated at a table in Cioppino's, perusing the menu. They had ordered a bottle of Pinot Grigio and both agreed they were in no rush to head back over across the street to the Nesbitt Inn. They discussed their wonderful lunch and the whole enchanting day before they even ordered.

A couple was seated shortly after them at the next table. They said, "Pardon us for interrupting you but it's always a pleasure to meet others here on Nantucket. We are Rita and Don Mignosa. Are you visiting or are you here for the season?"

Wendy smiled and replied, "No, we only arrived today and have just a couple of days left to our vacation. Already we were wishing we could have more time to explore the island!" They engaged in a very nice conversation with the couple and found out they owned Mignosa's Market on Main Street. After a bit of chit chat, Wendy concluded the conversation with thanks for being so friendly.

Hunter Laroche

Wendy then asked their server rather secretively if he would please send over two glasses of Prosecco to their new friends. Don Mignosa thought that it was such a thoughtful gesture that he invited them to join him and his wife at the Galley Restaurant the following day for lunch. They nodded and accepted the invitation with plans to meet at the specified time.

Their dinner turned out to be an excellent affair. Wendy had the grilled lobster tails over a pesto pasta with jumbo shrimp. Nancy had the Cioppino, the namesake dish of the restaurant. After an enjoyable dinner and a bit more conversation with Don and Rita, they parted ways, saying they would meet them at The Galley at one p.m. sharp!

After dinner they went to Bookworks right across the street and looked at many of the books in the gardening section. There were several on Nantucket's homes and gardens. They made mental notes to come back the next day and purchase a few books to take back home with them.

They strolled back to the Nesbitt Inn. On an antique table by the front desk, they found a plate of homemade cookies and a personal note from Dolly stating that she and Nobby had to retire early but hoped their evening turned out nicely. They opened the doors to their rooms and simultaneously laughed and said, "How amazing is this? We both have handwritten notes on our pillows saying, 'Sweet dreams, and see you in the morning!'"

Around nine a.m. they met and enjoyed a lovely buffet of different breakfast breads along with fresh cut fruits, jams, marmalades and a selection of tea. Over the breakfast they made their plans to visit the Whaling Museum and one of the churches. Then they would refresh themselves and walk the mile to the Galley Restaurant.

They enjoyed their visit to the museum and the tall white church on Center Street. They even walked all the way up the steeple to catch the amazing view of the harbor!

Upon returning to the inn, they saw Dolly and Nobby sitting on two green metal rocking chairs on the front porch. They thanked them both for the restaurant recommendation along with the great homemade cookies! Then they mentioned that they were going to walk to the Galley Restaurant.

Dolly said, "You had better bring a lot of money as it's one pricey place."

Nancy mentioned that they were guests of Don and Rita from the market on Main Street as they had met them at Cioppino's the night before.

"Oh," Nobby said. "Well, you will be in great company. They are really very lovely people."

Dolly added, "The Galley is a topnotch place. However," she smiled and shrugged her shoulders, "we only go if we are someone's guest. Now, it's about a mile from here. Nobby could drive you there if you'd like."

"No, thank you," Nancy responded. "We want to enjoy the scenery of Nantucket, so we will walk. I'm pretty sure we can make it there on time!"

They refreshed themselves in their rooms and headed out, taking in the fresh air and picture-perfect island scenery. They arriving at the perfect time just as Rita and Don pulled into the parking lot.

"What a view!" both women exclaimed as the restaurant was situated directly on the ocean's edge. They were all seated at a great table, and the host said smilingly, "Nothing but the best for Don and Rita and their friends!"

As they settled in Don ordered a bottle of French champagne. They offered cheers to each other and no one picked up the menu. Soon a bottle of French Chablis was being opened. Rita called the server over and ordered some calamari, cod beignets and some assorted olives.

Nancy and Wendy looked at each other, raised their glasses in a second toast and smiled.

As the appetizers arrived the conversations started flowing. Don asked the gals where they grew up, what they did for work, and what brought them to Nantucket.

They both started talking at the same time, then laughed, They took turns explaining that they both still lived at home with their parents, and if they ever moved out both of their mothers would have a meltdown, so to speak. They had been friends since kindergarten, and they both worked in extremely dull jobs at Aetna Life and Casualty in Hartford. Their workspace consisted of small windowless cubicles, and every day was the same routine: up at five-thirty, take the seven a.m. bus to the office, work until four p.m. and then return home. Every evening they would have dinner with their parents, except on the weekends when they would hop in Nancy's old green Rambler hatchback and escape to different areas of Connecticut.

They both had boyfriends who never seemed to have any money to take them out for a dinner. All they wanted to do was talk sports and drink beer on the weekends. So, both young women really enjoyed it when they could escape their parents and the boyfriends for a few days.

They had planned this trip for a few months, explaining they had first headed to Mystic, Connecticut, and toured a few of the gardens. They recalled spending the night at the Griswold Inn, then driving to Newport, Rhode Island, to stay with an old high school friend. Then they continued onto Chatham on the Cape. They had considered earlier going to Martha's Vineyard, but the more people they spoke with about their plans the more people recommended Nantucket as a nicer option.

"And, now here we are, like two nomads just traveling around for a few weeks. Time sure does go by quickly when you're having fun!" Nancy concluded.

As lunch continued so did the many choices of food. Rita said, "Let me order a few different items and we can graze the afternoon away, unless you have other plans?"

Wendy and Nancy, feeling like they hit the 'food and wine jackpot', just looked at each other, clicked their glasses together and said, "We have nowhere to go!"

Lunch lasted almost four hours! At one point Wendy revealed, "You know, Rita and Don, we would love to pack up our belongings and land out here for the whole summer! We saw a few nice window boxes on our tour around 'Sconset, but we honestly think that between the two of us we could really assist some people and make their flower arrangements spectacular! We both have gardens at home and have attended numerous flower shows. But where would we find a place for us to rent with our limited budget? This is one expensive island, beautiful, but pricey!"

Don looked over at Rita, and as she knew what he was thinking, gave him a smile and a wink. Don then proposed, "Well, ladies, we just might have solution for you. What is your approximate housing budget?"

"Oh, my goodness," Nancy replied, feeling a bit embarrassed. "We have never really thought about it. If we give up our jobs, well money will be kind of tight. We both have savings, but giving everything up to become vagabonds on Nantucket - well, it's a fun thought but I don't think it's in our realm of possibilities!"

Don then asked Jake, their server, to bring the wine list over. With a slight smile he offered, "Ladies, it's truth or dare! Here's how this works: I will make you a one-time deal. If you agree to the deal, then we are going to have one superb bottle of red wine. If you do not agree to the deal, we will have a moderate bottle of red wine and then lunch will be over."

Nancy and Wendy turned to each other, and their jaws dropped.

Rita offered to clarify the situation a bit. "Let me say one thing. When Don makes an offer in this manner to someone, it's usually a great deal. So just relax and listen!"

Nancy and Wendy sat up straight and focused on their host. They had no idea as to what to expect.

Don then said, "Here we go. Rita and I purchased a home on Quince Street about a month ago. It was owned by Dr. Tom Sollas and his wife, Ann, for years and was beautifully maintained. But about five years ago they sold it. The people who purchased it ended up getting divorced a very short time afterwards. During the divorce proceedings there was a dispute as who would own it as a part of the settlement. The husband stopped coming to the island. The wife took off for Europe and refused all contact during the divorce proceedings. The house sat there year after year, with the paint peeling, weeds growing out of the gutters, lawn not mowed, and zero landscaping. Rita and I knew the home when Dr. Sollas owned it and it was a beauty. As we walked past it almost weekly it was a very sad sight to see. Now for the latest update . . ."

At that point Jake appeared asking if Don had made a selection. Don replied, "I need five minutes. Then it's either a great bottle or a moderate bottle . . ." Jake winked and backed away.

Don resumed his tale. "Soon the taxes on the property were in arrears, and despite numerous attempts by the bank to get them paid and the mortgage as well, unfortunately payments had ceased almost three years before when the couple departed from the island.

Luckily, I had a friend at the bank who had been watching the property slipping more and more into ruin. He called me said it's going to hit the auction block in a couple weeks, and bemoaned that everyone was going to be in a losing position, including the bank. So, early the next morning I went to the bank with a checkbook, made them an offer before the auction even was announced, and now we are the new owners of the Quince Street property as of last week!" Don's eyes were twinkling a bit and his smile was bigger than before.

Don ended the story saying, "The following day an envelope was delivered to Tom Kendrick, owner of Kendrick Real Estate Office on Main Street. Enclosed were ten one hundred dollar bills with a note saying, 'Tom, thanks for the tip on the house going up for auction. Yours, Don.' So, ladies, as of now the house sits as is. Some furnishings are in there, but it needs some upgrades which is a project we were going to begin in the fall. Now, here's the deal: Quince Street is right here in town. We will let both of you stay there. We would get the hot water and plumbing up to par. All we ask of you is to clean up the exterior grounds, and clean up, dust, mop and scrub the inside. It needs a lot of TLC as it's been empty for over five years now. I will also get my guys to go through it from top to bottom just to make sure no mice decided to make nests in there, that type of thing."

He paused, looked at the women directly and held up two fingers. "So, you have two options here: one you make an agreement with us now, and tomorrow you get the keys from us and take a walk through. Secondly, if it's not what you were expecting and too much of a project to take on, you can just walk away from this idea. No feelings hurt."

Nancy and Wendy turned their heads away from Don to look at each other, then turned back to Don. Nancy asked, "Do you think we could excuse ourselves for a couple of minutes to talk this over?"

Don nodded, and Rita indicated that at the end of the bar there was a small space that would work for a private conversation. Once there, they hugged each other and held each other at arm's length.

Wendy went first. "This is hard to believe! We've only been here for a bit over a day and now we have the chance of a lifetime to consider moving here! What do you think, Nancy? Should we make a list of pros and cons? Or just go with our gut feeling?"

Nancy took a deep breath. "Well, like Don said, if it seems overwhelming, we can change our minds. I think, given that we don't have a lot tying us down – well, you know our parents will have a minor fit, and the men in our lives won't understand it in the least – that it's high time we bailed out of our cubby-holes and made the most of an amazing offer."

Wendy shook her head and said, "I totally agree! I'm nervous as heck but I'm game if you are!"

They gave each other a high five and said simultaneously, "Let's go for it!"

Grinning, they headed back down to their table and to their hosts who were watching them in anticipation. Wendy and Nancy gave them both the thumbs up signal and almost shouted, "We're going to go for it! What do you think?"

They all agreed it was a deal.

Don ordered a very fine French Bordeaux, a 1966 Château Haut-Brion, and they once again toasted each other. Don gave them a few leads as to what might work best on transitioning into this proposition. They shook hands and then Rita drove them to the Nesbit Inn, where they took a long and restful nap. Who knew where this adventure would lead them?

BLOOD FALLS, TAYLOR GLACIER, ANTARCTICA

Blood Falls, named for its ruddy color, is not in fact a gush of blood from some unseen wound. The color was initially chalked up to red algae, but a study in the Journal of Glaciology has uncovered its true origin using radar to scan the layers of ice from which the river pours.

Located in Antarctica's McMurdo Dry Valleys, the falls pour forth from Taylor Glacier, and the liquid bubbles up from fissures in the glacier's surface. The flow was previously a mystery, as the mean temperature is 1.4 degrees Fahrenheit (-17 degrees Celsius) and little glacial melting can be seen at the surface. Imaging from underneath the glacier helped solve the mystery, revealing a complex network of subglacial rivers and a subglacial lake—all filled with brine high in iron, giving the falls its reddish tint. According to the study, the makeup of the brine explains the fact that it flows instead of freezes.

Mark Donato dialed the station where Beth was on dispatch duty. She picked up the phone and said, "Hey, Mark, can you hold a second? Dolores Frechette is here. Her dog, Teddy, is missing again, and we have to help her out."

Constable Kosmo, who happened to be standing at the dispatch desk when Mark called asked Beth to get Mrs. Frechette some water and then seat her in his office. With a smirk on his face, he picked up the phone, and in a quiet muffled higher-pitched voice said, "OK, sweetie, what's up?"

Mark, not noticing anything different, replied, "Hey Babe, how's about you getting all dolled up tonight and we can hit the town? Maybe you can wear that black leather skirt with the little slit on the side, and your red low neckline sweater? I mean we only live once, Babe. We can make this a hot night, just like that show *Cat on a Hot Tin Roof.* We can make kissy-kissy in the back booth of The Mad Hatter when no one is around us!"

Shifting to his normal voice Kosmo responded, "Oh, that sounds lovely, really lovely. What time do you want to pick me up?"

Mark was so startled he started turning all red in his face and almost dropped the phone. "Funny, really funny, big man. Don't you know that personal calls are just that-*personal*?

"Well," Kosmo laughed, "if you're going to be all huffy about it, then I will just stay home! We'll see you here at the station when you arrive." Then he hung up.

Mark grumbled to himself, "Sheesh! I can't believe I fell for that."

Right then Beth returned to her desk. Kosmo winked and said, "Old Romeo, he's got big plans for you two this evening. He'll be in at checkout time but I don't think he's going to be happy with me." He chuckled and headed to his office.

Beth then rolled her eyes and asked, "So he did fell for it again?"

"Yup," Kosmo replied. "Some jokes just never get old!"

Kosmo settled Mrs. Frechette down by explaining, "Rick Blair will take his dog Madaket out to the beach area with you. You will track Teddy down in no time, as we all know Teddy likes Madaket a lot! Just give me a minute or two to radio Rick. He'll meet you here promptly. You may wait out front."

"Oh, thank you, Constable. I just hate it when Teddy runs off on me like that!" Mrs. Frechette tottered out to the front room.

Later in the afternoon, after Beth had departed, Jimmy Jaksic was on the dispatch desk. He buzzed Kosmos in his office.

"What's up Jimmy?"

"Chief, Judy's calling. She's on line one. Want me to patch her through?"

"Yes, thanks."

"Hey, Koz," Judy greeted him. She was one of the very few people allowed to address him as Koz.

"Hey, Judy how's things?"

She continued, "All is well here, but I've got to tell you something."

"OK, fire away."

"Well, last month I bought some tickets for a raffle. I purchased twenty tickets as it's for a good cause - the Boys and Girls Club." She paused.

"OK," Kosmo said, "what gives?"

Judy continued. "Well, they had six things for prizes ranging from a bird feeder to a free commuter book on the ferry, a dinner at the Straight Wharf, and the grand prize was a three day stay at The Chatham Inn on the Cape."

"OK, sounds nice. Did you win the bird feeder?" Kosmo asked, chuckling.

"So, smarty pants, the owners of the Chatham Inn sent me a letter saying that I was the recipient of the three-night stay! Their names are Peter and Kathy Bauer, and enclosed in the envelope was a gift certificate to dinner at the Weaquasset Inn, two complimentary massages at the Chatham Inn as well, and a bottle of wine each evening delivered to my room: white, red, rose, or a sparkling wine."

Kosmo whistled, "So, you hit the jackpot! Good for you!"

"Now that you've heard the big news, here are my thoughts," Judy added. "The deal is good through November. So, if you could manage some free time, I will add a room for you as my treat! It might be fun! You know I could ask a slew of other people, but they most likely won't want to shell out the money as the Chatham Inn is really top notch. you should see the brochure! I mean this place is the cat's meow!"

Kosmo replied, "Well, I could join you and I'm glad you offered, but I can pay for my own room."

"No," Judy quickly stated. "I have had a tremendous run here at Hatch's, and my bank account is just overflowing with cash. So, you spring for a lunch or a dinner the rest is my treat!"

"Deal!" Kosmo told her. "Let's shoot for right after Halloween. It will be extremely quiet here on the island, so slipping away for a few days will not be a problem at all. I'll get it into the work log right away, but for now, I won't let on to where I'll be headed."

"AOK, Number One Constable on The Rock!"

When Nancy and Wendy woke up later that afternoon, feeling refreshed, they met on the front porch where Dolly and Nobby were enjoying a slice of Key Lime pie sent over from Cioppino's. Dolly asked what their plans were for the evening. They told them about the long, long fabulous lunch and about the Sollas house on Quince Street.

Nobby piped right up saying, "What a shame! How such a beautiful piece of property could have fallen into disrepair is just beyond me."

Both Wendy and Nancy did not mention anything about the offer that Don had made them, but asked if they could tell them how to get to Quince Street. As it turned out it was a quick short walk from the inn.

Off they headed when Dolly called after them, "You can't miss it, about three quarters of the way up on the left. At one point it was the Quince School. Now it's all overgrown, just a shame, a real shame. Dr. Sollas would have a heart attack if he saw it now."

They thanked their hosts and proceeded on to Quince Street. They found the property with ease. At one glance they were in heaven, what a beautiful home! Yes, it was in total neglect, but they could make it into a beautiful property in no time at all. It would take some grunt work, but they would accept the challenge.

They entered the broken picket fence gate and walked around the entire home. On the back side was a hatch door leading to the basement, and it was unlocked. There was a light switch, they clicked it on and, lo and behold there was light!

Both of them remembered Don's comment about the mice so they clapped their hands to make some noise to scare any possible mice away. The basement was dry, though there were some cobwebs and quite a bit of sheet-covered furniture. They turned on any light switch and pull-string they could find. Then they headed upstairs. The door opened into the kitchen area which, too, was quite dusty with cobwebs but nothing a good vacuum and dusting could not fix.

They toured the entire space, opening every cabinet cautiously, not knowing what might have nested inside. It was exciting and amazing to think they'd be living there in no time at all.

The next morning at eight a.m. they met with Don and Rita and said, "We will take it! We're going to hustle home and figure things out. We should see you in a few days. Thank you ever so much for proposing this venture to us!"

They were packed and got to their ferry on time. From Hyannis they headed back to West Hartford, and each of the girls met with their parents. They called in their work resignations and, lastly, explained to their boyfriends that life was taking a fast and amazing turn for them. Two days later they packed up Nancy's car and headed back to Cape Cod. Don had tipped them off about making ferry reservations for their car as well.

When they arrived back on Nantucket, they found the keys to the Quince Street house in the mailbox. Upon entering they picked up an envelope with a note saying that Rita had stocked the refrigerator with some staples to hold them over for a few days. It said the outside gas grill was oiled and ready for use and the fireplace in the living room had been stocked with wood. There was a good amount of food stocked in the freezer as well. Rita had also dropped off four bottles each of white and bottles of red wine.

Wendy commented, "Well, it sure doesn't hurt that our landlords own and run a grocery store! Wasn't that super thoughtful of them to take care of our needs right away?"

By late afternoon they had moved all their belongings into the house. Nancy suggested they open a bottle of white wine and they went to work. They made a quick to-do list and started right in. Luckily there were a lot of cleaning supplies that they figured Rita had left as well.

By eight p.m. they were feeling quite pleased with the progress they had made. Wendy had begun upstairs with the two bathrooms. They chose their bedrooms, gave them a once-over and found some sheets that had been stored in a zip-shut case and seemed to be still fresh. After a few quick shakes the sheets and blankets were placed on the queen beds in each of their bedrooms. The girls made a very quick job of unpacking their clothes, and Wendy said she was done cleaning, vacuuming, and dusting both bedrooms

By nine p.m. Nancy had whipped up a simple dinner of grilled chicken breasts, sauteed with fresh green beans and a saffron rice mix. They settled down to their dinner. The second bottle of white wine was open, toasts to their new venture given, and dinner was quickly consumed. They retired soon, after both of them managed a quick hot shower. What a transition day it had been!

FREIHUNG, GERMANY

The White Lady of Freihung supposedly used to drift around the town's old mining tunnels. After the complaints by the residents, the tunnels were destroyed. But the White Lady appeared above ground shortly afterward. Today, she regularly appears in car rearview mirrors as a passenger in the back seat, and she probably is the main reason for the increased number of traffic accidents in the region.

Kosmo entered the station quite early. Mike DiFronzo was almost finished with his night shift on dispatch. "Good morning, Mike," Kosmo greeted him.

"Hey, Chief!"

"Much of anything happen over the evening shift?"

"Well, I hate to tell you but Eelskin Joe and Hunter Laroche kind of got into it with two guys down at the Rose and Crown. We got a call from the bartender, Marie."

"Oh, really? Fill me in," Kosmo requested.

Mike explained, "I guess Marie Lafrontiere was bartending. These two thugs, as Hunter put it, were being quite rude and crude. Eelskin relayed that these guys were making all sorts of rude and nasty comments to her. So, Hunter went over and politely asked them to finish their drinks and leave the bar. Now, as the report states, everyone in the bar confirmed that Hunter was very polite but stern with his request. I guess things escalated, and next thing you know, Hunter grabbed the larger of the two men and used his head as a battering ram to toss him out the back door. Apparently, his pal, another bruiser, jumped Hunter from behind. But that did not work out too well for him. Marie called the station and Deputy Donato, Rick Blair, and Jimmy Jaksic were over there in minutes. However, by that time, the party was over. Eel Skin leveled the other bruiser with a knock-out punch. The guy Hunter rammed out the door was seeing stars! He did not even seem to know his name! To make a long story short, the two thugs are sleeping it off in the cage. No one wants to press any charges. Jack McElderry, you know, the owner, is calling Eel Skin and Hunter two honorable gentlemen!"

Kosmo rolled his eyes, and thought to himself, "It's going to be a long day." Turning to Mike he suggested, "OK, let's see if we can rouse these two visitors and get a little more information about them. Were they checked into a hotel?"

Mike then explained, "Deputy Donato wrote them up pretty well. He stated to them that Marie Lafrontiere was highly regarded in the community as she is always donating her time to numerous local charities, along with singing in the church choir on Sunday. He gave them a little sermon on morals and so forth. One guy asked if Mark could leave them alone as his head felt like he was run over by a truck. The other clown said he thought his jaw was broken! Mark told him he was just a wimp and to quiet down."

"Apparently Deputy Donato also removed the cash they had on them, paid the bar tab and left Marie quite a generous tip on top of it. It turns out that these guys were staying at The House of Orange Inn. So, Mark called Peter there and said just pack their bags as they were going to be spending the night compliments of the Nantucket Police Department's free lodging program. Mark told him in the morning we would send someone up to collect their belongings, settle their bill for them with cash they had in their wallets, and would be put on a one-way ferry off the island. Quite a night, I'd say!"

Kosmo headed for the back cell to check on the occupants when the phone rang. Mike called to him, "Excuse me, Chief, but Harbor Master Ted Hudgins is on line one and wants to talk with you.

Kosmo took a deep breath and thought, "Oh, Nantucket, a funny little island with funny little people." Out loud he said, "OK, patch him through." He picked up the phone.

"Hey, Ted, what's up?"

Ted said loudly, "'There is no security on this earth, only opportunity!'"

Kosmo drummed his fingers on his desk and asked, "OK, Ted, what is this call about? I've got business to tend to in the shop this morning."

"Well, Chief, I am still memorizing a lot of different quotes. You never know when you are at a cocktail party they might come in handy!"

"So, what do you want with me, Ted?"

"Oh, I wanted to let you know that yesterday the surfer out by Cisco who was missing after falling into a rising wave was found safe by Sheila Lucy's crew of the Coast Guard a few hundred yards off shore on his board. He was a little shaken, but he was wearing a wet suit, and all in all, he's fine.

"OK, Ted, thanks for the update." Before Kosmo hung up he heard Ted say, "'The pen is mightier than the sword!'"

Earlier that morning, around five a.m. the sun started to rise and was glowing in both Nancy and Wendy's east-facing bedrooms. After trying to catch some more rest they found themselves in the kitchen by five forty-five.

Nancy said, "Well, it's like we are back in Connecticut, but this time our office is the great outdoors!"

After a quick breakfast of fresh coffee and a toasted English muffin with peanut butter, they headed outside to the shed in the back of the property. They hadn't looked into it when they first walked the property. They were hoping they'd find some yard tools in it. It took a small nudge of Nancy's shoulder to force the rusted lock (that was not actually closed) free from the hasp that was holding it shut. What they discovered inside was almost a gardener's paradise! There were all sorts of shovels, trowels, rakes, a push lawn mower, garden shears, large clippers and other tools to keep a yard crew busy all summer!

Here it was only six fifteen in the morning, and they made their plan: first the front hedges, just a rough cut. They would cut, trim, and rake as they went. In the shed were two boxes of large garden trash bags. After two hours of non-stop cutting and bagging, a sliver of light started to show through the picket fence. At this point they already had ten completely filled yard waste bags, and this was only the beginning!

Luckily, Don and Rita also had noted that they had a charge account at Hardy's Hardware where they could charge things if needed in the landscape project. They made a list of items that would help move the work along from day to day. They took a coffee and water break and discussed how much they had accomplished, although to anyone else it might not look like a lot. They both figured by noon it would be time to break for the day, have lunch and re-evaluate their progress. After all, they weren't full-time landscapers in their previous careers! They would have to ease into this new situation.

That afternoon, after making a new list including getting some supplies, they headed to the Brotherhood of Thieves Restaurant for a cold beer. While they were enjoying the first full day back on the island and their drinks, at the table next to them was a group of five men. When Nancy and Wendy clinked their beer mug, one of the men reached over to the girls, added his glass and said, "I'm not sure what you're celebrating, but 'cheers,' nonetheless!"

The man introduced himself as Reg Marden, stating that he was a retired lawyer. Pointing to his tablemates he explained that the rest of the gang were friends who met at the Brotherhood every week for a beverage. Most of the group were all retired and enjoying life on the island. Admittedly, they all got bored from time to time as one can only play so much golf or fish on a regular basis. Reg then asked the girls, "What they were doing? Here for a long weekend?"

Nancy replied, "Well, we are actually kind of new here. We were given an offer to live for free in exchange for some repairs, or actually gardening and landscape work, on a house on Quince Street."

Reg paused then asked, "Not the old Sollas house?"

"Exactly!" Wendy said. "A friend we know just purchased it. He said it would be empty for the summer and in exchange we moved in and are going to see what magic we can work."

Another guy at the table introduced himself as George Williams and said, "We heard that Donny Mignosa had his eye on that piece of property. Well, if he now owns it, you can be sure it will turn out to be a beautiful renovation! He and Rita have quite the eye for details!"

Then George introduced the other men at the table: Mark McGarvey, Joe Hassey, and Al Lussier.

Wendy said politely, "Well, it's nice to meet all of you. If you are in the neighborhood tomorrow or anytime in the near future, stop by! You will see we have our work cut out for us, but we are eager to see what improvements we can make on the property." Then everyone went back to their own conversations.

After finishing their beer and paying the tab, Nancy suggested, "Let's head to the seafood market on Main Street and pick up a nice piece of fish. We have some rice and vegetables, plus the lettuce for a salad. So, all we need is the entrée."

Wendy added, "Let's not forget to chill some more wine in the fridge! And let's redo the list of the landscaping details. We should make a time frame and a shopping list for things we will need. We should update it every morning so our work time is productive. Back at it, best buddy!"

ISLAND OF GHOSTS, POVEGLIA ISLAND, ITALY

Poveglia Island is one of 166 islets in the Venice Lagoon off the eastern coast of Northern Italy. Although it has served various purposes, this place is well-known for its macabre past. Tens of thousands of dead and living Black Plague victims were brought here across centuries. Corpses piled up in pits were burned in large fires. In later years, mentally ill patients in the institution suffered heinous tortures and experiments at the hands of a mad doctor. The locals say Poveglia is an "island of ghosts," cursed with many unhealthy spirits. Its dark reputation can be traced to a history filled with death and drama.

The girls were up enjoying their coffee and some Downy Flake doughnuts. Soon after they were out in the yard, measuring the flower beds for the amount of mulch needed after weeding was completed. Nancy made a note to ask Rita about whom they can call for the yard waste pickup, along with a lot of old bricks, some broken window glass and some rotting wood that they removed off the back deck.

They both agreed on some nice lattice wood to be added so the rose plants would be able to grow up on both sides of the home's front exterior. They actually had compiled their list the night before, and they were moving along just as they planned to when, at eight a.m., three pickup trucks pulled into the driveway of the Quince Street house.

"What's going on?" Wendy wondered out loud.

"Beats me," replied Nancy, holding her hand over her eyebrows to cut out the sun from her view. "We'll see!"

Kosmo entered the station that same morning. Rick Blair was on the dispatch desk.

"Good morning, Chief!" With that, his dog, Madaket, popped up from under the desk. Wagging his tail, he ran right up to Kosmo. Madaket had a huge liking for Kosmo.

Bending over to pet Madaket, the chief asked Rick, "OK, give me the rundown. Any bank robberies last night?"

"Nope. The only thing of any interest was that Lilly Baker called saying her horse had escaped sometime between five and eight p.m. She called all the usual neighbors, and everyone was on the lookout. Well, it turns out Midnight had strolled into town and found himself on Main Street eating the flowers from the center monument on lower Main! He was also seen drinking the water out of the trough, pleased as punch with himself! Lilly came down with her trailer, loaded old Midnight into it, and all was quiet the rest of the night in Nantucket!" Madaket thumped his tail as if to say, "And that's all, Chief!"

"Thanks, Rick. I'm glad it was a relatively quiet night after that bar brawl at the Rose and Crown recently. I'm headed out for a stretch of the legs up Main Street. Back soon."

Kosmo strolled over to Mignosa's Market to join Rita and Don for coffee. As he entered, he spotted the Harbor Master right as Ted spotted him. Approaching Kosmo Ted said, "'The greatest glory in living lies not in never falling, but in rising every time we fall!'"

Kosmo nodded and replied, "Very nice, Ted," and walked past him. Rita was arranging a few items on a shelf and waved to the chief, knowing what he would enjoy next.

At the Quince Street property, the men started piling out of their trucks wearing outdoor work clothes. Al Lussier was the first to greet them both.

"Good morning!" Al said in a loud boisterous tone. "We are all here with rakes, shovels, hedge clippers, hoes, hammers, saws, wheelbarrows, you name it - we have it! After meeting you two yesterday, we all thought we might as well lend you a hand as we've got nothing better to do! I also have a large sketch pad that we can use for garden design if you might like. I, myself, am quite an avid gardener."

Al turned and pointed to another one of the fellows.

Hunter Laroche

"George here likes to play the foreman. Tell us how we can help you both. We have no plans so for the rest of the day we are all yours! Except, we might all need to take a lunch break and run down to the counter lunch deli at the pharmacy. But other than that, we are good to go!"

Wendy and Nancy welcomed the group and started to go over their plan-of-attack list with George.

Mark McGarvey said, "Let me go check all the drain pipes and their connections and fittings. I have a large pile of nice stones I could bring over if Al thinks they might look nice under the bottom of the drain spouts.

Joe Hassey said he was going to walk around with Reg and check for broken shingles on the roof, along with rotting window trim and missing cedar shakes from the siding.

With that, the yard was a buzz of excitement! The guys were in their glory showing off their skills and abilities.

Wendy pulled Nancy aside and said, "We can't let these guy go and pay for their lunch. Why don't I run down to the A&P and pick up a mixture of some nice ground hamburger, buns, pickles, and chips, some more beer, and sodas? I'll come back and pull out that Webber grill and fire it up. There is a bag of charcoal but I need to see if it's still dry. I will get some catsup, mustard and relish, some sliced cheddar and a head of iceburg lettuce and we should be good to go. I'll make them a burger that's fit for a king!" She popped into the car and headed out.

Everyone was working away. When she got back, Wendy pulled the grill out, found that there was a full can of lighter fluid, and the charcoal briquettes looked nice and dry. Around noon, she brought out a pitcher of iced lemonade and iced tea with fresh sliced lemons along with a few sprigs of fresh mint as she found a small plant for sale at the market.

After they all settled inside at the kitchen table, Al was back to his sketching, talking with Nancy as Wendy brought in a rather large platter of burgers right off the grill. The men were amazed at the size of the burgers! Wendy told them that it was a mix of chuck and porterhouse steak that she asked the butcher to grind.

The men were still licking their lips when Mark asked, "How many ounces each are those burgers? Approximately, I mean. They are huge!"

Wendy said, "About twelve-ounces each."

Al replied, "Well, that's about two and a half times the size of what Sylvia makes at home! I won't be so hungry for supper, though if we keep up the pace we did this morning, maybe I will!"

As they all dug into their meal, napkins were passed around, the condiments were slopped on, and some had cheese. The chips were devoured, and every burger, pitcher of iced tea and lemonade were consumed.

They discussed the other details needed for the home's repair, from rotting wood to a tree stump that needed to be dug out. They agreed to attach it to one of the truck's frames and pull it out with a chain. Several cedar shingles on the home needed to be replaced, and a four-by-four section of the black tar roof shingles needed replacing as well.

When they got up from the table, Joe and Reg went thru the home inspecting all the ceilings for water damage. They only found one area in the smallest of the four bedrooms upstairs that had some damage. It wasn't much but the roof needed to be patched and then the ceiling repainted.

George sat with Nancy and Al and compiled the list for the following day. They decided that the tree, the roof and the shingles would be a priority. Mark and Wendy went through the outside garden, weeding and removing some small shrubs. Al joined them shortly. He told them he had an abundance of tomato and other vegetable plants as well as some roses he would be glad to donate if they included another fabulous lunch in the deal!

Around four p.m. Nancy had a bucket filled with beer and ice and brought it out to the back deck. They all called it a day. They discussed how Don and Rita were going to be pretty impressed with the final outcome if it continued shaping up the way it was headed. They all agreed not to tell Don and Rita anything about the newest landscape progress, especially as 'the helpers' were a great boost to all their efforts. So, Nancy and Wendy would get in touch with them and ask them not to stop by the property until they were able to make a good dent in the project. Everyone felt that ten days would be their best estimate on having the landscape area ready for viewing. Nancy said they would both stop into Mignosa's Market after the men were packed up and ready to depart.

Once the girls got cleaned up, they headed to town. As they entered the store Rita was arranging a nice bouquet of flowers, and she gave them a smile.

"Howdy!" she said. "How's the house shaping up?

Have you gotten a chance to start in on things yet?"

Nancy replied, trying to keep a serious face about it all, "Well, we sat down today and started our plan of attack. We figure it will take at least ten days until we start to see any favorable results. We know we will be trimming bushes, mowing the lawn, plus a mish-mash of work until, hopefully, it all comes together in the end. So, Rita, we have one question. Who do we call for yard waste removal? We figure it's going to take several days of bagging the waste once we get started." Then Nancy thought to herself, "Little did Rita know there were already fifteen bags stuffed full, and numerous more to follow!"

So, Rita gave them the name and number of the trash pickup service they used for their other property. Then Rita gave them a large bouquet of flowers in a glass vase and said, "Here, maybe this will cheer up that dismal atmosphere inside of the house. Any mice spotted?"

Wendy answered, "Nope, not a thing! There are a few spiders, lots of cobwebs, but nothing we can't handle. It's going to be one room at a time: open the windows, air it out, get the rust out of the flowing water in the pipes. We did find the circuit for the hot water heater, and, wow, it gets toasty! Our showers will be quite refreshing after a day in the garden weeding. And thank you for the flowers, they will spruce up the kitchen enormously!"

"Oh, one more thing, Rita," Nancy interjected. "We have one request, and we are hoping it's OK with you both."

"What's that?" asked Rita.

Nancy explained," Would you and Don not walk or drive by the house until we are much farther along with the project? I mean, it's going to look like a bomb went off when we start trimming and pruning. There will piles of plant cuttings, limbs, old shrubs pulled out, things will be scattered everywhere! It will not look very appealing until we can make some sort of order out of the yard."

Rita nodded. "Sure, I will tell Don, and we will not go anywhere near the property until we get the green light from both of you! We'll be eager to see the results!"

Back on Quince Street they dined on pan-seared scallops with fresh herbs and lemon-peel zest cooked in a black cast iron skillet. The main dish was accompanied by lightly sautéed asparagus and a wild rice blend. Finishing off their Vermentino white wine, they called it a night.

Nancy started reading a book she found on one of the bookshelves in the library. It was called *The Wauwinet Caper* penned by Hunter Laroche. She enjoyed reading a few pages, planning to set it down and head off to bed in a short bit of time. The next thing she knew, the bottle of red wine that she had just opened was now half finished, and two hours had slipped by! She had read one-third of the book as well!

HOIA-BACIU HAUNTED FOREST, CLUJ, ROMANIA A PORTAL WHERE VISITORS DISAPPEAR!

Just three kilometers away from Cluj, Romania, lies the Hoia – Baciu Forest, emerging from somewhere in a broken time. It is a mysterious and wonderful place, where the normal and paranormal merge and the conventional and unconventional cannot be distinguished from each other. Once you enter the strange forest, it captures your immediate attention because of the strange shape of the trees. In no other forest do the trees turn so unnaturally in the way they do here. Everywhere you look, six or eight trees spring from the same root system. Instead of growing towards the sky, the trees become arched as if into a silent prayer, bent to the ground by an unknown force.

Since ancient times, the inhabitants felt the strange powers of the forest and shunned it because it was beyond their power of comprehension. For a long period of time, people had not really talked about the forest, as they were afraid to mention the place they believed fell under a curse. In the early 1950's, a lone biologist named Alexandru Sift, during his long pioneering research, lifted the veil of mystery that had fallen upon the forest. His investigations were continued into the 1970's by several research teams as well as by solitary researchers from Romania.

Kosmo took a leisurely morning walk from the station. He stopped down to see Duke at the hardware store. Once again, the first thing he did was run into Ted Hudgins who quickly said, "'The way to get started is to quit talking and begin doing!'"

Kosmo nodded at Ted, and said, "Yeah, I know, another great quote to have up one's sleeve. Well, I've got things to do, so please quit talking, quotes or no quotes!"

Kosmo flagged down Duke to explain, "Hey, Duke, the handle on my screen porch off the backside of the house is, well, to put it mildly, shot. I guess it's time for a new one. And, you know, I can barely use a screwdriver. Would you know someone who's handy with carpentry tools?"

Rusty Riddleberger happened to be standing there. He offered, "I could fix that for you if you need a hand."

Duke confirmed, "Hey, Kosmo, this guy Rusty can fix anything, and I mean <u>anything</u>!"

"Really?" Kosmo asked, looking up at the tall red-haired fellow.

"Sure thing!" replied Rusty. "Give me the address and I will have it fixed in no time!"

Kosmo wondered aloud, "How much would I owe you?"

Rusty brushed it off saying, "No charge. Won't take me but a minute."

Kosmo countered, "Sorry, but I am not allowed to accept any type of gifts from Nantucket residents."

Rusty laughed and corrected him, "Gift? This is not a gift. I am just replacing your door handle."

Duke stepped in and clarified things. "Well, Rusty, Kosmo is the Chief of Police, so he cannot accept anything for free."

"It might be interpreted as "bribing an officer of the law," Kosmo explained further.

"OK, ten bucks," Rusty tossed out a basic fee.

Duke gave Rusty the door handle, Kosmo gave him the address and ten dollars, then the two new acquaintances headed out the door to their respective jobs. Rusty was down at the police station forty-five minutes later, a new door handle in his hand, and the ten dollars. Mike DiFronzo greeted Rusty who asked to speak with Kosmo.

Kosmo came out smiling and said, "Hey, Rusty!" Then he noticed the handle in Rusty's hand and asked, "Couldn't you find the house?"

Rusty replied, "Oh, I found it OK, but excuse me for saying, it's not the door handle that needs replacing."

Kosmo looked a little puzzled and said, "Well, it looked pretty well shot to me. What's the problem?"

Rusty grinned and wiggled the door handle. "In a way you're correct, but you see it's a little more involved than that. The entire screen door's hinges and frame are pretty well rotted out."

The chief continued, "OK, let me know the situation."

Then Rusty inquired, "How long have you lived at that house?"

"Just about ten years now," Kosmo answered.

Rusty then asked, "Well, do you know how long the previous owners lived there?"

Kosmo scratched his head a bit and replied, "Well, best I can remember it was built by their grandfather. Then their parents lived there, and then this couple lived there and sold it to me. I remember the inspection guy telling me something about some repairs that were needed. The house definitely had some issues but I closed on it pretty quickly at a really good price. Unfortunately, not being handy with household tools, I really have done nothing to fix it up. My days start early and end late, and you know I'm more or less on-call 24 hours a day! My friend Judy is always telling me that I need to get a carpenter over to take a good gander at the entire house. And, Duke down at his store, actually has mentioned that to me on a few occasions. I guess it hasn't been my top priority since moving here."

Rusty nodded understandingly. "Well, here's the way I see it. You need *a lot,* not a little, but *a lot* of repairs, sorry to say. From the roof to the foundation there are all sorts of issues going on. If over time they are not attended to, things will just get much much worse. I noticed you have a hole behind a light fixture on the back porch, so every time it rains it's letting water in between the outside and the inside of the walls. That has 'disaster' written all over it! And that's just the tip of the iceberg. You really need to get your caretaker on top of this. Actually, you might seriously want to find a new caretaker. Whomever you're using has let the house slip so far into disrepair, he's not doing you any service."

"You could ask Duke who he likes for that line of work. I am sure he knows of some of some good qualified people."

Kosmo bit to the quick and asked, "Could you do it?"

Rusty jiggled his head from left to right. "I could, but it will take some time. Seeing as how you don't really know me, I would feel better if you would call a few of my references first. For one, Tom Kendrick, of the real estate office, has me on retainer for numerous properties he manages when people are away for the season."

"OK," Kosmo said, "give me a moment." He went into his office, shut the door, and five minutes later he was back out saying, "You're hired!"

"Really?" asked Rusty. "You work fast!"

"Yes, Tom Kendrick just gave you a glowing review! When might you start on this project?"

Rusty pulled out a small notebook from his back pocket. "OK, well, here's what I've got going on. I am presently working on four other projects; two are just about wrapped up and the other two are to be done at my leisure. So, I can do this: I work at my own pace, I tackle the job my way, not the owner's way. Most owners don't know how to replace a light bulb, and when they do, it's the wrong wattage or not an outdoor bulb. They start to act like your mother-in-law in the back seat, telling you how to drive!"

He grinned and continued. "I will write down any issues you want me to attend to and listen to your thoughts, but that's just the way I work. So, if you agree to that, I will take the job. If so, I will need a key to the house. So many issues are approached from the inside and the outside: roofing, attics, crawl spaces, electrical, plumbing, termites, etcetera. The list goes on and on, but I will get it done the correct way the first time, not after numerous times of jacking up your bill." He looked to see if Kosmo was following him on his expectations which the constable seemed to be doing.

Rusty went on. "Also, I would like to make a list to get your house back up to par and have Duke come over. The three of us would go through my list from top to bottom. This way I think I would feel better with Duke reassuring you that my plans will work for you, and that I am not taking advantage of you. And here's an important caveat: sometimes I get into something and a whole can of worms emerges. The way it looks now, that is definitely going to happen from time to time. For example, you have about six broken windows, along with rotted sills. And it's possibly more as I was not counting. So, what do you think, Chief?"

Kosmo agreed, knowing that now was the time to pay the piper. His house had been neglected far too long.

The men shook hands, and Rusty headed out with his notebook in hand, making a list as he left the station.

That morning Nancy and Wendy were also up bright and early, fixing some scrambled eggs mixed with diced ham and a couple of toasted English muffins. Then they were at it once again. This time Mark McGarvey backed his truck in with a load of fresh stone for around the drain pipes. and He had a good amount of blue slate left over from a few other jobs which he figured would work into the paths. Right behind him Joe Hassey arrived with Al Lussier who had his extra plants in the back of his car. Al was eager to see exactly where to place them. Reg Marden and George Williams arrived with a few bundles of cedar shingles. Reg told the girls that a contractor friend of his had a son, Cody Affeldt, who was going to stop by around noon and replace the missing shingles. And he added that Cody was bringing some black-tar roof shingles and would repair the roof area. Reg assured them that Cody was extremely limber and could balance on a ladder or a roof like a tight-rope walker.

As everyone started their tasks, Reg picked up a drop cloth and headed upstairs to repaint the bedroom ceiling. He was smiling a bit secretively to himself and looked at his watch. For, lo and behold, just as Nancy was getting ready trim a tree in desperate need of some attention, two cars pulled up. Out of them emerged six ladies all carrying some sort of cleaning supplies: buckets, vacuum cleaners, dust brushes, mops and spray bottles.

Sheila Egan introduced herself. "Howdy! We heard about your big project here. We're either related or are good friends of the retired men's group. Mary Williams is married to George, Sylvia Lussier is married to Al, Kathy Legg and Donna Affeldt are also married, but their husbands are off doing other projects. I do believe Donna's son, Cody, will be stopping by later on to patch up a spot on the roof."

The other women all smiled and lifted up their cleaning gear in lieu of a wave. "Welcome to our favorite island! We'll be glad to be of help if you don't mind," Donna said. Then she explained that they were going to give the inner working of the old house a good touch up and shine.

Wendy, after hearing all the introductions, said, "This is just amazing! Nancy and I thought we'd be working for weeks to get this lovely house back into shape. Let me give you the two-cent tour!"

Sylvia said, "Oh, there's no need to do that! I've been here before as Ann Sollas was an old Garden Club friend. It's just such a shame how the last owners just let it get into terrible disrepair."

And off the ladies went into the house like the Seven Dwarves with all their work gear in hand!

Wendy went to Nancy and said, "Now what are we? A party of thirteen including Donna's son? I'd better get to the market pronto and get lunch supplies. And I'll go to the A&P so Rita and Don don't see me buying food to feed an army!"

At the end of the morning Wendy called, "Lunch time!" She even rang an old handbell she found in a cupboard. She had sliced and grilled chicken breasts, and placed them on two large platters, dressed with a light vinaigrette. Additionally, there were some grilled sweet Italian sausages and buttered rolls for the sausages. She placed out a dish of mustard, and some garlic bread she found in the frozen section of the store. Now it was nicely warmed up. For drinks she set out a selection of sodas along with pitchers of iced tea and lemonade. They had to divide the group up as the kitchen table would only seat eight. The men sat together, and the ladies gossiped away at small tables out back by the grill. After they finished, Wendy placed out two platters of brownies, gingerbread cookies and chocolate chip cookies. Everyone reached for their favorites!

After about an hour, Cody Affeldt arrived and went straight to work on the roof. He seemed to fix it up in a very timely manner as next thing they knew, he was on the ladder replacing the cedar shakes. Nancy and Wendy gave him a thumbs up in appreciation for his talents.

Mark and Al were digging around the tree stump they knew had to be removed. After an hour the chain was double wrapped about the base as deep as it could go. They attached it to the steel frame of Mark's Dodge Power Wagon and slowly managed to get the old rotted tree trunk free from its hole. Then Mark filled the hole with small stones, and they covered it with some dirt. The workers agreed that it was going to take at least a half of his truck bed full of dirt to fill it up to the surrounding grassy area. Joe said that he had lots of extra dirt he would love to get out from behind his work shed.

Reg appeared from the house with some white paint speckles in his hair and on his face. He beamed saying, "One heavy coat did the trick! The ceiling looks good as new!"

Cody told George that the leak in the roof was from a knot in the plywood on the roof that had rotted out. He patched it with some heavy-duty rubber roofing tape and also added a coat of wet black tar before he added the black shingles. He stated, "It should be good as new! And," he noted, "as I walked over the roof, there were some soft spots. The owners would need to get T&T Roofing Company, or someone else to look those over. I'm glad I could help."

Meanwhile, the ladies had finished cleaning the upstairs except the room where Reg had painted. Sheila explained to Nancy they would do that as the last thing. They moved to the downstairs and were cleaning like a whirlwind: mopping, vacuuming, dusting, and washing the inside windows. The outside of the windows would be cleaned in a few days by Cody and three of his friends in trade for lunch. They would get the *best* burgers according to Al. Lunch would include ice cream sodas that Nancy said are over the top! Wendy makes them with root beer soda and vanilla-bean ice cream!

At the end of the work day two bottles of Pinot Grigio were opened and beers were on ice. Wendy had prepared some antipasti with sliced ham, turkey, salami, olives, Pecorino cheese, and mini gherkin pickles. She hollered out, "Time to stop for today! Snack time!"

The teams of workers filed into the kitchen to wash their hands after putting away an assortment of tools and cleaning gear. Then they all went outside and stood looking in amazement at what had transformed in such a short time. They grabbed a drink and a snack and circled up to talk about where things stood.

"Next on the list," Al said, "was to touch up the painting, remove a few more weeds, and edge the driveway. The windows will get finished by Cody and his group."

Mark said, "I'll arrange with Joe to bring the rest of the dirt fill tomorrow. There's some mulch readily available at the dump for free, so maybe Reg and George, would you see to that? We need to put up the lattice work for the rose bushes, too. The painting will take a good two days and then we really should be more or less finished. Hard to believe we've done so much in just two days' time! Great job, everyone!"

Before everyone bid their good-byes, Nancy reminded them, "Not a word to Don and Rita! And, lunch for the next two days is on us again. Everyone is invited, whether you're working or not!"

The next day Cody Affeldt arrived with his three friends, bringing rags, sponges, squeegees and ladders, and they worked at a record pace. Mark and Joe arrived with the dirt. Reg grabbed a shovel and proceeded to fill the stump hole, grade it, seed and water it and covered the area with a light netting around the newly seed dirt.

Al Lussier was nailing up the lattice work for his rose bushes. Reg and George were painting the trim where it was needed. Then Reg replaced the rotted wood boards on the back deck. He stated, "Well, it's not a perfect match but it's better than falling through the deck!"

By late morning Wendy was making an array of sandwiches when Donna and her husband, Randy, arrived to see If Cody needed any help on the window project. Then Sheila, Kathy and her husband, Brian, and Sylvia arrived. Sylvia started laughing as she got out of her car. "Well, you invited us for lunch, working or not!" She saw Wendy setting out food in the backyard and went to help her.

Brian grabbed a paint brush and joined in the party. Randy assisted Al with the lattice work, and then went and helped Reg with the deck planks.

Mark did the final project on his list as he had brought more stone to place in the driveway. That certainly gave the yard some real sparkle!

At last lunch was served, and what a spread! It consisted of: roast beef sandwiches on Portuguese bread, ham and cheddar sandwiches, egg salad sandwiches, pretzels, chips, a roasted corn and tomato salad, sliced beets with goat cheese and a bowl of sweet bread and butter pickles. The drinks included sodas, iced tea, lemonade, and cranberry or grape juice. Randy saw the pickles and devoured a bunch of them! To top it off there were deviled eggs and pan-fried French fries with a cayenne and mayonnaise dipping sauce. Every platter was picked clean!

Cody reminded them all, "In two hours it should be ice cream float time! We're on the final stretch of the windows. Back at it, good buddies!"

Everyone in the group found a project to attend to for the afternoon. By five p.m. they were done! They cleaned up their work space, and once again everyone admired the transformation. It is just utterly amazing, they all agreed. It was starting to look like a classic Nantucket post card! All it lacked were the pink roses reaching up the trellises. The place was spotless, and the ice cream floats were a huge hit!

Then the happy crews packed up their stuff and pulled out, leaving a quiet but totally cleaned up classic Nantucket house to its new residents. Wendy and Nancy sighed and slapped each other on the back. Who would have figured they would get all that help? What an amazing community they had found!

Nancy grinned at Wendy and said, "I'm on my way to the wine shop. When I get back, I'll place a bottle on ice. While I'm in town I'll ask Don and Rita to stop by at six. I'll tell them we have a question on the landscape project and that we are just beginning to make some headway, slowly but surely. Wendy, you'll have time to catch a quick shower. They'll just have to put up with my dusty outfit!"

Don was at the counter when she arrived. He said, "Rita is out in 'Sconset delivering some flowers to friends. Sure, we'll be happy to stop by. Are there any issues?"

Nancy replied, "No, not really, but this is a rather large project, and we do not want to start moving forward until we have a solid plan in place. Actually, we are ready to go full force tomorrow. We have been designing and reworking our ideas. I know it's been five days, but we want to study and approach the project carefully as it will make for fewer needed changes the end. Oh, and pardon my appearance, I was going through the attic and basement trying to get a few cobwebs cleared out!"

Six o'clock arrived, and Nancy and Wendy were standing at the end of the driveway when Don and Rita walked up the street. "Fingers crossed!" Nancy wished. "Let's hope they like it!"

Don and Rita stopped at the entrance to the yard and were at a loss for words. Rita stood there with her jaw dropped open. Then she spoke first. "How, I mean, *how* did you manage this? I mean, this is unbelievable! We are both in shock!" She continued to exclaim, "This is impossible! This can't be the same house you moved into five days ago! It's impossible! Don, look at all this work they figured out! I think we have two Superwomen who have moved in!"

Nancy and Wendy beamed. Wendy said enthusiastically, "Let's go inside. We have a chilled bottle of wine and we can discuss the whole process for how this actually took place."

She explained how they met the guys at the Brotherhood and how they invited them to stop by if they were in the neighborhood. She shared how one thing led to another and suddenly they had a small army working on the house!

Don asked, "Who repaired the screens? Who did the painting?" He continued with a whole host of questions. Then he hit a sensitive nail on the head. "How much money did you pay out?"

"We are not expecting you to pay for any repairs," Wendy assured him. "The only cash we paid out was for beer, wine, beverages and food to feed them all. No one wanted financial compensation, believe it or not!"

Don shook his head in amazement, looking out the windows at the trim and tidy yard.

Rita declared, "This place is sparkling clean! I mean, we are in awe here!"

Wendy and Nancy went over just about every detail, from the hole in plywood on the roof to the broken and missing shingles to the removal of the dead tree stump.

After the wine was consumed, Don said, "OK, here's the next deal. I would like both of you to reach out to everyone who worked on this project. Their phone numbers are in the directory. We know all of them, but if you could make a date so we can take everyone out to dinner, we can put that in motion. I mean it, this is unbelievable what you have accomplished, and I mean it truly!" Don raised his empty glass to show his appreciation to the hard-working women who had totally salvaged a sad situation.

SNAKE ISLAND, BRAZIL WHERE NO HUMAN SHOULD EVER GO...

About 25 miles off the coast of Brazil there is an island where no local would ever dare tread. Legend has it that the last fisherman who strayed too close to its shores was found days later adrift in his own boat, lifeless in a pool of blood. The mysterious island is known as Ilha da Queimada Grande, and it is in fact so dangerous to set foot there that Brazil has made it illegal for anyone to visit. The danger on the island comes in the form of the golden lancehead snake – a species of pit viper and one of the deadliest serpents in the world. The lanceheads can grow to be over a foot-and-a-half long and it's estimated that there are between 2,000 and 4,000 snakes on the island, which unsurprisingly is known as Snake Island. The lanceheads are so venomous that a human bitten by one could be dead within an hour.

Kosmo was sitting at his desk reading the prior night's report.

First his phone buzzed. Mike DiFronzo told Kosmo, "Sorry to tell ya, Chief, but Harbor Master Ted Hudgins is wants to speak personally to you. He's on line one."

Kosmo sighed and said obligingly, "OK, put him through. Kosmo held the receiver well away from his ear.

Ted came on the line and said, "Tell me, and I forget. Teach me, and I remember. Involve me, and I learn.'"

Kosmo countered, "Very creative, Ted. Are you taking evening classes at the high school?"

"No, nothing like that, Kosmo. Just little tidbits I pick up here and there. Maybe we can go to lunch, just the two of us? We can discuss some nice theories on different topics. I have lots of time this week!"

Kosmo rolled his eyes and replied, "I will get back to you on that invite, Ted. So, what's the reason for your call?"

"Well, they are calling for a late nor'easter' to be possibly heading up the coast on Wednesday. I have my crew on stand-by, so if anything happens, we are covered. Sheila Lucey and I are in contact every morning and afternoon before she signs off the Coast Guard airwaves. I just wanted to let you know of the upcoming situation and that we have our plans in place. Over and out," Ted signed off before hanging up the phone.

A few minutes later, Deputy Donato stood in the chief's doorway. He cleared his throat so that Kosmo would look up. Kosmo greeted him, "Good morning, Deputy. I'm just reading the report from last night. Yet another quiet night here on the Grey Lady. What's up?"

Mark held out a yellow legal pad. "Well, I just finished up my little report here. It has not been added yet to last night's log."

"OK, what do you have to add?" inquired Kosmo.

"Well, it seems old Lynne MacVicar, well she tied one on pretty good last night. When she was driving back out to 'Sconset around seven-fifteen or so, she plowed right into the 'Sconset rotary! Her old Ford wagon, well, the front was crushed, the two front tires were blown out and when someone called it in, she was nowhere to be found! You could smell the aroma of vodka in the car. I mean it reeked like a still! I guess she managed to walk home a little banged up but it must have been helped by the booze. When I got to her house, she seemed to be feeling no pain. There she was at her kitchen table holding a cloth to her head with a glass in front of her and slurring her words. She tried to tell me she swerved to miss hitting a baby fawn. Ha! I will 'baby fawn' her! She was smashed!"

Mark shifted his position in the doorway and continued. "But she's a sly one. She muttered she was sober as a judge, and she had just run to town to get a bottle of vodka at Hatch's. So, when I arrived, she had tried the latest trick that Eileen Berg, the attorney, is telling some of her DUI clients. If you crash into something and you have been drinking, rush home, sit at the kitchen table, pour some vodka down the drain but leave a bit in a glass. Tell the police when they show up you were so distressed that you just chugged a big glass of booze. That way they can't prove you were drinking and driving. What a conniver she is, drunk or not!"

Kosmo questioned Mark, "So, do you think that actually could be the case?"

Mark laughed. "Oh, come on, Chief, it's the oldest game in the book! Old Lynne MacVicar, she's a booze hound! I mean, it's all over town! I've heard that she took a cruise and drank them dry and almost fell overboard. And she went into some bar on one of the islands and almost missed getting back on the boat! It was just about ready to pull out of port, and she comes staggering out, yelling 'Wait for me!'"

Mark continued with his collection of island gossip. "Then I heard that she also stayed at some all-inclusive resort in Mexico, and she drank so much that she was asked never to return. Rumor has it that on the cruise ship the bartenders nicknamed her 'Glug, Glug, Glug' when they saw her coming. And get this! At one point when I was in her kitchen she asked if I wanted to dance! The old broad, she could not even stand up."

Kosmo interrupted. "So, what did you do about it all?"

Mark explained, "I called Norman Moore to come and tow the car away. Sadly, it's shot, totaled. But she will just go to Don Allen Ford and pick out a shiny new one, she's got a ton of dough." And he handed his report page to the chief.

"OK, Mark, thanks for handling that. Do you think there will be any charges against her?"

Mark shrugged his shoulders. "Not sure. You're welcome. Another busy night in the foggy village of 'Sconset! That's all I have to report."

A few days later, Wendy and Nancy were happily seated with a party of fourteen, consisting of the retired men's group and the women's cleaning group for dinner at Cioppino's. Rita had planned the menu with Tracy Root, the owner, and with the chef. It began with a large sliced smoked salmon platter with toasted buttered breads off the grill. It was accompanied by a platter of carpaccio of beef. The next course was individual plates of lobster salad along with several dishes of vegetables. The specialty Italian condiments were supplied by Rita from their market. The entrées were served family style and included sliced tenderloin of beef with a red wine mushroom reduction, grilled scallops and pork picatta, along with a beautiful plate of grilled lobster tails served halved!

Rita had insisted that they were not to run short on anything. If the server saw a platter of food running low, it was to be replenished as needed. All was done to perfection, and the guests were moaning in delight at how it all tasted.

Right before the dessert course was going to be placed on the table, Constable Kosmo and Judy Brownell poked their heads into the entrance of the small private dining room to say a quick hello to Don and Rita. They had been dining in the larger room next to their little soirée. Don, as the host, stood up and asked the two of them to join them for an after-dinner drink.

Kosmo, who was close friend with both hosts, looked at Judy who nodded. He accepted, saying, "Why not? But only a quick one. We don't want to intrude on your party." Kosmo looked at the long table and nodded at folks he knew. They pulled up a couple of extra chairs, and he asked, "So what's the occasion?"

Don then explained the whole transformation of the house on Quince Street in deep detail. He introduced Wendy and Nancy to Judy and Kosmo. After such a glowing report on the final outcome, Judy asked if the guests of honor might to stop over to her liquor store and advise her on her window boxes, as they were in desperate need of some TLC. Nancy and Wendy nodded emphatically. Then Kosmo and Judy headed out. Judy handed her card to Nancy.

The dessert was a lovely tiramisu along with fresh bowls of raspberries. To top it off, Cioppino's famous chocolate Kahlua cake was set on the table. Also, ever the thoughtful hostess, Rita had made up boxes of chocolate truffles to be given to each guest at the end of the meal. Each box had a personalized note to each recipient thanking them for all their hard work and effort on the Quince Street property. Lastly, in each of the envelopes with the notecards was a hundred-dollar gift certificate to Le Languedoc. The Mignosas knew that the work that was completed was worth even more than what they were sharing that evening.

Throughout the meal the wines never seemed to end. A toast with Dom Ruinart Champagne started the party off, and was followed by a French Corton-Charlemagne. Next the waiter brought an Italian Brunello Di Montalcino. After dinner drinks and scotches were also offered. It was a Class A meal! George made a very nice toast to Don and Rita on behalf of the group for such a lovely dinner.

The next day Nancy and Wendy stopped by Mignosa's Market to thank Rita and Don for such a grand evening.

Don was on the way out when they arrived and only said to them, "OK, you two, just to let you know you have an unlimited, never to expire, house charge account here at the market. We've set one up at Les's Lunchbox, too. It has a zero balance that you can never exceed, and it can be used three hundred sixty-five days a year! This is our personal gift for two such wonderful friends. Please use it and enjoy it!

They did not know what to say, but as Rita had told them since their new friendship had developed, Don is a man of means. If you're under his wing, you're all set in life! His nickname is 'Dondola', as he believes in giving back. Don is always doling out cash. If a person has earned his gratitude, as have many of our employees, then many of them never leave us. His best-known quote about our workers is, 'Pay them and keep them, don't screw them and lose them!'"

THE GHOST OF RAYNHAM HALL, NORFOLK, ENGLAND

One of the oldest halls in Norfolk, it was the first in England to be heavily influenced by European architecture. The hall is also famed for its spooky visitors, most notably the ghost of Lady Dorothy, the wife of the second viscount of the estate.

"No one has proven the picture taken of her is a fake," said Lord Charles Raynham of Raynham Hall.

The 17th century hall, near Fakenham, has been home to the Townshend family for more than 300 years.

Raynham is located near the source of River Wensum. Raynham Hall was built by Sir Roger Townshend in 1620, more than 100 years before the foundations of Holkham Hall were laid. Raynham was built in an entirely new style following the Italian form with a more contemporary red brick design.

Deputy Donato entered the station and went to the chief's doorway. He was quietly humming.

Kosmo looked up and said, "OK, Deputy what's on your mind?"

Mark quickly asked, "How often do you clean your gun?"

Kosmo looked at him with a puzzled expression and said, "Excuse me? Why do you ask?"

Mark replied, "I'm just curious. How often do you take your gun apart, oil it and put it completely back together?"

Kosmo informed him, "Well, not all that often. As you know, in the ten years I have been here, I have never fired it."

Mark tapped on his holster. "Well, let me tell you something. He elucidated, "These 'babies' can jam up on you. And that's the last thing you need when you're in a showdown with a criminal pointing a gun at you!"

"I guess you have a point there," Kosmo replied. "I might just have to go straight home and oil my 'baby' up!"

Mark continued with a serious face. "I am not kidding there, Chief. I take mine apart almost twice a month. Old Betsy here won't jam up on me-she's ready for action!"

The chief smiled. "It's a good thing to know that the loyal citizens of Nantucket are in safe surroundings with you and Old Betsy."

Kosmo shifted his focus. "Now, do you think you and Old Betsy could take these papers to the owners of The Skipper? It's their liquor license renewal papers."

Mark stepped in and picked up the forms, patted Old Betsy in its holster and strutted out.

Beth English who was on duty at the front desk knocked on Kosmos' door frame. "Sorry to bother you, Chief, but Ted Hudgins is here. He wants to speak with you."

Kosmo nodded. "OK, let's see what Ted has on his mind. Send him in." Beth gave him a thumbs up.

"'It is during our darkest moments that we must focus to see the light,'" Ted blurted out even before saying hello.

"Very nice, Ted. What's on your mind?"

"Well, Chief, it seems that some kids, most likely early summer visitors are hanging out down at the end of Old North Wharf and having a get together at night. I want to see if you could print a sign saying, "Per order of the Nantucket Police Department this area is closed after ten p.m.?"

Kosmo nodded. "OK, I will look into it. Give me a few days. How many posters would you want?"

Ted replied, "I would say about six will do the trick. Also, we will patrol the end of the dock every night before closing up shop at the office. Sheila Lucey is also going to spread the word about it being a 'no trespassing zone' after ten p.m. Thanks, Chief, I knew you'd be in agreement. See ya."

The next few days the girls finished up a few minor things around the property. Then they paid a visit to Judy at Hatch's Liquor Store. They agreed that the window boxes themselves and the liners were, well to put it mildly, in terrible shape, so they would be glad to revamp them. But in actuality Judy really needed new boxes, liners, plants and soil from top to bottom, in other words, soup to nuts!

Judy then said, without any hesitation, "If you go ask for Duke at the hardware store-he's the garden shop manager-tell him I sent you and to just place everything on my house" charge. Oh, and before you leave, could you please drop off this bottle of Beaujolais to him with my compliments? And one more thing. Here is a bottle for you two. It's quite refreshing if you chill it in the refrigerator for twenty minutes so it's not cold but cool to the touch."

The girls set out on their first window box job. By four p.m. Hatch's window boxes had totally been redone and mounted. Judy actually had no idea that they were already replaced until it seemed like, every few minutes, someone was saying to her, "Love the new look!"

She kept wondering what they were talking about since she already had her hair done with a slight trim four days ago.

Finally, the light dawned when Bunny Meyercord said, "Oh, my gosh, Judy! I love your new window boxes! They are superb! I had no idea you had such a green thumb!"

Judy went outside to see them and was quite amazed at the wonderful display of flowers Wendy and Nancy had planted. Judy explained to Bunny about the women who had actually done the work and went back inside the store.

That same day Bunny went home and called the 'Flower Box' girls and left a message asking if she could order four of them. She also inquired if would they ship to North Carolina to her off-island home there if she ordered some.

The next day reality set in as to what were they going to do. They had certainly enjoyed the lunches out and the beauty of the island. They knew the house, as of now, was more or less in excellent condition, and they had made new friends. But what were they going to DO? They were happy but realized they would not be earning weekly pay checks as they had been in

Connecticut. They could only walk around town, mow the lawn and work in the garden so many times. Boredom might soon set in!

Nancy was tossing ideas around when she went out to the back shed. She figured she could find some things to get rid of and make less clutter when she spotted a roll of what looked like thin copper. She didn't pay much attention to it as she moved some old rusted chains and a few useless flower pots to the trash area.

Back inside Wendy was making a kettle of hot water for a cup of tea. Nancy asked her, "Are you thinking what I am thinking? What's the next move here? We need to keep ourselves occupied. Any ideas?"

Wendy added, "Well, some income would also be a positive step here."

They enjoyed their tea, then Nancy picked up the drawing pad that Al Lussier had left for them. She started a rough sketch, crossed it out and started again. After a few rough drawings she said, "I have an idea!"

"What gives?" Wendy asked.

"Well, you know it's the time of year when Nantucketers are into spring plantings and window boxes. Several of them I noticed when we were in 'Sconset were nice but nothing over the top. It almost looked to me like the imagination was an afterthought. They bought some plants, planted them and that was it. So, maybe if we started a small gardening service, nothing too big, possibly giving consultations, and make up some window boxes, then we could sell them from the back of the Rambler on Main Street?"

Wendy replied, "Not a bad idea, not a bad idea at all. It seems the ones we did at Hatch's were easy enough. We'd have to research flower sources, and the hardware store seems to have a good gardening section. Let's get going!"

Nancy explored the idea further, looking at her sketches. "Starting up should be a relatively cheap investment. We make a sign reading, '*Dow & Eblen Garden Designs*', we tape the signs on the side of the Rambler, park it with the trunk facing the sidewalk with a couple of small model boxes in it. If Don and Rita OK it in front of their store, next thing you know, we are in business!"

Wendy sat silent for a moment and said, "Heck, why not? I'll make up some order forms and perhaps we should call the town office to see if they require business permits for on-street sales. And once we've purchased some of the equipment, we can figure out our pricing. I think, as that was our brainstorm when we first visited 'Sconset, that it's time to hatch this little baby!"

Nancy started to make a list. She figured they would purchase four window box containers and make two different colorful plantings in each one. They would price it at a two hundred percent mark up and see what happened.

She thought out loud, "The worst thing that might occur is, if we don't sell them then we are only out a small amount and we hang them up here at the house. Or if worse comes to worst, we can place them on the picket fence out front with a 'For Sale' sign and see what happens."

They finished their list. The first thing was to go and ask Rita if they could park their car out front and possibly put handmade signs on both doors of the car reading, '*Dow & Eblen Garden Designs*'. They would make sure that they would not block the store's prime front door parking space.

Rita loved the idea!

Next, they went to the variety store and purchased some magic markers in several different colors, along with some clear plastic tape, and some poster board in pink and blue.

The following stop was Hardy's Hardware Store. They wanted to price out window boxes and liners. After jotting down the costs they asked to speak with Duke in the garden center. They told him their thoughts on costs for the boxes, and he said since they were friends of Judy's, he would give them the 'friends and family rate' which chopped off an additional twenty-five percent. He said if business took off, he would throw in all sorts of extra perks. So, they purchased everything they needed to make the four flower box planters. They asked him who sold bedding plants wholesale and he sent them to the edge of town to Granny's Greenhouses. They were amazed at the variety of plants that 'Granny Alice' had on hand! It was hard for them to limit their purchase to just three dozen starter plants.

Lastly, they went to the Town Office and spoke with the clerk. She provided them with a basic 'Street Vending' form and assured them that small appropriate operations usually got approved quickly by the town officials. It had a small fee attached.

After returning home they both went to separate areas of the house, agreeing to meet in the kitchen in about thirty minutes with their hand designed logo to enlarge onto the poster board for the sides of the car. After the thirty minutes was up, they both reviewed each other's ideas. Both of their sketches were almost identical! They just started laughing, and Nancy combined their ideas and started to draw away! Soon their logo, incorporated into a larger design, was completed.

Wendy went out back to the shed which had a small but usable table. She placed a layer of small rocks at the bottom of each box line, added two different types of potting soil and then placed the flowers in with a nice balance of colors. She added a bit more soil to hold the plants in firmly, and, *voilá!* She was done! The whole process took under fifteen minutes, and all four boxes were completed in one hour. Everything they did per box was to be priced out for costs and time of labor. Plants ran around three dollars per window box; soil and stones about two dollars as they had purchased some bulk bags; cost of the window boxes and liners with the twenty-five percent discount ran six each and the total was eleven dollars, not including labor.

The gals discussed labor cost. "Well, how could they put a figure on that, including the travel and shopping time?" Wendy wondered out loud. "It only took me fifteen minutes to put one box together. So, if we put labor at twelve dollars an hour, and knowing we're marking them up, that will cover gas and shopping time easily."

Now, if they priced them at twenty-eight dollars each, they would have their one hundred percent markup covered. At eight a.m. the next morning, the two eager beavers were parked on Main Street with their car backed in and signs taped on both sides of the car windows. The town was quiet, and Rita was headed down Main Street to the store. She was smiling ear to ear when she saw them with their new 'stand' all set up. She asked how much they were charging for the boxes. When they said twenty-eight dollars each, she started laughing!

Wendy and Nancy started to look worried.

Wendy asked, "Are the boxes that overpriced?"

Rita then said, "I will take two, but ladies, ladies, ladies! This is Nantucket! No one sells a thing of beauty like these for anywhere less than forty-five dollars! I sell flowers that are wrapped in paper for fourteen dollars, and here you have way more materials and time invested in each box. Let's just see what happens with the remaining two boxes."

Rita asked if they could mount the two boxes she purchased on her front window ledges in front of the store.

Nancy nodded, "Sure thing, Rita, if you have some basic tools in the back of your store. We will see how the other two sell, and rethink our pricing if they sell quickly. How does that sound?"

Rita said she'd go see what tools and hardware she might have in their back work room to mount the boxes.

After about twenty minutes an older lady came up to the car, looked at the remaining two window boxes, and asked the prices for them. After Wendy told her twenty-eight dollars each, the lady loudly said, "Rubbish, complete rubbish!"

Wendy and Nancy were quite affected by this and did not know how to reply.

Then the lady explained, "The ones I have at home are complete rubbish! I bought all the necessary soil and fertilizers, and the plants just rotted and wilted away. Do you deliver?"

"Yes, we do!" they both chorused in unison.

The woman continued in a no-nonsense voice, "I will take six of them. If you can deliver by tomorrow, I would be grateful, as I am going off-island in two days. But I'll be back soon after that so the plants shouldn't dry out."

Thus, in less than one hour, they were sold out. They still had the two on display in the car, plus the two that were going to be mounted in front of Mignosa's Market. Rita had come out to see how they were doing and asked if they could pick up some brackets to hold the planters. So, they would need to get down to the hardware store and buy some more supplies from Duke and Granny's Garden. They would have to hustle in the afternoon to fill their first order at least!

The plan was to remain parked on Main Street for another hour. Nancy pulled out a pad from the car. With their two samples at hand, they were ready to take orders for free delivery or pick up on Main Street. Their idea of one hour longer turned into three more hours. By noontime they had twelve orders for delivery, promising that if the customer paid right then and there, they would have the window boxes delivered within forty-eight hours.

They went home after visiting Duke and Granny Alice yet once again as they needed more supplies than they thought earlier on. 'Dow & Eblen Garden Design' was in business!

After their first week they had raised their price to thirty- eight dollars per planted window box. They were averaging close to eight orders per day. They realized they were on a roll, so why take a day off? Nantucket has a short season, so they should 'make hay while the sun shines!'

Several customers asked if the gals could stop by their home and give them gardening suggestions? Duke was handing out the girls' new business cards like candy. They decided every Monday would be their "house call" day with a minimal charge for them to drive out and consult on each customer's landscaping needs. Not one customer batted an eye. All they wanted was for Wendy and Nancy to stop by and give them some ideas and thoughts on their gardens.

After three weeks of continuous non-stop inquiries, Judy at Hatch's was telling everyone who commented on her new window boxes about 'Dow & Eblen Garden Design' and handed their business card to anyone who asked. And the gals continued to have their car trunk display visible each morning. They were keeping busy!

A few days later Wendy walked into the kitchen of the Quince Street house. She nestled a copper flower box liner inside of a maple window box, which had white and blue gingham checked cloth encasing it. She called Nancy into the kitchen, and said, "What do you think? With a little tweaking, maybe we could put something like this into our inventory, put a very high price tag on it and call it our 'Reserve Vintage Model.' I found this copper in the shed. It took about forty- five minutes from start to finish. We can get some more of the cloth and possibly branch out to other colors that make the copper stand out. We can make two and see how they sell. If they do sell at all, I am thinking we should price each one at eighty-five dollars each. Our cost from start to finish is around is twenty-two dollars. That's just a mere four hundred percent mark-up!"

Nancy encouraged her. "That's gorgeous! Let's make two and bring them to town tomorrow!"

Once again Rita was walking down Main Street. She saw the girls setting up shop. As the Town Clerk had said, they never ran into any permit issues to sell their window boxes on Main Street. Perhaps that was partly due to the fact that Kosmo was a personal friend of Don and Rita's, and Judy was still raving to him about the flower boxes they did at Hatch's.

When Rita got closer to their car, she saw something reflecting off the sun. Seeing the two copper-lined flower boxes she asked, "What the heck are those beauties?"

"Oh," Nancy said a bit proudly and with a twinkle in her eye, "That's our new 'Reserve Vintage Model.' We thought the classic blue and white cloth would fit in well with what we have seen of Nantucket house interiors. They go for eighty-five dollars each, quite pricey we know, but we thought we would do it as a fun project!"

Rita looked at her store front window and said, "I will take six of them as soon as possible! I am going to put fresh fruits and vegetables in each one inside the store, and in the front window I'll make a new display with them. Filled with our fresh fruit or your flowers, they are gorgeous!"

Nancy said, "We can get you the cost price. After all, you have done so much to help us get established on the island this summer!"

Rita quickly said, "Don't you dare! It's full price or nothing!" She headed into the store and started clearing space by the front windows.

They had not even finished setting up the display off the back of the Rambler, and they had already sold six of the 'Reserve Vintage Models'! True, it was Rita's order, but if she liked them, most likely some other folks would, too! Within two days the new 'Reserve' boxes were selling like hot cakes. Duke, at the hardware store, asked if they would contract the store out for fifty pieces at a wholesale price. The store would get their carpenter to make more boxes if the girls would do the liners and covers.

Wendy told him, "But you will put us out of business on Main Street!" Then she offered, "We will cut you a twenty percent discount, and you will have no problem selling them at even a higher price than we sell them for out of the back of the Rambler."

Now, over the several weeks that just seemed to fly by, they were in a dilemma. Summer was coming to an end, and they needed much more space to keep producing their crafts if they were to continue. They also needed more landscape operating equipment as their gardening business

Hunter Laroche

was growing at a pretty good clip. And, to add to the problem of how to maintain their business, several people were hinting around and asking a few realtors if the home that was so beautifully restored on Quince Street might be for sale? It made them nervous about where they would end up if Don and Rita had to accept an offer they couldn't refuse. What might their future hold on the small island?

Around that time, Robert Romanos entered Kendrick's Real Estate Office on Main Street. "Hey, Tom, how's things?" he asked.

Tom Kendrick nodded at Robert. "Pretty good, can't really complain. Season is winding down, which make it a good time for me. There will be a lot fewer 'tire-kickers' just wasting my time pretending they are interested in buying a home when in fact they just want to see how the other half lives!" He continued with a quizzical look on his face, "What can I do for you, Bobby?"

Bobby scratched his head. "Well, I am not really sure at this time. You know, five years ago, when my uncle left me the five-acre property in Quaise, I thought it would be a nice thing to possibly fix it up and rent it out. At one point I had Pierre Garneau, who was interested in possibly living there in the main house, thinking he would do renovations on the property for a reduced rent cost. But he found a great deal within walking distance to town that has a garage he can store some of his tools in. Furthermore, you know that living out in Quaise it can be quite desolate, especially in the winter."

"You've got that right," Tom replied.

Bobby continued. "Well, I've have been paying the real estate taxes on it for the last five years, and I have no desire to do anything with the property. It's a real 'diamond in the rough'- nice piece of property but not what everyone is seeking these days. People want to be closer to town and prefer a much more of a modern living space. As you know, it has the one smaller barn that really needs some structural work. Then there's the larger barn that is fine structurally, but that's about it. The windows are all in place, there's water for the sink, but no hot running water. The stairs to the upper loft need to be reworked as they are pretty well rotted, and someone might fall through them if they walked up them. In the house, itself, the four bedrooms are really more like three as one is quite tiny. Best thing would be for someone to knock the adjoining wall out, secure the upper beams and make it into the master suite. The driveway, well, that totally needs to be graded and filled with crushed shell or pea stone. It's two hundred yards long, so that's a pretty penny and a fair amount labor to boot." He took a breath and peered off while picturing the entire property.

"There are two sheds that are of a pretty good size, at least ten-by-fifteen feet each. I never even tried to open the rusted locks. I've looked through the windows and there are lot of garden tools, wheel barrows, hoses, the usual stuff. The other shed does not have any windows, so who knows what's inside of it? I don't know and I don't care. There is also a long bed truck trailer with black steel heavy-duty mesh sides. All the tires are flat, and it looks like at one point the brake lights were wired. But now there is just a lot of debris piled up around the old trailer." He shrugged and rolled his eyes as if the thought of it all was just overwhelming.

He rambled on, but Tom was following his train of thought. "The main house is quite antiquated, to say the least, and who knows what the basement looks like. Probably a foot or two of water has collected over time. I never once set foot down there. I do go and run the water in the barn and the house every month or so. It kind of comes out orange brackish in color! The electrical outlets all work, but the wires for the house are from ancient times. I don't think you can plug in a toaster oven and a mixer bowl at the same time. You would definitely blow a fuse or two!" He sighed.

"Other than that, she's a real beauty. The property is a very nice spot up on that knoll. Of course, you can see the ocean from it, too. But I have no desire to keep it. So, my question is, can you get me a fair estimate on what it's worth? I am interested in selling it sometime, actually sooner than later, as the end of the year comes quickly, and no one looks to purchase any real estate here from November to April as you well know. And, one other thing - if you can put out some feelers, of someone possibly looking for a fixer-upper, I will get you some cash for the referral if it goes through. Maybe we can get the purchaser to ante up some as well to you. Maybe we could arrange it as an all-cash sale with no real estate selling fee?"

Tom replied, "Well, let's see where this leads to. You're correct about trying to move it to a sale quicker than later. And, as long as it's priced to move, that's a positive factor as well. But it is going to be a tough sell."

Bobby said, "It's going to be sold 'as is', so if someone thinks I am paying for an inspection they are totally off base. If they make an offer and I like it we will move forward to closing as soon as possible after a title search is completed."

"OK," Tom replied. "Let me take a drive out there this afternoon. I am headed to 'Sconset, anyway, so I will swing by on my way back."

Bob tipped him off. "There is a key to the house under the clay pot on the back porch. You know, in a way it's kind of a shame that no one would really want it. I am sure back in the day it was quite a lovely place," Bob said. "I'll really appreciate anything you can do to help me out. It has been a bit of an albatross hanging from my neck these few years. Thanks, Tom. Let me know what you think." He headed out of Tom's office with a slight hope that something would come of this revelation.

THE MYSTERIOUS HAUNTING OF THE RIDDLE HOUSE WEST PALM BEACH, FLORIDA

The history of what has become known as the Riddle House goes back to 1905, when it was commissioned and built by hotel owner, Henry Flagler, in West Palm Beach, Florida. The quaint Victorian-style house was situated across from the eerie Woodlawn Cemetery. It originally served as a mortuary and funeral parlor, giving it a taste of death from the very beginning. Oddly enough it boasted a cheerful, bright paint job on the outside, earning it the nickname "The Painted Lady." Considering that the cemetery was the final resting place for many of society's elite, there was a habit at one time of burying corpses with jewelry and other valuables. Thus, Woodlawn Cemetery began to attract more and more nefarious elements. Grave robberies became common place, and so the Riddle House became a Gatekeeper's Cottage, a sort of base for security guards from which to launch patrols to ward off trespassers.

Officials of West Palm Beach sold the house to Karl Riddle in 1920 to have it moved, allowing for other development of the site. One of Karl Riddle's employees apparently hanged himself in the attic due to economic hardship. The house was moved to "Yesteryear Village", and, even now, docents dress in period costume and tell stories of ghostly doings in the house.

Tom Kendrick found the property on Quaise Pasture Road as Mr. Romanos had given him good directions.

There was a pretty beat up rusted red mailbox at the beginning of the driveway on the left as you entered, and a very large rock anchoring the right side of the driveway entrance. He drove in slowly as the center of the lane was pitched high with over grown grass. With no one other than Bobby going into the place just occasionally, it just became more overgrown. He did not want to rip the muffler off the bottom of his car.

When he pulled up in front of the house, he had to admit to himself the setting did take one's breath away. He could hear the ocean waves making gentle noises off at a short distance. The property, according to the town map parcel he had stopped and picked up at the Registry, showed it as 5.2 acres. All taxes were current and paid for, well water, and a septic system were in place, but he guessed that the entire property could use quite a bit of updating. Bobby had said the electricity was installed, but then again, the person who purchased it would do well to call the electric company to see about an inspection on the old original wires to the home.

Tom got out and walked around the property. He could make out that most likely, many years in the past, there had been some large gardens, most likely for vegetables. Bobby had mentioned that his uncle had left Nantucket some eight or so years prior to his passing, in which case that meant the property had been vacant about thirteen years or so. The home had no visibly broken windows but was in a pretty sad state. The shingles and several roof patches looked extremely rough, and most of the screens were torn. No doubt there were bird nests in the eaves of all the buildings.

He pulled the plot map out and took a good long walk around the property. He found old stone walls that were most likely the boundary lines. Overall, it really was a magnificent piece of property! He noted the way it was situated such that the early morning sun would rise on the front of the home. It had a large deck facing west off the back that would certainly provide for some beautiful sunsets.

Tom then went to the smaller of the two sheds. It was locked, and had no windows, but seemed to be in fairly decent condition as the roof overhung the walls quite adequately. Next, he walked a short distance to the larger shed which had double-wide barn-style doors locked with a rusted padlock. He looked into the extremely dusty windows and could see a good amount of garden equipment.

He then wandered to the large barn. He entered through the side door that was shut tight with a wooden block nailed to it to keep it from blowing open. He recalled that Bobby had described the interior quite clearly. Inside there were piles of beautiful rough-cut wide pine boards stored off to one side, the kind of wide boards one did not see commonly on Nantucket as very few large softwood trees still grew there. There were a few long work tables, some old furniture, and in the back part of the barn was a tractor covered with about three tarps. There was a smaller tractor and several other gasoline-operated farm vehicles. He walked back to the right side of the barn and tested the steps leading up to the loft. They squeaked but seemed to hold his weight.

He very cautiously went upstairs, and at the top was amazed by a very large set of windows overlooking to the west. What a spectacular view! He saw a few deer grazing as if they not a care in the world. He also spied a tiny black and white kitten running around chasing a blowing leaf. The deer did not pay any attention even as it ran between their legs! Tom thought, "What a spunky little cat that is!"

There was a sink with a single spigot off in the corner near the windows. Tom turned it to the 'on' position and waited a few minutes. After a little gurgling some blackish-brown water spilled out. Slowly he let it run for a short time as he was curious if it might run clear. It started to become slightly clearer but still had a yellow hue to it. He figured there must be a spring that built up enough pressure to allow the water to flow out.

Looking around he saw numerous boxes, some wicker furniture that looked as if it had seen better days, an old single bed with some faded sheets on it and an old moth-eaten Army-style dark green wool blanket. There was even a pillow that definitely had seen better nights!

He descended the stairs as carefully as he had climbed them and exited the barn, closing the door as he had found it. Tom then found the key under the clay pot to the front door entrance. It turned quite easily, and the door was unlocked.

He stepped inside, sniffing the air which smelled dusty but not moldy. Straight ahead was a mahogany staircase leading to the second floor. He took a moment to adjust his eyes to the dimmer light. He figured the best way to get the lay of the house was to start in the basement. He located the creaky old door off the kitchen and hit the light switch, but nothing came on. So, being prepared, he used the flashlight he had brought with him as a safety precaution. The basement smelled extremely musty but almost seemed like a dry musty aroma. When he got to the bottom of the stairs, he saw it was completely dry, which was a relief. Just that much less trouble for a prospective owner.

He shined the flashlight beam around and marveled at how pristine the basement area looked-almost like a step back in time! The old washer and dryer were an olive-green color. There was a large plastic double sink and folding table next to it. He found an overhead fluorescent light with a pull string and pulled it ever so gently, and there was light! Bobby had said he kept the electricity paid up, perhaps just so he could make the rounds from time to time. But quite likely some bulbs had burned out.

There were also some boxes piled up on a small homemade stoop to keep them off the floor. He noted some other old furniture and bed frames, a few cinder blocks, a room that enclosed the oil burner, a hot water heater which was cold to the touch, miscellaneous tools on a few shelves, and a work bench and stool to sit upon. And, as in many storage spaces on the island, there were numerous large plant pots, some of nice ceramic styles.

Tom headed upstairs and toured the main floor. It had a very nice den with a small fireplace, and there were several books on the shelves along with a desk and chair. He moved into the living area which had another larger fireplace, a couch and two easy chairs. The upholstery was a good leather, so these items had not suffered mice damage. The room contained a few tables with out-of-date magazines on them, two ottomans, and more book shelves with cabinets underneath them. It was quite a large room, well laid out, facing the western part of the property.

The kitchen faced the barn areas. He could still see the deer, and the little kitten was laying in the sunshine. He then went upstairs which had two good sized bedrooms, each with a full bath with a combination shower and tub. A third bedroom was on the smaller size but still a good space. The fourth bedroom was the smallest and could best be described as a 'knitting room'. There was also one more full bath on the floor.

Looking a little harder, Tom noted in the smallest room there was a door that might lead to the attic. Tom turned on the light switch and ventured up. He just poked his head to see above the floor line and saw lots of open storage space. That was good as there would be less junk to move out of the house. The attic needed new light bulbs as three of them seemed to be burnt out. He went back downstairs to the main floor, thinking to himself, "This place has potential, but the location is not in very desirable place on the island. Beautiful setting, but pretty far off the beaten track."

Tom returned to the office and jotted down a few notes, made a Manila file folder labeled 'Romanos-Quaise property' and left it on his desk. It was just after four-thirty so he decided to head to Cy's for a cold beer. Deep down he was thinking that the Romanos property was going to be a hard sell. The property, even though nicely situated, really had no draw. It was definitely a 'fixer upper', but unless he could find a builder who might want to take on a project like that, would they have enough money to purchase it? Mr. Romanos made it clear that he expected a cash deal.

Tom reached over and took a cocktail napkin from the stack in front of him. He wrote down a few figures and crossed them out, refiguring. He felt that, even with all the buildings on the property, one hundred and ten thousand dollars would be the high value, and eighty thousand would be the low value. So, meeting that number in the middle, at ninety-five thousand, was to be the asking price. That needed to be a cash deal as the bank was not loaning money much in these times, only on secured mortgage deals.

He finished his beer, went back to the office and put the Romanos file away. He thought to himself, "This is not going to happen overnight, even if it comes close to a deal being offered." Then he decided to call it quits for the day. He sighed, "No money made today, that's for sure."

During the same day Ted Hudgins pulled up in front of the police station on Water Street. In his motorcycle with the side car, his dog, Bella, was sitting in the lap of Ted's lawyer friend who was visiting from Naples, Florida.

Ted walked into the station and asked Mike DiFronzo, "Is the 'big guy' in?"

"Yes, he is. Let me buzz him. Hold on a second."

Kosmo told Mike to send him in.

Ted saluted Kosmo and said, "'Many of life's failures are people who did not realize how close they were to success when they gave up.'"

Kosmo acknowledged him. "Very nice, Ted. Now, what can I do for you?"

Ted pointed in the general direction of the harbor. "Well, just a heads up for you. We have a mega-yacht due in port tomorrow. It is one hundred eighty-seven feet long. It's owned by the oil baron, Faust Goskowsky. The guy is loaded! Made his money in Denver Oil and Gas. I just got the word from my buddy who is the harbor master over in Newport. Says she's a thing of beauty! Going to tie up here for three nights. And his guest is, from what I understand, a contessa from Italy. My friend told me that the Contessa - just a sec, her name is on this piece paper - Contessa Mariangela Biagiotti Iacopucci-Ruggeri and her family own half of Italy in the Tuscany region. I guess they are in the wine business big time. They say she's wealthier than the oil baron's wife who is, of course, also on the yacht." He stopped and put the paper back in his pocket. Then he continued.

"So, Chief, what I am going to do is have them park the yacht at the end sloop, backing her in. I will also put up an extra 'No Trespassing' sign at the gate that leads to the end of the dock. I'll have one of my staff stand guard during the day so none of these looky-loo's can just try to take pictures of the Contessa and Mrs. Goskowsky."

Kosmo nodded. "OK, Ted that's fine. Just don't go making a big fuss over their visit. I mean remember that fiasco when Bob Dylan was here on his yacht? You had everyone and their mother jamming the street on the way to his boat, *Thirty-Acres*. So, Ted, give these ladies their space!"

"Roger that, Chief!" Ted said saluting Kosmo. He finished with, "'If life were predictable it would cease to be life and be without flavor.'" Then he turned around and headed out of the station.

John Vega and Bella were still seated in the side car. Ted said, "I got the green light to treat the incoming yacht like royalty. This is going to be something, I tell ya! What do you think, Bella baby? We're headed out, John. Hang on!"

Kosmo returned to the station to find Deputy Donato almost asleep behind his desk. He knocked rather loudly on Mark's door frame and the deputy almost fell off his chair! Mark picked up his head, looked at his boss and quickly started shuffling some papers on his desk when Kosmo asked him, "Late night?"

"Well, kind of," Mark acknowledged. "I was out doing night reconnaissance in my neighborhood, just trying to keep my skills toned and intact. I'll bet it was not until ten-thirty when my head hit the pillow!"

Kosmo chuckled, "OK, well, glad to know we are in good hands!"

Kosmo went into his office, and two minutes later his phone buzzed. Rick Blair was on dispatch and told him Ted Hudgins was on the line. Kosmo took a big breath, let it out and said, "Put him through."

"'Do not go where the path may lead. Go instead where there is no path and leave a trail,'" Ted stated in a boisterous tone.

Kosmo, with his usual reply said, "Well, that's very creative, Ted. What's on your mind?"

"Well, Chief, I just want to let you know if any hostage situations arise, my good friend, John Vega, is still visiting. I've got to tell you, he's a top guy in negotiations. He's here on his yacht, *Lawyer Up*, for the next month. So, if any tough situation arises, give me a buzz. He would be happy to help. The guy is bright as they come, top in his class at law school, top in the state for college graduates, and he is also a member in the *MENSA* society.

Kosmo concluded, "Thanks for that info, Ted. If any hostage situations come my way, I will give you a buzz. Over and out." Kosmo looked up at the ceiling and shook his head.

Wendy and Nancy met with Rita the next morning for coffee at Les's Lunch Box which was an area leased to Les Zablazkai right in the store. His successful eatery been there now for five years. They stated their plight about the end of season and the fact they needed to make a decision on what direction they were headed. They knew from the whispers around town that people were inquiring about the Quince Street house. They both knew sweet deal that they had all summer might come to an end at any time. Rita agreed that Don might sell the property, but told them he was also very keen on seeing that both Wendy and Nancy had a place to move into.

Don entered the store right as Tom Kendrick was walking in as well. Tom and Don exchanged hellos, and Tom said to Don, "Hey, Don, do you have a minute?"

Don nodded. "Yes, Tom, what's up?"

Tom explained, "Well, I have a couple who are looking to buy a house in town. They actually walked by your Quince Street property and asked me if it was for sale. They also looked at two houses on Fair Street, but really are interested in yours. I told them I knew the owner but did not think it was for sale at this time. And to tell you the truth, several people are also inquiring with other realtors about your house.

Don, who saw that Wendy and Nancy were in the store, told him, "Well, Tom, at this point we have the two "window box" girls living there. I really do not have the heart to sell it out from underneath them. You must realize that they were the ones who transformed it to what it is today. I'll let you know if anything changes. Thanks for coming to see me directly." He then went and joined Rita, Nancy and Wendy for coffee and a Danish. Tom took a seat at the counter for a morning coffee.

Rita told Don about their concerns with the season winding down and the fact that the buzz around town was people were looking to try and purchase the Quince Street property. They shared that if they were going to stick around, their business was expanding and so were their storage needs. Don told them he would never leave them homeless as he and Rita were so grateful for how they turned an eyesore into a masterpiece!

Tom Kendrick finished his coffee and toast, ordered one large coffee to go and headed back across the street to his office.

Don watched Tom exit the store, sat back for a minute and then hurriedly said, "I got to run!"

Rita laughed. "Well, there he goes, 'greased lightning!' Who knows what he's planning!"

Don walked across the street and entered Kendrick's Real Estate Office.

Tom was just taking the lid off his coffee when he saw Don. "So, Don, did I forget to pay?"

Don laughed, and replied, "No, but I have a question.

The couple who are interested in Quince Street-are they serious or just lookers?"

Tom looked directly at Don. "I believe they are serious, as they told me I could request a background check with their bank if needed."

Don countered, "OK, for the sake of seeing where this might lead, do you know of any rentals where I could move the gals? Their small business has grown, and they need more storage space for their gardening and landscape business."

Tom replied, "Well, I can ask around, but most rentals are really in the core district downtown. There's not much out of town to rent that is worth looking into if they need more space for landscaping equipment."

Don suggested, "Well, let's do this. If you'd do a little research and get me a fair price offer on the Quince Street property first. Then, if seems like a solid offer, maybe we can make a deal on selling it. Then I will see what we can do with the girls."

Tom told him he would have all the information early the next day. He added, "One thing, Don. There is one property that has just been presented to me, and with the right offer, I believe it would be a very good value. This might work out for you if it's handled correctly."

Don asked, intrigued, "What do you mean, if it's handled correctly?"

"Well, the thing is this guy who's selling his land with a house, barn and a couple of sheds will only deal in a cash transaction. He prefers to keep it off the radar. He is looking for a very quick turn-around. I told him there is not much demand in the market right now for a five-acre piece of property with a neglected house in Quaise."

"Quaise?" Don asked. "Well, that's not too far out of the way. These girls have a car and could use a barn. What is the asking price?"

Tom explained, "To tell you the truth, I have just spent a short amount of time reviewing the property. The taxes are all up to date. Yesterday I drove out to view it. Many possibilities are there for someone creative to fix it up. The drawbacks are: it's five miles out of town, it's almost remote, and the buyer has to be able to agree to it being sold "*as is*". It would be a nice place for an artist or a wood worker to set up a shop, but all the artists I know are not financially established to come up with a cash payment. You must know banks are not loaning to any one unless they have a solid credit line. You could guess the credit line the of a starving artist, and most builders these days are just doing several odd jobs at a time.

Then Don asked again, "So, what are we talking about, price-wise?"

Tom replied, "I fiddled around with it briefly in my head, and I figure around $90,000 is about where it lands. However, if someone had cash, and if I do not make it an official listing, and if both parties make a donation to my favorite charity - which is *me* - the prospective buyer might just be able to offer less."

Don, who really enjoyed the chase of a piece of interesting real estate, wondered, "Might you be free anytime soon to take a drive out so I could view it for myself?"

One hour later, Don, Rita, and Tom were walking the Quaise property. Rita gave Don a slight wink as they headed back to town. Another good deal was in the making!

BORLEY RECTORY, BORLEY, ENGLAND THE MOST HAUNTED MANOR IN ENGLAND!

In 1862-1863, a year after being named rector of his somewhat secluded parish, Bull Borley built what would be later become known as the Borley Rectory. Little did he know, unfortunately, that the land he chose to exercise his holy duty on was anything but sacred. In fact, Borley Rectory is now widely known as one of the most haunted places in the whole of England. From witches to ghosts to many other paranormal phenomena, the Rectory has become a site of unexplained experiences and a favorite of paranormal investigators across the world.

Rita and Don sat in their personal booth at Les's Lunch Box. Don, with his pad and a pencil started sketching out a rough plan for the property.

Rita said, "That place would be a perfect fit for the girls! What do you think about the price?"

Don sipped his coffee and then replied, "Well, I happen to know Bobby Romanos. He loves cash, and right now no one is going to even consider purchasing that property. However, Rita, you and I both never know. One minute you think a piece is going to sit on the market for a year or two. Then, a week later, someone walks in and buys it, someone like us!" He gave her a wink.

Don finished his sketches on four different pieces of paper. He showed them to Rita and explained some of his ideas for each building and the general property. He posed the question, "Yea? Or nay?"

"Do it!" Rita nudged him. "All the guy can do is turn down the offer."

"OK, I'll put this in motion. I'll tell Tom not to mention our names at all. I will also tell him that this will be a one-time offer, nothing higher. I will agree to paying all costs, and Bobby will net the offered amount one hundred percent."

Don then went to the triple-walled five-foot tall safe in the back room of the store. It weighed around two thousand pounds and was bolted onto a cement slab. It would take a crane to move it! He quickly moved some funds into a small briefcase. Next, he walked across the street, explained to Tom the deal, left the briefcase with him and said, "My offer expires at noon tomorrow."

They shook hands, and Tom added, "Both parties are to give me seven hundred fifty dollars in cash at the final signing of the papers if the deal goes through. That's my commission."

Don then asked Tom, "Would you please ask Bobby to come down to your office at one point, and open the briefcase so he can visually see the money? And, if you set a time for Bobby to arrive, call me at the market so I could see the look on Bobby's face. That way, when Bobby leaves this place, I'll know the answer from his facial expression. That alone will be worth the seven-fifty to me!"

Thirty minutes later, Tom called the store. Fifteen minutes later, Bobby Romanos arrived at his office. Ten minutes after that, Bobby walked out, all smiles. Don had his answer.

Tom walked across the street to Mignosa's Market. Both men were all smiles. Tom said that Bobby saw the sixty thousand dollars and said, "Deal!" Tom then said he could have all the necessary papers drawn up with Eileen Berg as she was the attorney that handled all his real estate closings. This would be a simple one-page legal document of the sale, and it could be signed, sealed and delivered as early the beginning of next week. The men shook hands.

Don and Rita made reservations at the Chanticleer for dinner at six p.m., and they also arranged for a bottle of Pol Roger champagne, and a plate of hors d'oeuvres to be served with the champagne. They had arranged for the girls to meet them at four p.m. at the market. Rita told them that they wanted to take them to dinner but had to make one stop on the way.

Not having any idea what was up, the girls met them at the market. Don had the plot plans and sketches all rolled together on the front seat of the car. He glanced at his watch, hit the trip odometer to zero and off they went. It took sixteen minutes, with the odometer registering seven and a half miles to the driveway entrance.

The old red mailbox was at the driveway entrance. Don already had plans for a new one to be stenciled *Dow & Eblen Garden and Landscape Services* if they accepted their offer. It would be much bigger and shiny. The large boulder would remain in place, but some very nice plantings would be placed around it, with a sign reading *Dow & Eblen Landscaping*. The sign would be placed in back of the boulder on two poles. It was in the sketches, but only Rita and Don knew about it. They drove into the driveway. Don explained that a friend had suggested they take a look at this property.

Right away both Wendy and Nancy said, "Wow! Nice piece of property!" As they got out of the car, several deer a short distance away glanced over to in their direction. What they did not see was the little black and white kitten running through the tall grass.

The sun was just setting, and Nancy observed, "It looks like the morning sun hits the front of the house, and the sun sets at the back side of the home. Is there a deck on the back of the house?"

Don replied, "Good question. Yes, I think it spans the whole width of the house. Right about now the sun should be in perfect alignment. Let's walk to the back and check it out."

Then Nancy wondered, "Who owns this place? Are we here to meet them? This is really quite the cool spot!

Maybe we could see if the owners might want to rent us some space in one of the barns. It would be perfect for our growing business! Well, I didn't mean to make a pun of it."

Don looked over at Rita and said nothing. He did say, "Let's check out the back deck and see if the sun sets on it."

All three of them were in a tranquil state of mind. The sun was brightly shining right on the deck. It felt mesmerizing to Wendy and she said, "You know, it's like a Chagall painting with the sun's light radiating off the clouds."

Don then said, "Let me show you something. Meet me around front." He went to the car, picked up the plans and sketches. They all went to the front porch of the house. Unexpectedly, Don took the key from underneath the clay pot and led everyone into the kitchen. He then said, "This place needs some work, but it has a great layout. I was put in touch with the owner and I bought it!"

Wendy responded, "No kidding! What a great find! Good going, Don. I hope it was a good deal!"

Then he proceeded to show Wendy and Nancy some of the sketches. He excluded the entrance of the driveway with the sign and new flowers surrounding the large boulder. The girls focused on all his ideas and were impressed with his vision.

He followed by saying, "So, if Rita and I are the new owners and if you're interested in possibly renting, maybe we can make a great deal!"

Wendy looked at Nancy then to Don and Rita and asked, "What do you mean?"

Don explained, "We're sorry to say but the rumor is true about people asking if the Quince Street house is for sale. As of now it's is not. We would not sell it until we had a place for you both to relocate if you wanted to stay on island for now and continue your business. So, here is the deal. I thought we might possibly make improvements on this property, but before we get that far, we want to make you an offer. We will sell this place to you for sixty thousand dollars. We will forgive ten thousand of that, making it fifty thousand dollars. We would hold the money on paper, payable to us at a very low percentage rate. We would also add five thousand dollars towards improvements that you can charge at any account that we use."

Then Don rolled out the last sketch. "We will also have this sign made for you as a house warming present!" He showed them the *Dow & Eblen Landscape Design* sign sketch with the new red mail box and flower plantings around the boulder at the driveway entrance.

Wendy had tears rolling down her cheeks. "Don, Rita, I just can't believe this! It's incredible! I don't know how we could refuse such an offer!"

Nancy just stood there, almost in shock. "This place would really give us lots of room to expand our business. I can already imagine us living and working here!"

With smiles on their faces, they finished up the complete tour of the property, and headed to the Chanticleer. The champagne was served, the glasses were clinked, the hors d'oeuvres were consumed and the dinner was wonderful. There was a lot to celebrate all around that evening.

The days began to move forward rather quickly.

Tom Kendrick made the sale proposal of the property on Quince Street to the couple from Washington, D.C., and they were ecstatic. They said to draw up the contract. However, coincidentally, Bill "Pully" Pullman, a realtor whom Tom knew well called him and said he had someone who was interested in the Quince Street property. The next thing Don knew, there was a bidding competition going on! The property went for twenty-five percent higher than the asking price! That was no issue for Don and Rita when they sold it.

The girls were in their new digs within three days. Don ordered the new sign for the entrance of the driveway. He also had one of his crew send down a large shiny red mailbox from a retail outfit off island. Then Rita called George Williams of the 'retired men's club' and told him the latest news of the gals' new home in Quaise. George got on the phone, and word spread rapidly among the team. The group went over with two bottles of champagne celebrate the girls' new living situation. While they were there, each of the men had a pad of paper. They set to work making notes for their chosen designated projects, from painting to woodwork, to roofing, screens and cedar shingles. It was 'déjà vu' all over again!

Mark McGarvey said one of his friends owed him 'big time', so he was going to have him bring over a road grader and work the driveway from the house to the street. They would level it so it was easily passable for any vehicle. He then told the girls he had another friend who had a whole mess of crushed shells that would certainly be enough to cover the whole driveway. He insisted that it be his house warming gift to them.

The first Saturday after Wendy and Nancy moved in, each of the men invited a friend who had some sort of trade skill. The ladies also showed up with four of their friends to scrub the 'dickens' out of that old forlorn house. Next thing the girls knew, the whole property was buzzing with people! It almost looked like an Amish barn raising.

Cody Affeldt showed up with six of his friends after speaking with Wendy, asking if she might be able to make them some roast beef sandwiches and root beer floats. Equipped with ladders and rags, they went after the window cleaning job with a vengeance. Additionally, Randy Affeldt went to work on the oil burner and water system.

Wendy had made a new friend, Karen Grant, whom she met at the grocery store on a few occasions. They had gotten to talking about different ways to prepare dishes for extra flavor. So, she called her and asked if she might like to come out a few different times and help prepare a feast. She explained about the house and all the people working on it. She admitted it would be much easier to feed them a good meal than to have them bring a boring sandwich. Wendy explained the ins and outs of the kitchen.

Karen asked, "How's the electrical situation?" Then she added, "I've got a very good friend who is a whiz at electrical work. He's employed by Kevin Dineen, loves to pick up extra electrical jobs and always seemed happier working with plugs and wires than anything else, besides eating!"

When Karen and Wendy put their culinary skills together, it was truly unbelievable the meals they prepared! And it was fun as well as a challenge. Wendy set up two large plywood boards into two long tables able to sit ten persons each. The chairs they found around the house and barn were a little sketchy but they managed to do the trick!

The food seemed endless to their wonderful helpers. They kept one table replenished with sandwiches, chips, and other snacks, along with pitchers of water, iced tea and lemonade. It kept the workers going and made for great camaraderie.

Within three weeks the property was absolutely radiating. Some of the people driving past were quite curious about the *Dow & Eblen Landscaping* sign, and several actually drove on to the property to ask about their company.

Kathy Legg, Sylvia and Sheila went to the Hospital Thrift Shop one hour before it opened on Monday as Kathy donated some of her time working there. She had begun to make a stash of things she thought would fit nicely into the girls' new home. Sheila and Sylvia proceeded to do their own shopping inside the store, and within forty-five minutes they had managed quite the haul.

Kathy made a list of what they had taken and left a note that read, "I'll be back tomorrow with cash to settle up! Your volunteer, K.L."

THE SUICIDE FOREST, AOKIGAHARA, JAPAN

While the density of the trees and the often-treacherous terrain in Aokigahara Forest on the slopes of Mount Fugi make it hard to determine an exact number of suicides, the number of dead bodies that are found is shockingly high. In 2003 alone, 105 bodies were found in the forest.

Mike DiFronzo, one of the police department dispatchers, was enjoying the last of his lunch at The Chanticleer. He had begun his meal with a peach and cranberry salad tossed with an apple-sherry vinaigrette. He had asked the bus boy instead of bringing him a new bread roll every few minutes, if he could have a full basket just left on the table with more butter. Mike had mopped up every last morsel of the salad dressing, using a few rolls.

The lobster roll was, as he proclaimed to the server, top-notch. When the server went to remove the breadbasket, Mike said, "You can leave that here. Why let it go to waste?" This was his first experience dining at the Chanticleer, and as he sat out in the garden, he did not want it to end. He buttered up the last two rolls and sipped on his sixth glass of iced tea.He had been given a gift certificate for twenty-five dollars from Sheila Egan a few days after Mike had stopped on Fair Street to help her change a flat tire.

Mike had priced out his spending so that the bill would come to just about the total of the gift certificate's value. His meal would include the Chocolate Marquise cake. He finished his entire meal, all rolls and every dab of butter, drained his iced tea, paid the bill and was content to remain seated for a little while longer.

All of a sudden, Mike heard someone coughing. Three ladies, who were seated at a table across from him in rose garden, seemed to be in turmoil. Susanna Goskowsky was in a state of panic! Sylvia Lussier was holding the Contessa's arms over her head. Susanna was holding a glass of water, but the Contessa was choking despite the pats on her back. She pushed away the offered glass of water. Her coughing was getting worse and turned into a gurgling sound. She was gasping for air!

Mike, despite his bulky frame, sprang out of his chair and went to assist the Contessa who was starting to turn from red to blue in her face. Mike told the ladies to step aside. While turning the Contessa around, he began to wrap his arms around her from behind. He clasped his hands together and started to pull in from below her ribs. After three pretty good tugs, the Contessa was still blue and gasping.

Mike then changed tactics as he did not want to risk breaking the lady's ribs. He laid her down on her back and opened her mouth. He looked inside her mouth and knew he had two choices: one was to use a sharp knife and to try a mock tracheotomy; the other was to try to pull out the piece of food that was stuck in her throat with his fingers. His best choice by far was to use his fingers.

He reached inside her mouth and prayed, "I hope this works!" He locked his two fingers on what he was the piece of wedged food and said softly, "Here we go."

In one smooth pull he succeeded in removing a piece of meat from her throat. He held the lady's head off the ground. He reached up and took a wet towel from the wine bucket, drenched it in the cold water and applied it to the woman's forehead. Then he reached up, grabbed a linen napkin off the table, soaked it in the ice water and placed it on the back side of her neck. It might not have been a pretty picture of the lady with the soaking wet towels adorning her, but within a few moments the lady's color returned to her face and her breathing was back to normal.

Susanna and Sylvia were then attending to their friend while Mike just quietly slipped out of the restaurant's front gate and departed. After Mike left, Susanna asked the server who was just standing around watching the situation unfold, "Where is the gentleman that assisted in this matter of urgency?"

The waiter said, "Well, Madam, I'm sorry. With all the commotion I do not know where he went."

Another waiter stepped forward. "Let me check the men's room." He returned, saying, "I'm sorry, he's not there." After the waiters helped the Contessa back on her feet and checked to see if she was truly all right, the ladies returned to their seats. The Contessa, feeling somewhat embarrassed, apologized to the staff for the commotion that she caused.

She then told Sylvia and Susanna to finish their meals. She asked the server to remove he plate and bring her a pot of chamomile tea.

Susanna asked her server, "Can you could tell me who the person was that came to the rescue?"

The server asked around, but no one seemed to know who the man was. Sylvia asked, "Did he pay with a credit card? If so, his name would be on the copy."

The server returned and said no credit card, but they were in luck as he paid with a gift certificate from Sheila Egan. The server would ask the restaurant owner later on if they could contact Sheila and find out for whom she purchased the gift certificate.

Susanna informed the waiter that she was staying in the harbor on her yacht named *Black Gold,* and if they obtained the information about the man, they could leave word with the Harbor Master.

The ladies resumed their luncheon, and Sylvia was so relieved that the choking ordeal was over as the Contessa Mariangela Biagiotti was her favorite cousin. Sylvia was also pleased to meet Susanna Goskowsky. Mariangela had grown up with Sylvia, and both of their maiden names were Iacopucci. They were both born in the same house in the northern part of Tuscany in a small village. They had been inseparable during their childhood time together.

However, at the age of twenty, Mariangela had moved to Florence to study wine making at the *Accademia del Vino.* On one of the outings to a vineyard she met the owner, Count Reggeri. One year later, after studying intensely, she applied for a position of a 'viticoltori assistente' at the Count's vineyard. He was quite attracted to his new employee, and a year later after they had courted, they were married.

Mariangela's new title was Contessa Mariangela Biagiotti Iacopucci-Ruggeri, and with that title came wealth that people could only dream about. Sylvia was her Maid of Honor and cried during the whole ceremony.

Over time Mariangela took a project on as her own personal venture in the wine business. The property was a vineyard that had fallen into disrepair. First, she went to the area on Montepulciano and sought out the property which was for sale. She was used an alias so that the current owner would not inflate the selling price if he realized who she was. She brought with her, on her second visit to the dilapidated property, a wine maker from one of their vineyards.

The vigneron made several passes through the vineyard. It consisted of two hundred hectares, and there was an option to purchase another parcel of two hundred more hectares. Mariangela drove a hard bargain and was able to get the property and the additional two hundred hectares at a very good price. She named it *La Cessca* from the coat of arms of Count Cessca who had originally owned the property many years in the past. The winery, after a few years of hard work, paid off and was successful in producing one of Tuscany's finest Vino Nobile Di Montepulciano wines consistently year after year.

Sylvia returned home after lunch at the Chanticleer to tell her husband, Al, about the threatening issue with her cousin. She also shared that they had been invited as guests of Susanna Goskowsky to her yacht *Black Gold* the following evening for dinner. When Al heard that it was a mega-yacht, he called all the guys that afternoon from the 'Retired Men's Club' and bragged that he and Sylvia had been invited to dine on a huge yacht. Al then went to his closet and started to pick out what he would wear on the yacht. He was almost jumping for joy!

The following day Susanna had been informed that the person who had saved the Contessa from choking to death was a man named Mike DiFronzo and that he worked at the police station. Susanna, on behalf of the Contessa made a call to the station. She learned that Mr. DiFronzo was not working at that time and was actually off the island since early that morning. She stated that she had an issue of importance to relate so she was put through to Constable Kosmo.

After she explained in great detail about the heroic effort by Mr. DiFronzo, Susanna said that the Contessa wanted to show her gratitude but was departing the following morning. They were taking the yacht and heading down the Intracoastal Waterway. She asked if it would be permissible for the Contessa to send a note of thanks via the police station.

Kosmo said, "Most certainly, and I'm glad you called to tell us of this event."

Susanna then asked if Kosmo might know of anything that Mr. Difronzo liked in life, such as any hobbies or such.

Kosmo told her that Mike was a superb person, but he always seemed to get the short end of the stick in life. He lived at home with his mother, and his only hobby in life was food. Kosmo clarified, "And when I say food, this guy, well, I believe he dreams about it in his sleep."

Kosmo went on to say Mike had been all excited the entire week about going to lunch at the Chanticleer. He talked about it all week. He could never afford to even, as Kosmo put it, walk past the Chanticleer or the Galley Restaurant as well.

Susanna thanked Kosmo for his time and disengaged the call.

Mike DiFronzo arrived back from Hyannis on the last ferry. The next morning, he reported to work. He had himself all set up with his cooler containing two sandwiches, three chocolate milks and another bag with some Fritos and potato chips.

Kosmo arrived shortly after and sat down in front of Mike's desk. He started a conversation with Mike asking, "How was your trip yesterday off island?"

Mike explained that he got everything on his shopping list and enjoyed a great pepperoni and mushroom pizza which cost less than half of what it would on the island. He had thought of buying an extra one to bring back home with him, but he had so many shopping bags he did not think he could carry it.

The chief nodded in understanding. Then he asked, "Didn't you go to the Chanticleer the other day for lunch? I think I heard you got a nice gift certificate for helping Sheila Egan with a flat tire."

Mike's eyes lit up. He loved to talk about food as well as consume it. "Oh, boy, did I!" He described everything down to the smallest detail about his lunch, everything but the ice cubes in his tea. He was going on again about his lobster roll when Kosmo interrupted.

The constable said, "Well, Mike, it sounds like you had a nice time."

Mike nodded enthusiastically. "I sure did, though I think that was my first and last time there. It's a little out of my pay scale range to dine at the Chanticleer."

Then Kosmo raised his eyebrows in curiosity. "Was there a situation with a customer choking while you were there?"

Mike looked down at his desk and rubbed his hands together a bit nervously. "Well, yeah. I mean there was, kind of."

"Can you fill me in?" Kosmo asked gently, noticing Mike's nervous reaction.

"Oh, boy, the lady is not going to sue me, is she?" He rushed to give Kosmo an explanation of his actions.

"After I got the piece of food out of her throat, I did dunk some towels in the ice bucket and put one on her forehead and one underneath her neck. First, I did try to force it out by giving her some abdominal thrusts that I read about in a magazine. Don't tell me I broke one of her ribs! If she sues me, I don't know how I will explain that to my mom!"

Kosmo reassured him. "No, nothing like that, Mike. It seems to me is after you saved this lady's life, as it was explained to me yesterday when you were gone, you just left the restaurant. She wanted to thank you for what you did. So, the women tracked your information down by contacting Sheila Egan as they found out that you used a gift certificate and the envelope had your name on it."

Mike let out a big sigh. "Wow, that's a relief that I am not getting sued. I knew a guy who was sued, and it was a real mess."

Kosmo grinned and continued. "Well, Mike, it turns out that your very good deed has not gone unrewarded. You see, the group of ladies included Sylvia Lussier from 'Sconset, and the lady who was hosting the lunch is Susanna Goskowsky. She is married to a Denver oil baron, and that's whose mega yacht, *Black Gold*, was in the harbor until early this morning. So, Mike, yesterday afternoon, after I had a very nice call from Mrs. Goskowsky. I was invited down to her yacht to pick up this personal letter to you from the lady whose life you saved."

Mike smiled back at Kosmo. "That sounds nice. Were you invited on board?"

"Yes, I was, and I have to say, it's an exquisite yacht." Kosmo cleared his throat in expectation of what would come next. "Now, there is a little more

Hunter Laroche

to this story, and before you open up this envelope, I think you might want to know that Mrs. Goskowsky is considered to be one of the wealthiest ladies in America, and she is deeply grateful to you."

Mike said modestly, "Well, that's very kind of her."

Kosmo went on. "Now, the second part is about the lady whose life you saved. She's not too shady herself. You see, Mike, she's a contessa, and her name is . . ." Kosmo had it written down on a piece of paper in his hand. "Contessa Mariangela Iacopucci Biagotti-Ruggeri and she is from a royal Italian family. Amazingly enough, she is a cousin of Sylvia Lussier!"

Kosmo handed the letter over to Mike and invited him to open it right there. "So, let's see what she has to say to you in this letter. Susanna said that she had her personal secretary write it in correct English as dictated by the Contessa so that it would translate correctly."

Mike opened the envelope with his hands shaking a bit. He had never had such a fancy letter addressed to him!

"Dear Mr. DiFronzo,

Words cannot even to begin to describe your kindness and quick thinking to come to my rescue.

I believed at one point that the incident that transpired was possibly going to take my last "breath" of life out of me. I started to see darkness, and with that comes the loss of oxygen to one's brain, and after that life can be taken away in an instance.

After the incident passed, we tried to locate your whereabouts, but it seemed that you had vanished as quickly as you appeared! When we did find out who you were, as we did not know anything about you personally, we contacted your supervisor who told us what a gentle soul you are and that one of your hobbies is dining. So, as a small token of my appreciation for your gallant act, I have secured for you a "never-expires" dining account at two restaurants on the island. The first one is at the Chanticleer, and the second one is at The Galley.

Now, so you fully understand the outlay of this gift, you may dine as often as you wish at either place. There is no limit on this gift. All gratuities to the staff and maître d' are also included. All you do is let them know when you are planning on coming. They have my credit card on file, and, as a back-up, they have Susanna's just in case of an expired date on one of them. They also have a direct phone line to Susanna if any type of payment issue ever arises. Now, Mr. DiFronzo, please do not feel embarrassed to indulge in this thank you gift, as the monies to fund this are practically endless.

It is also understood by me that you reside with your mother. Given the fact that she has raised such an honorable son, enclosed find a personal note to her. And, I have also arranged for Flowers on Chestnut to deliver every ten days a fresh bouquet of flowers for her to place for her dining room table. This also is an endless delivery, never to expire.

Lastly, I want to personally invite you and a guest as my treat with two round trip tickets to Italy any time you would like. This is not limited to a one-time journey. My husband, the Count Ruggeri, and I will welcome you with open arms on every visit you make. If we are traveling abroad, my personal secretary will attend to you and your guest's every whim! Presently, we own fourteen wineries and six châteaus in Italy as well as one in Provence, France. All transportation will be taken care of, and if you would like to visit the château in Provence, that is easily arranged.

In closing, Mr. DiFronzo, I cannot thank you enough for your noble act of saving my life. My husband and I shall always be grateful to you.

Sincerely,

Contessa Mariangela Iacopucci Biagotti-Ruggeri"

Mike was at a loss for words, as was Kosmo. They both looked at each other in disbelief.

Kosmo broke the silence. "Oh, I almost forgot, Mike! There is another envelope. This one from Mrs. Goskowsky."

Mike opened it up, still a little shocked from the first letter he had just finished reading.

"Dear Mr. DiFronzo,

This is a short note, in addition to the letter you must have just finished reading from the Contessa.

Your act with such a quick decisive response and the potential severity of that unfortunate situation at the "Chanticleer" was, just to say at the least, an act of an angel. That situation, most likely, would have had a much worse conclusion if you had not intervened. I could write a long detailed letter to you saying how you saved the day and a life as well. The Contessa is one of my closest and dearest friends in life. If something drastic had happened to her, it would have sent me into a downward spiral for many years to come.

But, to save myself from the many tears that would fall onto this page with the thought of losing her, I will make it short. I would like to offer you, and up ta total of six couples, a two-week trip upon our yacht, Black Gold. She is one hundred eighty-seven feet long, and we employ a crew of eight. My contact information is enclosed. All we would need to secure your voyage is for you to tell us if would you like it in one time span or for two separate weeks. We can have the yacht in Nantucket Harbor within a few days' time during the sailing season, barring bad sailing weather.

Once again, my heart reaches out to you for your kindness. My phone number is enclosed. Feel free to reach out to me at any time.

Most sincerely,
Susanna Goskowsky"

Later that afternoon Sylvia Lussier called Constable Kosmo, relaying the story he already knew. She said that she and her husband would like to take Mike and his mother out for a nice dinner, and could he have Mike call her in the next few days?

Three weeks into their new venture in Quaise, the girls figured it was time to tackle the large barn. With a sketch pad in hand, they had been in there a few times. They had not paid it much attention as it was a low priority project on their list at first. Now they were ready. With flashlights in hand, they opened the wide barn doors. A decent amount of natural light filled the dusty old barn. As they started to walk around, so much dust kicked up they had to step outside to let the air clear.

That when Nancy first heard it. She asked Wendy, "Did you hear that?"

Wendy looked at her. "Did I hear what?"

Nancy said, "Shhh. It sounded like a cat. It's very faint but I'm sure I heard a cat's meow."

They both stood there for a moment, and then they both head it. Again, the noise was faint but definitely it was a cat. But where is it coming from?

Wendy pointed back in the barn. "Maybe it went up the stairs?"

They first searched the main floor of the barn, behind all the boxes, under all the tarps covering the lawn equipment but found nothing. They made kissing sounds, but nothing came back in return.

They ventured up the creaky old stairs, searched top to bottom in the loft, but again found nothing. So, down they went and walked all around the outside of the large barn. But to no avail. No cat showed up.

Nancy shrugged. "Well, enough of that. Let's get back to work."

They entered the barn once again, and within a minute they heard the faint meow. But this time they remined still, and Nancy said softly, "It's coming from underneath the floor! Oh my, the cat must be trapped! How are we ever going to get these heavy floor boards up?"

Wendy suggested, "There must be some type of trap door somewhere." They looked over every square inch of the floor and detected nothing like a trap door.

Right then, Al, George and Joe pulled up in George's pick-up truck. The girls rushed out and started talking all at once. They explained that there was a cat trapped under the floor of the barn, and that they looked for a trap door but found nothing. So, they had walked all around the barn, looking for a spot where the cat could have crawled under, but again found nothing.

Joe tried to reassure them. "Well, if the cat got in, then the cat can get out. Don't worry too much about it."

Wendy and Nancy were not too thrilled with that statement. Yet they knew George had a soft spot for animals, so Wendy asked, "Would you grab a shovel and see if you could possibly dig a small hole under one part of the barn's foundation to let it get out?"

Al sided with Joe saying, "Ladies, the cat will find its own way out soon enough. We came to get some work done, not rescue a barn cat!"

Nancy replied, "What if some big snake or a rat eats the cat? Then how are you going to feel?"

George chuckled, went into the barn, grabbed a shovel and proceeded to find a soft spot to dig a hole under the foundation of the barn. He ended up at the back side of the barn. The dirt was firm but still softer than any of the other areas he had poked the shovel into.

So, with Al and Joe remaining out front of the barn's entrance, Nancy and Wendy followed George. He started to dig, but then he noticed that where he was digging seemed as though it had been filled in from a previous hole at an earlier time.

So, his little project all of a sudden became a much larger project. Joe and Al walked to where they were standing and asked George, "What's up?"

George stating that all the soil around that side of the barn was pretty dense like it had not ever been disturbed. However, where he was digging was not nearly as hard packed. It felt as though the soil had been dug up in the past.

Al decided that he wanted to be part of this mysterious hole, and he didn't want the girls to think poorly of him for not caring about the cat. He stepped forward and said, "OK, George take a break. I will dig for a while."

Just then Randy and Mark also pulled into the driveway with a truck bed full of stones. "What's going on?" Randy called from the truck window.

At that a big digging party began. When they were about two feet below the ground level, they noticed that the foundation was much deeper than they thought. They discovered there was a steel plate covering what seemed to them as an entrance to the barn's basement, like an underground hatchway.

Mark said, "We are going to need a chain and a truck to pull that steel door off. But first we need to get to the bottom of the steel plate. I will need to get the stones out of the back of my truck bed before I try and add more weight to it by pulling the steel plate away from the barn."

Thirty minutes later, after Al and George had cleared away almost all the dirt that surrounded the steel plate, Mark backed his truck up attached the heavy metal chain he kept in the boot of his truck bed, secured it to the steel plate's edge where there were two thick handles and ever so slowly pulled it away from the stone foundation. He worked slowly, and asked Randy to make sure the surrounding foundation was not going to cave in. The steel cover slid up from the hole that the men had dug.

Randy asked Mark if he had a flashlight in his truck. He asked the same to the others, though just George had one in his truck, and Nancy and Wendy still had theirs.

Al wanted to be the 'team leader', as he put it, to go in and scout it out now that the steel plate was removed and it seemed safe for them to enter the barn's crawl space. No one else particularly wanted to be first as they thought it possibly could be full of rats that might be living in there.

The opening was a good five feet in height and four feet wide. Al entered and found that he could easily stand up. Joe really had no desire to go into the dark dreary space, but Randy and Mark had a bit of curiosity built up, so they followed Al. Then Nancy and Wendy entered. They discovered some old crates with rusted tools, a good amount of cobweb covered furniture that looked like it had been there for a hundred years, and some old dishes in wooden boxes. There was some other miscellaneous stuff piled off to the side, clearly nothing of any value or interest to them. They agreed it was just more stuff for the next dump run.

Then Nancy asked, "What about the cat? Anyone see a cat?"

Wendy started making kissing sounds but did not have any luck. They decided to climb up the dirt ramp that they had had made while digging and go have a beverage on the back porch of the house. Then they could discuss how to deal with that lower level of the barn.

Wendy set the pitcher of iced tea out with a bowl of ice and sliced lemons along with some spoons and sugar.

While they were seated, Wendy suddenly jumped up in startled manner out of her seat. Everyone looked at her and asked, "What's the matter?"

She exclaimed, "Ewwww! I think a rat just ran across my feet!"

Everyone looked down, and Nancy picked her feet up off the ground and tucked them under her knees. Then Randy started laughing, reached down and picked up a tiny dirt-covered black and white kitten!

"Hey, you little feller," Randy said affectionately.

"You must be the culprit we have been looking for!" Holding the kitten up a little higher he said, "You see that large hole by the barn? That's all your fault!"

Right then the little kitten gave out a meow, and everyone started laughing. Then the kitten curled itself into the nape of Randy's neck and started purring away. Nancy murmured, "Oh, you poor little thing! You must be lost! I wonder where your mother is?"

Randy handed the kitten over to Nancy and offered, "You know, he or she reminds me of a marshmallow, all black and white like a s'more. We would make those when we were kids."

Nancy agreed, "That's a cute name, but I wonder where her mother is? The poor thing is all dirty and scared. I'll bet she's hungry."

She handed the kitten to Wendy and went in the house. She diced up a very small amount of leftover chicken breast and poured a small saucer of milk. She brought it outside and placed it down on the deck. The kitten finished every morsel, lapped up all the milk, looked at Nancy and ran off into the field.

Everyone chatted about Marshmallow for a short time. Then George suggested, "Let's go and haul all that stuff out of the basement of the barn. The ladies can hose it all down and decide whether to reseal the basement or perhaps build some steps or a hatch way going down. It's a good useable space." They all got up to tackle the job.

An hour later everything was out from the basement area of the barn and was laying outside. The girls said they would go through all the junk in a day or two. Al commented, "The only strange thing down there is that locked metal rectangular box. It was actually buried under some dirt. I only noticed it as I stepped on it, and the ground felt soft. But it seemed like something sturdy was under the soft dirt under my shoe. So, I scuffed off the dirt and saw it was a box! I would be careful opening it, as way back then there were a lot of old ships firing missiles. Possibly some previous owner of this property brought one back as a souvenir. The box looks like something from the Navy. They still find them around New England buried on some beaches. Some poor slouch probably had no use for it, had no idea how to get rid of it, so he buried it under all the junk stored in the barn's basement."

The next morning, after they finished their tea and toasted English muffins, the girls went to sort out all the new junk they had now acquired sitting along the side of the barn. They knew this would add to the more than twenty or so dump runs that Cody and his friends had made. The boys were ecstatic at getting cold hard cash, as one of Cody's friends referred to their payment at the end of every day, along with the root beer floats and the roast beef sandwiches. Each day, working at the house, they felt as though they hit the lottery.

Wendy and Nancy were slowly going through the piles of dishes and serving platters. They made a few separate piles, one for the dump, one for the thrift shop, and one for the items that they might keep and use in the house.

The sorting was going well when Wendy asked, "What do you think we should do with the 'bomb' box?"

Nancy suggested, "Maybe we should contact someone at the VFW and ask if they might like it. You know those old guys, they need some new excitement in their daily lives. First, we could gently break the lock off. We know the thing was stepped on by Big Al, and even though it was buried under a few inches of dirt, if that didn't set it off, nothing will!" They smiled at each other.

"Well, let's do this," Wendy replied. "Let me get a pair of pliers and a screwdriver. As you just said, it's been moved, buried, uprooted and hauled outside, and with all that movement nothing set it off. Even with Al stepping on it, the thing has to be disengaged from firing!" She crossed her fingers and held them up.

"OK," Nancy said, "let's move it into the barn and place it on the plywood table." They hoisted it up and brought it into the barn. It was relatively light, maybe weighing twenty pounds or so.

Wendy did a little drum roll on the tabletop. Then, using the screwdriver and the pliers, within three tries, the lock broke free!

Nancy picked up the ancient looking lock and said, "This thing has got to be a hundred years old!"

Opening the old rusted metal box, they found a cloth wrapped ever so tightly around a wooden box of finely designed inlaid wood. The outside of the box was in extremely good shape, not dampened or moldy in any form. The girls gave each other a puzzled look, and Nancy stated with a bit of relief, "I have no clue what we're looking at, but this does not look like any firing missile box to me!"

It took them a moment to get the inner box out of the metal box as it was packed in quite snugly. Laying it on the table, they removed the cloth wrapping. There were two heavy-duty pewter clasps on each of the ends of the wooden box lid. Each clasp was sealed with metal tie enclosures and an unbroken, very thick red wax seal.

"Whoa!" Wendy exclaimed. "What *is* this? I have never seen anything like this, only in a movie!"

Nancy looked over the inlaid box. She queried, "Do you think we should take this to an antiques guy? Maybe he would know something about it or its contents, as there definitely may be something of value inside from the looks of this ornate box!"

Wendy pondered that thought for a moment and said, "Hold on, I will be right back." She returned with her Nikon camera and said, "Let's do this. I will document everything from the outer box, the lock, the cloth, and the wax seal. Then we will open it. I will document it step by step, and if there is nothing mysterious about the findings inside, we are good. But if it holds something that might be valuable, we can make a decision on our next move. You know this island, if we've found something valuable, the gossip mill will be churning up interest in our discovery in no time flat. I'm just glad we're doing this on our own."

The wax-sealed box, Wendy figured, was about two and a half feet long and sixteen inches wide. She was snapping photos of it from every angle: top, sides and bottom, with the box standing up and laying down.

Then Nancy whispered, "The moment of truth! Who wants to cut the steel ties?"

Wendy volunteered, "Let me get some wire cutters to cut through them, and then you can do the honors!"

Nancy said, "Drum roll, please!"

The first cut of the steel ties went easily, as did the second. They placed them aside to keep if they were to be taking the box and contents to someone for evaluation. Then using a screwdriver Wendy broke the red wax seal.

Nancy opened the box ever so gently. Inside was another cloth tucked around what, at first glance, looked like a long rectangular object. There was a beautiful dark green lining of some type of fine woven material encompassing the interior of the box.

Nancy looked over at Wendy and surmised, "This is no cheap find. I don't know what's under this cloth, but for anyone to take the time to use such a fine inlaid box, seal it with a wax seal and use metal tie closures, and then wrap it in another cloth inside with such a fine interior lining – it's amazing. We are possibly looking at something *very* valuable!"

Right as they were about to do the unveiling, Marshmallow jumped up onto the plywood table and scared both of them! She let out a big meow and started poking her nose into the box.

Nancy picked up Marshmallow and commanded her, "Go and chase a field mouse!" She put her down, but the kitten looked up at the girls and jumped right back onto the plywood table. Once again, she poked her nose into the mysterious box. Yet, as determined as Marshmallow was to explore the box, they just moved her aside on the plywood table.

"Now for the moment of truth! Here we go! Cross your fingers!" Nancy slowly and cautiously removed the final cloth covering. Their eyes grew big. Under it was revealed the most amazing enameled gold staff which was around two feet long. It had some beautiful ornamental filigree. At the top of the sword-like object was an eagle and looked like it was carrying a young man holding the world and a small statue.

They both looked at each other. Wendy asked puzzledly, "What exactly *is* this thing? And why was it buried under all the dirt in a sealed off barn basement?"

They were both clueless about what the object was, but they knew that it had to be rather old and possibly quite valuable. They removed the object from the box and admired it. Nancy suggested, "You know, it looks like some type of baton!"

Right then a car pulled into the driveway. They quickly put object back into the box and placed it under a tarp off to the side of the barn. "Let's not say anything about this to anyone," Wendy cautioned.

Bobby Romanos stepped out of his car. The girls had not met him before, so were at a loss as who this person could be.

Bobby quickly took a look around and said, "Amazing! Truly spectacular!"

Nancy and Wendy were at a loss for words. Nancy asked, "Excuse me, and whom might you be? I'm Nancy Eblen, and this is my business partner, Wendy Dow."

"Oh, I'm sorry. I'm Bobby Romanos," he said. "I am the person that just sold this property. I guess you're the new owners?"

"Well, yes, we are," confirmed Nancy. She decided not to say a thing to Mr. Romanos about Don and Rita who actually purchased it for them, as Don had said he bought it under an anonymous corporation to keep their identity private from town records.

"Well," he said, "All of this - the sign, the big red mailbox and the flowers, along with grading the driveway was an excellent idea. I cannot believe what you have done with the place in, what, four weeks now?"

Wendy admitted, "Well, we had a lot of help from our friends. At one point, we had sixteen people puttering around here doing all sorts of jobs. We started some days at six a.m., and we sometimes worked until eight at night. We all worked together, and we fed them very well! We served lemonade, water, sodas and iced tea, and we kept the inside of the barn set up with sandwiches and snacks all day long. Some of our friends could give us a few hours every few days, and others stuck with it multiple days in a row. Sometimes we did a large BBQ out back in the sunshine. We set up two tables on the back porch. We have come quite the distance, as you've noted, but there is a long way to go. And thank you for the compliments."

"Wait a minute, Bob said. "Are you the two girls that do the window planters, especially the copper-lined ones with some type of colored cloth covers as well?"

"Yes, that's us," Wendy confirmed.

"I've seen your Rambler parked on Main Street a few times when walking past Mignosa's Market. I noticed they have four of them in their store front window filled with fresh vegetables. They are really quite eye-catching.

I used to have one of those Ramblers in yellow!" Then he shifted his focus.

"Mind if I have a look around? I see you have new hardware on the shed doors. Was there anything of use to you in the sheds? I certainly had no use for any of that old stuff."

Nancy replied, "Well, we mostly found some old rusted tools, a roll of screening, some plant pots, and fertilizer. Whoever lived here must have done some gardening and yard work."

Bobby went on to explain his connection to the place. "I never opened the sheds since my uncle left this property to me. Heck, I never even went into the basement of the house, and I only went up once into the attic. The only thing I did was stop by here every month or so and turn on the water for a few minutes. I would flush out the old rusty water but it never came totally clear. I did drain the pipes every fall, and I would have never had the water turned back on, but I read an article that said it was not good to leave the pipes empty for more than three or four months. So, I would fork out the dough to have the water turned on. I never really used any except to flush out the pipes every few weeks, flush the toilets, stuff like that. Each fall I had the house lines drained. To me it seemed like a total a waste of time and money, but I guess it's the way it has to be done. How's the old barn holding up?" He looked in that direction.

He advised, "You might want to keep a good eye on it. With one good storm, even though it's still pretty solid, I would be cautious as it might just blow over. And be mindful of the stairs leading up to the loft. They are pretty rickety! The loft has great windows! Some wonderful lighting come through, but the windows are caked in dirt."

"Well, not anymore!" Wendy declared. "They have been triple washed inside and out! And, you're right, they are lovely windows with a great view over the meadow."

Bob started walking towards the closed barn doors.

Right away Nancy looked at Wendy with a worried look on her face.

Then Nancy spoke up quickly. "Well, the barn seems fine, but it has lots of cobwebs and spiders, maybe ticks. It is on our list to-do list when we can get the funds to do some repairs." She was attempting to deter him from going into the barn. But Bobby started moving closer to the barn doors.

Wendy quickly blurted out, "Our insurance company came by for an inspection of the property a few days ago. The inspector told us that under *no circumstances* are we to let anyone into the barn until we get some structural improvements made. If they come back and see that there's a deep crawl space under it, well, they might really start asking questions. So, we are going to make one more walk through it and then replace the steel plate. That will take around five of us due to the weight of it, and we will seal it off for good."

Nancy added, "We might have the pipes and the drain for the hand sink relocated to a better location so we won't have to ever dig it up again to get to the pipes."

Bobby agreed, "That's a good idea," and started walking around the outside of the barn.

Wendy and Nancy were trying to figure out exactly what he was doing back here after he had let the property go. He then spotted the pile of dirt leading to the incline that led under the barn. "What's going on here?" he inquired.

"Oh, that's the crawl space we were talking about,"

Nancy replied. "It turns out a cat was stuck under the barn! Right about the same time as we heard the cat crying, a couple of friends came over. So, we all took turns digging at the edge of the foundation to try to get at the cat. That's when we uncovered a steel door, or more like a large metal plate which seemed to be covering an entry way underneath the barn. It led to what we thought must have been a crawl space. So, lo and behold, we uncovered a huge six-foot deep basement with rock walls. All this junk you see piled here was found down there. We are going to take it to the dump this week, except for a few plates and a decent China platter or two. The rest is useless clutter. Whoever put it there should have disposed of it. I'll bet it's been there for a hundred years!"

Bobby added, "Well, I had no idea that there was any crawl space not even to mention a six-foot deep crawl space under this barn. I don't believe my uncle had any idea either. I was told by my uncle that this place was built in the early 1800's by a man who had traveled here from France. Or, at least that's what my uncle mentioned to me quite a long time ago. He had found an old diary written by the man. I think his name was Gerard Dubois. My uncle even hinted to me that it seemed like this guy was on the run from Europe, but that's all I know. I was rather young when he told me that story." Bobby paused and continued to look around.

"I never saw the diary, but then after my uncle moved away, I had a group of ladies from the Hospital Thrift Shop come over and remove tons of stuff from here. I had zero use for any of it. I bet they took four or more pickup trucks of junk away-some to the thrift shop, the rest to the dump. It's odd, but there is one closet up in the attic that was locked, and I never found a key to it. But with all the junk that was cluttered around here, if I had to guess, there's just more junk in there. So, I just let it be." He moved away from the barn and headed a bit towards the house which gave the girls some relief.

"How about the basement in the house?" Bobby asked. He continued to share his stories about the place.

"I only ventured down there once. I used to come and visit my uncle every three or four years, spend the night and then head back off island. He owned this place for over fifty years! He loved it, but his age became a factor. He was quite the handy man, so he kept things in pretty good working order. When he passed away, he left it to me, and I just held on to it for a few years. As I had no interest in living here, it just sat empty. I was paying the taxes, and I would stop out about once a month just to check for broken windows or to see if anyone tried to squat on the property. It's a beautiful place but it does nothing for me."

"Well, the basement," Wendy picked up on his last question, "at least it's dry. It was full of spiders, tons of dust, but no mold. There were some more carpentry and gardening tools and a very old washer and dryer which were just sitting there collecting dust. We did not even try to plug them in. They were taken to the dump last week. We have friends who are remodeling their home, and they have a washer and dryer which they have offered to us. They are getting new models next week, so it's perfect timing. They will have theirs delivered here, but we need an electrician to recheck all the wiring so we don't short the place out and start a fire."

"OK, well it has been nice to meet you," Bobby said. He turned back as if he was going to pay more attention to the opening underneath the barn. "I was just stopping by to say I received a notarized letter from the law office of Eileen Berg that the property is now free and clear of any association of my ownership and the taxes are all current. She also stated that the electric bill has been transferred out of my name and registered to you.

One question-is it worth a look to go down there under the barn?"

"No," Wendy said firmly to discourage him. "There are a couple of pretty well rusted pipes that lead down from the sink in the barn. And it looks like the drain from the sink just goes directly into a small pile of rocks in the corner of the basement. It's not very sanitary, if you ask me, but at least it's only a hand-washing sink. Above it there is also a cold-water spigot. We turned on the spigot, and after a lot of gurgling, about a minute or two later dark brackish water slowly flowed out. We let it run for several minutes, and the water started to run clearer, but it's still cloudy. It really needs a good flush!"

OBVOGNY CANAL OF WASTE WATER, ST. PETERSBURG, RUSSIA

Obvodny Canal (Russian: Обводный канал, lit. Bypass Canal) is the longest canal in Saint Petersburg, Russia, which, in the 19th century, served as the southern limit of the city. It is 8 kilometres (5 mi) long and flows from the Neva River near Alexander Nevsky Lavra to the Yekaterinhofka not far from the sea port. The canal was dug in 1769–80 and 1805–33. By the late 19th century, after the Industrial Revolution, it had effectively become a sewer collecting wastewater of adjacent industrial enterprises. Eventually the canal became shallow and no longer navigable. The banks of the canal are lined with granite.

Wendy and Nancy waited until Mr. Romanos had driven away. Then they eagerly went back to the tarp covering their new found object to pull it out and place it back on the plywood table when another car pulled in! This time is was a red Jeep with a hard top. A lady around forty years old stepped out and started looking around as if the house might be for sale. Wendy shut the barn door after they both exited the building and asked the lady if they could be of some assistance?

"Oh, yes, my name is Lynn Pearl, and I was informed by Rita at Mignosa's Market that you are the ladies who make those gorgeous copper lined window boxes. I think they are absolutely stunning!"

"Yes, we are the creators of them," Nancy replied. "It's nice to hear that you like them."

Lynn then explained, "My family owns Claudette's Sandwich Shop out in 'Sconset. We would love to have two of them created for our store front!"

Nancy responded, "We can certainly make that happen. Right now we are on a short hiatus getting this property up to snuff. We have had a lot of help! If you could have seen this place four weeks ago, it was in pretty rough shape. Now we are making plans for our landscaping company. Of course, we will be modifying the barn into our window box production area. At this point we have seven orders on our list, so it will be at least eight weeks before we can complete yours. It takes us about a week to fill an order."

Looking a bit disappointed, knowing that the summer season was moving right along, Lynn replied, "Oh well, it is what it is. I will only need two boxes."

Nancy tried to make the situation a little lighter. "We also enjoy your place! We have been there three times now, and I just love the lemon cake squares!"

Then Lynn made an offer. "How about this? I drive the Polpis Road route at least once a week. I would be more than happy to drop off a few sandwiches as my treat if you could find yourselves bumping up my order in the queue! Also, I would be more than happy to pay for the order one hundred percent right now if that might help your cash flow with all these projects. Lastly, to go one step further, if you would like to display your new business cards on our counter, a friend of mine a makes beautiful calligraphy signs. I could have her make a very nice one saying these window boxes were made by Dow & Eblen with your phone number and address written on it. So, what do you think, ladies? From one business woman to two others?"

Wendy looked over at Nancy, smiled, and recalled, "You know, I just remembered we had an order that is not scheduled until when those customers return to the island, which is not until next week! I think that just moved your order to first in line, which means it will be ready in seven days! Oops, made a mistake it should be ready in two days! And, can we tell you our preferred sandwich fillings?" All three of them started laughing, the deal was done!

They wrote down all the information that Mrs. Pearl had requested for the style, size and colored cloth lining. As she got back into in her car, the girls desperately wanted to get back to their discovery. However, yet another car pulled in, but this time it gave them a little start. It was the town water department inspector's vehicle. A man sat behind the steering wheel reviewing something on a clip board.

Mrs. Pearl got back out of her car, walked up to the man and said casually, "Hey, Mr. Cokonis! What's going on?"

Mr. Cokonis waved, leaned his head out the window and said, "Hi, Lynn. Not much new these days. How's John?"

She replied logically, "By this time of day, I can say he's most likely up to his elbows making sandwiches! Tourist traffic has picked up very nicely, I must admit!"

The inspector started laughing and got out of his truck.

"What brings you out here, Dave?" asked Lynn. The girls were listening, and they were glad Lynn knew the man.

"I'll tell you. Joe Hassey and Al Lussier stopped by my office earlier this morning and told me about these two women - a Ms. Nancy and a Ms. Wendy - who are living here. They said that their water system was pumping out some pretty nasty rust-colored water. So, they asked if I could bring out a couple of pumps and put some good pressure into the system to clean the old pipes. I researched this property and found that it's on a well that must be over a hundred years old!"

Right then, Al and Joe and Reg arrived. Al got out and acted like he worked for the town! Soon introductions were made. Lynn stated that these two lovely young ladies were to be given the VIP treatment or else Lynn was not going to vote for Dave as the next elected town Water Department head.

David saluted her and said, "I will give them my most professional services possible!" The men all laughed.

Then the men headed to the basement of the house, led by Nancy and Wendy, with Lynn tagging along out of sheer curiosity. Al offered all sorts of suggestions, and Joe just nodded, though he hardly had any clue as to what they were talking about. From his work toolbox, David took out a water testing kit. After a few simple steps, he found the water was very heavy with iron minerals. He tested for water hardness, alkalinity, toxicity and heavy metals. He also tested for nitrates and nitrites, coliform bacteria. Lastly, he checked the water for silica content, oil and gas indicators, and its general chemistry.

Al kept asking, "What's the verdict?" each time David shook a sample in a little vial which he labeled for each test.

David only thought to himself, saying, "Hmmm . . ."

Joe and Reg stood there thinking it was just about time to go to Cy's Green Coffee Pot for a cold beer. Nancy and Wendy had drifted off to another part of the basement to sort through some of the old pots stored down there.

David once again said, "Hmm."

"Well?" Al asked, getting anxious and feeling like he was the foreman of the job.

David said, "Guys, it's not too good. Let me go speak with them."

They all gathered around David with his clip board in hand. Once again, he said "Hmm, well, ladies," as he reviewed his notes. He began a report of all of the elements of his water quality tests when Don and Rita came down the basement stairs. Now it was turning into a water party so to speak!

Rita sidled over to Nancy and Wendy and asked, "What's going on?" She noticed Lynn was there, too. "Oh, hi, Lynn. I guess you found your way to the window box ladies! They sure get a lot of fellows following them around, wouldn't you say?"

Al offered an explanation to Don and Rita. "We asked David if he could come out and check on their water quality, and he is just about to give us his findings."

David resumed. "Girls, I hope you have not been drinking the water out of the faucet."

"No, we have not," Wendy replied. "We have been using the five-gallon plastic jugs from the A&P."

Nancy chimed in. "We noticed it doesn't smell so good, and when we shower it leaves our hair a mess! We are using Irish Spring soap so we don't smell like the sulfur-like rotten eggs aroma it leaves in the air! What's in the water, anyways?"

David explained, "That's a good thing that you're not consuming the water. There are some pretty high, though not really toxic, levels of several minerals that aren't so desirable in the water."

Al asked, "So, what's the solution?"

David again looked at his clipboard and said, "Hmm. I need to find the opening for the well, drag up a good sample and take it to the laboratory. It's quite possible that, after all these years, certain soil chemicals have leached into it along with any number of possible dead organisms."

Nancy and Wendy looked at each other and Wendy exclaimed, "Yuck, that's disgusting! What are we going to have do about it? I mean, how can it be fixed?"

"*Is* it fixable?" Reg asked.

David rubbed his chin and said, "From what I know, you have a few options.

"Which are?" Al asked.

"One, you could dig a new well," David replied.

"And how much will that cost us?" wondered Nancy, now getting worried that they were getting in over their heads financially with this important issue.

David tapped his clipboard. "One never knows, as you have to go down at least one hundred feet to avoid salt water infiltration, so it gets pricey." He continued,

"The second option is to call David McCoy and see if he might be able to pump it dry. Then he could lower someone into the dry well and dig it out a good ten feet or so. That would remove all the sludge and deposits that have been building up over the years. Then you have to wait for the groundwater to refill the well."

Don looked at David and asked quietly, "Can you and I have a word?" They walked a little ways away from the group. Al started to join them, but Don gave him a look and said, "It's just going to be David and me."

Everyone watched them from a distance. David looked at his clip board and then at Don. Then he rubbed his chin. Rita figured she knew where this conversation was heading, so she just made small talk with Nancy and Wendy.

After a few minutes David and Don came back. David said, "I will be here with a crew at seven a.m. sharp. It's going to take a good half-day, if not longer, to tackle this problem. You will not have running water for at least two days, possibly three."

Wendy looked at him and asked, "How much will this set us back, financially?"

"If you have to stay at a hotel, it might run you a few hundred dollars as it's high season on island right now."

"No," Wendy wanted to clarify. "How much for the half or full day's work?"

"Oh, that," David replied casually. "Mr. Mignosa and I have come to an understanding, so you will have to discuss that with him." He headed up the stairs, and everyone followed him. As he got in his truck he repeated, "There will be around ten of us here at seven a.mm. sharp with several trucks. So, make sure your car is parked in a spot where you can drive out." And he left.

Everyone began talking at once. Al boldly asked Don, "So, what's the deal you made with David?"

Don replied, "Now, Al, it's something we are keeping private between the two of us. But let's just say he will enjoy many a lunch at Les's Lunchbox!"

Lynn turned to Nancy and Wendy with a smile. "I have an idea for you two. We have a two-bedroom apartment above Claudette's that's sitting empty for the next couple of weeks until one of my cousins arrives. It's fresh and ready to go! Why don't you pack up what you need for a few days and stay there? It has a full kitchen as well. Why don't you stay there tonight? Then you can head back here tomorrow to check on the progress of the well. I have to go into town for food supplies. The stairs to the apartment are on the backside of our building. The key is under the mat." And she headed for her car.

Wendy and Nancy did just that.

At seven the next morning, David Cokonis arrived with what seemed to be an army of town sewer and water department trucks. Wendy and Nancy arrived at nine, allowing enough time for the circus to get set up. What they saw made them stop in their tracks! There were trucks and more trucks, all sorts of pumps, hoses, and men scurrying around every which way! Some were blowing out the water pipes, others were sucking out the well with a large black hose. They saw sludge being expelled into one of the large round cylindrical sewage trucks. It was amazing!

Luckily, the girls had taken their newfound object after the previous day's commotion had died down and hidden it up in the attic of the house.

They covered it with some old blankets and set a box on top of it. They did not even tempt themselves to take another peek at the object.

With all the men hard at work, they decided that it was no safe environment to be hang around. So, they decided that a few errands ending with a nice lunch was on the agenda and headed back out, hoping all would go well on the property.

In the car, they made a short list of items they needed for their upcoming projects. They headed to see their new found friend, Duke, at Hardy's Hardware. He had heard about the Quince Street project that the girls had transformed. He also liked their window boxes that he noticed when he headed to Les's Lunch Box for Hot Pastrami Day! Each time they went to Hardy's, Duke was their personal shopper. He told that at least once a week or so, something was on deep discount!

He had followed what they did on the Quince Street property. When he found out from Al that they had moved onto the new Quaise project, he was there within a few days. He took a good look at the house and its surroundings. Then he made his decision as to what to get them as a house warming gift. He found a toaster oven at the store, gave himself a very big employee discount, wrapped it up and brought it to them. Within thirty minutes Wendy had made what he claimed to be the best sourdough candied bacon, tomato, and swiss cheese sandwich. Their friendship was sealed forever after that lunch!

The girls stopped in afterwards to see Don and Rita. Nancy ventured to say, "Don, we don't know what you said to Mr. Cokonis, but it seems like the whole town is working on our property!" Don gave them the AOK sign and smiled.

Then they walked over to the Nesbitt Inn to say hi to Dolly and Nobby who invited them to enjoy some tea and cookies. Their hosts rather prided themselves on being the first ones to really welcome the girls to the island. And they realized how much had happened to Nancy and Wendy since their first night on Nantucket! They were really becoming a part of the island community.

Lastly, they drove out to the Westender Restaurant for lunch. "I guess we'll survive away from home right here on the island for a bit longer," Wendy acknowledged.

Kosmo was off island for a one day overnight for a Police Chiefs' conference in Bourne, by the Cape Cod Bridge. He had left specific instructions with Jimmy Jaksic and Beth English to only notify him if it was a true emergency. Otherwise, they could just keep everything correctly entered into the daily log. Deputy Donato was also left in charge, but he was not to overstep his boundaries. That meant no giving jay-walking tickets, no excessive parking tickets, and no 'secret missions!'

Nancy and Wendy returned home around four p.m., and it seemed like the project was still in full swing. David told them that they were just about finished up. He said they drained the well dry and sucked out every inch of sludge. Then they lowered two guys alternately down the narrow shaft and hauled out an easy seventy-five buckets of wet muck and slime.

David continued his review of the day's work. After the crew had dug down a good six feet or so below the bottom of the well, they added three different layers of rocks and sand. The plans were to bring in several water trucks the next day, again promptly at seven, add numerous water filtration enzymes, and let it sit. Then they would repump the water out after two hours and repeat the process two more times. After that it would take a day for the last water with the enzymes to settle.

David also told them that they replaced a good fifty feet of pipe in different areas of the current water lines. They added two pumps courtesy of the lovely town of Nantucket. By the following day, they would flush the entire water system one final time. He mentioned that the sink in the barn now had a hot water line added along with new piping, and a whole new sink and drainage system to boot. "The sink," David told them, "was sent over by Duke at Hardy's as a gift!"

He concluded, "On a final note, Don kindly requested that I inspect the pump for the well system. I was going to check on it, anyway, but it was barely running. I am surprised that you even had any water coming out of the spigots. So, we installed a two-pump system as you have water for the barn as well as the house. They are brand new, and they have been in our warehouse forever! I don't even know why we had them in the warehouse, but they are now installed, all oiled, wired and ready to go! This should provide you with at least twice the water pressure, and hopefully, by tomorrow midday you will have crystal clear drinking water everywhere! Oh, by the way, we added four new water spigots around the house and the barn's exterior. Two of my men are master plumbers, and they tackled those tasks. Here is my card. If I do not see you tomorrow while I'm here for the final check of all systems, pumps and water quality, just give me a call about any other problems-day or night. My home phone is written on the back of the card as well.

Good luck with your new enterprises out here in Quaise. You are two ambitious young ladies, that's all I can say!"

They thanked him and headed back to 'Sconset to unwind from all the hustle and bustle of the last two days. They could organize their work schedule so that once they were back home, they could use their time well to tackle the waiting flower box order list.

NAGORO, JAPAN A CREEPY JAPANESE VILLAGE WHERE DOLLS REPLACE THE DEPARTED

Nagoro is a slowly shrinking village located in the valley of Shikoku, Japan. Populated by creepy dolls, it might make you question the reality of the place. Its inhabitants left the village in a search of employment or else they had died. Eleven years ago, Tsukimi Ayano returned home to Nagoro. Faced with loneliness, she populated the village with dolls, each representing a former resident. About 350 life-size dolls currently reside in the village.

The local school is now filled with a few dozen dolls, patiently waiting for class to begin. Made of straw, the bizarre dolls are dressed in old clothes. Once, when working in her garden, Tsukimi made the first doll in the likeness of her father. Then she came up with the idea to replace the other family members with similar dolls. Ten years later, her work continues. Every doll is located in the place where that person would have resided. So, while one is strolling along the village, one will find quite unique monuments to the former inhabitant, either appearing to be working in the field, fishing in the river or simply sitting along the road and staring at you.

Later the following day, Nancy and Wendy drove back to their house and waited patiently until everyone had packed up and departed. Then they went into the house and, without even turning on a single faucet, headed up to the attic. Who should they find up there but Marshmallow!

She sitting on top of the things that covered the mysterious newly found object.

When she saw Wendy and Nancy, she let out a meow and started scratching at the blanket covering the box. Nancy gently picked up the kitten and placed her on the floor, but Marshmallow promptly hopped right back on top. "What is it about this mystery object?" Wendy pondered. "Does no one want us to ever get a good look at our new treasure? Even the cat?"

Nancy picked up Marshmallow once again and placed her on a table off to the side by one of the windows. "Well, at least she can see what we are doing here."

Wendy uncovered the old box and placed it on the other table. Then they removed the cylindrical object. Even though there was good light coming in from the windows of the attic, it did not seem bright enough.

Nancy then offered, "Let me grab the step stool out of the kitchen and bring up three lightbulbs. I will replace the one in the lamp there. I am sure there is a plug around here somewhere. Then we'll replace two of the burned-out overhead lights. That should brighten up this dingy room!"

Five minutes later they were in business. The bulb in the lamp actually worked and was quite bright. With the three overhead lights all now working, the new object glistened and was very shiny.

All of a sudden, they heard a car pull into the drive. Wendy joked, "What *is* this place these days? Times Square? Just how many people can find us way out here in Quaise?"

They quickly placed the staff back into the box, covered it up once again and headed downstairs.

"Hello! Anyone home?" They heard a man's voice cry out.

Nancy opened the front door to find Tom Kendrick just about to knock on the door. Marshmallow was right at her side.

Tom looked down and said, "That looks like the little kitten I saw hanging out with the deer when I was here looking at the property last month."

"Yep, it's the one and same," Nancy replied. "We've adopted her, or she has adopted us, and we call her Marshmallow."

"Well, it's nice to meet you, Marshmallow." Reaching out his hand to Nancy, he continued, "I am the realtor who sold this place to Don and

Rita. My name is Tom Kendrick and I run Kendrick Real Estate on Main Street, across from Mignosa's Market." He pointed behind him and around the yard. "This place looks amazing! It's unbelievable what you have done to the property. It's almost unimaginable how you accomplished so much in such a short time. I just can't believe it. Don told me you had an army of people working here. Great results!"

"So, I'm Nancy Eblen, and this is my business partner, Wendy Dow." She continued, nodding, "Yes, we did have a lot of help. But there is still a long way to go. It seems like every time we cross one thing off our list, we add two more!"

Wendy spoke up. "So, what can we do for you Mr. Kendrick?"

"I have some papers that go with the property. Don asked me to drop them off to you. They include some tax records and plot plans. Additionally, here is some history of the property that I went and researched for you at the Atheneum and the Town Hall. I thought that as no one really knows much about this old property, you might enjoy looking over it sometime. I took some time to read through it and it's quite interesting."

Marshmallow meowed, and Nancy invited Tom to come in and set the papers on the kitchen table.

Tom shared what he had learned. "The property was actually deeded way back in 1810, purchased on a trade of livestock and some money. Then a Frenchman named Gerard Dubois purchased it in 1875 and built the house and barns over time. There are some articles included with all this stuff that I copied from the *Inquirer and Mirror* about this man. Sorry, but it's rather vague details about him. There's really not much of substance, but after the man passed away, rumors started going around that he actually was on the run from France. I talked with Bob Rully, one of our town historians, who told me that the gossip was this Frenchman was a jewelry and art thief and used to fence everything to a dealer in England." He shrugged his shoulders and closed up his file folder which he handed over to Wendy. "But I am sure they are just what they say - rumors."

Mr. Kendrick asked if they would show him around the property and point out what improvements they had made. However, very politely, Nancy said they were just about to run into town. But if he left his card maybe he could join them for an afternoon glass of wine on a sunny day on the back porch in the very near future! She knew how eager she and Wendy wanted to get back to their treasure.

Tom said, "Thank you very much, I'll take you up on that invitation. I'm sorry I didn't forewarn you of my visit. I'm sure you have a lot to do here. And, it is nice to know the new occupants of this place!"

As he got up to leave Wendy asked, "Excuse me, Mr. Kendrick. We are wondering who would we might talk to in town who has a good knowledge of antiques?"

Without a moment's hesitation he said, "Oh, that would be Bob Tonkin. He has a shop on the corner of Main and Federal Street called Tonkin's Antiques. He is also a good friend of Don and Rita's and a very honest person to deal with. He has a vast knowledge of antiques from all over the globe." Then Tom raised both eyebrows and inquired, "Why, did you find a few antique pieces here? I could have a gander at them. My uncle in Dartmouth-Cornwall, England, where I actually am from, dealt in antiques for fifty years. So, I know a thing or two about old artifacts and furniture. Would you like me to have a look?"

Now the girls were in a tight spot. Thinking quickly on her feet, Nancy blurted out, "No, actually we might want to pick up a small piece of furniture here and there in the future. We think some older used pieces might fit in better with the look and feel of the house. Where we come from, in West Hartford, Connecticut, everyone's houses have modern items from the 1950's and '60's. Nothing that works for a house in the country."

"Oh, OK," Tom replied. Well, let me leave you with this information and I will await your call. Any day of the week is fine with me for coming back for a glass of wine. Actually, I will bring a bottle from my collection, a nice red Bordeaux to celebrate! This was the quickest real estate transaction I have ever done! It was very nice to meet the two of you, and you, too, Marshmallow!"

After Mr. Kendrick left, the girls locked the front door and hastily went back upstairs, only to find Marshmallow, once again, on top of the treasure.

They went through the same motions again, moving Marshmallow to the table. Then they removed the shaft from the box.

"What do you actually think *is* this thing?" Nancy asked, staring at the ornate designs on it and feeling overwhelmed looking at the gold staff.

"I don't have a clue," Wendy declared. "I think, to act on the side of caution, we should quietly nose around Mr. Tonkin's store. We can just appear to be two curious tourists. I will make a sketch similar to this staff, but not anything so accurate that it would give it away. Then we can ask him what he possibly think it might be. If he gives us a clue about it, we can venture from there and try and move forward. I can sketch this thing out in about an hour, on a regular legal-sized pad of paper,

"What do we do if he asks what we are referring to?" Nancy countered.

Wendy shrugged. "That's the million-dollar question. Hmmm, I have a thought. We can say that our niece sent us this drawing and asked is if I know what it is as I studied some art in college, and she is curious."

Nancy tipped her head side to side, pondering the idea. "Well, it's a thought and perhaps it's a bit lame, but we can work on it. Go and get the things you need to sketch this thing. Then we'll run into town and pay old Tonkin's Antiques a visit! It can't hurt to try! Come on down, Marshmallow. Wendy needs to focus."

A while later, the girls were walking through the shop of Tonkin's Antiques. Mr. Tonkin was there and introduced himself. He said, "Take your time, ladies, and browse all you'd like."

After five minutes, Wendy went to his desk and said, "Excuse me, if you would please, Mr. Tonkin. I am wondering if you might be able to shed some light on a drawing I have here. It's a rough sketch, but we are curious as to what it might be. She pulled the sketch out of her purse and unfolded the drawing.

Mr. Tonkin took a moment to look at the sketch. Then he suggested, "It certainly looks like a scepter."

"What's a scepter?" Wendy asked? Nancy was looking over Wendy's shoulder.

Mr. Tonkin replied thoughtfully, "I think the best way to describe it is as a staff that someone would hold for some purpose or ceremony. You can look it up in the dictionary or an encyclopedia."

He went on to tell them more about their uses. "Real ones are quite old, hundreds of years old. Many a scepter has been duplicated and sold in tourist shops in France and England. They are like a staff, a stick or a baton. They come in many different designs and materials, though usually somewhat elaborate made out of a good metal. Kings used to have large ones and would wave their visitors towards them with their scepter as it indicates authority. There are some sayings that they symbolize God's rule on earth, showing dominion over people, their rulers and their nations."

He looked up from the sketch, feeling curious.

"Might I ask why you are interested in them? Does someone you know have one? Perhaps that's a silly question for if so, it must be a copy of one sold in a tourist shop. If it was an original scepter from some kingdom, it would be worth a fortune. More like something out of a fairy tale, I'd have to say!"

Wendy smiled at the thought. "It turns out we just found this sketch we had of it in an old book that we bought while in Boston a while ago. Actually, we forgot all about it until a week ago it when we found in in one of our boxes."

Mr. Tomkins held up his index finger and pointed it toward them. "You mentioned Boston. Were you in a rare books store or another antiques store? I know several dealers in Boston in the business. There is many a fine shop on Newbury Street and those surroundings. One person in particular I know has a vast wealth of knowledge on all sorts of antiques. His background is not just furniture but artifacts, jewelry, pendants, crests and things such as scepters. He owns Caselli's Fine and Rare Antiques. He is a truly wonderful man, full of knowledge and a real world history buff. If your friend has a scepter, he will know in a second if it's a fake. There are a few originals around, but all of them are privately owned or in a museum."

Wendy finished up their inquiry. "Well, thanks for the input. It's all quite interesting. And what did you say was the name of your friend in Boston?"

"It's Caselli, Nick Caselli. He can tell you just about anything with regard to ancient artifacts."

Nancy commented, "OK, thanks. Well, lovely store! We will be back for some more browsing soon!"

THE DEATH ROAD, BOLIVIA

Officially known as The North Yungas Road, the route was constructed by Paraguayan prisoners of war from the deadly Chaco conflict of the 1930's. It was built in order to connect La Paz with Las Yungas and the Amazon. In 1995, the Interamerican Development Bank declared it the "World's Most Dangerous Road", an unenviable moniker which is still in use today. An estimated 300 people per year have perished along the road from various causes!

The girls went back to 'Sconset for what they believed was their last evening stay above Claudette's.

They discussed their next steps, both of them wondering what they should do.

"Do we take the Scepter up to Boston and just take a chance on this guy Caselli?" Nancy proposed. "Hmm, maybe we can take the film from your photos and have it developed in Boston. Then we could go to his store, not say anything about Nantucket, and slowly breach the subject of the photos. We won't tell him a thing about us, and watch his reaction."

Wendy nodded. "I will take some really good close-up shots of the scepter and see what pans out. He will have no clue who we are, so if it's valuable we are anonymous and can just walk away with some insight. We could also visit the libraries up there and do some research on scepters. It sounds like there's a lot more to that staff than meets our eyes, at least! And what it was doing buried in the barn sure has me intrigued!"

"Me, too!" agreed Nancy. "OK, let's get our trip plans laid out and make it an overnight in Boston."

The next morning the girls packed up, wiped the apartment down squeaky clean, put the key under the mat, and then slipped a card with a gift card to Lynn for The North Shore Restaurant under the door of Claudette's.

They arrived at the house in Quaise where they found David Cokonis and four other men putting all the hoses and tools away into their trucks. David greeted them and announced, "Your water is crystal clear and should remain so for the next twenty years! Also, your water pressure is very good, about ten times what it was a few days ago. Every waterline, pipe, sink, hose, and even the washer line in the basement was refitted, so when you hitch up your unit it should be perfect."

Right as he said that, a truck pulled in and David McCoy, the 'Well Digger Guy' said, "Hey! I got a washer and dryer for this place. Where do you want it?"

"Hi, McCoy!" Mr. Cokonis called to him. "We almost had to call you. The well system here was in pretty bad shape."

McCoy tossed out, "Why didn't you? I could have had this place fixed up in no time!" He pulled out his card, handed it to Nancy and said, "McCoy's the name, 'Water' is the game!"

Nancy asked, "Why are you delivering our washer and dryer?"

"Oh, I got paid twenty-five dollars to drop this off, not including a tip. For another fifteen dollars I can install it off in your basement. I got my nephew, Poindexter, here with me - strong as an ox, this one!"

Mr. Cokonis whispered to Nancy, "This guy will do anything for a buck! By the way, don't give him a dime! He tries to chisel a nickel out of anyone he can. I am surprised he has not started sitting on some old box on Main Street asking for change. He's a real piece of work, this one, but he can find water anywhere! He has a natural talent for it."

Mr. Cokonis said to his men, "One more job, boys! Get those machines downstairs into the basement, make them level and set them up!"

McCoy, who thought he was going to lose out on some extra money and a tip to boot said, "I can handle it! I brought our little Poindexter all the way out here and promised him he would get ten dollars."

Right then, Poindexter chimed in, "You did *not* tell me I was going to get ten dollars. All you said was that I would get a couple chocolate bars for helping!"

McCoy weaseled in, "Aw, don't listen to him. He's not all right in the head, gets it from his mother's side, and he don't hear too well, either."

"I hear real well," Poindexter argued back. "I just got my ears tested last month in school!"

"Pipe down, you little whippersnapper!" McCoy responded angrily.

Mr. Cokonis stepped in and interrupted their bickering. "No, I'm sorry, Mr. McCoy. These people have zero property insurance set up yet. So, if you twist an ankle or something, it would be terrible for you. A lot of out-of- pocket expense with a visit to the emergency room. As we are with the town, we are covered."

Frowning, but knowing when he was beat, Mr. McCoy barked, "OK, let's get this dog and pony show moving. Time is money, and I got lots of work that needs finishing up." He got out to open his truck tailgate.

Wendy, who had been quite uncomfortable with the exchange between McCoy and his nephew, asked Poindexter, "Would you like an ice cream sandwich?"

"Oh, boy, yes! I sure would!"

"Well, seeing how I have not had any lunch, I could go for one as well," his uncle said said over his shoulder.

Wendy headed to the house with Marshmallow following right behind.

It seemed to take no time at all to get the washer and dryer installed up and running. The next thing the gals knew, the men getting ready to leave.

Mr. McCoy, ever looking for a deal, asked Wendy if maybe she had another couple of the ice cream sandwiches for the drive back to town.

Wendy said, "Sorry, those were the last two we had!"

Before he got into his car, Wendy stopped Mr. Cokonis and asked if they could do a huge BBQ on a Saturday or Sunday afternoon for all the men that worked on their well system. Each of them could invite a spouse or girlfriend. Wendy told Mr. Cokonis, "We will make it a great afternoon as your guys did a lot of work! We will supply beer, wine, sodas and a very nice BBQ with chicken, burgers - the whole enchilada!"

Mr. Cokonis accepted the invitation on behalf of his crew. "Sure! That sounds swell, really swell! I'll figure out a date that will work for all of us and let you know well in advance. Thanks so much for the offer. See you then!"

When the last truck rolled out of the driveway, the girls took their small bags into the house and turned on the kitchen tap. Mr. Cokonis was true to his word!

They took long showers in each of the upstairs full bathrooms. There was absolutely no loss in water pressure while both showers were running at the same time. They also gave the new washer a test run, and it seemed to work just fine.

The girls repacked and made plans for taking the six a.m. boat to Hyannis. From there they would take a Peter Pan bus to Boston. They called Lynn and asked if she could stop in to check on Marshmallow and refill her bowls if needed. They didn't plan to be gone more than a day and a half or so.

They arrived in Boston at eleven a.m. and checked into the Newbury Street Guest House. They asked where the nearest film developing place would be. They were directed to the Rexall Drugstore on Commonwealth Avenue. A man took their information, had them fill out their name and address just in case the film went missing and was found at a later date. That way they could be contacted either by mail or phone. Wendy also asked if she could request the expedited processing service for an extra fee. The man said yes, and she was told that her order would be ready by ten a.m. the following day.

Then they went to the Boston Public Library. The woman behind the main desk was extremely helpful. She guided them to the area on books that would give them information about scepters and other old artifacts.

They read as quickly as they could through numerous books and articles, hoping to make a match with the one they were researching. Some had photos of actual scepters and where they were now housed such as museums or private collections. The article that most interested them was called "The Scepter of Dagobert." Here is what it said:

The Scepter of Dagobert: Originally part of the <u>French Crown Jewels</u>, sometimes considered its oldest part. Dating from the 7th Century, the Scepter of Dagobert was stored in the treasury of the <u>Basilica of Saint-Denis</u> (also known as Basilique royale de Saint-Denis) until 1795, when it disappeared, stolen from the Basilica. It was never seen again. Its name comes from <u>Dagobert I</u> (629-639), the French king for whom it was supposedly created by Master Goldsmith, Éloi de Noyon, better known as <u>Saint Eligius</u>.

When they felt as though they had taken as many notes as they could, they realized it was late in the afternoon. In their eagerness to learn more about the scepter at a fine library, they hadn't eaten any lunch.

They asked the desk attendant where would be a good place to get a hearty dinner. The woman recommended Durgin Park in Faneuil Hall Marketplace. It was a few blocks to the restaurant, and as they walked, they discussed their strategy for the following day. They enjoyed their dinner and called it an early night back at the inn.

They got up at eight, showered and enjoyed the inn's scrumptious breakfast. Carrying their notes along, they arrived at the Rexall Drugstore and their order was ready. Auriello LaValencia was the photo department manager according to his name tag. He was the man who had them fill out the information when they dropped off the film. He was smiling away. He said to them, "Everyone calls me 'Smiling Al.'" He handed them the photo package and told them the charge.

"Well, it's nice to meet you, 'Smiling Al'," Wendy replied to him.

Al then asked, "Who took those photos?"

Nancy pointed to Wendy and said, "She did. 'Smiling Al' asked her what type of camera and lens she used as the photos were very clear and precise. He shared that he developed them himself.

Wendy responded, "I have a Nikon single lens reflex camera. It takes really precise shots."

Al inquired further, "You must work for a museum, no? Those gemstones in the photos almost look real!"

Wendy told him she did not, and then Nancy gave her foot a light tap. Nancy interrupted and said, "We have got to get moving, lots of thing to see. We might even take one of those Duckboat tours. Nancy quickly paid the amount due and they departed the store.

Wendy commented out on the street, "He was quite friendly for a city person, don't you think?"

Nancy replied a bit impatiently, "Yes, he was, but we have more important things to do. So, let's get this show on the road. Remember, we aren't going to say too much to anybody about this business."

They went back to the Newbury Street Guest House, laid all the photos out on the dresser and selected six of just the inlaid gold baton.

They put the rest securely away in Wendy's luggage. They headed back out and found Caselli's Rare Antiques just a little way down the street.

They stood across the street from the shop for a few minutes, watching to see if anyone was entering or exiting the store. "All looks quiet on the western front," Nancy quoted the title from an old movie and novel of the same name.

"OK, here we go! Step Two of our mystery investigation!" Wendy declared.

They rang the buzzer to enter into the shop. A lady who introduced herself as JoAnn Caselli had buzzed them in. She asked what she could do for them. Nancy explained to JoAnn that they had some questions about some photos that were given to her by a friend. They wondered if Mr. Caselli might be able to tell them what the object was in the photos. Nancy said it looks like an old baton. She did not mention that they had done a little research on this mysterious object. JoAnn said he would be arriving at the shop quite soon, so if they didn't mind waiting, that would be fine.

Luckily, Nick Caselli entered the store soon afterwards. He introduced himself to the girls who said their names were Donna and Diane. They explained their predicament in a manner they had rehearsed prior numerous times. Then they brought out the photos.

Mr. Caselli gave a slight chuckle and declared, "Well, ladies, you have photos of yet one more 'knock off' of a famous European artifact."

Wendy and Nancy looked at each other, not yet wanting to reveal any information on how it was discovered or details about the inlaid box and the wax seal. But it was frustrating not being ready to share their story!

However, Mr. Caselli added, "These photos are really quite fine quality. It makes it almost look like the real thing!"

Nancy asked, "Well, what *is* the real thing?"

Mr. Caselli then gave them the whole story of the 'Scepter of Dagobert', and how it's been missing since the late 1700's. He explained it was part of the royal French king's jewels and that it was stored in a French Basilica in the year 1795. He then finished by saying, "Amazingly, it has not been seen since. It's rumored to have been stolen from the Louvre Museum in Paris. And, once again, you may tell your friend she has a very fine reproduction of it! If she would like a fair value offer of the staff, then I could recommend someone here in Boston who might be able to fetch her a good price for it."

Wendy asked, "What is so special about this scepter?"

Nick expanded on the story. "Just the fact that it has been missing for almost two hundred years is one thing. The other is that it possibly holds a clue to where some mysterious gold coins are hidden. The rumors state that there is a piece of a puzzle in a part of the scepter that holds the clue. First, one would have to first find the original scepter, and people have been puzzling over that for almost two hundred years! Should it ever be found, then one would have to know where to look for the clue which is, supposedly, in a chamber in the scepter. This part of the legend could all be just a fantasy conjured up over time by those who have been searching for the 'Scepter of Dagobert'."

Nancy wondered out loud, "If the real one was ever discovered, what might the value be?"

Nick chuckled. "It's almost impossible to place a value on it as it's never been discovered. It is certainly a one-of-a-kind artifact, probably priceless. I can see you are intrigued by this on-going mystery that has captivated the imagination of many historians and treasure hunters for a long time! But, again, sad to say, these photos can only be of a replica of the real thing. But thanks for stopping by to inquire. There are many old mysteries in this world that will probably never get solved! It was nice talking with you both and seeing those photos." Nancy and Wendy thanked Mr. and Mrs. Caselli and returned to the guest house. They went into Nancy's room and started reviewing what they knew in an excited manner. Nancy encapsulated their knowledge. "Our house was built by a Frenchman. Rumors on Nantucket say he might have been on the run as he was possibly a thief. We know it was very well hidden. It is an artifact he could not easily pass along due to the history and speculation about it. This staff or scepter was in a sealed box with metal ties and a wax seal. It's apparently a very fine inlaid box. I can't imagine that someone would place an imitation scepter, or whatever it is, inside such an intricate box, seal it up and bury it. Of that, I am very sure!" she declared to Wendy.

That evening they dined at Anthony's Pier Four Restaurant, splitting a dozen oysters and a three- pound lobster, served with a bottle of Liebfraumilch wine. Skipping dessert they headed back to the guest house, still feeling totally confused as to where the next step would lead them.

THE HILL OF CROSSES IN LITHUANIA

Tucked away in a little corner in northern Lithuania is a place like no other in the world. The Hill of Crosses combines thousands upon thousands of crosses, all woven together into legends and fables. This sacred place is unique not only for its size, but also for its history, filled with tragedy and death, hope and redemption.

Mark Donato and Beth English had opted for one of their 'spy' nights out on the town. Earlier that week, Mark had visited the thrift shop and picked out a red velvet smoking jacket smelling of moth balls, along with a pair of velvet black pants for a whopping total of three dollars! Beth was wearing a leopard-print short jacket, black tight-fitting jeans, dark ruby colored ankle boots and was sporting a black beret. They walked into town.

First stop was the Ships Inn where they each had a Kir royale. Everyone in the restaurants truly enjoyed the evenings when 'Boris' and 'Natasha' would arrive in costume for their 'spy' night adventure.

They walked hand in hand as they ventured from place to place, Beth with her cigarette holder, (even though she did not smoke), and they would speak in foreign accents, talking about the mere peasants they were walking amongst. As per their usual route, the next stop was the Tap Room where June Hutton, the hostess, was seating people.

"Hello, Natasha," she said giving Beth a big hug, "and to you as well, Boris," addressing Mark with a smile. "What brings you back to Nantucket?"

"Oh, darling," Natasha exhaled, "we were just in the Caribbean, and the heat and the humidity was dreadful! I mean, you can't do a *thing* with your hair! Dreadful, I tell you darling!"

"Were you on a mission?" asked June, enjoying playing along with the scene.

"Yes, but our target - let's just say he could not with- stand the will of Natasha! He gave up all the information so easily. But such is life - tsk, tsk. Well, he died anyway. Such a shame, the poor man. But when one does not see it Natasha's way, well, such is life . . ."

June looked around and tilted her head towards Beth. "Well, follow me. Your secret is safe with me, and I have a lovely corner table for you!"

Beth ordered one very cold shaken, not stirred, Stolichnaya vodka martini poured into two chilled glasses with blue-cheese stuffed olives. She commanded the waiter to tell the barkeeper not to be short on the pour!

The next venture for them was the Club Car. The bartender was alerted by a call from June Hutton that the couple was on their way and to have a table towards the back door near the piano waiting for them.

They totally enjoyed their evening, and Mark actually awoke the following morning without a hangover.

Following their trip to Boston, Wendy and Nancy returned home to a very excited and happy Marshmallow. You would think they had been gone a week! They went right up to the attic and looked over their discovery. Pondering their next move, the decision was made.

Bob Tonkin had given them a very good lead, and now they felt like they could trust him for guidance. They went to visit him first thing the next morning. They asked him if he could be very confidential regarding the matter they were going to discuss with him. He readily agreed. He went to the front door, locked it and flipped the 'Open' sign to 'Back in 30 Minutes.' He led the girls to a section in the back of the store.

First, they pulled out the original sketch they had showed him. He stated, "OK, I remember that."

Then Wendy pulled out every photo that was taken from start to finish, all in black and white.

He exclaimed, "Wow! Nice photos! Very clear and precise." Then he stood back and asked in a more serious tone, "But what is this leading to, may I ask?"

Wendy responded, "Well, we will get to that. We actually took these photos to your friend, Mr. Caselli, in Boston. He said the same thing. We did not let on as to who we were, or where we were from, even. We used fake names. You will see why we kept an air of secrecy about what we were doing. We even had the photos developed in a drug store in Boston so no one would start to question where they were taken or what they were showing. We didn't want any links to Nantucket at this point."

"OK," Mr. Tonkin said in a puzzled voice. "So, is there more to this story?"

"Well, yes," Nancy assured him. "Here's the story from start to finish, but we need your total confidence in not revealing anything that we are about to share with you."

"Ladies, it's not often that I close the shop during business hours. You have it, I can promise you," Mr. Tonkin replied.

Nancy retold the story from the cat's meow to Al Lussier stepping on the 'bomb box', pointing to it in the first photos.

Wendy picked up by explaining that the house was built by a Frenchmen. "This was told to us by Bob Rully who is kind of a local historian."

Mr. Tonkin nodded and shared that he knew Bob Rully quite well.

Wendy continued. "The Frenchman was named Gerard Dubois. It seemed to some here on the island that he had had questionable dealings over in Europe. It's rumored that he could have been a possible art or jewel thief. It's also rumored that he could, as they say, have been "on the run" from authorities. Somehow, upon his arrival to the US, he found Nantucket a safe haven way back then. So, there you have it, that's the complete story, at least as far as we have been able to decipher it," Wendy said.

"Well, that's a heck of a story! Where is this supposed scepter now?" he inquired, trying to get a jump on where this tale might lead.

Nancy looked towards the front door. "It's sitting in the boot of our old Rambler wagon parked right out front."

"Would you be OK with bringing it inside?" asked Mr. Tonkin. He was rather dubious of what he might see next but wanted to go along with these two adventurous young women.

Wendy summarized where things were at. "Well, we have gone this far. Please remember, even if it's a fake, we still want your one hundred percent confidence on this deal."

"You have my word," he replied, raising his right hand as if he were testifying in court.

He led them to the front door, unlocked it, and Nancy went out. She removed the 'bomb case' from the car, looking around to see if anyone near the car paid any attention to her, but it did not seem so. She carried it carefully back into the store.

Mr. Tonkin locked the front door again, and left the "Back in 30 minutes" sign in place. Once again, they went out of sight of the front windows to his office. With knowledgeable hands, and following Wendy and Nancy's cautious instructions, he very slowly removed the staff from the 'bomb case' and examined the piece.

He looked at it right-side up, sideways, upside down and from every angle he could think of. He studied the inlaid box and the very soft silk-like lining. He took a jeweler's eyepiece and closely looked at the intricate stones that adorned the scepter.

After examining the piece for a good five minutes, he placed it on his desk, looked at both of them and declared, "Wendy and Nancy, either this is the most amazing replica of the 'Scepter of Dagobert', or, and this is just a farfetched theory, it's the original. How on earth that could be is beyond me!"

Wendy and Nancy looked at each other and asked, "OK, how do we find out?"

"Well," Bob ventured, "to authenticate this scepter we need a true professional, a person who has great knowledge in this field, someone we can trust one hundred percent not to disclose what we might possibly have here. I could reach out to a few museum curators, but I am afraid that word would spread instantly as someone is always looking to take credit for the next big find in the museum world. To me, they are good at what they do, well at least some of them are, but there are also a lot of "wannabes" who somehow slide into a position that is on a lower pay scale. They have no other choices where to work as they are not very good and their knowledge is quite limited. They are usually the most flamboyant ones, all talk, but with no real knowledge to back up their work." He took a breath, trying to think through the best approach to this challenge.

"I could also try a few private consultants, but then again, if I do not know them personally, well, things could get ugly to say the least. They would find a private buyer, and, well, I don't like the odds of small Nantucket being mentioned in the latest museum discovery news. We don't want to attract the wrong clientele here."

He paused again. "I truly think we might consider Mr. Nick Caselli. He owns a very nice shop in Back Bay, Boston. He was in Cambridge, across the river, many years ago when I met him through friends. He is my first choice, the one person whom I have known for years and feel we could trust. We will most likely will have to pay him an appraisal fee. However, he is extremely fair and honest. As they say, no pain, no guts, no glory! We will have to take what comes with the task. There may be a bit of a financial risk, but at this point, I feel we should move forward."

The three of them discussed the next steps. Wendy would accompany Mr. Tonkin to Boston as she took the photos. She, with Mr. Tonkin to substantiate what they had discovered, would make another visit to Caselli Rare Antiques. Bob said he would call ahead for a private viewing. He would explain to Mr. Caselli that this artifact was something he needed another set of trained eyes to authenticate. Nancy would stay behind to tend to things at the house.

FIRE MUMMIES THE SMOKED HUMAN REMAINS OF THE KABAYAN CAVES

Mummification of the deceased is a fairly well-known practice from ancient times. Most notably, the Egyptians utilized a mummification process that led to today's cliché image of a deceased body covered in gauzy wrappings. The discovery of mummified remains in several caves in the Philippines represents a different type of mummy – the fire mummy.

Found in caves in the town of Kabayan, in the Benguet province of the Philippines, the fire mummies are human remains that were preserved through a lengthy dehydration and smoking process. These well-preserved remains have given researchers insight into a unique mummification process, and into the tribal people who engaged in those methods.

The Kabayan mummies are also known as the Ibaloi mummies, Benguet mummies, or Fire mummies. They were located in many caves in the area including Timbak, Bangao, Tenongchol, Naapay, and Opdas.

Ted Hudgins walked into the police station promptly at nine a.m., telling Rick Blair that he had an appointment with Constable Kosmo.

Rick replied, "Yes, Harbor Master, I have it right here on the calendar. Let me tell him you have arrived."

Kosmo was seated reading over the prior evening's log book. Ted walked in and abruptly declared, "'You will face many defeats in life, but never let yourself be defeated.'"

Kosmo smiled up at him and said, "Still at the old quotes, I see."

Ted nodded emphatically. "Yes, I am studying at least three a day. I do my best to memorize them. What I do is start every day with the first one I read, and then repeat them from start to finish. As of now I am up to seventy-five different quotes." He stood as if waiting to be praised, but Kosmo only shuffled the forms in front of him.

"Well, that's all fine and dandy, Ted, but what I want to discuss with you is the upcoming town meeting focusing on the Coast Guard funding. They asked me to see if I could sit down with you and Sheila Lucey to review how it all synchronizes together."

"That would be great," Ted said. "My books are always open for town scrutiny."

"Well, here's the thing Ted. Last time at the meeting you got all fired up. Everyone thought you had way too much coffee. The things on your list, well, to put it mildly, were way off base. Where did you come up with some of the funding requests for such crazy things? You know, Bonnie Rizzo thought you had read way too many spy thrillers! For example, mine sweepers?"

Ted shrugged. "Well, one never knows! A small Russian sub might penetrate the waters of New England's coastline."

"Well, Ted, here's the deal. The three of us are going to meet this week at Sheila Lucey's office and review each department head's requests and budget before we go into the town meeting. Once the three of us each agree on each other's budget amount we will be ready. Let's schedule the meeting for early next week around ten am. I will have Sheila Lucey set it up. And, by the way, we don't need a small PT boat sitting in the harbor, manned at all times, Ted. See you around. I appreciate you stopping in."

Going with the plan of investigation into the big investigation of the scepter, Wendy and Mr. Tonkin arrived at Caselli Rare Antiques in Boston. JoAnn greeted them, and she gave Mr. Tonkin a strange look when she remembered seeing Wendy just a few days ago. She wondered what on earth the connection might be! Mr. Tonkin greeted her as well, introduced Wendy to JoAnn, and then said they had an appointment with Nick. JoAnn confirmed it and took them to Nick's office.

Bob greeted Nick warmly and introduced Wendy to him as well. Nick maintained a professional demeanor when he shook hands with her, but he, too, was mildly puzzled to have her return to his office with his colleague.

Bob laid all the cards on the table, retelling the story of the girls' discovery from start to finish. Occasionally he would turn to Wendy to confirm that the details were accurate. Then the time of truth arrived. Bob laid the 'bomb box' gently on the desk and told Nick, "She's all yours."

Nick replied, "Well, we shall see what we have here." He put on a pair of gloves, and with JoAnn watching closely, Nick started to work his magic.

He had several magnifying glasses and a variety of measuring tools for the stones. He also had a type of oil or resin and used a bright overhead light pulled down close to the box. Nick wiped the inlaid box with a cloth, and then used a different type of metal assessor for the gold staff. He never made a sound or a comment the entire time. He just kept measuring and examining the staff over and over.

Then he got up from his desk and retuned about five minutes later with a book opened to a certain page. He asked Wendy, "When you opened the box as you have shown here in these photographs, did you, at any time, use any cleaning substance on the inlaid wood box or the gold scepter?"

Wendy shook her head emphatically. "No, it was never touched other than when we removed it out of the box. We used a clean washcloth, not an oil-stained rag. Otherwise, it's just as we found it."

With a serious demeanor, Nick asked again, "Are you one hundred percent sure? Are you sure neither you nor the other lady you were here with decided to give it a wipe down?"

Wendy answered in all sincerity, even though she was feeling a little nervous at this point, "No, we did not put anything on the box or the scepter. How you see it is how we found it."

Nick took a deep breath and looked firmly at both Bob and Wendy. "First of all, it is critical that what I am about to say remains strictly confidential. I have got to tell you, and this is my most educated hunch, that I am ninety-nine percent sure that this is the original 'Scepter of Dagobert!' The stones are real, the gold has not tarnished, and it's in impeccable shape. When one adds to it the facts about the Frenchman building the house where this was discovered certainly leads to the likelihood of the discovery. The metal ties that close the box are quite old. Additionally, using the wax seal was an historic means of doing such a task. No one would hide such a magnificent piece of art in this world, unless they could not fence it or sell it illegally due to the rarity of the piece. Possibly he was waiting until later date to sell it, but he had to be very cautious to whom he offered it. If it was to be discovered on his property, he possibly could have been placed in jail until his dying day." Nick shook his head, almost in disbelief, as he continued to study the rare and extremely valuable artifact.

He asked Wendy and Bob, "Can you ask your local historian the name of the Frenchman and how he died? If he had lived a long life, he could have fenced it at any time."

Bob replied "Yes, we know the man's name. It was Gerard Dubois." And then Bob ventured, "But if he met an untimely death, that might explain why it was never sold."

Nick nodded thoughtfully and looked at JoAnn. "Well, I am going to need few more hours to do some very discreet research on the scepter. Bob, I would like you to stay with me here for a while so we can bounce things off each other."

Nick turned to Wendy. "Trust me, this treasure is in good hands. I will have Bob back at your hotel by two this afternoon with a definitive answer. Thank you, both, for relying on me to investigate this marvelous device."

JoAnn led Wendy back to the front of the office. She realized that Wendy might be a bit overwhelmed by what was going on, so she offered her a cup of tea or coffee. Wendy took some tea, sat down in an antique chair in the room and took a deep breath.

"It's all quite something," JoAnn started to say. "It's not every day that an item like that one arrives here in our office. How are you feeling, Wendy?"

Wendy shook her head as if to settle her thoughts. "I'm overwhelmed, even now, though we don't have Mr. Caselli's final opinion. It's just hard to believe the chain of events that led me to end up here again! I don't know what to think!"

JoAnn nodded in agreement. "We will just have to wait and see what my husband determines. It might be quite a story, one way or the other. If you need a bite to eat on your way back to the hotel, may I recommend a nice café that's along the way?" She saw Wendy to the door.

After stopping at the café to get a light bite to eat, Wendy walked back to the inn and waited anxiously to hear back from Bob about the latest information regarding the scepter. She felt antsy and decided to call Nancy.

Back on Nantucket, Marshmallow jumped onto the countertop, let out a meow, and a few seconds later the phone rang. Nancy picked it up quickly, as she had stayed close to the phone, hoping to hear from Wendy.

Wendy explained what had transpired with Mr. Caselli, and gave her the latest update. Wendy had time to spare so she went back over to the Boston Library again, to research a bit more about scepters. Lo and behold, there was a short but very informative chapter on 'The Scepter of Dagobert' in one of the books she found. She had taken numerous notes and then had walked back to the guest house.

Nancy quickly asked her, "So are they thinking it *is* the original scepter?"

Wendy spoke in a soft voice, "I will tell you one thing. Even though Bob and Nick might be experts, I, myself, believe almost one hundred percent that it is the original. We know the guy was French who built the house, and the scepter came from France. We learned it was rumored that he was possibly a thief on the run, and the amazing appearance of the box and its contents - I mean, it has *got* to be the 'Scepter of Dagobert!'"

Wendy continued, "The good thing that we did was document it and photograph it from start to finish. Mr. Caselli said that was a smart thing we did."

"Oh, my god!" Nancy exclaimed in a rush. "What are we going to do with it? I mean, it's got to be worth a fortune!"

"Well, just stay near the phone, Nancy. I will call you back after I get all the final information from Bob and Mr. Caselli. We'll know soon, I promise."

Five minutes later the phone in Wendy's room rang. She answered it and said, "I just hung up, Nancy. What do you need now?"

Instead of Nancy on the line, it was Nick Caselli. "Hello, Wendy," he said. You might want to sit down for this. Bob and I have come to the conclusion that this is the original 'Scepter of Dagobert!' It has to be, it just *has* to be, with all that we've verified."

"Oh, my!" Wendy replied. "Oh, my, my! Well, now what do we do with it? I've never been in a situation like this, and I don't think my friend Nancy has either! We're going to need your help!"

Nick continued very calmly on the phone, realizing that he had a potential client with an extremely valuable artifact that would need unimaginable care and keeping. "Bob has a few thoughts, but as of now this will strictly remain confidential with JoAnn and myself, and I imagine the same for the three of you. Bob will be back at the Newbury Guest House soon, and he will give the scepter to you for safe keeping. I would not breathe a word to anyone about this, not even a whisper to friends or family until the three of you decide what your plans are going to be. I can, for a small retainer, help you along in any process you might choose as a course of action. And I would also be one hundred percent discreet on my part. I would refer to you both as an anonymous party."

Wendy again spoke softly so as not to be overheard in the inn. "Do you have any idea of the value that could be placed on it?"

Nick answered, "Not at this point, but it will be in the millions to say the least. I am going to do some more research on this. I have many friends in the business field. I know some college professors who love the chase of undiscovered treasures. One man in particular lives outside of London, Mr. Rolf Achilles. He has a wealth of knowledge. I am going to find his number and give him a call. I will just explain to him that I am personally researching history on several different of artifacts. I will ask about a few different ones, so that he does not pick up on the fact that I am referring to 'The Scepter of Dagobert.' I will assure you is he is a true genius with respect to such artifacts, and he would never suspect any other reason for me inquiring about artifacts along this line other than to expand my knowledge of special antiques."

THE CAPUCHIN CATACOMBS OF PALERMO

Human beings have always had a fascination with death. In some cultures, the dead are never left alone, but continue to interact with the living. For instance, some cultures set up ancestor cults to memorialize their dead forebearers. Others believe that the living can communicate with the dead via mediums. While these forms of interaction deal with the dead in their ethereal forms, the living also interact with the physical remains of the dead. One of the most common modes of this interaction is the preservation of dead bodies. Although the most famous mummies belong to the ancient Egyptian civilization, they are certainly not the only ones that have been produced by mankind. Mummies have been made in different time periods by various cultures. One such example would be the mummies in the Capuchin Catacombs of Palermo (The Catacombe dei Cappuccini.)

*The Capuchin Catacombs of Palermo are located in Sicily, Italy. In the 16*th *century, the Capuchin monks of Palermo discovered that their catacombs contained a natural preservative that helped mummify their dead. One of their brethren, Brother Silvestro, was the first to be mummified. Apparently, he was a particularly holy monk, and the preservation of his body would have been useful in attracting pilgrims to Palermo. Apart from attracting pilgrims, it also attracted the attention of locals who wanted to be preserved in the same manner. Since then, over 8000 Sicilians of various walks of life have been mummified in the catacombs.*

Wendy made a quick call to Nancy and relayed the latest news. She went on to say, "OK, Bob and I are going to take the bus back to Hyannis and catch the six p.m. boat. Please pick us up when we arrive. Let's take

Mr. Tonkins out for a bite to eat. I think the Madhatter is open until ten. Give them a call, ask for a quiet table away from the bar area. Then we can see what our next move will be. Just one note—Mr. Tonkin was correct in saying that Nick Caselli and his wife are really wonderful people.

When the researchers returned to the island, the three of them sat in a corner table at the Mad Hatter Restaurant. The scepter was locked securely in the Rambler's trunk space. They ordered a bottle of Pouilly-Fuisse and quietly cheered each other. Wendy and Nancy thanked Mr. Tonkin over and over for all his help.

They talked quietly. "So, what do you think should be our next move, Mr. Tonkin?" pondered Nancy.

He replied, "Well, Nancy and Wendy, first of all I'd be most happy if you called me Bob. He started tapping a spare straw on the table, "Well, that's the million-dollar question, but until we decide what you need to do, we need a place that's safe to keep the treasure and be sure it's away from prying eyes.

Wendy offered, "We can hide it at our house, and no one would ever be going through it for any reason.

Bob nodded, "That might work out well and in our favor, as you live a bit out of town. As of now, no one but the Caselli's and we know it's in our hands. So, no one is going to be searching for it. As for the next step, it's going to be important to keep my name silent as well in this deal. One whisper of Nantucket combined with the word 'treasure' and there would be all sorts of people descending upon my store! I have to admit, it's not all that burglar proof to say the least. Then, if word got out, there would be the newspapers and the TV stations from New England. We would have quite the circus going on here-a real dog and pony show! People will go to great lengths searching for a treasure like this."

Their server approached the table and they quickly dropped their conversation. All three of them ordered the prime rib special. They quietly agreed it would be best to sit silently on this for a few days and not rush into any hasty decisions. They agreed to meet in two days at Bob's store and see if any of them had some new thoughts or suggestions.

The girls took the scepter in the box to their house, and they packed it up under the old blanket in the attic.

The next day they were cracking the whip on moving forward with the planter boxes. They set up the new workspace in the barn and were making the copper lined window boxes. It helped get their mind off the treasure.

During the morning Rita arrived at the house and said, "Oh, by the way, girls, I started selling your window boxes at the store. Well, I'm not really selling them but taking orders and deposits. I know the price of them. So, as of now, I now have fourteen orders with the name and address, and phone number and the color of the lining requested for each. I also took down how many per order as several people want at least two if not more.

I also gave them your cards and told them you were possibly about eight weeks out for delivery or pick up based on the day they placed the order. Some of them asked if you could hold them for a later date, possibly springtime pickup, if they were departing for the season. I said I did not believe it would be much of a problem."

Wendy responded, "Oh, thanks so much, Rita! How many orders did you say?"

Rita confirmed, "Fourteen, and that was just in the last week. I think you are going to get a bunch more orders. Looks like you're right at it! Good luck!"

Two days later, at ten a.m., Wendy and Nancy were seated in the office of Tonkin's Antiques. They had already dropped off two finished window boxes to Claudette's, and two more for a customer who had ordered them a few weeks before. They also went to see Duke at the hardware store and picked up more copper and a few other items they needed. They were so grateful for such a large working space in the barn now that the orders were coming in. Duke told them he would bulk up their orders to get the maximum discount and put their business under contractor sales for even a deeper discount. He was now becoming one of their weekly dinner guests at their home in Quaise, and he never arrived without a bottle of nice wine, chocolates, or a bouquet of flowers in hand. He was certainly loving life and enjoying getting to know these girls better every week.

As they sat in Bob's office, he had a sheet of paper in front of him on his desk. He told them that earlier he had called Nick and discussed different avenues along which they might possibly proceed. Nick had suggested to Bob that he could write a very impressive single page letter to some elite museum curators. He would explain that an article of great renown that has hitherto been in a private setting was to be expected to be presented to several potential museums that might want to acquire the object for a loan. The loan would be under a specific financial arrangement for a specified period of time. This way the rare scepter could be admired all over the world."

Nancy looked a bit puzzled. "Bob, exactly what does that mean?"

Bob continued. "Well, you would loan it to different museums for a royalty payment so they can place it in their museum. It's like they are renting it from you, for a period ranging from two weeks to two months, depending on the size and the popularity of each museum. This would not be limited to just the United States, but Canada and Europe as well. We would hire a reliable transport company that carries good insurance. Plus, I would have a personal insurance company deal with us directly. We are best to be safer than sorry with coverage. I have used Krauter and Company out of New York numerous times in the past. I deal directly with Neil Krauter, the owner. They have been in business for a long time."

He went on. "Nick and I would confer with the curators at the different museums. We would try to do it logistically, moving it from one region to another nearby region so the shipping, and transport would be minimized, like going the shortest route from A to B."

"Do you and Nick think there is any real demand for museums to want to rent the scepter?" Wendy asked.

Her nodded in the affirmative. "Good question, and yes, we think it will be in high demand. We believe that, if our assumptions are correct, the scepter's travel will go on for at least ten years or more. You would have the right to either stop the viewings or to sell it to a museum or a private party at any point.

"So, just for fun, what are we looking at for a two-week rental?" Nancy inquired.

"Let's put it at a ballpark figure: net in your pocket, after Nick's and my consultant fees, about fifty-two thousand dollars a year, give or take ten percent. And you still own it."

Nancy looked at Wendy and then to Bob. "Really, do you truly think that much?"

Wendy realized that the prospects were something that were more in Bob and Nick's line of work. "Well, you two are the professionals. We will follow your lead."

Bob then said, "I would like to invite Nick and JoAnn down to the island for a couple of nights. I have plenty of room for them to stay with me. We could finalize the details and let Nick run with it, even though I would be involved every step of the way."

"That's a great idea!" Nancy chimed in. "We will plan dinner out one night and the first dinner in our home in Quaise where we can talk freely."

Bob said, "I will let you know tomorrow of the plans. This is going to be quite an undertaking but one that should be well worth the effort."

Wendy and Nancy went back to Quaise, worked a few more hours and called it a day. The sun was setting, and Marshmallow was chasing leaves all over the back of the house. The girls cracked open a bottle of Vino Nobile Montepulciano from La Braccesca winery, an Italian wine which was a given to them. They actually received a whole case from Don and Rita as a house warming gift. As they sipped away, trying to relax on the porch, they were still in awe over the fact that they might pull in fifty-two thousand dollars a year from the traveling scepter. They both laughed, and Wendy declared, "We have come a long way from our cubicles at Aetna Insurance Company! If old man Wooldridge could see us now! There's no more telling us to quit talking and keep working!" Giggles followed, and the wine went down quickly.

The sun was starting to set when Marshmallow stopped in her tracks and started looking into the brush behind the house. Wendy asked, "What is it, 'Tiger'?"

Nancy suggested, "A big bear?", and the girls started laughing. But Marshmallow did not budge. Both of the girls thought it might be a deer, but the cat had never acted that way towards any deer. Actually, she was friendly with them. The girls picked up their wine glasses and thought it was time to start the fireplace in the living room. They called for Marshmallow, but she just sat down and stared into the brush.

Nancy went back outside and picked Marshmallow up and was looking towards the area the cat was fixated on. She thought she saw someone in the brush, but then she thought that the light was just playing tricks on her eyes. "Nothing there, sweetie pie. Come on in, it's supper time."

Mark Donato was pulling people over every thirty minutes as cars drove out of town on Milestone Road. His first stop turned out to be Isky Santos.

Isky rolled down his window and said, "Hey, Deputy, it was so nice to see you last week at the Lions Club Raffle. Did you end up winning anything?" They had a nice conversation, and Isky drove off.

Sean Divine and Colin Keenan were the next car to be stopped. Deputy Donato could not believe it, only his luck. Colin rolled down the truck window and said, "Hey, Deputy, you got any tickets to the Policemen's Ball?" and started laughing.

"Funny, really funny," Deputy Donato replied. Sean Divine was about to add something when Mark barked, "Zip it!" and ran his fingers across his lips. "Both of you just drive off, get out of here, skedaddle now!" They revved up their engine and headed out.

The next stop was Sylvia Lussier, who had Kathy Legg and Sheila Egan in the car with her. Sylvia rolled down her window and everyone stated talking at once. Sylvia asked when he and Beth could come to dinner. Kathy then told him they were going out fishing and would Beth like to join her and Brian. Sheila started in asking when Beth could join her out at Miacomet to drive a bucket of balls and have lunch. As if Mark was the keeper of Beth's social schedule, he thought to himself. A few minutes later, without allowing Mark to get a word in edgewise, Sylvia drove off saying, "Ciao!"

For his next stop he hit it big. It was old Lynne MacVicar. He radioed into the station to Mike DiFronzo, saying he had a possible "10-27" and a "10-81". That conveyed that he was detaining a motor vehicle driver and a possible "driving under the influence." Oh, this was good, really good, Mark thought to himself. Now he had Old Lady MacVicar right where he wanted her—no running home and chugging down some vodka so she could not be arrested for a DUI, nope not this time!

Rick Blair was out riding his bike as he was off duty with Madaket, his dog, following him on the bike path. Rick had his radio scanner attached to the basket on the front handlebars. He heard the call and the location, and as he was close by to the incident, he said, "OK, Madaket, let's step up the pace and see what Deputy Donato has going this time."

When Mike DiFronzo heard this, he got the numbers mixed up from the code book. He radioed the deputy, but Mark was so excited about bagging Old Lady MacVicar with a DUI he left his portable radio sitting on the front seat of the squad car with the windows up. He did not hear Mike DiFronzo radio him back about the 'Paramedics assistance' radio call. Mike placed a call to the hospital requesting an ambulance, and as is standard procedure, the Fire Department was notified.

The police scanner at the *Inquirer and Mirror* was on. Dorleen Burliss thought to herself, "We have not had any type of story all week and deadline is tomorrow. Good, this might do it." So, she said to her co-worker,

"Turrentine, we are up! Let's move it! Someone had a heart attack, it seems, while driving down Milestone Road and possibly hit a deer or a tree. Grab your camera and let's go."

Doreen made a very quick call to the police station and asked, "Is the radio call about a heart attack victim? Possibly hitting a deer or tree, or another vehicle?"

Mike DiFronzo started to tell Doreen a long dragged- out story when she said, "Out with it, DiFronzo! I don't have all day to gab."

Right then, Steve Turrentine with cameras hanging off his neck and his back pack said, "I'm ready!"

Mike DiFronzo started to say something about a heart attack when the cord on his phone knocked his chocolate milk all over the desk onto his mother's *Good Housekeeping* magazine that she had not even read yet. Worrying about the magazine, he muttered, "Oh boy, this is bad, really bad."

Doreen Burliss took that for well things are not looking too good. She cheered to Steve, "Finally, some action around this sleepy little island! Thanks, Mike."

She and Steve flew out the door, and Doreen urged Steve, "When we get close to the accident which must be right around the Rotary, just start snapping away. We will figure out the photo lineup for the paper later."

Lynne MacVicar had just been to her doctor's office for a routine check-up and physical. She knew how beat the system, and fool the doctor. Every time she had an appointment, she would stop drinking three days prior to it. Then she would eat salads, a lot of fresh vegetables, and cook without butter. Her main course would be grilled chicken with rosemary.

For lunch she would have soup and no bread. She also would drink lots of water and juices, prune and cranberry, which was like a mini-detox and would clean her system out. She figured she'd get by with a clean bill of health.

When Deputy Donato approached her car, he had he place her hands on the steering wheel. He said calmly, "Now don't move, Mrs. MacVicar. I am just going to perform a safety check to make sure you don't have any weapons in the vehicle." What the deputy was actually searching for was an open liquor bottle, so he could nail her for drinking and driving. He searched the back seat, under both sides of the front seat, then the passenger's side, the glove compartment and door pockets, but found nothing. Figuring she had either tossed the bottle out or was coming from a bar, he ordered her out of the car for a sobriety test.

Mrs. MacVicar knew she was sober as a judge driving her new car. She stepped out and Deputy Donato puffed up his chest and stated in his most authoritative voice, "OK, Mrs. MacVicar, we are going to do this by the book as the Commonwealth of Massachusetts requires."

The part came when she was to stand on one leg and count backwards from twenty. The thing that added to this difficulty was she had only had water since the blood test required no food for at least twelve hours prior to the appointment. On top of that, she was delayed getting her blood work taken due to some call requiring her doctor to go down to the emergency room for an extended time. Before he left, the doctor asked Mrs. MacVicar if she wanted to reschedule for another time, but she told him she'd rather get it done with as she was already at his office.

To herself she thought, "I can't bear the hassle of another fast from butter, salt, steak, and liquor!"

So, standing next to her car, she started to raise her leg up, and she fainted! This occurred right as Dorleen Burliss arrived and pulled onto the grass. Seeing the lifeless body on the road she told Steve start shooting photos fast! She pulled out her note pad, and then the circus started! Cars were stopping, putting on their four- way flashers. Several people knew Mrs. MacVicar.

Rick Blair arrived on his bike. Madaket thought, "Wow, this is fun!" He started barking and jumping as Rick tied him to a tree. The first thing Rick noticed was a lady laying in the road, not moving. Then he heard the word 'dead'. Dorleen Burliss also heard the word 'dead' and that really got her going. She was already working angles on the story to hit the next day's paper. The fire department arrived next, followed by the ambulance crew.

Doreen instructed Steve, "Take a few more photos of the lady on the ground. Then get a bunch of them loading the body onto the stretcher."

Mark was now not feeling so good himself. He heard the word "dead" and almost fainted, thinking Mrs. MacVicar had a heart attack. He worried that, if there was an official inquiry, he might be blamed for it.

Within minutes the phone at the police station was ringing non-stop with callers asking if they had any information on the dead body on the Milestone Road.

Bobby Lamb was flying over the island doing some touch-and-go landings at the airport. Looking down he spotted all the flashing lights and the crowd below. He circled over twice at a low altitude. Someone said they must be bringing in Med-flight. Bobby Lamb radioed the airport tower requesting information on the commotion on Milestone Road with all the police, fire truck, and ambulance vehicles.

Allan Costa at the tower radioed back, "It's all over the scanners. A lady died of a heart attack after being pulled over, or something close to that."

Constable Kosmo was sitting and enjoying the movie *The Man With the Golden Gun* when the usher came to his seat and whispered, "Chief, you're being requested on the phone."

Kosmo took a big breath, sighed, went to the lobby and picked up the phone.

Mike DiFronzo addressed him a bit breathlessly. "Chief, Rick Blair who had been riding his bike with Madaket on the Milestone Road, just radioed in. It seems Deputy Donato is there on scene with a dead body in the street."

Kosmo said, "OK, Mike, tell Rick and Mark I will be right there."

The usher considerately told Kosmo, "The movie is playing all week. You're free to come see it anytime."

Kosmo nodded and thanked the usher. Out in his cruiser, Kosmo spoke briefly again with Mike, trying to get the correct story. He then radioed Rick Blair asking for an update. Rick replied, "The paramedics are working giving CPR right now. It appears to be a woman in her mid-sixties. Deputy Donato is off to the side with the fire chief, Dan Connor."

"OK, how does Deputy Donato look?"

"Well, I think he might faint," Rick replied. "I'll go stand by his side and make sure he doesn't."

Kosmo then radioed Dan Connor. Dan explained to him, "The lady does not seem to be deceased, or that's about the best conclusion I can determine at this point. The EMT's are doing CPR on her now. My guess is that she fainted."

"OK, thanks, Dan. I am on my way. Tell Deputy Donato not to speak with anyone until I get there. It would be best if you stay close to him. I am switching to Channel Seven. I will leave it open so you can give me a play-by-play of what's developing until I arrive."

"Got it, Chief!" Dan acknowledged. A couple of minutes later he radioed Kosmo and said, "They gave the lady some smelling salts, and she seems to be coming back to life. Also, from what I understand, her name is Lynne MacVicar.

Kosmo rolled his eyes and put the picture together in his head. He thought, Mark must have pulled her over, and to get the goods on her must have asked her to perform a sobriety test. Either she was drunk and passed out or fainted. Well, with all the drama that has incurred during this mess, which he would get to the bottom of rather quickly, he said once again to himself, "*Nantucket, a funny little island with funny little people!*"

When Kosmo arrived, he went over to Mark and pulled him aside. Mark detailed the whole police stop from start to finish. Kosmo then went to the paramedic attending to Mrs. MacVicar and asked him very quietly if he could perform an alcohol breathalyzer on her, very discreetly. The EMT told Mrs. MacVicar to breathe quite normally into the bag he was holding. Mrs. MacVicar, still feeling a little woozy had no idea what she was doing. A few minutes later the paramedic told Kosmo she was not under any influence of alcohol.

Finally, Kosmo was able to speak with her. She calmly stated that all she can remember was stepping out of the car.

Kosmo then asked Mark, "What code did you request at dispatch?"

Mark said, "I called in a 10-27 and a possible 10-81."

"That's it?" Kosmo replied.

"Yes, that's it," Mark nodded, feeling rather glad to see Old Lady McVicar starting to get up with help from the paramedic.

Kosmo then radioed the station. At this point Beth was now there with Mike.

"Hey, Mike," he asked. "What were the codes that Deputy Donato radioed in?"

Mike answered, "Well, let me see. I think it was a 20-87 which I don't even think exists, and I, for the life of me, cannot remember the other code but it had something to do with paramedics being called to the scene."

"Ok, Mike, we'll hash this out later. Over and out."

Kosmo told Mrs. MacVicar that she could have a ride home, if she preferred, with someone she might know in the crowd here, or take a few sips of water and drive herself home.

She said, "Thank you, Chief. Just give me a few minutes to catch my breath and I will be on my way."

Doreen Burliss nodded her head towards the office and called out, "OK, Turrentine, we are out of here."

Steve at this point was now off in the brush area taking a few pictures of some birds that were also watching the show. He turned to Doreen who reiterated, "Let's move it, Turrentine! We've got a deadline to meet."

As they were driving away, Doreen grumbled, "That Donato, he gets on my nerves! He is always starting some big commotion, and it turns out to be nothing but a big fat goose egg. And that other bozo in the department, what's his name? Oh yeah, DiFronzo. I run into him all the time at the A&P. He seems to think I am his best friend. Last week I was buying some cereal, and he was in the same aisle. He starts telling me that Cocoa Puffs were his favorite but he also liked Lucky Charms. He kept blabbering away. Then he started on something like pancakes, butter, and maple syrup that his mom makes him every Sunday morning. Really? This is who we have to protect us if something serious goes down? Those two are lucky they don't end up shooting themselves or each other!"

Steve shrugged his shoulders and merely replied, "Well, I really liked Cocoa Puffs when I was a kid."

Upon returning to the station, Kosmo called Beth into his office. He instructed her, "Beginning on Monday I want you to perform a code review with every single member of this force, including me. One on one, even if you have to break it up into a few different time periods. We can't afford to have mix ups like this every time a car gets stopped."

Beth nodded, "Got it, Chief. I'll bring my code book home and brush up on it before then. Do you want to be my first student? See you later."

THE HAUNTING OF BELL WITCH CAVE, TENNESSEE

There's a constant and substantial fascination with the paranormal around the globe. This is especially true for the United States, which has a number of haunted tours across the country including the famous town of Salem, Massachusetts. Fans of the macabre know this as the place of the Salem Witch Trials. But Salem is far from the only place in the country where one can experience the downright creepy and unsettling history of witches. Another truly eerie location is in Adams, Tennessee, which is home to the Bell Witch Cave....

About a week later Wendy woke up at two a.m. and went down to the kitchen to get a glass of water. She did not turn any lights on as the moonbeams were giving off enough natural light. Staring out of the window she could have sworn that she saw a person walking out by the large barn. She quickly and quietly went upstairs and gently woke Nancy up, saying, "I think there is someone outside. Don't turn on any lights. Let's go to the front bedroom and stand in the shadows. We can glance over the whole area without being seen."

They did just that, and, sure enough, there was someone creeping around.

Wendy whispered, "OK, let's startle him before he startles us!"

With that they went and began turning on every light they could find. Nancy grabbed two pans and started banging them together. Wendy opened the front door, waved a flashlight and yelled, "We see you! The cops are on the way!"

The person was off and running into the brush in no time.

They quickly called the police station. Mike DiFronzo answered and told Nancy to stay inside, lock the doors and remain on the line until a squad car shows up. Given their location, that would take about ten minutes.

The police car arrived with its lights on but no siren. Jimmy Jaksic, the officer responding, walked the property and checked the barns and sheds, even though the girls stated the person ran off through the brush. They could not describe him, only suggested that it most likely was a male, and the person did not seem tall or heavy.

Jimmy Jaksic also did a complete walk through the house, but the girls said there was no need for him to venture up into the attic as they spotted the person just outside lurking through the property. Additionally, Officer Jaksic checked to make sure all the windows and the basement hatch door and solid door at the bottom of the hatchway were securely locked. He also suggested they leave a few lights on in different areas of the house.

Lastly, he recommended that they might want to pick up some more exterior lights for the house and the barn area.

The next day they made a quick stop to see Bob Tonkin and told him the story of someone sneaking around their property in the middle of the night.

Wendy wondered, "Bob, you don't think someone caught wind of our discovery, do you?"

Bob shook his head. "That's almost impossible as no one but the five of us know about it, and we are all sworn to secrecy. Maybe the culprit was just casing out houses in the area thinking a lot of people have started closing up their homes. But the thing is, I can hardly ever remember reading about any home break-ins lately in the newspaper or hearing anything about burglaries

But, if I were you, I would keep some lights on all night and double-check the windows and lock your doors."

They told him that's what Jimmy Jaksic had suggested and thanked him for his feedback.

On their next stop they went to see Duke at the hardware store. He recalled noting that all the fixtures were good out at the girls' house, so they could add additional lighting. They purchased a set of six bright outside lights. Using the phone in Duke's office, Nancy called Al Lussier at home out in 'Sconset to see if any of the guys were free to install some new outside lights. They had all the 'fixings' as Duke called the wiring and switches. Wendy then called her friend, Karen Grant, and asked if her boyfriend was free to assist the guys with the new lighting installation. They then headed home.

Within thirty minutes, George Williams with Reg Marden had arrived. Marshmallow came galloping up and let out a big meow for him. George reached down and scooped her up and said smilingly, "Hey you little rascal! What have you been up to these days?"

They were the first ones on the scene. The girls told them the story of the prowler on their property and that was the reason for the lights. Reg volunteered to take a look around outside, thinking that maybe the prowler had dropped something or left tire tracks somewhere.

George stated, "Well, it certainly is strange why someone would be way out here at that time of night. Maybe, if it was a burglar, he was looking for an out-of-the-way home that the occupants have left for the season. But it's a rare thing out here or almost anywhere on the island. Most things that are ever stolen are bikes from someone leaving a downtown establishment, seeking an easy way home."

He looked around. "I was going to mention to you that I have a friend, Rusty Riddleberger. He is a real jack-of-all-trades. With this sized property there is always something that is going to need fixed or replaced. I tell you, he's the person to call. Here's what I'm thinking. In the smaller barn, the loft upstairs could easily be made into a large one or two-bedroom apartment. It has got to be an easy sixteen hundred square feet up there. With his skills and your design imagination, I am sure it could be very nice. Then you could rent it out, maybe to some fellow who needs a small place to stay."

Nancy nodded. "Well, that sounds good, George, but at this point we are watching our expenses. We need to keep the correct intake and outflow of cash for the next year."

George nodded but persisted. "Well, here's the kicker. First off, he has done a lot of work for Mary and me on all our properties. He has also worked for, I don't know, maybe eight or ten of our friends. Everyone swears by him. Perhaps, in lieu of cash for his labor, he could build the apartment and live in it. You might want to talk with him. He is very easy going. He also manages to find all sorts of usable wood, appliances, doors, windows, and plumbing items like sinks and faucets, even new pipes, at unbelievable prices in the back of Marine Hardware, or with Duke or free at the 'Madaket Mall.' I'd like to invite him to come over with me to meet you both. You could show him the upstairs loft space, and if the three of you hit it off it might be a win-win for you gals. Plus, he could watch the property if you ever go off island. Why don't you consider this?"

Wendy and Nancy looked at each other and nodded. Wendy said, "OK, sure, invite him over."

George went into the house and called Rusty who was just heading out the door. "Hey, Rusty! You know that property in Quaise I told you all of us guys were working at?"

Rusty replied, "Yes?"

George continued. "Well, they have a great loft space that they might be interested in building out.

And the idea I pitched to the girls was you could stay there rent free if you tackle the renovations. They would pay for materials. Want to come and take a look?"

"OK," Rusty responded. "I am just heading out to Tom Nevers to work on a deck. But I could take the Polpis route and be there in thirty minutes or so. Where is it exactly?"

George gave him the directions and disengaged the call.

An hour later the Quaise property was abuzz with all the guys and the lighting situation. Everyone had thoughts, ideas, and discussed the angles at which to mount them. Even Rusty got engaged in the project. The lights were installed, angled, and wired outside the house and the barn in under three hours.

Wendy managed to set up a big lunch spread with beer, sodas, and iced tea in the barn, and the party continued for a bit. Some of them a bit more worked then headed out. Reg got a ride home from Al.

Rusty, George, Wendy and Nancy had a very productive meeting after that. The girls liked Rusty from the get-go. He just jumped into action of the lighting party without even inquiring about the loft space he might inhabit. Nancy had a pad of paper to sketch out the new living space. She figured the meeting would be rather short, but that was not the case. Rusty tossed out some ideas from the very first step going up to the loft. Then the list began. His thoughts and design ideas were right alongside that of the girls.

After about an hour, Nancy had five rough sketches on her legal pad. Rusty explained that the costs could be lowered for plumbing, electrical, and numerous other things as he could provide all those services. Wendy added that, any evening after working on the property, if he wanted to stay over that they had a bright and cheery bedroom with access to a full bathroom that was not being used. He could come and go as he pleased.

Nancy said, "And if you do stay here, dinner is every night around seven and you are more than welcome to join us."

Rusty smiled and added, "Well, I am quite the grill master and would be happy to assist. Now, I've got to head out to do my work on someone's deck. I'll call you when I think I can get started. Thanks, this should work out great. Nice to meet you both!"

That night, the house was aglow with new lights. Per Bob's advice, they even left a few on inside the house.

Later that same evening, Kosmo was having wild dreams. He had not eaten any red onions which always gave him nightmares. However, in one dream the cobble-stone street was red, not with water but with blood flowing down Main Street. He awoke in a damp sweat. He tried to think if he had read something, seen something that might have his thoughts turning his dream into something so gory, but to no avail. He did remember walking up Main Street the day before and glancing into an art gallery. He noticed a deep dark painting with a hint of red flowing through it, and he thought it was kind of eerie but remembered that art is in the eye of the beholder. Additionally, he was looking at a few books in Mitchell's Book Corner which was also closed. Possibly a subliminal memory from a book cover was the reason for his dream. He had also window shopped at a few of the antiques shops on Main Street as well. Maybe something from one of the stores slipped into the dream. He wished he knew the source of his nightmares.

The next morning Wendy went to town to do some banking. Rusty arrived with a box of tools and a ladder. He had said he could start off working a few hours a day as he was working on three projects that were nearly completed. He had told the girls that he would take the them up on the offer on spending a few nights in the spare bedroom. He figured it would take at least two weeks before he could get things set up for Randy to run the pipe for a hot water shower up in the loft. After that he could set up a cot and a sleeping bag and would be comfortable staying up his new living quarters.

Wendy had countered, "No, you're not sleeping on a cot! You stay in the spare bedroom as long as it takes!"

Rusty commented, "I am not much of a night owl. After working all day, a cold beer, a hot meal and I am off to read and then fall asleep. I am up early, so I will try and accomplish the quieter projects ones early in the morning."

Nancy had laughed. "Who are you kidding? The sun rises so early we are up before the birds, it seems. So just do what you need to do whenever you're ready."

Wendy returned from the bank and told Nancy, "You know what? A strange thing happed on my trip into town." She looked a little anxious.

"So, what's up?" asked Nancy.

Wendy shrugged. "Well, I don't know. Maybe it's my imagination, but I thought someone was following me in a car. I looked in the rearview mirror and the car joined me when I turned off Quaise Pasture Road. It followed me, but not very closely, all the way to Main Street. I parked by the Pacific National Bank up at the top of Main. And I looked down the street and saw the driver had parked on the lower part of Main. I really was not really paying it any mind, but I just had a strange feeling about it." She went over and sat in a comfortable chair in the living room.

"So, I went into the bank and when I came out, I walked across the other side of the street. The car was still parked there with a man inside. He had a large floppy hat on so I could not see his face, but it was a Ford, four-door, kind of rust-colored. I guess I am just a little jumpy. First the prowler, and now someone following me. It must just be the fact we are dealing with the scepter."

Nancy replied, "Well, maybe it was someone waiting to pick up his wife from Miller's Hair Salon. It's right next to Main and Union Street. I can't see how anyone else would know about our big mystery item."

Wendy nodded. "That's most likely it. I did walk back up and stopped in to see Mr. Tonkin. He said he spoke with Nick Caselli, and Nick was slowly working through his plan of action for the treasure."

Nancy tried to reassure her. "Well, as of now it's secure in the trunk of the old Rambler. Did the car follow you when you left?"

"Nope. I was free and clear of my stalker." They started laughing.

CHÂTEAU DE BRISSAC, BRISSAC-QUINCÉ, FRANCE, AND THE GHOST OF THE GREEN LADY

Château de Brissac is a castle located in the commune of Brissac-Quincé, the department of Maine-et-Loire, France. The castle is recorded to have been built during the 11th century and has a long and interesting history. Like many castles around the world, the Château de Brissac is said to possess its own resident ghost. This is 'La Dame Verte' or Green Lady, who is said to be the ghost of an unfaithful wife murdered by her husband during the 15th century.

Bob Tonkin had the door to his shop open and was enjoying a lovely warm fall morning. A man walked in, wearing an old light-gray trench coat and a hat and sunglasses. He was browsing around, so Bob introduced himself. Bob said, "If you have any questions or find something that interests you, feel free to ask me any questions."

The man did not really offer much of a reply, so Bob thought he would just let the man be. The man spent a good fifteen minutes looking around the store, then asked Bob if he had any swords or daggers, ones that had inlaid stones.

Bob replied, "The only sword I have is one from the Civil War. I acquired it from a garage sale. It's in good shape and the price is twenty dollars. It's in the back of the store near the basket of canes if you'd like to see it."

The man replied, "No, I've got my mind set on something more intricate, more on the line of a really historic antique, perhaps from Europe."

Bob noticed that the man had a slight accent and politely asked him where he was from.

"Oh, me? Well, Boston. Just down here visiting for a couple days."

Bob clarified what he meant. "No, I am curious about your accent. Is it South American?"

The man nodded. "Well, yes, Peru to be exact."

Bob told the man if he left his name and number then if anything of interest came across his desk, he could call him. The man shook his head and said, "No, thank you. It was just a whim, nothing really that important." He then exited the shop.

That evening Bob Tonkin did his nightly ritual. After securing his most valuable pieces in the small safe, he locked up and took the short stroll to the Ship's Inn.

Greeted at the door by Bob Moulder, he took his regular seat at the bar, already knowing that the Monday evening special was pan-seared sea scallops. He had a quick Scotch, ordered the scallops and a glass of Steele Sauvignon Blanc. Bob Moulder asked him how his day went.

Bob replied, "Oh, nothing new, but it was a beautiful day. I took in a very nice original Marshal DuBock painting. It's on consignment. So, it was a quiet day, even though I did have a gentleman in from Peru. I think that's the first time I ever had a customer from Peru."

Mr. Tonkin then paused and reflected. "You know, Bob, all day I had this weird feeling like I was being watched. I can't explain it or put my finger on it. It's just some weird feeling. Oh well, maybe I spend too much time in that shop by myself."

They made some more small talk, and then the antique dealer mentioned, "I might have access to a private, one-of-a kind artifact coming my way."

"Oh, really?" his host replied. "What is it?"

Bob shrugged. "Well, at this point I cannot comment, but I would receive a royalty check every month for many years to come if it pans out."

"Well, that sounds exciting! I hope it happens!" His host went into the kitchen to place his dinner order.

Bob Tonkin did not notice the man who quietly entered the lounge and sat behind him, newspaper in hand, wearing a hat.

The following day Wendy and Nancy drove out to the dump with a car full of stuff. What they did not notice as they pulled onto the Polpis Road was a car parked near the junction, backed into one of the dirt roads.

Bob Tonkin began his day as normal, coffee and a Danish at Jared's dining room. Then he went to open up his shop by eight a.m.

Upon returning to their home in Quaise, Nancy and Wendy went straight into the barn to start work on more of their copper lined window boxes. Rita kept giving them more orders! She had priced them out at a ten percent mark-up, explaining to Wendy and Nancy that it did not affect their selling cost. Her markup was a handling fee for the customer not having to drive all the way out to Quaise to place an order.

However, what they did not notice was that the basement door below the hatch on backside of the house had been jimmied open. Around lunch time the girls unlocked the kitchen door, not noticing anything awry. But then this feeling came over Wendy that something was not correct. Upon entering the house, they both noticed Marshmallow greeted them in a panicked state. She was not meowing to the delight of their arrival. She made a low growl and was in an agitated state. The girls now definitely knew something was not correct.

Wendy stood stock still. "Nancy," she whispered, "someone's been in here."

"What do you mean?" asked Nancy.

Wendy explained her suspicion. "When we pulled out, I saw Marshmallow laying up on the small barn loft window ledge, enjoying the warmth of the sun, and the house was locked when we left. So, Marshmallow couldn't have gotten back in."

Nancy looked around and gasped, "Oh, my god, that means that there might be someone in the house!"

She grabbed a heavy frying pan. Wendy quickly called the police station and said they think it's a possibility that someone had broken into their house and might still be inside. What should we do?"

Mike DiFronzo took the call and radioed Deputy Donato who was on patrol near the airport. Hearing this Mark said quickly, "Call for back up! I'm headed there now."

Mike instructed the ladies to leave the house as quick as possible but Wendy disagreed. "No way! We've got the basement stairs and the stairs leading up to the second floor covered. We have large heavy frying pans, and if anyone comes near us, they will pay the price big time!"

Mark turned around. He fishtailed the patrol car almost out of control, just barely missing the mail truck stopped on the side of the road. He turned on the sirens and started pressing the gas petal to the metal. "OK, baby," he urged the car, "let's get this party on the road!" He took a left onto Old South Road and cut Tom Santos off as he was preparing to turn onto Airport Road. He then pushed the accelerator to the floor, hitting a small bump in the road which jostled him almost out of his seat. He went to grab the radio's mic but dropped it. Going at that speed he dared not to try to pick it up off the passenger side floor. At the same time the radio came alive.

"Station to Donato. Over."

Mark was wide-eyed. His mind was racing, thinking: Gun, check. Billy club, no. Mace, check. Bullet proof vest, check. Handcuffs, check.

He had just passed Valero's when a truck pulled out of Island Seafoods, moving about twenty miles per hour. He started honking his horn yelling, "Move over, you stupid imbecile! Then he went to pass, only to see a large Toscana cement truck coming right at him! With the truck being such a mammoth vehicle there was no way for it to slow down and pull over very quickly. Again, the radio came alive.

"Base to Deputy Donato. Come in, Deputy."

Mark was in a pickle. He did not want to slow down in his chase to the scene, but he needed to respond. So, he abruptly slammed on the brakes and came to a screeching halt.

He picked up the mic and said in a rush, "Donato to base," while cursing under his breath about Mike DiFronzo. The old busybody probably wanted to also report a cat stuck up in a tree.

Mike responded excitedly, feeling high to be involved in a live break-in. "Kosmo has been alerted and is on the way in his personal car. What's your ETA? Over."

Mark feeling flustered as now was not the time for chit chat replied, "About seven minutes. Over and out."

He dropped the mic on the front passenger seat and hit the gas. He was coming up to the Rotary, and as he was about to enter, a group of bicyclists crossing the street, with zero regard to the sirens and the lights of the squad car. Mark started blowing the car's horn which only made matters worse as a lady then fell off her bike. All the other cyclists stopped and were waving at Mark to stop his approach. Mark sneered and said, "The heck with this!" He pulled a fast careless U-turn and then hit a hard left, cutting through the Miacomet Water Company dirt road. Coming out onto Milestone Road, he hit the gas, made a fast left on the Polpis Road and floored it.

He reached over, picked up the mic and almost dropping it again, said, "Donato to base. Over.'"

Mike DiFronzo, ever so anxiously awaiting new updates on the big break in, replied, "Base here. What's the latest? Over."

Mark demanded, "Just get ahold of Beth, and tell her if I don't make it that I love her and my last Will and Testament is in the shoebox in my closet. Over."

Mike now thought to himself that something had happened to the Deputy. He replied, "Base here. What's happened?"

By then Mark was driving so fast that he almost ran off the road twice. Dropping the mic on the floor he did not respond back.

Again, Mike DiFronzo radioed, "Base to Deputy Donato." But he got no reply.

Mike now thought that Mark might have been shot. He quickly dialed Beth at home, saying in an agitated voice, "Beth, I think Mark has been shot, and he might not make it!"

"Shot?" Beth screamed. "What do you mean, *shot*?"

"Well, he just radioed in that he might not make it and his will is in the shoebox in his closet."

Beth now had tears flowing down her face. She asked, "Where is he? What's going on? Where's Constable Kosmo? Tell me what's going on!" she screamed again.

Mike explained, "Kosmo is on the way to the shooting. You see, there was a burglar inside of a house and he must have had a gun. Mark was there trying to disarm him, I guess. I don't have all the facts yet, but I just radioed for fire and ambulance to get to the scene."

Beth asked quickly, "Where is the property located?

Oh, my poor Mark! What am I going to do without him?

We were planning on going to the Club Car to celebrate our anniversary next week! What am I going to do? I don't have a car! I can't get out there. What am I going to do?" And she started crying even more.

Mike offered, "I could get my mom to drive you out there, but she a little slow getting ready, always messing with her hair and deciding what shoes to wear."

Beth just dropped the phone and kept sobbing away and whispering, "Mark, oh, Mark!" which made her sob harder.

Deputy Donato made the turn on to Quaise Pasture Road. He made the turn into the driveway, going so fast he almost clipped the bumper on the large boulder. Mark came to a screeching halt, put the car in park, undid the clip to his holster, pulled out the megaphone from the trunk and shouted, "This is Deputy Donato from the Nantucket Police Department! The house is surrounded! Come out with your hands up and you will not be harmed!"

No one came outside, so he repeated it again and nothing happened. Now he was hoping he got the correct address, but at that moment Constable Kosmo arrived in his black Jeep and asked for the latest update. Mark shrugged, "Zero response from our intruder. Should we break out the tear gas, Chief?"

Kosmo saw all of Mark's gear at hand. "No, not just yet. Mike told me the girls are inside holding the exit points in check. Let me go inside. I want you to go to the back side of the house, and keep your eyes and ears open."

Kosmo opened the front door announcing his presence and saw the two girls holding frying pans. He asked, "What seems to be going on here?"

Wendy and Nancy put down the pans, and, sounding relieved, they explained about the house being locked while they were in the barn, yet, when they arrived back, Marshmallow the cat was inside though when they left she was in the barn window soaking up the sun.

Kosmo asked, "Is there an open window the cat could have entered through? Does anyone else have a key or reside here?"

Nancy answered, "Well, Rusty Riddleberger is going to start staying here soon, but not yet. No one has a key unless the previous owner still has one, that's a Mr. Robert Romanos. But he would have no need to return here."

"OK, well here's what I would like you to do. Exit the house through the front door and shut it. One of you stand a good fifty feet from the front door the other on the corner watching the north and west sides of the house. One of you do the same from the back side of the house facing the east and south sides of the house. Now if you see anyone coming out a window, door or basement entrance, you do not go near them. Just start yelling your heads off. Deputy Donato and I will comb the house starting from the basement, through every nook and cranny. We will be out in a few minutes."

In the meantime, Beth English was on the phone to her mother, sobbing away, explaining that Mark was killed 'in the line of duty' and most likely will receive a 'full honors' memorial burial. "Oh, Mom, what *am* I going to do?" Beth wailed and then blew her nose.

Beth's mother said, "Don't you do anything yet, Honey. Your father and I leave soon. We will drive straight through the night and will be there tomorrow morning. Mind you, Honey, we won't be near any phones until we reach the ferry terminal. So, don't fret, dear. We are on the way."

Beth hung up and flopped onto her bed and sobbed some more into her pillow.

Constable Kosmo and Deputy Donato headed down to the basement. Right then, Dan Connor, the fire chief, pulled up and so did an ambulance. Kosmo asked Mark, "Did you call them?"

"No, not me," replied Mark, fingering the handle of his gun.

"Oh no, let's hope Mike DiFronzo did not get all riled up and make a big deal out of this," the chief muttered.

He radioed Mike at the dispatch desk. "Constable Kosmo to Dispatch. Over."

"Dispatch here, Chief. Over." Mike sat eagerly by his radio.

"I don't know what's going on as of yet, Mike, but please radio Fire Chief Connor and tell him to just sit tight for a few minutes. Over."

"Roger that, but what's the prognosis, Chief? Over."

"Look, Mike, tell everyone to sit tight. Over and out."

Mike DiFronzo called his mother to inform her of Deputy Donato's passing. She was taken quite aback, telling him she was on the way to the

Ladies Club luncheon and would not return home for at least two hours. She said Mike really should wear a bulletproof vest while working. Then she hung up.

Mrs. DiFronzo was the center of the talk at the Ladies Club luncheon. They voted to take up a donation drive to help with the funeral arrangements. Then they held a moment of silence in memory of Mark Donato.

Back at the house in Quaise, Fire Chief Connor and his crew as well as the paramedics were all on standby.

Kosmo descended the stairs into the basement and found nothing except the fact that the door had been jimmied open. He deduced that it most likely was a burglary and maybe the cat snuck in while the back hatch to the basement stairs was opened. They then went through the entire first floor. Every closet was opened and nothing was discovered. Nothing really seemed to be out of place.

Back in town, one of the servers at the Jared Coffin, who was on his day off, just happened to be passing through the ladies' luncheon and heard the news about Deputy Donato's demise. He raced down to the Rose & Crown. Soon the bartenders were on the phone calling every bar in town, spreading the news of Deputy Donato's demise. People were adding that he put up a good fight but that the guy riddled him with holes using a tommy gun. In a matter of thirty minutes the news seemed to be all over the island like a wildfire on a dry windy day.

Doreen Burliss from the Inquire & Mirror called the station, and Mike confirmed the passing of Deputy Mark Donato. He looked at the time he wrote down that Mark asked him to call Beth, placing the time of death close to ten thirty that morning, God rest his soul. Doreen told Steve Turrentine to grab his camera, and they were out of the door in a flash, racing to the Quaise property.

Meanwhile, Kosmo and Mark made their way slowly and cautiously up to the second floor of the house. But their search again revealed nothing other than the fact that one closet door had been left open. Nothing seemed to be tossed about or disturbed. Kosmo now opened the door leading to the attic. The items up there seemed to be slightly out of order, but they did not encounter any burglar. What they did find was a locked door that had been pried open. It looked like it had been rummaged through but they had no idea what it looked like beforehand. Kosmo said he would go outside and give the latest update to the fire chief. Mark should go down to the basement and exit through the jimmied door up out through the hatchway, and look for anything out of the ordinary.

Kosmo walked out into chaos. Dan Connor asked about the body. Kosmo stated that they did not find the intruder. Dan then said, "No, we heard that someone had been shot in the house."

"And who told you that?" demanded Kosmo.

Dan explained, "The call came in from your dispatch desk."

Right then a jeep came barreling in the driveway. Steve Turrentine jumped out of the car, snapping photos of the fire chief, Constable Kosmo, the fire trucks, the ambulance, along with Wendy and Nancy.

Doreen Burliss, not seeing Deputy Donato, quickly barged in on the constable's conversation with Dan. She addressed Kosmo, "So sorry to hear about Deputy Donato, but you can be assured we will write up a very moving and positive article about him." She flipped her note pad open with a pen and started firing off numerous questions.

Dan Connor offered, "I will let you handle this. Good luck!" and walked off grinning.

Kosmo was trying to get the whole underlying story that led up to all this. He asked Doreen, "What have you heard?"

She looked up at Kosmo. "Only the fact that Deputy Donato was trying to apprehend a burglar and he was shot multiple times." Then she added, "Is the suspect in custody or still at large?" And softly she asked, "Where is the deputy's body?" She added, "In respect to the department, we will not take any photos of him in his deceased state."

All of Main Street was buzzing with the latest news. Everyone at Mignosa's Market and at Les's Lunchbox was shocked. Don and Rita were off island, so they were not in the loop with the latest news. People were stopping work for the day and suddenly the bars were packed. The liquor stores were doing a brisk business from people buying pints of everything from Peppermint Schnapps to Rumplemintz along with beer to drown their sorrows over the passing of Deputy Donato. At every bar in town, it seemed that people were doing shots after a toast to Deputy Donato.

Beth was just curled up on her bed under a blanket holding a framed photo of them taken at the Chanticleer a few months before. Her phone was ringing off the hook. She finally just placed the receiver on the kitchen table covering it with a pillow so as not to hear the busy tone.

Kosmo slowly assessed the latest information, and told Doreen that the information that she had been given was misconstrued. He told her Deputy Donato was alive and well, the intruder broke into the home by breaking into the basement door, and at that point they did not know if anything was taken, nor did they have any suspects.

Almost the same time, bouquets of flower arrangements were being delivered to the police station almost nonstop. The phone was ringing off the hook. Mike DiFronzo had called Rick Blair and asked if he could hurry down to the station, adding that Deputy Donato had been killed in the line of duty.

At the girls' house, Deputy Donato walked around to the front only to encounter a quite agitated Doreen Burliss. She rolled her eyes and put her hands on her hips. "It's always something with you, Deputy, always something!" and stormed back to her car.

Steve Turrentine was out walking the fields of the property taking all sorts of photos. At one point he got a nice photo of a fawn and its mother standing by some trees. Doreen yelled out of the car window, "Anytime you're ready, Turrentine!" He ambled back in her direction.

Kosmo, at this point, had no idea what was happening in town or what the gossip mill had started up. He decided that he would deal with Mike DiFronzo later.

Around the house all was settling back to normal. The frying pans lay on the front steps. Deputy Donato said the basement door was the entry point for the intruder. Wendy and Nancy mentioned that the other night Patrolman Jaksic had come out after their call about a prowler on the property around two that morning.

Kosmo nodded. "Well, it's a good possibility that they could be connected. Would you accompany me on a walk-through of the house just as Mark and I have searched it?"

As they reviewed the search, Kosmo pointed out that nothing except the broken door lock in the basement seemed out of place. A few things were moved in some of the closets. They hadn't noticed much awry, nothing until they reached the attic. The original blanket that covered the scepter had been hastily tossed onto the floor. A few things were moved away from the walls of the attic, and the lock was broken off the closet door.

Kosmo asked them, "What could this person been searching for? Any ideas?"

They told him they had nothing of value in the house and were clueless.

Kosmo added, "I doubt the intruder will be back, as it seems they had plenty of time to go through the house. Were you gone today at any time?"

"Yes," Nancy answered. "We made a dump run which easily took over an hour."

"Well, it seems the person might have been watching your movements," Kosmo surmised.

Then Wendy added, "I thought someone was following me the other day, when I pulled out of here. It seemed to me the guy, who was in a rusty brown-colored four-door Ford, followed me all the way into town when I was headed to the bank. I was not one hundred percent sure, but I just had this weird feeling. He parked on lower Main, and I parked up by the bank near Orange Street. But then, I decided to take a casual stroll after leaving the bank. So, I crossed the street and slowly walked down the sidewalk, trying to get a closer look at him without drawing any attention to myself. Nancy and I discussed it, and it could have been some guy just waiting for his wife to come out of Miller's Hair Salon. I left it at that. But now this is the third incident: first, the late-night prowler; secondly, the car following me; and the third is this apparent break-in. I'm starting to get the creeps about this whole situation, Chief." Wendy wrapped her arms around her body as if she had the shivers.

Kosmo attempted to refocus her attention on the situation. "Do you have someone that can repair the basement hatchway and the door?"

Nancy nodded. "Yes, we have several people, and the upper wooden hatchway locks from the inside. But we don't ever lock it, and with the steel door we just use the simple hasp closure to secure it so it will not blow open if the hatchway cover was left open overnight or during the day. There is no way anyone can get through the door it if it's locked. It's solid metal, but I will have Rusty take a closer look at it."

Kosmo added, "Also, you might want to see if your friend, Rusty, can start staying here with you. It might be a good idea just until we can see if we can clear this situation up."

Kosmo looked around the room. "One thing that bothers me is the fact nothing was taken. Usually, a thief will go through dresser drawers or jewelry boxes to snag watches, change containers, things that are easy to fit into a small bag. Then off they go. This person is looking for a specific object, it seems to me," Kosmo continued.

Deputy Donato cleared his throat as if to speak. He had tried adding small bits and pieces into the conversation, but mostly was asking himself why he did not think of those clues. "Hmm, well, I was just wondering . . . No, never mind."

Kosmo pointed up the stairs. "One question - was there anything in the locked closet in the attic that was missing?"

Wendy replied, "Well, we have no idea. Mr. Romanos told us he did not have a key to it and thought it was most likely filled with more junk, so he never tried to open it. However, Mr. Romanos figured that closet has been locked for over ten years. So, if someone was searching for a certain object, why would they wait over ten years? This house was vacant for the last six or so.

But I guess now we might as well clear the junk out of that old closet."

"OK, well thanks for your time, ladies," Mark said. "We didn't mean to create such a big scene here, thought it could have been quite a situation if we had caught the crook."

As he and Kosmo headed to their cars to go back to the station, Kosmo told Mark that they had had enough excitement for the day. Mark could go home and take a break. The chief said he had some things on his mind that he wanted make note of back in the office, and that he'd see Mark the next day.

Little did Mark know, but by now the whole town was mourning the loss of him, except Doreen Burliss who was still fuming when she arrived back at the *Inquirer & Mirror* office. He had yet to come face to face with the rumor of his own death!

As Kosmo was driving back, Mike DiFronzo came on the radio. He still thought that the deputy was deceased. Mike said he had a call for the chief from Judy Brownell from Hatch's.

Kosmo radioed back, "Call her back and tell her I will be back at the station in about twenty minutes and will get in touch. Over."

Upon his arrival back at the station people were laying flowers in piles in front of the station, paying homage to the passing of Deputy Donato. He was not prepared for the onslaught of attention he would get. Flowers were piled up on the entrance to the station, and there were about forty people holding candles. The minister from the church was there reading from the Scriptures. The group all rushed Kosmo as he was exiting his vehicle. Now what? Kosmo shook his head at the scene in front of the station.

Mark, being released for the rest of the day, thought it would be a great thing to stop by Beth's apartment to tell her of the big intruder search out in Quaise. He was still clueless about the rumors floating all over the island of his untimely death. He went to her apartment, all smiles, and did his little three knocks and then two more. It was kind of like their private signal to say who was at the door. He waited, humming away, all smiles and smirk of pride on his face. When she did not answer the door, he gently repeated it. What he did not know was that Beth had shut her bedroom door and covered her head with a large pillow to shut out the light and sounds of the day.

Mark figured out that she must have gone out, so he figured he would go home. He would get himself all gussied up and take her out for an afternoon beverage at one of the local watering holes. That way he could let anyone within earshot overhear him telling Beth about his big day with the burglar.

He took a shower and got himself all set to hit the town. He was ready to find anyone who might be interested in his latest adventure. He walked into town and headed down to the pier to the Ropewalk where the party was still going on. People were passed out in chairs. A few people were asleep with their heads on the tables. Others were mumbling in useless conversations about nothing. Marie Lafrontiere, who was working one of her numerous bartending gigs, looked up and saw Mark walk in wearing his fedora. She did a double take and felt a little pale. She reached for the bartop to steady herself. She thought she was seeing a ghost!

Mark went up to the bar and commented to the wide-eyed and speechless Marie, "Wow! What kind of party is going on here? I hope you're taking all their car keys!"

At that moment, Colin Keenan and Sean Divine, who had been leading numerous toasts, looked over at Mark and said rather drunkenly, "Hi ya, Deputy Dawg!", not even realizing why they were even there at the bar.

Mark sensed that this would not be the place to see if he could relate his story to anyone of importance. He turned on his heels and continued up to Bosun's Locker. It was the same deal there! He peeked through the window and saw people in different stages of drunkenness, even some sleeping at the bar. He shook his head, saying to himself, "Why don't these people get a job?" He then said to himself, "Ahh, the Tap Room! That's the ticket!"

He walked up to Center Street only passing a few lone souls walking the streets. Upon his arrival, June Hutton, the hostess said excitedly, "Mark! You're OK?

Oh my, everyone in town was so upset about the news! I mean, we heard that . . ."

Right then, Chris Morris walked up with four people. Not noticing Mark wearing his fedora, he asked June if they could have a table for four.

June said, "Sure thing. It's kind of quiet in here. Everyone is down at the Rose & Crown, having a shot and beer party."

Mark, overhearing that the bar was quiet and the Rose & Crown was a zoo, decided to just to go back home and call Beth. Town seemed a bit strange right then. Maybe she had returned home and would go out with him.

Back at the station, Kosmo had spoken to all the curious people telling them that the information, as was usual of island gossip, was way over done. Deputy Donato was just home resting after quite the interesting turn of events of the day out in Quaise.

Some people began picking up the flowers, saying, "Well, these will look nice on my dining room table." Some looked disappointed that the big to-do was nothing more than the usual gossip mill going into full tilt.

Kosmo chuckled to himself, knowing that some of the flowers being removed were not even ones they had purchased.

Kosmo then brought Mike DiFronzo into his office. He told Mike to turnup the volume on the dispatch telephone ring signal so they would hear it if a call came in. Mike held his head down at first. He started saying that even though Deputy Donato used to give him a hard time now and then, he, Beth, and Mark were like three amigos. He wiped a tear from his eye and looked up.

Kosmo then broke the good news that Mark was alive and well and back at home. "Look, Mike, I'm sure this was all a communication breakdown. But from this point on, you are *not* to give out any information until it's confirmed from a reliable source. I'll bet the whole town is now drowning their sorrows like a hurricane party at the local watering holes. We can't have rumors like this one showing up and impacting our professional roles in this town. Get back on to your phone duty, OK?"

"Yeah, sorry, Chief. It must have been something that Mark said to me that I misunderstood. I'll be OK."

Next, Kosmo called Judy at Hatch's to inform her of Mark's well-being.

Judy said, "Oh, my, will you go figure? The minute the news broke of Mark being shot, the store was filled with people buying nips and pints of just about everything I could imagine. You know this island will do anything to get out of work and have a party! Thanks for filling me in, Kosmo."

Kosmo realized he hadn't yet thought about Beth. He told Mike to get on the phone at once and contact her, and when he did, he was to patch the call to his office, immediately!

Mike patched the call through to Kosmo. It took a few minutes but he finally was able to calm Beth down. She then said, "Oh no! My parents are driving straight through from Virginia as I called them when I got the news about Mark. What am I going to do?"

Kosmo reassured her, "Well, the best condolence is the good news that this was all a misunderstanding. Given what the department has put you and your parents through, I will secure a nice room for two nights and pay for dinner for both nights for them. It will be out our spending allotments we have. Now that I think of it, there is quite a good amount in that account as we hardly ever use it. As the old saying goes, if someone in the town treasurer's office sees how much we have, they might just want to appropriate some of those funds to a different department, and we cannot have that happening can we?"

Beth, through some sniffles said, "No, Chief, we can't!"

Kosmo, now that all the excitement in the station had calmed down, realized that Mike DiFronzo felt so poorly for this embarrassing event that transpired. The chief figured that maybe he should take advantage of this opportunity and make this into a staff party with a dinner celebration.

Mike DiFronzo went out front of the station and picked up two lovely flower bouquets that were laying in tribute. He placed them in a vase he had gotten from the back storage closet. He wrote an apology note to Beth, taped it on the vase and placed it on Mark's desk.

Just a few minutes later, Mark came into the station. "Has anyone seen or heard from Beth lately? I stopped by her apartment and I didn't get any response from her. I've walked around this town full of drunks and did not see her anywhere!"

Kosmo stuck his head out of his office door and crooked his finger to summon Mark into his office. "Well, Mark, there's something I need to inform you about. Luckily, it's all good at this point."

The following day Beth's parents called from a pay phone at the Steamship office. After a reassuring conversation that all was well with Mark, Beth told them of their nice suite awaiting them at the Jared Coffin Hotel along with dinners for two nights, all compliments of the Nantucket Police Department!

GHOSTS OF THE HAUNTED EDINBURGH CASTLE, SCOTLAND

The haunted Edinburgh Castle sits upon Castle Rock in Scotland. Since Edinburgh Castle was such an important stronghold for ruling Scotland, the rival English and Scottish Monarchies have fought over and taken turns in occupying the castle throughout history. This resulted in many sieges and battles being fought at the castle. There is historical evidence suggesting that at least 26 sieges took place at the castle, making it one of the most besieged landmarks in the world. With so many battles, suffering and deaths having occurred at Edinburgh Castle, it really comes as no surprise that it is considered to be haunted.

Bob Tonkin was on his usual daily ritual, locking the store. He left his briefcase inside on the office desk and headed to the Ships Inn for the evenings special of slow roasted prime rib. He had his Scotch, then a glass of a red French Bordeaux. Bob Moulder sat and chatted with him and asked, "So, how's it working out with your latest find for the antique store?"

The dealer said, "Oh, things are in the works, moving forward slowly but surely. It will provide a nice monthly check for years to come."

His host inquired, "I'm curious. What is it?"

Tonkin looked up over his glad of wine and explained, "Well, at this time I am not free to elaborate on it. Hopefully in a few weeks or a month I will have this deal all signed, sealed and delivered. It's a little different than most of my other transactions."

"Well, I hope it works out for you. I'll let you enjoy your meal in peace. See you, later, sport."

Bob Tonkin finished his meal and headed out. He turned around thinking he was being followed, but then thought it was just the rustling of the wind. He shrugged his shoulders and thought, "I must just be tired."

He returned to the store, placed Daisy, his dog, into the front seat of the Jeep Wagoneer, then placed his briefcase in the backseat. He then returned to the shop to get some magazines from the Antiques Guild that he had wanted to catch up on. Leaving the front door ajar, he walked back to his office. Daisy watched his every move.

As he walked back towards the front door a man entered. Bob said, "Sorry, we are closed for the day but I'll reopen at eight a.m. tomorrow."

Out of the blue the man inquired threateningly, "Where is it?" and locked the door behind him from the inside.

"Where's what"? Bob asked, wondering who this person was and what he wanted.

"You know what I am talking about," the man replied seriously, still in that threatening tone.

"Well, I don't have any idea what you're talking about, honestly," Bob replied, hoping the guy would turn around and leave the store.

"Yes, you do! I am talking about the jeweled inlaid sword or whatever you call it," the man demanded.

"Look, sir, you definitely have the wrong store, and the wrong person. And I have no clue about what you are talking about. If you don't turn around and leave right now, I am calling the police," Bob stated firmly.

The man did not move but just kept staring at Bob, Bob waited a few moments and started moving towards the phone by the front desk of the store.

When his back was turned the man picked up a heavy candlestick holder and smashed Bob on back of his head, knocking him to the floor! The man, thinking that Bob was down for the count, started rummaging through the store. Bob regained consciousness and pulled himself up by a chair. Hearing the racket the intruder was making, he went the find him and once again confronted him. The man picked up a fireplace poker and proceeded to bludgeon Bob to his death.

Hunter Laroche

LEAP CASTLE, COUNTY OFFALY, IRELAND ONE OF THE MOST NOTORIOUSLY HAUNTED CASTLES IN IRELAND

There are many incredible castles in Ireland, offering interesting ancient stories worth discovering. One that won't let you down is Leap Castle in County Offaly.

Leap Castle is one of the most popular castles in Ireland as it is famous for being known as one of the most notoriously haunted castles to ever exist. Every year people all around Ireland and from further afield flock to Leap Castle to uncover its ghostly stories and stunning beauty. It is forever captivating people on their visit to that part of Ireland.

Wendy Dow was pulling up Main Street to make a bank deposit when she saw all the commotion with the ambulance and fire truck up ahead on the street. She saw yellow crime scene tape blocking off the upper part of Main and Federal Streets. Then she spotted Rita, hurrying up the street. She waved to Rita who stopped and told her the distressing news of Bob Tonkin's demise.

Rita went on to say, "It looks like a robbery gone bad, but it's too early to tell."

Wendy felt weak in the knees and her stomach was not doing much better. She aimlessly continued up to the bank, made her transactions then headed back to the car. She rushed back to Quaise and told the unsettling news to Nancy. They both deduced rather quickly that there was way more to this story than meets the eye.

Sitting down in the living room, Nancy started. "OK, let's review what's been going on. We have had the prowler, then the break in, and now this. Well, for whatever reason, I suspect it has got to be the same person that killed Bob Tonkin."

Wendy wailed with her face all wrinkled up, "So what do we do now?"

Ted Hudgins, the harbormaster, heard about the incident over his police scanner as he was driving his old Willy's Jeep down Union Street. He was riding along with a brilliant lawyer friend from Florida, John Vega, when he heard the scanner. He told John, "Buckle up, old boy, we are putting the petal to the metal!" He reached in the back seat, pulled out his old trusty civil defense helmet and strapped it tight onto his head. Then he turned on the old siren he personally wired up on the Jeep and went flying around the corner onto Main Street. He raced up the cobblestones, all one hundred yards or so, and jumped out of the Jeep, megaphone in hand.

Kosmo heard and then saw Ted's Jeep. He said out loud to no one in particular, "What now? Really?"

Ted already had his megaphone turned on to high volume. He then saw Kosmo, gave him a salute and said, "Hey, Chief. I will take care of crowd control! You've got your hands full here with the shooter!"

Ted then told John Vega to take cover behind the Jeep until he could better access the situation and to keep himself out of harm's way when the bullets started flying.

Kosmo strode over to tell Ted to just go back to his office. But just then, a fire engine and the ambulance pulled up. Main Street was becoming utter chaos! His radio then started squawking as every department was now on the same channel. The firemen were unreeling hoses and everyone was shouting at once. Kosmo could not even hear himself think! Things were quickly spiraling into great disarray!

Ted Hudgins was shouting through his megaphone, "Everyone remain calm! Seek shelter behind a tree or an automobile as bullets could spray in any direction!"

Dan Connor, the fire chief, was reacting along the same line as Kosmo, still trying to figure out exactly what was going on. But he knew if there was a shooter Kosmo would have the street locked down in an instant! He was trying to figure out the best way to help restore order.

Don Mignosa was with Les, looking out from the stores window across the street. He started laughing and said, "This looks like a Laurel and Hardy skit or the Keystone Cops!" He then added, "Poor Kosmo! This is all he needs! Harbor Master Ted Hudgins with his civil defense helmet on and his megaphone." He and Les were having quite the laugh about the whole situation, still unclear what set it off.

Kosmo and Dan Connor finally managed to get Ted Hudgins to shut off his megaphone and move his Jeep out of the center of the street. Within twenty minutes Main Street started to quiet down and return back to normal. Kosmo still had a murder on his hands but the calamity in the streets was back to normal.

As Ted was departing, he told Kosmo, "If you need any back up, I keep my scanner on in the Jeep and office and house round the clock. Just call me and I'll be Johnny-on-the-spot!" He climbed into his Jeep, nodded to his buddy, John, and they motored up the road to head back around to the harbor.

MOOSHAM CASTLE, SALZBERG, AUSTRIA

The Moosham Castle witnessed some of the most gruesome witch trials in Austrian history. Interestingly, most of the accused victims kept in the castle were male, and a large portion of the ones killed were 21 or younger. Today, this castle is one of the most haunted places in Europe. Many people claim to have seen Anton, the castle caretaker, wandering around the castle and watching over the prisoners. Even more interestingly, oftentimes in the morning, when the staff would come to open the museum, they would find the guns in the hunting room hanging upside down, despite the castle being locked up overnight.

Nancy declared, "OK, I am calling Nick Caselli to tell him what has been going on. Then we need to proceed to get a bit of information out there."

"Have you checked the car's trunk for the object?" Wendy asked.

Nancy shook her head. "No and at this point we need too, but let's not look for it here, not out in the open. Our prowler might be lurking in the brush somewhere, watching out every move, so how are we going to get this done without anyone seeing us looking in the trunk?"

Wendy suggested, "Let's pull the Rambler into the barn, open the back hatch up and start loading some rakes and shovels into it. That way, if he's watching, it will look like we are headed out for a landscaping job. While I am taking my time loading the tools, you duck out of sight, and take a quick look under the trunk. Double check to be sure that it's still in place. Just do it quickly, then quietly shut it, and bring over a few more tools to load."

Nancy nodded. "OK, well we need to make a move sooner than later. This guy is not going to go away quietly. Let's pull the car around right out front of the barn. Also, we need to make sure Rusty is staying in the house every night. I don't want to be alone here and going through another chance meeting with this jerk ever again, especially at night."

Nancy pulled the nose of the Rambler inside the barn, acting like they had nothing to hide. She went to get the shovels and rakes from the wall of the barn.

Wendy went inside the house and called Nick Caselli. She relayed the story about the car that had followed her into town, the prowler, and the break in, and now Bob Tonkin's demise. It almost made her cry to think of the trouble they had caused.

After saying how sorry he was to hear that Bob had been killed, Nick suggested that they get the scepter off their property. That way it would be safer if they were to be possibly robbed if they were away or even at home.

Wendy said that they had made a rough plan how to get this done.

Nick also had told Wendy, "There is something else I've learned from my professor friend in Oxford, England. However, it would be best talked about in person. Just be careful," Nick advised. "I don't want anything to happen to either of you. Somehow, someone is onto this scheme. There's a lot at stake. I'll wait to hear more from you soon." And he hung up.

Wendy and Nancy discussed their final plan on where to hide the scepter. They would stop by the job site where Rusty was working and ask him to meet them at the dump out in Madaket. When they found him, they quietly told Rusty about an object they wanted to keep out of sight in case the prowler returned. Under the pretense of getting rid of stuff, they would remove the box from the Rambler rather quickly after they pulled in to the dump. Rusty was to very casually pick up the box that they would place near a junk pile. Then they would drive away. But they would not take their eyes off the box until he had picked it up.

Nancy suggested that he pick it up like it was something just laying around and place it in his truck, really paying no special attention to it. During that whole time, they would keep their eyes peeled on the dirt lane entrance to the dump to make sure their stalker was not on their trail.

After they instructed to Rusty, he did not fully understand what this whole 'cat and mouse game' was about. Yet he agreed and did not ask many questions.

But what would they then do with the box?

Wendy and Nancy discussed it among themselves. They did not want to draw any attention at all to the box, so they could not ask Don and Rita to lock it in their safe. All the men's club guys knew about the box from the discovery in the cellar, so they didn't want to get them involved. And, of course, they did not have a very good feeling about the box just lying around on the back seat of Rusty's truck, either.

On the way out to the dump they were both running ideas through their minds but they kept coming up blank. They kept saying, "Where can we store it where it will be safe and where we won't draw attention to it?"

They were tossing ideas back and forth when Nancy finally said, "You know what?"

Wendy asked hopefully, "What?"

Nancy continued. "Rusty is caretaking several properties, and I'll bet a bunch of the owners have already departed for the season. Some of the houses are locked up and pipes are drained. I am sure, until we figure out where to hide the scepter, he could put it in one of those basements. It doesn't take up any room, and no one is going to be going through their basements or garages this time of year. What do you think?"

Wendy nodded. "That's a good suggestion. I will ask him when we meet him at the dump. I am sure he is wondering what we are up to, but he is so quiet I bet he won't even ask what this is all about!"

Without any fanfare, they made the trade-off with Rusty at the dump. Then they pulled out, not seeing anyone trailing them.

Later that afternoon, while the gals were working on a few more window boxes, Rusty pulled in and met them in the barn. He quietly said, "It's all taken care of. Just let me know when you want to pick it up and I'll do that with you."

"Thanks, Rusty," Wendy said. "We really appreciate it."

That night they told Nick Caselli about moving the object. They were vague on the details and just said it was safe and sound.

Nick then added, "Well, I have something more to this story. I spoke in depth with my friend, Rolf Achilles, the professor at Oxford University in England. There may one more twist to this story. If it works out, then it will confirm my thoughts on the authenticity of our subject."

He paused to let the gals get focused. "So, here's a thought. JoAnn and I could come down to the island as soon as tomorrow or a few days later. I can relay the latest news to you both, and maybe take the object back with us to Boston. We have a large, very secure fireproof vault on the premise."

The next afternoon Nick and JoAnn arrived on Nantucket and stayed at Martin's Guest House. Wendy and Nancy drove to town, parked on Main Street and walked up and down numerous streets keeping an eye out for anyone following them. When they felt the coast was clear they entered the Jared Coffin Hotel and walked out the back door. They down the street to Martin's Guest House. Nick and JoAnn were seated in front of the fireplace and the lobby area was deserted. It turned out they were the only ones residing at the inn for the evening. The innkeeper left her number, and a platter of sliced assorted cheeses, as well bottles of red and white wine with them as she had gone out for dinner at a friend's house. So, the place was theirs for most of the evening.

Nick told them, in depth, the conversation he had with Professor Rolf Achilles. "Basically, there is some type of legend associated with the Scepter of Dagobert. Of course, it could also just a myth to make the story of the missing scepter even more intriguing. Given the amount of time that has passed since it was stolen, anything could have been said about the mystery."

Then Wendy asked, "So, what's the latest on it?"

Nick picked up the thread. "If this is even true, first off I will have to figure it out. But I have plenty of time on my hands and a private windowless office in back of the shop. Professor Achilles said that there might be a hidden chamber inside of the scepter. It has to do with a note that is written possibly in Latin, saying that someplace in Paris is a hidden treasure. The treasure is rumored to be one thousand gold coins from the royal family of France. The rumor goes on to say that it is hidden in one of the catacombs under the Place des Pyramides by the Joan of Arc statue which is a French gilded bronze equestrian sculpture. Now, ladies, I have read a few things about the possible hidden clue in the Scepter of Dagobert, but you know how rumors build up over time." Nick shook his head as if to suggest this was all a bit crazy.

He continued, looking at JoAnn for encouragement. "So, if I am possibly able to discover this hidden clue, then first off we will then know it's the original 'Scepter of Dagobert.' Then, and this is a huge proposition, I could possibly go and try to locate the gold coins. Then again, we could just be getting our hopes up on false information handed down over the years. People do things just to keep the story more intriguing. We'll have to proceed very slowly and cautiously no matter what we do from this point forward."

Nancy and Wendy looked at each other and nodded.

Nick suggested, "One other thing I would like to do is to meet the Mr. Rully who seemed to know some history on the Frenchmen who built the house. Also, I would like to see the property. However, the problem with this whole scenario is that if you are being watched or followed, it would not be a good idea for this person to see me. Who knows what this person has up their sleeve? He or she is certainly intent on gaining access to something they believe is in your possession."

THE HAUNTING OF CASTLE RESZEL, POLAND

This fascinating red structure looming over Reszel has a horrifying dark past. The town was burned in the 1800's, and a woman named Barbara Zdunk was arrested for committing arson and was later accused of witchcraft. In the castle, she was tortured and raped on multiple occasions, and eventually gave birth to two children. Many people claim that the ghost of Barbara and her children haunt the castle today. A strange smell of perfume was reported in the castle on multiple occasions, doors that were previously locked were found open the next morning, and some people even claim that they were touched by a strange force in the castle.

Nick nodded in the direction of the inn's front door. "You are both sure you were not followed here, correct?"

Wendy nodded emphatically. "We did a double check about four times while walking here. We cut through the Jared Coffin Hotel, entered the front and went out the private back door exit. There's no way we were followed." Nick gave a thumbs up and sat back on the couch.

They enjoyed the wine and the cheese, and the four of them walked over to the North Shore Restaurant for a nice dinner.

The next day Nick and JoAnn went to the Visitors Bureau and inquired about getting some local information from a man named Bob Rully. They were directed to the Nantucket Atheneum where Mr. Rully had an office. They were greeted by his secretary and shown right into his office.

Nick introduced JoAnn and himself to Mr. Rully. He said they were interested in any information that Mr. Rully might have on a Frenchmen who had built a home out in Quaise.

Mr. Rully was quick to pick up on the subject. "It's very nice to meet you both. I believe the fellow you are inquiring about was Gerard Dubois. It was rumored that he had a questionable reputation and had to flee France after escaping from a prison in the south of Paris. Then he supposedly traveled to England, then took a boat to America. It was rumored he had a good amount of cash on hand. He seemed to arrive on Nantucket rather quietly and built his home, doing most of the labor himself. The house is still out there, in case you are interested."

Nick's question he wanted an answer to was, "Do you happen to know how or when he died?" For Nick, the answer to this question might tie it all together. If Gerard had died suddenly, that might be the reason the scepter had not ever been sold, and therefore it was found hidden in the barn crawl space area.

Mr. Rully stated, "Well, it was quite a tragic and freak accident. It seems that Mr. Dubois was on a friend's trawler when a large swell rocked the boat at a pretty good angle. Overboard he went, never to surface again. His body was never recovered. The house, since then, has been owned by a few families but not many."

Now Nick was even more convinced that this was leading closer and closer to the final question of their object being the original 'Scepter of Dagobert.'

Nick thanked Mr. Rully for his time. As they were leaving Mr. Rully asked, "If you don't mind, why are you interested in the history of this gentleman?"

Nick knew that this question might come forth. He told Mr. Rully, "I happen to have a friend in Pennsylvania who thinks he might be related to a Frenchmen who lived on Nantucket, specifically in Quaise. He asked me if we ever were headed down to the island to inquire about this man. You've been helpful, Mr. Rully, though I don't know if my friend will be able to pick up any threads on this relationship." Nick left it at that.

Mr. Rully gave Nick one of his cards and said, "Please feel free to have him contact me if he would like me to dig around a bit more. Perhaps I can find out if Mr. Dubois had any known relations at the time of his death."

Nick and Joann went on to the Whaling Museum and took a guided tour. It was the last tour until the following month as the summer season had pretty much wound down. That evening they made plans to meet Nancy and Wendy at the Opera House for dinner.

Wendy was driving when she told Nancy, "We have company. It looks like the same old rust-colored Ford is trailing us!"

Nancy calmly advised her, "OK, here we go. Let's make it look like we are just taking our time, no sudden speed ups or turns. When we get to town, you drop me off at the Rose & Crown and park the car somewhere near there. I'll go in the Rose & Crown, then head out the back door and sneak over to the alley on the back side of the Opera House. There is a side door that you can enter into the patio of the restaurant. Then you will do the exact same thing: enter the Rose & Crown, and head out the back door. Don't talk to anyone. This stalker will never figure it out. When I called for the reservation, I asked if we could have that private table off to the side that cannot been seen from the hostess stand or the street. The reservation is under Achilles, so if our stalker tries to stop in places to spot us of see if we have a reservation under our name he won't get far!"

Wendy agreed. "Wow, this is like *Sherlock Holmes*! See you there in a few minutes."

Nick and JoAnn arrived, knowing the reservation name, and they all were seated. Nancy told Nick quietly, "Our stalker is back. We spotted him following us into town. He drives a four-door rust-colored Ford. Wendy will be here shortly. We had to take a detour on foot to slip into this place. It's a good thing we've gotten to know the island by now!"

Nick stood up when Wendy arrived, seeming a little breathless. He helped her get seated.

JoAnn asked, "Are you OK? Do you think anyone followed you?"

Wendy shook her head. "No, I think I outmaneuvered the guy."

Nancy went on to explain. "We've been planning for this. Rusty has all the outside lights on. Last week Duke, our friend from the hardware store, brought over some extra steel rods that were on deep discount. As an aside, it seems everything he finds for us is on deep discount!

He and Rusty made the hatch to the basement double strength for locking, as well as the door below that. It would take a full kick from a mule to try and break it open. Rusty is in the living room right by the phone if someone tries to break in!"

Nick then told them all the information he had gathered on the Frenchmen who originally built the house, and how his death was very sudden and that could be one of the reasons that he never was able to sell the object.

"Now, this calls for a celebration, but one thing," Nancy said. "We need you to meet up with Rusty so he can deliver the object to you. Then you can take it up to Boston and see if you can work your magic on locating the mysterious clue about the gold coins." She crossed her fingers and smiled.

JoAnn added, "Well, Nick has a talent for working with fine wood. His knowledge of antiques over the years has allowed him to repair many a damaged piece. He has a fairly good sense of how older objects made from wood, stone or metal fit together like a jigsaw puzzle. He has the time, the tools, magnifying glasses, jeweler's loupes and proper lighting. I feel pretty positive that if the object is concealing something, he will discover it!"

Their server, Kaci, asked if they might like a beverage while they were perusing the menus. Wendy asked if Nick and JoAnn might want to join them with Kir Royals to begin, and the evening began. They followed up the wines with a white Burgundy, then a red Cote's du Rhone. They selected a whole six-pound roast chicken of which the restaurant only cooked three per evening and were ready at forty-five minute intervals. When they were sold out, that was it for the evening. They were in time, and enjoyed the feast set before them.

When they departed the restaurant, Wendy and Nancy went out the patio side entrance. Nick and JoAnn waited ten minutes and went out the front door.

The next day Nancy called Martin's Guest House and told Nick that Rusty would meet them in the Steamship ticket office fifteen minutes prior to them boarding, and he would have the package in hand.

THE GARDETTE-LEPRETE MANSION, PHILADELPHIA, PENNSYLVANIA: AN HISTORIC HOME WITH A BLOOD-SOAKED LEGEND (RATED 'R' FOR ITS CONTENTS)

The house was built in 1836 for a dentist from Philadelphia named Joseph Coulton Gardette. He later sold it to Jean Baptiste LaPrete, a Creole and wealthy plantation owner, who bought the pink house as a vacation home. LaPrete invested a lot of time and money, transforming the residence in to a suitable place for his family. LaPrete decided to rent it for extra money when he began to fall on hard times after the Civil War. LaPrete would later lose the house to the bank.

A mysterious young man, allegedly from Turkey, approached LaPrete inquiring about renting his residence. An agreement was made and the man moved in with his treasure, harem of women and eunuchs. No one knows for sure who the man was, but he came to be known as "The Sultan". There are theories this man wasn't a sultan but actually, a brother of a Sultan.

Adjustments were made to the house upon his arrival. Doors and windows were covered and blocked. The balconies were closed off. The iron gates were chained and locked. Guards with curved daggers patrolled outside the house regularly. Soon, the air was filled with smell of incense, music and laughter trickling from the house every night.

It is said the 'Sultan's' harem was complete with women of all ages and sizes and men as well as young boys. Some say he went as far as to kidnap women and tortured them until they gave in to his pleasures. One night, the usual rowdy sounds turned to screams. Many people in the neighborhood were conditioned to the 'Sultan's' parties and didn't give it a second thought.

It took neighbors walking by the following morning to notice something was wrong. The gate was unlocked as it never was. Upon closer inspection, they noticed trickles of blood oozing from under the front door. It sent them running to notify the police. Knocks went unanswered, green-lighting their forced entry in to the house. Their eyes fell on one of the most gruesome sights ever. Blood coated the floors and walls. Body parts of the 'Sultan's' harem and guards were strewn about. It was later determined they were all raped prior to dismemberment. The 'Sultan', however, was not among them. Police wandered out in to the garden to find a hand sticking out of the soil. The 'Sultan' had been buried alive. Their killers were never determined.

Deputy Donato was making list after list. He was divided his legal pad into two sides. On the left he was writing motives, not really understanding what possible motives he had in mind. He more or less just started doodling. On the right side, he was going to add potential suspects, but then again that did not pan out very well. He did not know Bob Tonkin very well or any friends he might have had. The best he could come up with was his mechanic, possibly Daisy's dog groomer, or his housemaid. And that was just about it.

Beth walked into his office, and asked him what he was doing. He quickly turned over his pad of paper and said, "I'm making lists of different motives and suspects. It's a rough draft, but in all my home study courses for detective work, this is one of the chapters I excelled in!"

"Well," Beth said, "let me see your progress."

"No, not yet, it's still in the rough draft phase and I don't want to lose my train of thought."

"Well then," Beth asked teasingly, "what's a girl got do to have her fella take her out to lunch? And you know what today is? Pastrami sandwich day at Les's!"

Mark could not be happier that she had an excuse for him to stop making his lists!

Nick and JoAnn returned to Boston without a hitch. Wendy and Nancy kept look out for their stalker, never letting on in any way that they were on to him. They had made notes to turn over in a short time to Constable Kosmo via an incognito presence. They would slowly send information to the police station on this person who they thought would be of interest in the murder of Bob Tonkin. But if they knew if showed their cards too soon, it might be possible that this unknown person might spill the beans about the scepter, if that was even what he was after.

The day that Nick and JoAnn left, Nancy told Wendy, "Now it's time to turn the tables. Let's let the stalker become the prey." She smirked with the thought.

"And how are we going to do that?" Wendy asked.

"Well, my plan is simple. On the next drive to town if you spot him tailing you from Quaise, you put on your bright red cap. I will already be in town as I'll have Rusty bring me in an hour before you head out. I will have him lock my bike on a side street a day before the first trial run of this scheme. If I see you exit the car with a red hat on, I will be all bundled up with a hat covering my forehead and ears, collar up and my hair tucked under the hat. He will never spot me. He won't even know he's being watched. Then I will most likely easily be able to find where he's parked. Both times before he was on lower Main Street. He'll be clueless, not knowing we have him pegged." She nodded in excitement.

"I will write down his license plate, get a good description of him, and, if we are lucky, he will remain in town as he most likely knows that you will just head back to the house. Then if needed I will hop on my bike and trail him. I will carry a map in my back pocket or a backpack and should look like a normal bike riding tourist. He will pay no attention to me. Then he will most likely drive to the hotel or inn here in town where he is staying. I will hang back and watch him enter." She had a clear image in her head of the situation.

"So, then we'll have the car's information. It's most likely a rental. Then we will also know the hotel or inn where he is staying. We can get the information somehow or some way about who he is and where he is from. You know that almost everyplace here leaves the check-in register just on a desk or in an unlocked office.

We then find a time when he has gone out and we zip in, scan the register, find out who this clown is and out we go. Maybe you can take a picture of the page of the register. After you take it, we'll get it developed. I am sure we can find this guy's information out pretty easily."

Wendy nodded, though she wondered if they'd be able to pull off of this off.

Nancy was on a roll. "And we know one thing-that in this town there is nothing going on after eleven p.m. All we have to do is find out the inn or hotel, then we can ask or inquire if a certain single gentleman is staying there. We can say that a friend from off island is trying to send him a surprise. We'll let on that she told us but we forgot to bring the piece of paper we wrote his name on. We will ask if could they check it out for us, and for them not mention anything to him that someone was inquiring as we want to keep it a surprise. What do you think?"

Wendy replied, "That sounds simple enough. No one is going to question something as innocent as that

And by then I will most likely have gotten a pretty good view of what he looks like, so I can describe him to the front desk person."

Nancy continued her train of thought. "The next move will be-after we get that information, his room and name- well it gets a little dicey from there on out."

"Dicey?" Wendy asked a bit nervously.

Nancy explained, "Well, we get the room number. Then late at night we go and steal one of the extra keys to his room. You know they are always hanging in plain sight. No one ever pays any mind to them."

"And?" Wendy asked.

"Well, we watch him, beginning early in the morning. We get some walkie-talkies. I will call Duke later on."

"Walkie-talkies? What on earth for?"

"Yeah, when he heads out, you follow him and give me the update where he is. I go into his room. If by any chance he starts heading back to the hotel, you radio me. If he drives off, you stand away from the hotel keeping watch as he might come back. All I need is five minutes or less in his room."

Wendy hesitated. "I don't know about this. It's kind of risky, don't you think?"

"Piece of cake! In and out, sleek like a cat. That's why they are called "cat" burglars!"

Nick Caselli was busy. He had been two days out of the shop and he felt like it was a month. The office phone was ringing off the hook, and people were stopping in to shop and ask numerous questions. He had never seen business so brisk, though it was about the start of the holiday season. By the end of the third day, he put a sign on the front door, *'Please call for an appointment any time this week.'* There, that should help. JoAnn gave him a thumbs-up.

He needed time, a lot of quiet time, to examine the scepter. Whoever actually made the scepter did not make it easy to divulge its secrets, for if it fell into foreign hands it needed to be difficult to find the hidden clue. If there even was a clue to be found, Nick thought.

He closed himself in the back office. JoAnn answered all the calls, and told people, who after reading the sign on the front door may have still rapped on it, that Nick was a little under the weather. She said he would not be seeing anyone until Monday at the earliest unless it was something that needed immediate attention.

Nick started at the very top of the scepter which he now knew that in 1795 was stolen from the Louvre after being on display for two years. He had a printed page he had copied from an archived file from the Boston Library.

The text explained, "The golden scepter, named the 'Scepter of Dagobert', raises questions no longer answerable. Doublet describes it in detail, and Feligrands' engraving helps us to picture it. He notes that some antiquaries of his day thought it to have been a consular staff. On the top was a golden group of Ganymede carried by an eagle, each of whose wings was set with four emeralds and a garnet surrounded by eight pearls. This was planted on a globe held by a hand, with likewise a little branch garnished with pearls, enamels, and coral. The hand was at the end of a golden rod, also enameled and set with stones. Probably the summit group, and perhaps other parts of this scepter, were antique, but it is unlikely that we shall ever know more about it."

Nick's plan was to work thirty minutes on examining the intriguing artifact, and then take fifteen minutes of rest to get his eyes readjusted. This was tedious and time-consuming work, and he did not want to have to go back and repeat a step all over again. Slowly and surely was his plan, even if he only managed two hours a day. He figured it was going to take a while.

The second day into this project when he was studying very closely under the wings of the eagle, his eye caught something very faint. Below where the eagle perched, he thought he could make out a slight break in the filigree. Nick slowly and cautiously moved the scepter to try to get a better look at this spot. While wearing his white jeweler's soft gloves he called JoAnn into the back office. He gave her the magnifying loupe. She put it on while he shined a bright light on the scepter. He asked her if she thought she could see some type if break in the area he had studied a few moments earlier.

"Sorry, Nick, I think that is just a spot that is slightly marked holding the top to the shaft. If there was a way to get into the part under where the eagle is perched, it would have to be cut open and that would ruin this masterpiece." She kissed him on the forehead and said, "Let's wrap this up and call it a day. A fresh set of clear eyes in the morning will work wonders. I can see as of now your eyes are blood shot from looking at this scepter so intensely through the magnifying glass. Let's give it a rest!"

Nick nodded, and carefully repacked the scepter in its case and locked it up in his vault.

Kosmo, like Deputy Donato, had made a list. He had been back to the scene of the crime three times, walking all throughout the shop from every corner as well as from the basement to the second and third floor. The assailant definitely was someone looking for something specific.

On the day of the discovery of Mr. Tonkin's death he had also gone to Bob's home which had been searched. He could see things that were out of place. Rita had told Kosmo that she and Don had been guests for cocktails numerous times at Bob's home, and it was always neat and orderly. He also had a cleaning girl come in every week. The house had definitely been rifled through.

With that in mind Kosmo added some thoughts to his ongoing list. He knew it was not about a cash robbery as the petty cash box was still untouched under Bob's desk in the office. His wallet, with over two hundred dollars, had still been in Bob's back pocket when they took his body to the morgue. His watch and other jewelry in the store glass cases were left untouched. What was this mysterious person after to the point that he would have to kill Bob for it? This was a dangerous criminal, that's for sure. And, chances were good the crook didn't yet have what he was wanting.

Kosmo once again headed back to Bob's house. He looked for the way that the person had entered the house. He spotted it after realizing that someone had yet, again, gone through Mr. Tonkin's personal property. It had to be via the back door inside the screen porch. He heard a car pull in, and Deputy Donato joined him.

He told Mark, "Ahh our intruder has returned yet again. He's been searching, neatly, but still searching for something. What is it?"

Mark tried to sound knowledgeable on the subject of the intruder. "Yup, plain as day the intruder has returned yet once again." Yet he truly did not have a clue how Kosmo knew this fact.

Kosmo wanted to have a little fun with Mark. "So, Deputy, what gave it away for you?"

Mark was not expecting this question and started stammering. "Well, um, well you see what I was thinking was . . ." Then he said, "Did you hear that?"

Kosmo, knowing this was a ploy to throw him off the subject said, "Oh, I think that was just the wind. We're really starting to get some late autumn weather. So, you were saying?"

"Saying what?" Mark asked.

"About what tipped you off that the intruder seems to have returned?"

"Oh, that. Well, it just seems to me, with my photographic memory, that some of the magazines and things on his desk have been rearranged." Mark nodded in the direction of another room.

"His desk?" Kosmo asked. "We have not gotten to his den yet."

"Well, what I meant to say is, if I can see that some of the magazines have been moved, I'll bet things on his desk have been moved around as well. I mean, that it's just common sense." Mark was just fudging some ideas to try to come out of this awkward spot.

"OK, my other question is," Kosmo persisted, "why would a thief be moving magazines. He's not looking to steal a *National Geographic*, is he?"

Mark hemmed and hawed. "Maybe I have this all wrong, but perhaps the thief is just looking not to have to buy a magazine subscription. So he kills Mr. Tonkin for his magazines. This way he gets them for free." Mark looked at Kosmo rather sheepishly.

"Cute, really cute," Kosmo chuckled. "Let's just start looking around as we have some serious detective work to do."

Mark nudged him. "So, if you are so smart, how did you know the intruder has been back here?"

"Well," Kosmo replied, "first off, with the yellow tape over all the entry doors no one would breach that. So, additionally, when I was shutting this place up, I placed a small folded piece of paper in every door jamb. When I arrived today, I saw the back door paper had fallen out. So that's how our intruder got in most likely both times. Let's give this place a thorough combing over. And no time for reading *National Geographic!*"

Nick was back at work slowly turning the scepter around in his hands. With so many shiny stones it was hard to keep track where he was on the staff. It strained his eyes looking through the loupe which just made everything larger. But it also distorted the image in a way that made his eyes go blurry after looking through it for a while. Additionally, he would very gently clean every piece of the staff he looked at. Several times he thought to himself, this is either the biggest farce in the world, or it's really going to be worth the effort to figure it out.

He asked himself who would actually hide a clue written in Latin inside of a memorable piece of history?

But the chase was on for him, and he was determined to follow through. He now was taking only a few appointments a week until he thoroughly had completed the task that lay before him.

Kosmo and Mark once again went through the house top to bottom. Kosmo found a pad of paper in the top drawer of Bob's desk. It had been placed under a book inside the drawer. He did not pay much attention to it but stuck it in his briefcase to study later. They continued going through the shelves and all the closets, but nothing stood out in any way as to what this intruder could be looking for. Mark and Kosmo went back to the station, only after Kosmo wedged the paper back in the door frame.

Once they were in the office, Mark headed out on patrol. Kosmo picked up the phone, called Judy at Hatch's, and invited her to dinner at the India House. She readily accepted and said, "I will bring a nice bottle of wine from the 'Queen's' cellar."

He then told Mike DiFronzo that he was off to the Dreamland to see the movie *Klute*.

Mike quickly added, "You know, Chief, I could get Beth to hop down here and take over the phones as I was thinking of going to see that as well. We could buddy up and get the Big Pack."

"The Big Pack?" Kosmo asked, grinning to himself.

Mike shook his head eagerly. "Oh yeah, it's an extra-large popcorn, and I have them do three layers of butter! If they put it only on the top, by the time you're part way through it, there's no more butter farther down inside the carton. But what I do, and they know me there, I grab the salt shaker from over by the napkin holder and I have them do one third popcorn, butter and salt it, then same thing until it's all topped off. You really need some extra napkins with all that butter! Then you get the jumbo soda which you need as popcorn can really dry you out. My friend, Hector, always gives me free refills! He's such a nice guy, that Hector. And then," Mike went on as intently as a used car salesman, "as a bonus for the Big Pack you can select any candy bar as well! I always get the Snickers as it's one of my favorites. I would get the Kit-Kat but it goes down too quickly. Then I have to miss part of the movie to buy another one."

Kosmo nodded and looked at the clock. "Well, Mike, thanks for the tip on the Big Pack, but I am going to enjoy this alone. I have some things on my mind regarding the Tonkin murder, and it just might help me figure some things out if I do this solo. But let's keep it in mind for a future date! And I will spring for the Big Pack! And I won't tell you how the movie comes out. Thanks for keeping an eye on the shop." He headed down the street.

Nick Caselli was feeling restless. His eyes were burning looking through the magnifying lens, but he kept at it. As he was just working a few more minutes before taking a break, he noticed one of the smaller diamonds seemed to be dull, not sparkling like all the others. He thought to himself, "The person that made this fine artifact, how could he have so many beautiful diamonds embedded in the scepter and then have added a flawed one?"

He called for JoAnn to come in and give her thoughts on the stone. After a minute she asked Nick for one of his smaller jeweler's picks. A few seconds later out popped the flawed stone!

Nick picked the scepter up for a closer view. Looking through the loupe he told JoAnn, "Well, well, just as I thought. This is not a diamond! It's a cheap piece of glass! Why would this be placed in with all the fine diamonds?"

They both looked at the piece of glass. Then JoAnn said, "Hold on, Nick. Look where that piece has been removed. Is that a tiny screw in that setting?"

Nick nodded. "It looks like a tiny screw. Give me a small screwdriver."

JoAnn added a drop of denatured alcohol to the screw, a very small amount to clean it. Then she said, "OK, Nick, here we go! You're on stage, so see why that screw is placed there." She leaned over to watch him work.

Ever so cautiously, so as not to snap the screw off in place, Nick slowly turned the tiny screw. It was actually rather long for such a small-sized screw. After he successfully removed the screw, nothing happened. That was it. JoAnn wondered out loud, "Well, possibly it was just an added strengthening point for the staff."

Nick said, "Hmm, it seems that the screw must have a purpose. But tomorrow I'll just reset the piece of glass but in such a way that I can still remove it if anything comes to mind. Thanks, dear, for your help. This whole contraption sure is mystifying me!"

Nick was ready to call it a day when JoAnn picked up the scepter off his desk. She asked if he was going to replace the screw and the piece of glass the following day. Nick said, "Yes. My eyes are really tired. I'll put the loose pieces in this envelope. Let's get this scepter locked up tight."

Kosmo enjoyed the movie, avoiding the Big Pack, but ordered a small popcorn instead. After the movie had finished, he went back to the station. Beth English was just arriving for the shift on the dispatcher desk. She and Kosmo chatted for a while, then he went into his office and picked up his note pad. Something struck his thoughts but faded away almost as quickly as it had flashed into his mind. He then opened up his bottom desk drawer.

Underneath his daily journal was another note pad. It was one that he kept different scenarios written down relating to open and past cases, ranging as far back as when he was in Boston. Again, another though flashed in his mind, but yet too late for him to pick up on it. He just shook his head and took that pad of paper with him.

He met Judy at the India House at six-thirty. They split an appetizer of sautéed bay scallops served over a warm toasted Brioche bun, with diced tomatoes, garlic and some finely diced button mushrooms. The wine that Judy brought was a Chateau-Nerf-du-Pape. They enjoyed that with a roasted tenderloin of pork wrapped with spinach and prosciutto, served with grilled asparagus and Potatoes Anna.

Beth English enjoyed a meatloaf dinner prepared by Mark, with all the trimmings-mashed potatoes and gravy and two crisp cold cans of Canada Dry Ginger Ale which he brought down to the station.

Mike DiFronzo enjoyed a dinner with his mom which consisted of baked sliced maple glazed ham, with honey glazed carrots, oven roasted potatoes, and a big slice of a peach pie he had purchased at the church bake sale the day before.

ZVIKOV CASTLE, ZVÍKOVSKÉ PODHRADÍ, CZECH REPUBLIC CAN YOU SURVIVE A NIGHT THERE?

Legend has it that a supernatural being has haunted the residents of the Zvikov Castle since the 1500s. According to several sources, strange events still happen in the castle's tower. Visitors reported developing unusual photographs, seeing strange animal behavior and the unexplained extinguishing of candles and fire. Another legend says that anyone who is brave enough to spend the night in the tower will die within a year.

The next morning Mark arrived at the station with a suitcase. Mike DiFronzo saw the suitcase and asked if he was going off island. Mark just rushed past him and said, "Mind your own business!"

Mike had a few things on a list for his next trip off the island. He brought the extended phone cord into Mark's office so as not to miss a call. He started asking what boat Mark was taking, and, if his mom had time, she could bring the list of things he had been writing down for his next trip off the island. Mark just looked up at him and sneered.

Mike, a bit oblivious to Mark's body language, said, "You know in the strip mall on Main Street in Hyannis? There is this specialty popcorn shop there, and they make all different kinds of popcorn. My favorite is the caramel flavored popcorn. It's delicious! I have been craving it lately, and my mom likes the cookies-and-cream flavored variety. I'll bet she could get down here with some cash and maybe you could stop by there and buy some for us. I will pay for my mom's as she's doesn't charge me any rent. And, also, if you could . . ."

"Stop!" Mark yelled. "Go back to your desk and stay quiet! This is a police station, not a social club!"

Mike persisted with his wishful thinking. "But if you could at least get us the popcorn, I will save you some."

Mark pounded his fist on his desk. "Look, you dweeb, I am not going off island! And even if I was, I am not your personal shopper! You want popcorn? Go hop on the boat and sail away to Hyannis. Now out, out, out of my office!"

Mike asked, "Then why are you carrying your suitcase?"

Kosmo, who was in his office, was getting quite the chuckle out of this whole scene even though he didn't like the way Mark treated Mike. He stood in Mark's doorway after Mike had gone back to his desk and opened up a chocolate milk.

Kosmo said to Mark, "Oh, good! I heard you are going off island. I have some shirts that I would love to have dropped off at the dry cleaners."

Mark looked up at Kosmo and said, "Funny, very funny. And, just to let you know, this suitcase is for official business."

"Really?" Kosmo added, still smiling. "And what type of business are you performing?"

Mark stood up and crossed his arms over his chest. "Well, *Fact One:* We know somewhere hiding out on this island is a murderer.

Fact Two: We don't know who he or she is.

Fact Three: It's most likely a stranger to the island as no one here is a serial killer.

Fact Four: Is that no one seems to be doing anything about it."

He pointed at his suitcase. "So, inside this suitcase I have several changes of clothes. It's something I learned in one of my home-study police courses. I am going to go around to some of the inns and hotels and observe the comings and goings of people. If I spot someone rather shady looking, I am going to tail them to see what they are up to! There is more than one way to skin a rabbit."

Kosmo had a grin on his face but had to give Mark some credit for his effort. He left Mark alone and went back into his office. He sat at his desk and opened up the bottom drawer to pull out his pad of paper, which was covered by an old book. That's when it hit him.

"Of course," he said to himself, "that's the ticket. That's what has been bugging me."

The next day, feeling refreshed from a good night's rest, Nick and JoAnn entered the shop and put up the 'Appointment Required' sign. They went into the back room and carefully extricated the box with the scepter. As JoAnn placed the scepter standing up onto the floor something rattled from the bottom of the staff. Nick heard it ever so faintly. Nick picked up the scepter and gave it a very gentle shake.

JoAnn stated, "So, that screw that we removed yesterday holds something inside of the shaft. But what does it hold is the question!"

Nick suggested, "Let's do this. We'll start from the bottom." Nick placed the scepter standing up on his desk. JoAnn was holding it steady, and with his magnifying lens he studied the bottom where it seemed to have a loose fitting. Nick had JoAnn lift it off the desk, gave it a slight twist and the bottom of the shaft separated about 1/16th of an inch.

Kosmo grabbed his coat and was headed out the front door. He knew that Mike's feelings were hurt with Mark being so abrupt with him. This was an ongoing thing with the two of them-they were quite good friends, but when Mark got something into his head it was full throttle. He did not have the time or patience for people slowing him down. So he and Mike were like two kids, always bickering with each other.

Kosmo also felt badly that he was not able at the time to have Mike join him at the movies. He also recalled that Mike had gotten the whole town riled up thinking Mark had been shot. Mike had a heart of gold, but things, well sometimes the things he said did not turn out well for him.

Stopping at Mike's desk, he asked if he had any plans for lunch as he knew Mike's shift was ending at eleven a.m.

Mike said "I brought an egg salad sandwich to enjoy before I finished my shift, but actually I ate it a few hours ago. It was really quite tasty as my mom bought a few of the sweet onions on sale at the market. She added some sweet relish, put that all together on whole wheat bread, and well, it's like a slice of heaven!"

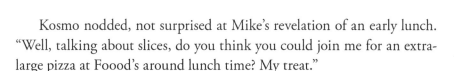

Kosmo nodded, not surprised at Mike's revelation of an early lunch. "Well, talking about slices, do you think you could join me for an extra-large pizza at Foood's around lunch time? My treat."

"Sure, I can do that! It would be swell!"

"OK, let's plan on noon. I will call Johnny Acton and tell him to give us his finest table!"

Mike chimed in. "You do know, Chief, it's really just a little sandwich and grinder and pizza type of place, don't you? I don't think they have special seating there."

Kosmo smiled. "Yes, I do Mike. It was just an expression of speech! I will see you at noon. Oh, by the way, do you think your mom would like to join us?"

Mike shook his head. "She can't today. It's the ladies knitting circle. They just knit and chat and knit and chat! She told me I should learn how to knit, as she was not going to be around my whole lifetime. And that I should learn how to darn my own socks when the time comes. So, no, it'll just be you and me, Chief. See you then, and thanks! I can't wait!"

Beth English picked up her telephone receiver at home. "Hello?"

"Hey, Babe, it's Marky-Pooh."

"Hey, Sweety, what's shakin'?"

Mark replied nonchalantly, "Oh, not much. It's just that Kosmo has me on a little 'recon' mission."

"Really? What do you mean?" Beth inquired.

"Well, Babe, old Marky-boy is going incognito—

undercover—and I am to scope out some of the inns and hotels to see if I can spot any questionable characters. You see, who we are looking for is the murderer of Bob Tonkin. Seeing how we have not tried this angle yet, he wants me to go deep undercover. So I brought in a suitcase full of different disguises-hats, sunglasses, shirts, jackets, stuff like that. I even brought along some other props like a book, a cane and different shoes. I am going deep, I tell you, deep! I almost don't recognize myself in the mirror!"

Beth nodded to herself, quite able to picture Mark getting into his disguise. "OK, Babe, you go get them! Call me later. I am making a corned beef and cabbage for dinner. See you at six!"

Mark's first outfit was a long black coat, a dark fedora, sunglasses, and a cane. And, to top it off, he was saying hello to the passers-by with a British accent. He made it to lower Main Street feeling very comfortable with his disguise. All of a sudden little Billy Marks came rushing by on his bike and slammed right into Mark!

Billy looked up and asked, "Deputy, why are you wearing sunglasses? It's really cloudy out today."

Mark replied, irritated, "Just quiet down and go away! I've got things to do."

Billy pouted, "I don't want to go away. I want to know why you're wearing sunglasses on a cloudy day, Mister?"

Mark, trying to be as inconspicuous as possible, barked at Billy. "Look, you little whippersnapper! You know I could lock you up for riding your bike on a sidewalk! Don't you know the laws?"

Billy started to cry and gently sobbed, "But I am only eight years old! How would I know the laws?" He picked up his bike and headed off, pumping for all he was worth.

Mark quickly walked away heading up Main Street. He acted as British as he could, using his cane for a proper walk and tipping his hat to the ladies saying, "Cheerio!"

Kosmo yet once again entered the back door of Bob Tonkin's home. This time the piece of paper was still wedged inside the door frame indicating that no one had entered since he and Deputy Donato were last there.

He went straight to Bob's desk in his office. He opened up the bottom right side deep drawer and removed a white pad of paper. He took a quick glance through it but knew there was nothing of interest on those pages. Below that pad were a few antiques magazines, And, underneath the magazines, was a black hard-covered book titled *Antique Trains from the 1900's*.

Kosmo placed the magazines on top of the desk with the other items he had already removed. Lying on the bottom of the drawer was a yellow-lined legal sized pad.

The top page had a few scribblings about upcoming auctions that were dated several months earlier. The second page had notes about some antique lamps and chairs that were going up for auction in Weymouth,

Cape Cod, again dated several months earlier. So far, so good Kosmo thought to himself. The next page was blank, but as he flipped to the fourth page he said aloud, "Bingo! This has got to be related to Bob's murder but why?"

He answered his own question realizing that when you want to hide something, you do it almost in plain sight just like his pad of crime notes he wanted to keep personal was under some useless things in a desk drawer.

It took Kosmo a good five minutes to decipher what was on the pages that lay in front of him, but he knew he was most likely on the right path. There was a list of things written down, a few crossed out and then written further down on the page. And, most notably, in fairly bold print on the top with question marks after it was written "**The Scepter of Dagobert???**"

Under that were a few notations with dates of its possible origin, its history, a book title and reference number at the Nantucket Atheneum. One note also said that it had been missing since it was stolen from the Louvre Museum in Paris since the late 1700's. There was a name scribbled next to this reading-Gerard Dubois.

Kosmo kept reading as the item was described as possibly a two-foot long staff embedded with diamonds and precious stones. Below that the word 'Nantucket' was written, and below that was 'Nantucket connection?'

Kosmo took the pad with him after putting everything back the way he found it.

He entered the station to find Beth English sitting at the switchboard ready the latest *Woman's World* magazine.

Kosmo checked in. "How's things, Beth? Any word from our undercover agent out in the field?"

"Yes, he said he was calling me from Checkpoint JC which I believe refers to the Jared Coffin Hotel. He said that, as of now, all seems cool and that this person of interest will be discovered soon enough. He also has a theory that it's possible that it's a two or three-man team. Perhaps one is acting as the lookout, and they could be casing a few of the other stores to hit before they make a break to get off the island." Beth shrugged her shoulders as if to say, "Who knows?"

She went on, "Mark stopped at a few of the inns asking what their rates were and was trying to blend in. In a different place he mentioned that he was waiting to meet a business associate so could he hang out in their lobby. He said he had one prime candidate couple, but it did not pan out as they were vising the lady's aunt at Our Island Home which he overheard the couple telling the innkeeper. He said he would report in by one p.m. by calling from Checkpoint CP, which I believe is the pay phone at Congdon's Pharmacy."

"OK. The next time he calls please tell our operative that I am doing some undercover work as well. I am going incognito to Foood's From Here and There to do a review on their extra-large pizza. I am taking the island's premier food expert, Mike DiFronzo, as the taste tester! Back in a while."

Kosmo arrived to find Mike sipping on a jumbo-sized rootbeer. Kosmo had made a quick call prior to arriving to Johnny Acton asking him if he could possibly make Mike feel welcome as he was still living down the embarrassment of spreading the word about Deputy Donato being killed in the line of duty. John had asked him if he was still getting ribbed about it. Kosmo then explained that the poor guy tries so hard, and, of course, his brother-in-arms, Deputy Donato, never lets up on him. They are like two kids squabbling all the time.

When he arrived at Foood's, Kosmo saw Mike looking like a kid in a candy store. He reached in his pocket to double-check that he had the lunch money.

He had taken the funds for lunch out of the petty cash which at this time was overflowing with money to be spent on whatever Kosmo decided on. There also a large amount in the station's checkbook for petty cash, as every month an allotment was sent to several departments in the form of a check. Kosmo thought he had enough funds for many years to come for personnel outings!

Mike exclaimed, "Boy, this is swell! You know, Chief, when I walked in, John, the owner, greeted me like a king! Then he offered me anything I wanted to drink- beer, soda, iced tea, or lemonade on the house! Boy, I wish my mom was here to see that!"

Kosmo was pleased that he asked Mike to join him for lunch. It made him feel good inside. Down the road he was going to have a chat with Beth to see if Mark and she could include him in some off-duty get-togethers.

John Acton made them a loaded half-pepperoni, and half-mushroom-and-sausage pizza. Mike told Kosmo how he loved root beer, and, when he was a kid, his mom used to make him root beer floats after he mowed the lawn. He said she still makes him one on Wednesday nights if he is not working at the station. Then he said how much he enjoyed pizza, but his mom does not as she says it gives her gas. So, any time he went for pizza he would always get her a chicken Caesar to enjoy. They finished their snack (as Mike referred to it).

In getting up, Kosmo said, "You know, Mike, the James Bond movie is playing at the Dreamland. I already have a couple of paid tickets. Maybe we could both go tomorrow and watch it."

"That would be great, really great!" Mike exclaimed, brushing the crumbs of pizza crust off his shirt. They headed out.

THE HAUNTED "SEAVIEW", A FORTY THOUSAND SQUARE FOOT MANSION IN RHODE ISLAND

From the 1850's to the early 20th century, wealthy families built elaborate mansions in Newport, Rhode Island to be used for entertaining during the summer season. In 1907, liquor millionaire, Edson Bradley, built a French-Gothic mansion, known as Aladdin's Palace because of its size, on the south side of Dupont Circle in Washington, D.C. It covered more than half a city block and included rooms with decor imported from France, a Gothic chapel with seating for 150, a large ballroom, an art gallery and a 500-seat theater.

Bradley decided to move his mansion to Newport, Rhode Island, in February, 1923. This move was so impressive it caught the attention of Ripley's Believe It or Not. At the age of 71, he began having his mansion dissembled and relocated to an already existing Elizabethan-revival mansion known as SeaView. SeaView was built in 1885 and previously owned by James Kernochan. The newer mansion was incorporated into the old building, and it took two years to finish the exterior. The interior was completed in 1928, and it consisted of 17 rooms on the first floor, 25 on the second and 12 on the third. The décor included turrets, Chippendale chairs, wrought iron torcheres, exotic hanging lamps, stained-glass windows and high arching doorways. SeaView Terrace cost $2,000,000 to complete.

Bradley's wife passed away in 1929. Her funeral was held in the mansion's chapel. Bradley himself spent five more summers at SeaView before his death in 1935. The couple's daughter, Julia Bradley Shipman, took over ownership with her husband, the Right Reverend Herbert Shipman (Protestant Episcopal bishop of New York and World War I army chaplain), until the late 1930's. They vacated the mansion after the great New England Hurricane of 1938, which caused severe damage to the roof and tower. During World War II, the U.S. Army used SeaView as officers' quarters. In 1949, it was sold for $8,000 after Shipman failed to pay taxes on it.

A year later, it became an exclusive all-girl summer boarding school, renamed Burnham-by-the-Sea. It was owned and operated by Mr. and Mrs. George Waldo Emerson. It remained a boarding school for many years, but the dilapidated condition of the mansion became a concern. Burnham-by-the-Sea gained notoriety after the Gothic horror soap opera Dark Shadows *chose the* mansion as the exterior set for the fictional Collinwood Mansion.

Martin and Millicent Carey purchased the former school and immediately began the restoration process. Being one of the largest of the Newport mansions, the cost of the upkeep was rather large. While 40,000 square feet of mansion tends to impress, the mansion has also become known for its resident ghosts, or at least one in particular. It is believed Mrs. Bradley loved her home so much she continues to live there…after her death! She has been seen playing her beloved Estey organ. Other witnesses have experienced hearing footsteps, banging, moving door handles, voices and dark shadows.

With much careful handling and by gently prying at the revealed slot on the artifact, Nick found the secret compartment inside the lower part of the shaft of the Scepter of Dagobert. He slowly unwound the folded parchment paper that was embedded in the compartment. JoAnn brought over a bright lamp and plugged it in. Nick placed the old paper flat and it read in Latin:

"Mille nummos a pectore containg magni sunt in Parisiensi sub Francorum Callistus deaurata sinistra equestrem sculptue Ioannae de Arc ima prima parte australi quintae catacomb"

Vae quem tenet Vivamus intelligendum est tenes et alia faciendi duplex, una subtiliter disquised super rasa animalis cutem tantum conspicitur quibusdam oleo adhibetur paucis minutis apparebit si enim animal pelle notas. Una est conplexio est oppidum seu Rungis, in outskirts Parisiensis, ut in "DÆmonibus 'Pub" et pone si talis homo adhuc existit, est masculus

Gloria nomine Danior et peto locum, ut emptio "nominis regem Aper Pheromone "et quod mutatum est necesse est non uti, si quis sic remaing" clue "numquam reperietur. Non musht esse Insecta a rara "Rex Aper" Et cum dicitur homo est uti a mollis panno, aut oleum cutis ad extergimus in cogitant tunica super corium et exspectare numerosis penduli tempus ante ultima verba ad clue veniam ad Superficiem. nullam aliam substituunt quae pro Insecta celare secretum in perpetuum."

Nick and JoAnn picked up the words for 'gold' and 'catacomb' along with the word for 'Paris', and they noted one or two other English-seeming words. That was about all their education allowed them to decipher.

Nick gave a low whistle. "Now this is the icing on the cake," he declared. "If we can get this carefully translated by a reliable source, we've got a huge lead on this mystery!" He quickly dialed Nancy and Wendy's phone number.

Marshmallow had hopped up by the phone, let out a loud 'meow', and a few moments later the phone rang, Nancy started laughing and said, as she frequently did, "Marshmallow, how do you know before the phone begins to ring that it actually is going to ring?" She picked it up.

Nick reported breathlessly, "We uncovered it, the clue!" he told Nancy. "I don't know exactly what it says, as it appears to be in Latin, but the words 'catacomb', 'gold', and 'Paris' we can understand! So now, unless I'm sadly mistaken, we know this must be the original Scepter of Dagobert!"

"Really?" Nancy exclaimed. "That's incredible! I mean, really incredible! What does it say exactly? Do you know if it's about gold coins? Listen, Nick, Wendy is in town, but as soon as she's back we will give you a call."

"OK," Nick said, "but now I will see if I can find a way to get it translated into English by a trusted source. We'll be here at the office."

Kosmo was now at home. He wanted time, time alone, quiet, no distractions. He had all the files laid out upon the kitchen table. His kitchen offered really great natural light, so it was a perfect place to study his notes on Bob Tonkin's murder and really think it through.

He made a fresh pot of coffee but only a couple of cups worth. Otherwise, he would be more wired than attentive. He poured himself a piping hot cup. He had his red marker, along with a black and a blue one, so he could mark different ideas as he made detailed notes.

As luck would have it, the phone rang. He went over to the wall phone and picked it up.

"Hey, Chief!" Ted Hudgins said loudly into the phone.

"'In the end, it's not the years in your life that count. It's the life in your years.'"

"OK, Ted, let's make this quick. I am in the middle of something and I need some peace and quiet."

"Oh, OK, roger that! Well, the reason for my call, and I will make this short, is there are weather reports coming in over the marine radio band that some storms are brewing from the northern Maritimes. that's the area way up in northeast Canada. There seems to be a major front possibly heading due south right towards old sweet home here, meaning Nantucket."

Drumming his fingers on the table, Kosmo replied,

"OK, so what does that have to do with me sitting at home right now?"

Ted continued, "Well, I called an old buddy I know who lives in Sydney, Nova Scotia. He says this thing might turn into one very powerful nor'easter', one of the strongest we might have ever encountered here on 'The Rock.' If it continues to gain gale-force winds, well we might be in for a big surprise if we are not prepared."

Kosmos' ears perked up. "OK, Ted, what is the latest time frame for this storm?"

"Well, my buddy says we might be seeing some action in forty-eight hours. We are usually at least seventy-two hours or eighty hours ahead of a storm with advance notice. So, what I have done is contacted Sheila Lucy at the Coast Guard, and she's in contact with the National Marine weather command in Maine. Also, she is putting out feelers to other Coast Guard stations up the northern coast, from Connecticut to Boston and including New Hampshire and Maine. She has been contacted by a commander from St. Johns, Newfoundland, and one from Dartmouth, Nova Scotia. From what she relayed to me is this is something not to take lightly."

Kosmo knew that if Sheila Lucey was talking to other Coast Guard commanders as well, there just possibly might be some serious issues heading towards Nantucket, Martha's Vineyard, and the Cape.

"'Never let the fear of striking out keep you from playing the game,'" quoted Ted.

Kosmo thanked Ted and told him that he would take a serious look at the situation.

Ted advised, "Well, you might want to take some course of action sooner than later. As you know, at the next election time people will remember when someone does not take the correct approach to an issue. Next thing you know, there is a disaster situation on the island, and secondly, you find out you lost your re-election. Just warning you, Chief. Let me know what you have in mind, OK?"

"Thanks, Ted, I'll get right on it."

Kosmo then replaced the receiver in its cradle. He picked up his coffee which was still almost too hot for him to drink, set it down and he dialed a number in Boston. "Can you put me in touch with Matthew Stuntsman?" He waited a short while.

The voice on the other end answered, "This is Matthew. How may I help you?"

"Hey, Matthew, it's Kosmo."

"Kosmo, you old dog! How are you? Still down on Nantucket chasing wild horses that roam the beaches? Or do I have my coastal islands mixed up?"

"Well, something like that," Kosmo laughed. "We actually have electricity in most of the homes, and some even have indoor plumbing," he said, pulling his friend's leg.

"So, what's the reason for the call?"

Kosmo explained, "I just got word, and I have to take it with a grain of salt as it came from my Harbor Master who at times gets a little overzealous, that there might possibly be a fast-moving storm coming down from the Maritimes in Canada?"

Matt chimed in, "Funny thing you should mention that. I was just in touch with a friend up there. He's in Halifax, Nova Scotia. And it's starting to form into a real beauty. They are calling it almost a Category 5 winter blizzard which is strange as it's still autumn. Temperatures may plunge by fifty degrees and there will be complete white-outs. The meteorologists also call them 'Arctic bombs.' The latest word is Coast Guard ships are all being called back into ports. Every state from Connecticut on up north is under a blizzard watch. It has more or less just developed over a period of twelve hours, and they say this one will possibly be one for the history books."

Kosmo interrupted. "So, as far as Maine, is there a weather advisory forecast forming for areas south of Maine?"

Matt informed him, "As of yet, everyone is still in the guessing game. But they are saying updates on the USCG channel will be every hour. This is like the hurricane watch time frame that they give you in Florida. You're still in the guessing game of where and when it might land, and they want you to take the precaution of not waiting until it's too late. Now for your area, you might want to get in touch with the local Coast Guard. They are usually spot on. They have their own telegraph system and the commanders all watch out for each other."

Kosmo concluded, "Thanks, Matthew, I am now going to take this seriously. How's the television station business treating you?"

"Pretty good. Even though I am the weather guy I have heard about the murder that took place on the island. Any arrests made yet?"

"Well, right now I am in the preliminary stages of targeting a culprit, but hopefully I will get it sorted out sooner than later. Oddly enough, given that it's a small island, I don't have a lot to go on as of yet. But the pieces will fall into place, hopefully sooner than later. Thanks again for your help, Matthew. I will be in touch."

Mathew asked, "Kosmo, give me a good contact number for you. If I get any updates that I think you might need I will give you a call. Good luck down there!"

GREYFRIAR'S KIRKYARD, EDINBURGH, SCOTLAND: THE MOST HAUNTED GRAVEYARD IN THE WORLD

Edinburgh has a whole lot of haunted history for tourists to explore: ghost walks, creepy castles and sites of witch burnings. But this city in Scotland also has what some consider to be the most haunted graveyard in the world — Greyfriars Kirkyard.

Most of the hauntings are linked to the ghost of George Mackenzie — a merciless judge who presided over the trials of the Presbyterian Covenanters in the 1670s. The Covenanters had petitioned the King to allow them freedom to practice their religion without interference. To crush this rebellion against the Crown, "Bloody Mackenzie" was brutal in meting out his punishments, and he imprisoned 1,200 Covenanters in a field next to Greyfriars Kirkyard.

Sighing, Kosmo looked over at the kitchen table. Minus the cup of coffee he was holding, it was going to remain like that, as least until he could figure out this Arctic blast situation.

He called Beth, who was on switchboard duty.

"Hey, Beth. It's me, I'm at home working."

"Hi, Chief, what's up? Are you getting the peace and quiet you needed to get your files on the Tonkin case in order?"

Kosmo replied enigmatically, "Well, in a way, yes, and in a way, no."

Beth questioned him, "What do you mean by that?

Oh, before I forget, Mark has started his 'personal thoughts' file on the murder as well. But what's the reason for the call?"

"Here's the deal. Ted Hudgins just called me and mentioned that there is a possibly very large Arctic bomb blizzard forming way up in the Canadian Maritimes.

I called my friend who does the weather reports on the Channel Five news station in Boston, and he confirmed it. This thing might extend all the way down to the Cape and the islands. Kind of freaky given the time of year, but I think we have to take it seriously."

Beth responded, "Really? I have not heard anything about it, and I was watching TV when I was home this morning."

"Well, to be better prepared, just in case this thing comes barreling our way, I want you to set up a meeting for today at five p.m. in the conference room. I want you to contact the following:

The Department of Public Works and the Mayor;

Dan Connor, the Fire Chief;

the Hospital nurses and doctors including Nurse Kate O'Riordin, Piper Raab Carol, and Lori Caputo;

both Sun Island and Harbor Fuel;

Sheila Lucy at the Coast Guard;

Ted Hudgins, Harbor Master;

the Nantucket Visitors Center;

the Nantucket Hotel Association President;

the Nantucket Chamber of Commerce;

Spyder Andresan at Steamship Authority;

and the Nantucket Airport Council.

Also, check the list over and see if I omitted anyone."

As she finished scribbling the list, Beth exclaimed, "Wow, is this possibly really something serious? Do you really think it is?"

"It very well could be. I will also have a meeting at ten a.m. tomorrow with everyone on our staff. Please let them know. Oh, Beth, and a few things: don't let Mark get all worked up about this. You know how he gets. And I know there is no way of avoiding this, but Ted Hudgins is going to go overboard with this whole situation. As he brought it to my attention, he will think he's in charge of the whole operation. I would not be surprised if he's not already in his Willys Jeep with his dog, Bella, racing out to the

VFW wearing that old World War I helmet with his 1940's siren blaring. And I would not put it past him to have started that land line call in place. I mean, once that starts, everyone on the list has to call the ten names which are on their list. And things just take off like wild fire." Kosmo was already dreading the upcoming scenarios.

"Oh, and Beth, you should also see if you can get Mike DiFronzo to come in and assist answering the phones. If they have not started ringing yet, they are going to at any moment. Ted has good intentions, but he can definitely get this island stirred up pretty quickly. So try to help him stay calm and just stick with what I want you two to say."

Beth said breathlessly, "Got it! I am on it! Oh boy, no sooner said than done! I already have two lines blinking and I have not had that happen in over a month."

Kosmo then dialed the Coast Guard office. Sheila Lucey's assistant answered, and Kosmo could hear numerous radio reports going off all at the same time.

Sheila was handed the phone. "Hey, Chief, I guess Ted contacted you about this storm that might be heading our way. What do you think?"

"Yes, Sheila, he did, and I have done some checking around. It seems that he is right on the mark. What's happening there?"

"Well, as of now I am patched in live to several Coast Guard divisions from Connecticut to Maine. I am also monitoring the Canadian Coast Guard channels. Everyone is relaying information, sharing the latest updates every thirty minutes. It seems to have hit the Maritimes very quickly and pretty forcefully. It's too soon to tell if it will stay at full strength or putter out and go out to sea."

She paused, then continued, "But this is a pretty big deal, and if it hits the island, well it could do some damage. As of now I am calling a marine forecast to all boaters that they need to head to a safe harbor sooner than later. If a trawler gets caught out in this storm things, well, let's just say they might not have a very good outcome."

"Well," Kosmo responded, "let's err on the precautionary side. Let's plan for the storm hitting at full force, and if it peters out or changes direction, at least we are covered. I have called for a five p.m. meeting with all the town and hospital department heads at the station today. If you think of any additional personnel who should be at the meeting, put them on the list that Beth has started. Thanks."

Sheila suggested, "One thought is we should get the information out to people living on the shorelines from Madaket to Eel Point to 'Sconset as they could take a direct hit if it comes barreling towards us."

Kosmo agreed. "Well, I am sure that Ted Hudgins has already started his land line call chain as the switchboard at the station is already lighting up with calls."

Ted Hudgins parked his Jeep directly in front of the entrance of the VFW Hall in Tom Nevers. His dog, Bella, was just pleased as punch to be going for a ride down Milestone Road. She just sat there happy as a dog could be.

Ted entered the VFW hall with his megaphone set on medium voice control and said, "May I have your attention, please?"

Al Lussier was sitting off to the side playing poker with a few of the guys, holding a winning hand of three aces. He looked up and said, "Oh boy, the reinforcements have arrived! I feel safe now!" All the guys at the table started laughing.

Ted repeated his request. "May I have your attention, please?"

Colin Keenan and Sean Divine were at the bar. They saw Ted and started laughing. "Did he say 'attention'?" Sean asked. They both stood up and held a salute like they were in the Army.

Despite the wisecracks, Ted went on. "This is an official announcement for the sake of public safety! It seems that an Arctic blast is forming in the Canadian Maritimes and it is headed directly towards Nantucket. The winds could possibly hit eighty plus miles per hours, and the temperature could drop fifty plus degrees in a very short amount of time. Rain could cause major flooding in low lying areas. Power is most likely to be out for anywhere from four to six days in some areas. It might be best for everyone here to notify a few people so we can get everyone who needs assistance covered. The grocery stores most likely will not be receiving any further food shipments, so if everyone is sensible and only purchases what they need, along with candles, matches, canned goods and water, just to name a few, we can all ride this out together. All of the towns' resource centers have been notified as well. The towns' departmental heads meeting will be held today at five p.m. at the police station. Thank you for your attention, and play it safe!" Ted put down his megaphone, looked around and headed back out to his Jeep where Bella was waiting, tail wagging.

Al Lussier just looked up, placed his cards down and said, "Three aces! Looks like I take this hand."

Sean and Colin started singing "God Bless America."

Back in town, at every bar and restaurant the phones were ringing like crazy. Managers were saying, "Big storm coming! Better bring in extra staff. This one is going to be a doozy." Nantucket partied heartily when a storm was about to role in.

Kosmo went out to his covered woodshed and brought in extra kindling and firewood, enough to last him if he was home, for at least a week. He never knew where he might be based or have to get to during a gale.

Then he went through the house and secured his storm windows, about which Rusty was correct: they definitely needed replacing. He secured the basement hatchway and then headed into town with a few extra articles of outer gear.

At the station he called Judy at Hatch's. He was going to tell her about the possible upcoming Arctic blast, but she said, "The store is like a mad house! Word Is spreading all over the island like this is going to be Armageddon. Paula just called me from Island Spirits and told me they are already running out of Grand Marnier, Schnapps, and Rumplemintz. Vodka is flying off the shelves, and people are buying the little nips by the bag full!"

"Well," Kosmo chuckled, "it doesn't take much to get this party started, does it? Well, let's keep the faith. I have a meeting here at the station at five p.m. with a lot of the town department personnel. You want to meet at Cioppino's for an early bite?"

Judy accepted. "That would be great. I mean this might be our last meal if Armageddon hits in a few days. We'll still close at the usual time, so see you at six!"

Kosmo was quite pleased with how well the departmental meeting went. Ted Hudgins was extremely reserved. Only at the end did he announce how he had personally called Kosmo at home to alert him of the upcoming situation. Kosmo nodded to Ted to acknowledge his helpfulness.

Judy was already seated when Kosmo arrived for dinner. She had taken the initiative to order two glasses of the house Chardonnay. They were both in no rush at all. Kosmo told Judy about how his original plans were to take a quiet afternoon at home and start really dissecting the Tonkin murder. But he had not even gotten into his first cup of coffee when Ted Hudgins had called him at home. And now was how the situation stood: his meeting was very productive. And tomorrow would be the station's employee's meeting which he suspected would more or less be the same as the town meeting today.

They split a lump crabmeat saute', and for their entrees Judy had a delicious fillet of halibut, while Kosmo had the fillet of sole française. They ordered a bottle of Patz & Hall Chardonnay and passed on dessert.

Kosmo heard a couple of familiar voices but could not see the restaurant's patrons. But, alas, there they were, in flesh and blood: Hunter Laroche, Krebs, Marty McGowen, and Eelskin Joe. Hunter spotted Kosmo and Judy rather quickly when they entered the restaurant, and the other three in his party went over to their corner table. Hunter greeted Judy and Kosmo. After Kosmo embraced Hunter, they made small talk. Kosmo looked over to see Eelskin with his usual briefcase being placed under the table.

Kosmo, who declined the offer for another bottle of wine with Hunter's compliments said, "You guys enjoy your evening, and if you are driving don't go getting all chinkered up! If you do, take a taxi. If you are driving, keep your eyes out for deer, as they are easily spooked with it being hunting season."

Hunter asked Kosmo quietly towards his ear, "Any updates on the Tonkin murder?"

Kosmo shook his head. "Nothing as of yet, but if you or any of the boys catch wind of anything, just give us an anonymous call at the station. I'd appreciate it."

"Got it," Hunter said with a nod and walked to his table.

Judy angled her head to Hunter's table then asked, "So how much cash do you think is in that briefcase?"

THE HAUNTED HISTORY OF DEADMAN'S ISLAND, VANCOUVER, BRITISH COLUMBIA

Think of the well-known Stanley Park on Vancouver Island and you probably picture sunny walks on the seawall and quiet afternoons exploring the Vancouver Aquarium. But did you know the park is actually home to one of the most haunted islands in North America?

Though closed to the public, Deadman's Island is home to ghostly lore centuries old. The list of spectral sightings and strange phenomena continues to grow such as loud clanging noises ringing out in the dead of night. Hurried footsteps pace back and forth. The unearthly moan of a young woman's sobs fills the still air. Tales of supernatural encounters stretch back more than a century...

One morning Wendy mentioned to Nancy, "You know, we still have not ventured into the attic closet. Now that it is unlocked, or shall I say, busted open, we should mosey up there and clean it out."

Nancy shrugged. "OK, well no time like the present. We can spend an hour up there, and then get back to the barn for a good four or five hours. We have so many window box orders, and I can't even believe we have now sold, or are in process of organizing, about eight orders for our reserve collection. I have to tell you, the people out here on the island are not shy with their spending!"

Wendy nodded enthusiastically. "All the better for our business! Though I'm glad it's 'off season' and we can get ahead on our box construction. Let's climb up to the attic."

The gals went to the attic. There were some old clothes hanging in the closet that had seen better days. Nancy found three dollars total in some of the pockets. They made three piles: one of junk which was going right to the dump on Rusty's next run; the second was miscellaneous dishes and things that they would bring to the kitchen to clean them up. Then they could see if there was any need at all for them between the main house and Rusty's new apartment. The last was a small pile of books. In it they came across what looked like a note book or daily planner. It was small, about ten inches by twelve inches in size. It was quite dusty with a ragged and well-worn cover. Nancy opened it up and was ready to toss it aside when she noticed the writing was not in English but what she was sure, thanks to her classes in high school, was in French script.

"Hey, Wendy, come look at this!" she called.

"I think this might have something to do with Gerard Dubois, the guy that built this house!"

Wendy said, "Bring it over to the window so we can get a better look at it."

Nancy handled it gently. Inside the cover in faded script were the initials, 'G.D.'

Wendy agreed. "I think you're right! I mean, who else that lived here would have written in French? I'll bet the answer is 'no one'!"

Nancy said, "I took some French classes in high school, but this is hard to understand as it's in cursive and pretty well faded. I am sure we could find someone to help us translate it, even if he or she did a small amount at a time rereading it to us. Now, the question is, who do we know that reads French fluently?"

Wendy said, "I don't have a clue, but let's do this: I will call George Williams from the men's group and have his group put feelers out. They love to be on a mission!

Plus, we could inquire at the high school or the Atheneum as well. I am on it! As soon as we finish up this closet, I will make the calls." She set the notebook at the top of the stairs. Marshmallow sniffed it, meowed loudly and then sat right on top of the old book!

Nancy considered their tasks at hand. "Well, the closet is just about done. Let me finish clearing out the stuff. I will haul the vacuum cleaner up here, give it a double cleaning, and let's hope I don't get a spider bite in the process!"

While Nancy continued the attic work, Wendy called George Williams. His wife, Mary, said he was out doing errands but she would relay the message. Then, looking in the phone book, Wendy left a message with the secretary at the high school. She then called the Athenueum. The librarian with whom Wendy spoke said she was quite well versed in French as it was one of her college two-year courses. She said even though it has been a good number of years and she might be a little out of practice, if they wanted to bring it down to the library, she would give it a gander.

The librarian went on to explain that she only worked two days a week as she was an avid gardener and she had a very nice garden at her home in Pocomo. That started off one great conversation. Wendy explained that she and Nancy had started 'Dow & Eblen', a small-scale landscape and window box business, and that they lived in Quaise. The next thing Wendy knew a wine and cheese get together was set for five p.m. at their home.

Sally Torpe arrived promptly at five. Wendy had dusted off the old worn diary as best as she could using a dry cloth so as not to damage the frail notebook.

The librarian was thrilled just to hold the diary and said, "Oh, I do hope I can be of some help with translating this! It's like a mystery!"

Wendy explained to her they found it in an old attic closet, and they believed the man who built and lived in the house could possibly be the author.

Sally slowly and cautiously opened the frail book. She read to them about twenty pages or so, emphasizing the fact that it actually seemed to be a diary which was written around 1875. It strongly pointed to the time the man spent in prison in France. There were some later entrees but they were vague. His writing rambled on about getting back to Paris and picking up his treasure! Then it described him scurrying off to London on a ferry, and then making his way to America.

The diary went on to say he had his treasure well hidden, and his plans were set forth to soon sell the 'exquisite item' to a very well-to-do private party in Newport, Rhode Island. Towards the end of the diary the man had entered a few short notes. His last one was that he was headed on the trip to Newport in a fortnight. And that was his last entry.

"Well, that's quite an intriguing story," Nancy said in amazement. "It's odd that we found this documentation of his time here but have not heard much from anyone on the island about this story. I wonder what happened to the old fellow? Thank you, Sally, for taking the time to review and translate this for us."

Following the very entrancing narration, the ladies enjoyed some wine. They then put on their coats and gave her a brief tour of the property as it was getting dark. Nancy explained how they had transformed it from basically an abandoned old place to how it stands now. She admitted they had a lot of help from friends. And, she added, they had numerous tasks to fix things up that would take them a good long time to accomplish.

Sally was quite interested in the window boxes. She said if they ever needed another set of hands, she had lots of free time and was actually only a short drive away. Having seen their 'Dow & Eblen Landscaping' sign, she suggested that they might want to contact Carol McGarvey who had a very successful landscaping business. Sally continued, "She's married to Mark McGarvey, one of the men who helped you in the projects here, I believe."

Sally went on to say, "I'm a friend of Carol's. She told me recently that she can't take on any more new jobs right now and asked me if I knew anyone who might be interested in picking up a client or two. She would probably also get you some additional orders for window boxes. She is feeling a bit overwhelmed with requests for landscaping work. I'm sure she has seen your copper-lined boxes all over town. And, she's a good friend of Rita at the market. Just a thought."

After Sally departed, Wendy called Rita and asked her about Carol McGarvey. Rita had nothing but rave reviews about Carol, and commented that she was an angel of a person and had one of the best landscaping businesses on the island. Rita, too, emphasized that Carol had more work than she could handle, and shared that between Carol's business and Mark's successful work, that couple could hardly keep their eyes open after dinner.

Rita suggested, "Why don't I get in touch with Carol. We could all go out to lunch sometime soon. Of course, it'll be my treat. I'm glad you called! I'll get back to you or perhaps Carol will contact you directly. Bye-bye!"

Having dealt with the work-related tip, Wendy dialed Nick and JoAnn in Boston. She relayed the finding of the diary and encapsulated his last entry. From that they were thinking that before old Gerard Dubois ever went to Newport to sell the treasure to a wealthy client, he met his demise.

Nick told them he also had some thoughts on the Latin inscription on the paper in the scepter. Perhaps it was a little more involved he originally thought. He couldn't help but think that it would be a challenging mystery to unravel. He also told them there was an extra small piece of blank animal hide or oilskin cloth folded up in the shaft. That item did not make any sense to them.

He was going to reach out to Professor Achilles and see if he might be able to meet his knowledgeable friend in London. If they could come up with any possible answers to the riddle of the coins, then possibly the two of them could head to Paris. But that was going to be a stretch both academically and physically. He was not sure if Rolf knew much Latin, but if not, he was sure that Rolf would most likely know of a way to decipher it. And he would make Rolf part of the privacy element they all had agreed upon.

Nick was trying to figure things out as much in advance as possible. If things progressed, a few issues would arise, one being that they would have to figure out a way to pay for Rolf's expedition with Nick to Paris. That would include a daily wage, lodging, all transportation costs and whatever else was incurred on the adventure.

Nick added that he was flush with cash, so if they all agreed, he would front expenses and get reimbursed later on from the monies received from the scepter's income from the museums. Also, if he succeeded in obtaining anything of value, thinking of the gold coins, then, after he sold them, the price would include a commission for Nick and also a flat fee to the professor.

Wendy took a moment to relay the financial arrangement to Nancy. "We agree one hundred percent. Before anything is decided would you draw up an agreement as to how you would receive as your percentage and how much to pay the professor if he agrees to join you on this quest?

Additionally, if something of value is found how much will be a bonus to the professor?"

Nick agreed and said he would not make any decisions until the four of them met in person. As for most of the conversation with the professor, he would keep it vague until they knew more. But he would also explain to him that he would get a daily rate, plus all expenses, along with a flat rate if they discovered something of value due to the professor's assistance.

After he hung up, Nick jotted down his thoughts. He called Professor Achilles and provided a more in-depth outline to him about this possible investigation. Nick would get a travel date to him soon so the professor could make time for Nick's visit and a possible follow up trip to Paris. He explained that he would provide a payment to Rolf of seventy-five dollars per day from the day they began the trip over to France until he was back on English soil. Nick also said that Rolf would also receive, in cash, two percent of the total value of the goods sold if they were to discover anything of value.

Lastly, Nick said he would have a very simple contract for him to sign, releasing him from any claims of rights to ownership of anything discovered with any value. He would just receive the two percent commission on top of his daily pay rate. All costs from food to beverages to travel and lodging would be covered by Nick until the end of the trip.

Rolf replied, "Well, as long as it's not going to be anything illegal then I'm up for the challenge! I'll wait for your next call. Thank you, Nick, for including me in your venture. I love a search related to an antique artifact!"

Two days before the predicted storm, Kosmo called Neil at the Languedoc Restaurant, and asked if he could have a table upstairs, out of the way, to review some things quietly with no outside distractions. He told Neil he tried to do that at home, but his phone kept ringing.

Neil responded, "Sure, Chief, the upstairs was vacuumed earlier on, all the tables are set with fresh linen, and seeing how we are closed this evening it should be just you and me in the building. Why don't you come up around eleven, work for as long as it takes, then the two of us have some lunch? I just got in some really nice gray sole, and some Brussells sprouts. We have not been able to get together since the spring!"

Kosmo said in an enthusiastic tone, "Deal!"

He arrived at the restaurant with his briefcase. He sat upstairs with a pot of coffee and pulled out his short list of notes. At this time, he had zero suspects, but he was going to define his search. He wrote down anyone he could think of who may have had recent interactions with Mr. Tonkin. He had asked Rita, and she had given him a short list of people with whom Bob had dealings to her knowledge. He unfolded it and jotted the names down. Then he began his own personal list of options:

1. Could Bob have been the target of another antique business owner on the island? As it seemed to him that this was not about money, but about a certain object he possibly had in his possession either at the store or his home. This he surmised due to the fact that at the store none of the jewelry in the display cases had been taken, and Bob's wallet was still on his person at the time of his death. Next he added,
2. Was he in debt?
3. Did he have any bad vices?
4. Was there a jilted lover?

He kept at it for a while, but nothing really came into his mind. He knew it would, sooner or later, but at this time he was at a loss for the most probable cause of the murder.

Neil came up and said, "How's it going, Kosmo? Lunch will be ready in a few minutes. Do you want any more coffee or anything else to drink?"

Kosmo flipped his notepad closed, looked up and said, "Thanks so much, Neil. I'm finished with the coffee, and some water will be fine."

During lunch Kosmo declared, "The sole is over the top!"

As Neil and Kosmo were good friends, Neil wondered out loud, "Why does it take us so long to get together?"

Kosmo nodded, "Yeah, I guess we're both busy guys."

At the end of their lunch while Kosmo was packing up his notes into his briefcase, Neil mentioned to Kosmo, "What sad news it was to hear about Bob Tonkin, a man with such great knowledge of the island, the local people and antiques. Now with his passing," Neil continued, "I wonder what will become of his shop and all the antiques there and in his warehouse."

Kosmo looked over at Neil and asked with raised eyebrows, "Warehouse? What warehouse? I didn't know he had other commercial property."

Neil filled him in. "It's out by the airport. Bob purchased a building several years ago as his shop was becoming crowded with his antique collection. I've been out there. In the warehouse he had a large wall full of beautiful oil paintings that he could not display in his store on Main Street. You know he had a keen eye for fine art."

Kosmo thanked Neil and said, "Sooner than later-you, Eddie, and Al, over on my back deck for some drinks!"

GHOSTS OF HAUNTED CORREGIDOR ISLAND, THE PHILIPPINES

The Old Corregidor Island Hospital is thought to harbor an incredible number of ghosts. The military hospital dates back to 1912 and played a pivotal role during times of war, treating injured soldiers. Many people still today have claimed to hear the cries, screams and footsteps of soldiers being treated at the hospital. Some have even claimed to hear noises that make it sound as though the hospital is still in operation. Yet now it only remains as a crumbling skeleton of a building. Many visual experiences have also been reported here with shadowy figures, apparitions and light anomalies all being common.

Two days later, Wendy and Nancy met up with Rita and Carol at the Languedoc. They enjoyed a tasty lunch ordered by Rita. Carol said to Nancy and Wendy, "Your window box projects are divine! I think it was clever of you to create different versions of them, and they seem to be have popped up all over the island this past summer. I'm sure, starting next spring, I could get you additional orders from my regular customers."

Nancy replied, "Thanks, so much, Carol. Coming from you that's a real compliment. We'd be glad to piggy-back some of our work onto yours if that helps. And, we'd definitely give you a commission for any orders you generate for us."

Carol reached across and patted Nancy's hand. "That's very sweet of you but it won't be necessary. Your work is going to be helpful to me, trust me. However, my husband, Mark, has raved about your cookouts. How about we try to get together for dinner once a month?"

"It's a deal!" Wendy chimed in.

The women finished their meal, and their waiter stopped by to give them a word of advice. "News has it that we're due for an unusual weather event. You ladies might want to go home and put away any stray yard items that you haven't yet stored for the winter. One never can tell when a storm is headed our way whether we're going to end up in its path or not. Take care!"

The storm hit with a vengeance. It came as predicted, fast and powerful. All department heads were on full alert. It started off with the temperature dropping at first at around ten degrees a day. Some winds kicked up but nothing much. People were crowding in the bars, thinking – "Well, it's another day off, let's party!"

The next night the temperature dropped rapidly at four a.m. another ten degrees. No one paid it much attention. Everyone felt that a little cooler fall weather was just the norm. Outside a few of the bars were chalkboard signs reading: Come and enjoy a "Blaster Burger", and try our drink of the day, "Arctic Freeze". Another sign read: Drink special: "The Deep Freeze" and "Arctic Apple Pie with Melted Cheddar." A third sign read: Take the chill off with a "Maritime Grand Marnier and Kahlua Coffee."

The grocery stores were almost wiped clean. Not a frozen pizza was to be found anywhere on the island. Beer was almost non-existent, liquor was running in very short supply along with cigarettes, batteries, flashlights, and gallon jugs of water.

The men at the VFW had formed their own rescue squad and were determined to assist as needed by any town departments. But when it really came down to it, most of them did not want to be trapped in their home for an extended amount of time with their wives.

So they made the VFW hall 'home base', telling their wives that they were making supply lists and were 'on call' for the island of Nantucket.

Furthermore, another good reason was that Marie Lafrontiere was on the next two shifts bartending, and with a fully stocked bar at discount prices and not the madness of the bars in town, they had plenty of seats at the counter. It felt like home away from home-several TV's and the food was actually pretty good there.

The third evening of the storm the temperature dropped in the blink of an eye thirty more degrees. The winds were not kind-they were killer winter artic blasts! The seas were churning and breaking over the sea walls in town. Brant Point was flooding almost as fast as a quick flash flood. The Rose & Crown was taking on water like a sinking ship.

The guys at the VFW, situated inside of the solid cement building were holding down the fort. At one point it was suggested by a patron of the bar that maybe a small group of them should pile in a car and make the rounds of 'Sconset. The idea was quickly abandoned as it had been mentioned.

Down near the docks Ted Hudgins was wearing his waders, a long raincoat, his World War I helmet, and goggles his neck. His dog, Bella, was curled up under his office desk with not a care in the world. Ted was ready for any emergency call.

Mike DiFronzo was home with his mother who was baking some chocolate chip cookies. Mike was just as glad not to have to be at work as he didn't really want to mess up any more emergency calls.

Sheila Lucey was monitoring Coast Guard stations up and down the coast relaying the Nantucket weather report every thirty minutes out to them.

Deputy Donato and Beth were both manning the dispatch desk and the incoming calls, trying to calm everyone as best they could.

Dolores Frechette, who took Mike DiFronzo's word of caution as he had told her it might be best if she moved into town for a couple of nights from her home in Madaket, called back in wondering if someone could go out and check on her house to make sure it was still standing. She wanted to relay her heartfelt thanks to Mike for his suggestion. She said her dog, Teddy, was just going to have to "hold it" as she was *not* going out to walk him in that mess of a storm for any reason.

Jimmy Jaksic and Rick Blair were in a patrol car sitting at the Milestone rotary awaiting any distress call that might come over the radio.

Kosmo was with Dan Connor at the fire station, all suited up if it might be necessary to go out in the elements.

Several trees early on knocked out the power to Surfside, Madaket and Polpis. 'Sconset was still holding on with power as were a few other areas. Boats were being tossed around the harbor like toys, and a few electrical transformers blew out. The storm was predicted to last about four hours, but then the news hit the Coast Guard airways. It was coming to a stall, and was not going to pass through as fast as predicted.

Straight Wharf was now so deep with water you could paddle a canoe from Easy Street all around the area.

The 'boys' at the VFW hall were not moving except to tip their elbows to drain their drinks. Marie Lafrontiere was keeping everyone amused and entertained.

Chris Morris called into the police station and said his wife was going into labor. Rick Blair and Jimmy Jaksic delivered the couple to the hospital just in the nick of time.

In the corner of the Languedoc, Hunter, Eelskin, Krebs, and Marty McGowen were counting out a rather large duffel bag full of cash. They weren't in any rush to go anywhere.

In two days' time, the storm passed and everyone awoke to a beautiful morning. The drunk-fest was over, and things slowly returned to normal.

The Morris couple had a very healthy baby girl and named her Theadora-Melanie.

The men from the VFW had perfected their stories on how they did their true duty to the citizens of Nantucket. They made Marie Lafrontiere swear that she would not repeat a word about their drinking at the VFW.

DEADMAN'S ISLAND, VANCOUVER, CANADA

While some people report that they hear sounds which resemble moving footsteps and shifting furniture on a supposedly abandoned island, others claim to see a strange glow from the trees which eventually takes the form of a human.

When things returned to normal, or so to speak, normal, after the storm, Kosmo returned to his task that still lay upon his kitchen table. He made fresh notes. He had made his rounds about the town trying to see if there was anyone who had a grudge against Bob Tonkin. Every time it came out the same- he was such a lovely man. He read over his pages of notes, and still could not find a motive. He knew it was robbery or an attempted robbery. But he had also narrowed his thoughts to the drawings on the pad of paper-the staff or the pole or the scepter-whatever Bob had written on his note pad with the sketches. Lastly, who was this guy Nick, the name that was also written on the page. He left home not anywhere closer to an answer to this mysterious murder than when he started.

He was on his way back to the station when he figured, "It can't hurt." He pulled up in front of Tonkin's Antiques Store. The yellow tape had been removed from the front door but there was a clear piece of plastic tape over the lock with a note saying "Not to be entered per the order of the Nantucket Police Department."

Kosmo went around to the back door where the yellow crime scene tape was still in place. But he looked and noticed that someone had taken a very small hacksaw and cut through the door's dead bolt that was between the two French doors.

"Walking past you would have never noticed this," he realized. Kosmo quietly walked away and radioed the station requesting for three people to quietly meet him in the back of Tonkin's.

Deputy Donato was at the dispatch desk when the request came in. He ran to his office closet and suited up with his bullet proof vest.

Mike DiFronzo was almost directly next door enjoying the last of his egg salad sandwich and vanilla coke when he heard it on his radio. Even though he was more or less just the dispatch officer, he was still a police officer in a lower official capacity. Mike told the lunch counter girl he would be right back and headed to the requested destination.

Jimmy Jaksic was coming into town in his car almost right at the intersection of Union Street and Main when he heard the message. He went up past Tonkin's and took a right onto Center Street, and everyone almost converged at the same time. Kosmo, who had his eyes on the back doors of Tonkin's the entire time, explained the situation.

Deputy Donato asked, "Don't you think that the lock must have been cut during the night at one point, not in broad daylight?"

Kosmo nodded. "Yes, I agree with you, but I am not taking any chances, and stranger things have happened. Can you imagine if we did nothing, only find out it only took us thirty minutes to secure this place and possibly find the intruder?"

He continued with these directions. "OK, here's how this will play out. Mike, you're in charge of guarding the front door. No one exits-got it? So, you go quietly now through the back door to the front door, blocking it from the inside."

Mike confirmed his understanding. "Like a linebacker, Chief!"

Kosmo went on. "Jimmy, Mark and I are going in through the back door and I want you to quietly close it and remain standing inside the door. If anyone comes running towards the exit, well, notify us with a large holler!"

"Got it." Jimmy headed down the back way with them.

Rick Blair showed up as they were getting ready to enter. He had his dog, Madaket, with him. Kosmo asked Rick, "If there was someone inside, would Madaket alert you to the person?"

Rick nodded enthusiastically. "Oh, yes, he would! You can hear him! He gets all excited when he meets a new friend."

Kosmo inquired, "How would you feel about releasing him off his leash inside the store?"

Rick agreed. "Fine, Madaket would love it!"

Two minutes after everyone was in place, Madaket took off inside the store with a gallop. Rick Blair followed Madaket as best as he could, but the dog was already on the hunt, all through the first floor and right up the stairs to the second floor. A few minutes later he was back re-scouting the first floor. He came upon a closed door and started whimpering. Rick opened it, and Madaket was charging down to the basement even before Rick could hit the light switch. Yet, after a few minutes with Kosmo, Mark and Rick as well as Madaket in the shop, no one was discovered on the premises.

Kosmo then asked Mark to get with Mike and take the squad car. "I want you to hit Valero's and Hardy's or anyplace you can think of that might sell a thin-bladed hacksaw. I am pretty sure that's what the intruder used to gain entrance to the store."

Mark was just about to ask why he had to drag Mike DiFronzo along with him, but Kosmo, out of Mike's sight, gave Mark a very deep intense stare, almost speaking with his eyes. "I don't want any guff out of you on this one."

Mark just shrugged his shoulders and said, "OK, DiFronzo, let's move it. We have work to do!" As they headed back down Main Street Mark started telling Mike, "Now look, we are all business here. You heard the chief- so no potato chips, snacks, sodas, chocolate milk, candy bars in the squad car! You got that?"

"Understood," Mike mumbled as Mike started pulling a half-eaten Snickers bar out of his top pocket.

Mark, seeing that move, said, "What did I just tell you?"

Mike shrugged. "I heard you, but you said no food in the squad car. We are not in the squad car, and I just figured I might as well finish this up on the way to the station. It's real tasty! You want a piece? I had a Kit-Kat earlier, but I finished that up before breakfast."

Mark just glared at him and said "Don't you dare throw any wrappers on the floor of the squad car. You got that?"

"Boy, you sound like my mom," Mike grumbled.

They did not have any luck with locating any shop that remembered selling a hacksaw. Back in the car Mike told Mark, "Well, this was quite the day! Some real action! You know I don't really get to be a part of anything that transpires outside of the station."

Mark said condescendingly, "Well, Mikey-O, you need years of training to become a real lawman like me."

"Well, it's all fine with me," Mike countered. "I am happy working at the station as I get to read my magazines. I went through the code book last week with Beth. She is a very good teacher. I mean, the way she puts the code system into perspective. And, besides, my mom, she really would be worried if I was out in the field. She's kind of weak-hearted and might not do too well if anything happened to me."

HART ISLAND, NEW YORK – ISLAND OF THE DEAD

Hart Island, sometimes referred to as Hart's Island, is an island in New York City at the western end of Long Island Sound. It is approximately a mile long and one quarter of a mile wide and is located to the northeast of City Island in the Pelham Islands group. The island is the easternmost part of the borough of the Bronx.

The island was used as a Union Civil War prison camp, a psychiatric institution, a tuberculosis sanatorium, a potter's field (i.e., a burial ground for poor people), and a boys' reformatory. The concept of having a mass burial ground which is completely cut off from the public obviously gives rise to lots of horror stories, involving torture and harsh handling and misusing of the corpses.

Over 850,000 bodies have been buried there, and during Hurricane Sandy, erosion from the storm uncovered many skeletal remains. New York City has worked to vastly improve the use of the land as a "city cemetery."

Nick Caselli managed to get a good crisp clear line to Oxford, England, and he had a very nice conversation with Professor Achilles. Nick proceeded to tell him that he wanted to include Rolf in a very private matter, one that included a very rare find. He declared he would stake his reputation that this find would go down in historical archives equivalent to finding King Tut's Tomb.

He would gladly include Rolf given his academic credentials. It had already been discussed with his partners with how he would be compensated in cash if he agreed to their terms. Nick told him that it was a very favorable deal he placed forth on Rolf's behalf.

Rolf asked a few questions and Nick answered them truthfully.

Rolf could not help but say, "Of course, I am extremely curious. So, without knowing all the details, I agree to the payment plan and the confidentially agreement. Once again, I will participate as long as there is nothing illegal about these dealings. I guess the expression, 'in for a penny, in for a pound' might be apropos at this point. So, what is the story, Nick?"

Taking a deep breath, Nick told him about the 'Scepter of Dagobert' which absolutely surprised Rolf to no end. Then Nick added the part about the note revealing some hidden gold coins somewhere in the catacombs of Paris. He explained that the note was written in what seemed to be old Latin script, and that he was now a bit up in the air as to where to go with it.

He explained to Rolf, "The note is quite faded and there are two types of animal-hide or parchment - one has the clues written on it, and one is blank." He paused to let the details sink in.

"So," Nick continued, "the question is: Would you possibly like to take this adventure on? And do you know anyone who can translate old Latin into English?" Nick waited in anticipation for his reply.

"Yes, and yes," were his answers. "Amazingly enough, I am up for the quest, and, yes, I do know a few people who could readily decipher the writing on the animal hide. With all the universities in the area we can find a Latin scholar."

"Professor Achilles, I look forward to having you join our research party. I will be in touch soon about travel dates. Thank you so much, you can't know how much this means to me professionally." Nick hung up and wondered where things would lead from that point on.

HOUSKA CASTLE, PRAGUE, CZECH REPUBLIC GATEWAY TO HELL.....

When mysterious haunted places in Europe are the topic, Houska Castle is another castle that gets a lot of mention. Located in the forests north of Prague, the Houska Castle is one of the most haunted places in the world. According to the legend, in one exact spot, there was a huge hole in the ground that was considered to be the 'Gateway to Hell.' Paranormal activities were disturbing the region, and the Bohemians thought they would solve the problems if they cover the hole. That's why they built the Houska Castle.

Hundreds of prisoners were forced to go into the pit to build the foundation for the castle. However, when they were taken out of the hole, they all looked like old men. Later on, the castle was the center of Nazi occult dabbling during WWII, and multiple dead bodies of Nazi soldiers were found on the site. Witnesses reported several different forms of paranormal activities, and some even claim that the site contains remains of demonic beasts who escaped the pit.

The day after the officers had cased-out Tonkin's Antiques, Kosmo drove to the office and called Deputy Donato on the radio. "Base to Deputy Donato. Over."

"Donato here. What's up, Chief?"

"I want you to meet me at the entrance to Teasdale Circle, the entrance closest to Milestone Road, over."

"Roger that, Chief. What's up? Murder? Robbery?

Should I suit up? My bullet proof vest is in the trunk. I can have it on in a jiffy, over."

Kosmo reassured him. "No, nothing like that, and don't use the sirens. I just want to check something out, over."

"OK, Chief I am on my way! ETA is about ten minutes. Over and out."

Mark was not taking any chances. He opened up the trunk of the squad car and put on his bulletproof vest.

He met Kosmo on the corner of Nobadeer Farm Road and Teasdale Circle. Then he quickly put on the patrol car's emergency lights.

Kosmo said, "Mark, shut those off. I just want to check out a building here, so don't go and draw any attention to us. Just nice and slowly follow me."

They arrived at an empty parking lot. Kosmo noticed since the rain had stopped the day before an automobile had then driven onto the dirt lot. He saw slightly wet tire marks from the mud puddle one had to drive through to get to the front of the building. He observed that it looked as if it had parked and then driven off, as the muddy tire tracks showed them entering onto Teasdale Circle. It must have been within the last twenty-four hours he figured.

Mark got out of the patrol car, and Kosmo saw the bulletproof vest but did not say anything about it. He knew of his deputy's propensity to overwork a situation.

As they approached the building, they saw some building numbers on the upper part of the warehouse. Other than that, it was non-descript.

Mark asked, "What is this place?"

Kosmo told him, "I just found out about it, and it apparently is an overflow storage of Tonkin's Antiques."

They did not have a key to the locked front door, so they walked around the backside of the building, where another double-wide sliding door was hung, but locked.

Kosmo and Mark walked the entire building's exterior, which had six windows. Kosmo wondered to himself, "Now, with the doors locked, would his hunch be correct?" He figured they would find that one of the windows had been forcibly opened from the outside.

Sure enough, one of the windows on the backside of the building had been, what looked like to Kosmo, forced open, most likely with a screwdriver.

He helped Deputy Donato gain entry to the warehouse. Mark commented, "Why would someone want to leave a window open? Someone could just break in!"

Kosmo did not say anything but had Mark go to the front door and unlock it. He entered and slowly and methodically scanned the interior of the warehouse.

Nothing seemed to be out of place, but then again it was a large place, and it would take a person a good amount of time to go through everything inside the building.

They looked around, taking their time. Mark thought to himself, "What was I thinking? The window is open, most likely, due to the person who broke into Tonkin's on Main Street. Mark then went to the window and started examining it more closely. He noticed some markings on the wood exterior frame, looking like it had been jimmied open.

He caught up with Kosmo and said, "It seems to me, Chief, that the window has been jimmied open, maybe with a screwdriver from the outside. I went and examined just a minute ago. My guess is that the same person who broke into Tonkin's is the same person who jimmied the back window of this warehouse, yes sirree, the one and the same."

Kosmo agreed. "I believe you might be correct. We know that someone first off kills Mr. Tonkin, and yet nothing seems to have been stolen from his store. Or as we at least know so far. Then the shop is yet again broken into with someone sawing through the French doors' deadbolt. But here a hack saw would not do the trick, so he uses something like a screwdriver to pry the window lock free. You sure have got a handle on this, Deputy, a very keen eye! Keep it up!" Kosmo knew he was subtly training Mark while making Mark feel good about taking a chance on his thinking.

They took one more walk through the warehouse, but not knowing what they were looking for, the effort felt fruitless. Nothing seemed out of place. Kosmo knew that Bob Tonkin was a man who was neat and orderly. He did notice, however, that some papers looked like they had been shuffled around on top of a desk there. When he opened the drawers, they seemed in disarray. Not knowing what they looked like at any time prior to their search, he again was at a loss. He was still keeping the information he read on the pad of paper he removed from the bottom of Bob's drawer in his home study private as of now. They left the warehouse as they found it, though they locked the window as a possible deterrent to the intruder should he return again.

In the parking lot he thanked Mark for coming along. He said, "Most often, two sets of eyes are better than one when it's not obvious what might be going on. See you back at the station."

Mark replied, "Right-o, Chief. Glad I could be of assistance. Any time!" Feeling quite self-confident, Mark spun out of the parking lot back onto Teasdale Circle.

On his way back to town Kosmo made a stop at the Ships Inn. He spoke with Bob Moulder, again asking if Bob ever mentioned anything that was out of the ordinary with his business or his life. It was a stab in the dark, but at this point and time he did not have much else to go on.

Bob just told Kosmo almost the same thing he had a while back. The only new thing he mentioned was Bob told him he had a customer from South America in his shop and that was a first for him, as he had people from Italy, France, and Germany often. Bob had also revealed he was awaiting some information from which he might be getting a steady monthly income. It was something he was slightly involved with at the time but it was too soon to tell. And then Bob was murdered.

Bob Moulder shrugged his shoulders and looked sad to think of his steady customer's passing. "And that's about all I can tell you." Kosmo thanked him for the update and departed.

Wendy and Nancy spent two days cleaning up all of the broken branches that had fallen during the storm. The house never leaked a drop, and the barns and sheds were still standing.

Wendy said with determination, "OK, tomorrow evening we are going to start our detective work. We will pick a street and enter every guest house we can find and see what we might be able to uncover. Maybe, with any luck, we will find our stalker. I am thinking around nine p.m. we have Rusty stay in the house, and we will make our first venture into our 'Nancy Drew' detective sleuthing!"

Marshmallow hopped up on the kitchen counter and let out a "meow". A few seconds later the phone rang. Nancy put her hands on her hips and looked at the cat. "How *do* you know the phone is going to ring?"

Nick was on the line. He explained that he had solidified the arrangements with Professor Achilles and he would review them right then. If the gals were good with the deal, they would get the wheels in motion.

He said he offered the professor the following:

Seventy-five dollars per diem if they were traveling, and all expenses including meals, hotels, and transportation. He said the Professor agreed to sign a contract stating that, no matter what they might discover, he had no legal claim to its value. He would be compensated two percent of the total sale value of such item(s) if anything was uncovered at all. As for Nick, he told Nancy that he would pay for all the expenses while traveling, and he would keep all the receipts. He would add it to the amount of the first few income checks that the museums paid to the girls directly. He said it might be best if they set up an off-island bank account to keep prying eyes away from their deposits from the monthly checks they would receive, but that was, of course, up to them. He also mentioned that the entire trip and all costs for the professor and were to be funded by Nancy and Wendy when all of their research was finished.

Nick went on to enumerate that his amount would still be the standard ten percent of the total that each museum paid until the time in which they stopped the touring scepter. If and when it was sold, he would get ten percent of the sale price, and he would also receive ten percent of the total sale price of the gold coins if any were be discovered.

Nick assured Nancy he had a lot of cash on hand, and he would have no problem taking sufficient funds with him to Europe. He also had credit cards, but he did not know how well they would work in Europe. He noted that JoAnn was also readily available to wire him funds through Thomas Cook, or any other travel company that offered that service. Every receipt would be kept for bookkeeping at the return of the trip.

Nancy had jotted down the key elements of Nick's accounting to review with Wendy. She said, "That's excellent, Nick. Thanks so much for all this strategizing. And, just to let you know, we are going to begin our search for our stalker tomorrow."

Nick warned her, "I know Nantucket is a small island, but still things can happen. Don't get in over your head. Get professional assistance if you need it. The police station is right there in town. I'll call you before I leave for Europe. Good luck!"

CURSED GHOSTS OF BHANGARH FORT: THE MOST HAUNTED PLACE IN INDIA!

Located at the border of the Sariska Tiger Reserve in the Alwar district of Rajasthan, the Bhangarh Fort is not for the faint-hearted. But, if there is not, as the phrase goes, a cowardly bone in your body and you greet danger with open arms, we invite you to explore the best among the most haunted places in India. Make your vacation all about getting acquainted with the mysterious stories behind this eerie fort!

Mark and Beth were approached by Marshal Dubock who, in addition to being a very fine artist, was the Town of Nantucket Visitor Services manager, and the president of the Chamber of Commerce. He had discussed with a few restaurant owners about possibly offering a 'theme night' along the lines of Mark and Beth's 'spy' nights that were the talk of the town every time they dressed up as Natasha and Boris and went out. June Hutton from the Jared Coffin told Marshal that it was really a great idea, as the Tap Room was always on their list of places to stop on such an evening, and the guests in the restaurant really enjoyed seeing them. And, so it was born: "Nantucket's Progressive Spy Night" dinner tour.

The first trial evening was limited to a party of two other couples to make the trial run. The cost was fifty dollars per couple plus any added alcohol if consumed. Carol and Mark McGarvey were the first to sign up, and the other couple to join in the fun was Randy and Donna Affeldt. The first place on the venue was Ships Inn where the tree couples enjoyed pan-seared scallops with black domestic caviar garnish. The next stop was the Club Car for a tableside-prepared Caesar salad.

Then the six of them progressed on to the Tap Room for a char-grilled sliced sirloin steak with buttermilk whipped potatoes and saute'ed broccoli in olive oil. This was followed by the final stop at the Languedoc for a warm Tart Tartin a la mode.

The evening was quite the hit. The entire event from each of the couple's arrival to the last restaurant course was documented by Steve Turrentine, and the newspaper was planning on a once-a-month spread on the "Spy Night" progressive dinners. Marshal Dubock was overrun with requests for couples wanting to be part of the "Spy Nights."

Wendy and Nancy were set on their sleuthing. They were headed into town, and Rusty was manning the fort.

He still was clueless about what was in the mysterious box that he had picked up while at the dump with Wendy and Nancy, or why someone would break into their home. But he never asked any questions as he just thought if they wanted for him to know, they would tell him eventually.

The plan was first to see if they could locate a single male staying at an inn. This would be done earlier in the day. If so, they would return later on in the evening and see if they could read the register and possibly find a key to the room.

Nancy entered the first guest house and told the girl at the check-in desk, "Hello. I'm wondering if you can help me out? A friend of mine wants me to drop off a gift to one of her friends who is staying on the island. I have a box to deliver to this gentleman, but somehow the paper and the guest house information for he is staying, along with his name is now among the missing. I cannot get in touch with my friend off island as she flew out yesterday to Europe. So, do you have any single men staying at the inn?"

All the innkeepers were very polite and kind and did not seem to suspect anything about her inquiries. After three negative responses, they called it an afternoon.

Wendy kept an eye out for the rust-colored Ford, but to no avail.

Nick Caselli made the arrangements to fly British Airlines from Boston to London Heathrow Airport. Rolf made reservations at a hotel in London. Nick called the girls and said, "The plans are set, no turning back now!"

A few days later Wendy and Nancy had not made any progress in their search for the stalker among the six inns they had now visited.

JoAnn drove Nick to the airport. He had a small checked bag and a carry-on bag and a briefcase. Inside the two bags he was keeping by his side Nick had five thousand dollars in currency in each of them along with two thousand dollars in his wallet. At first it seemed excessive, but JoAnn said better safe than sorry. She reminded him that it wouldn't put a dent into their cash supply, far from it. He boarded his flight with ease, and JoAnn had insisted at their expense he upgrade to first class. She jokingly reminded him, "If we don't go first class, our heirs will." Nick slept well on the flight and arrived to an early morning foggy London. He was fortunate that Rolf had a connection at the hotel, so he was able to check into his room upon his arrival.

The plan was for him to rest up for a few hours and meet with Rolf at one p.m. They would go to a nice pub for lunch and catch up on old times. After their lunch they went back to Nick's suite. He carefully took out a small box and showed Rolf the ancient writing that looked to be on animal hide. Nick had brought with him a powerful magnifying lens due to the fact the Latin writing was quite well faded in some places.

Rolf took his time deciphering the Latin. He asked Nick for a pen and paper from the desk and slowly wrote the clue out word for word which read (or as best as Rolf could decipher):

"One hundred coins from a metal chest are located in Paris, France, under the left Calixto gilded sculpture of Joan of Arc which can be found at the first base east- facing side of the fifth catacomb. Woe to the person who does not follow the following clue to the utmost as this could be a sign of bad fate. One should not take this information lightly, as the correct dealing with this situation is for someone who will only view the final clue. This clue will be seen only by the accurate use of the oil on the skin of the animal. If the correct oil is collected and used gently, it will unlock the final answer to this clue which will appear if the oil is used correctly on the animal hide presented here. On the animal's hide the answer will slowly appear within a half hour of a sand hour-glass timer.

One has to go forth to the town of Rungis, located on the outskirts of Paris proper. They shalt seek out a place known as the Demon Pub and locate, if such person still exists, a gypsy named Aberama. Then the seeker shall ask this such man about a place to purchase the oil of the Golden boar. It is a pheromone oil, but if a person should so use oil not from a Golden boar, the remaining clue will never will never be revealed. The hide will keep the secrets forever which will never be revealed to them."

Rolf was quiet for a few minutes after reading the transcribed note that lay before him.

Nick remained still, only asking, "Does any of this mean anything at all to you?"

Rolf said with a close-mouthed smile, "Oh, it is going to be quite easy. All we have to do is find a male gypsy that goes by the name of Aberama in Rungis, France, who is about one hundred and seventy years old! It will be a piece of cake, wouldn't you agree?" He laughed.

Then Nick said, "Well, as you say, like a piece of cake!

Now, do you happen to know anything about wild boar?"

Rolf shook his head. "Not really, except they do exist in the countryside of France and are quite delicious. Also, in Italy and Germany you see them on the menu as well here in England."

Nick, who after such a long journey, the jet lag and a big lunch, was feeling a bit fatigued and said, "Professor, let's do this: let me get some rest and we can meet tomorrow. Then we can see what we can figure out about this very strange note."

Rolf understood. "That's a plan. Tomorrow around ten a.m. I shall meet you in the lobby."

Nick gave a thumbs up. "Perfect! I am going to take another hot shower and rest. But I do not want to take too long of a nap for if I do, I will be awake at two a.m."

GHOSTS OF THE ANCIENT RAM INN
SALISBURY PLAIN, ENGLAND

The Ancient Ram Inn actually lies where two ley lines intersect, one of those also intersecting directly through Stone Henge. Ley lines are thought to be of spiritual significance with intentional alignments through sites of great importance. It is thought that the Ancient Ram Inn feeds off the energy produced by these ley lines and gains further energy from the ever-mysterious Stone Henge. Add to this the fact that the Ancient Ram Inn is built over wells, thus being constantly surrounded by water, is another factor thought to drive spiritual energy. Though it is also thought that this water has actually opened up a dark portal directly beneath the inn!

Another interesting piece of information that adds weight to the legends of the Ancient Ram Inn is that it is built right over the top of a 5000 years-old pagan burial ground. This claim was solidified after the skeletal remains of a woman and child were uncovered underneath the floor of the inn. An iron dagger was found lying within their bones, which gave life to rumors that the bodies were actually victims of a human sacrifice ritual.

Kosmo answered his phone after Jimmy Jaksic told him Ted Hudgins was on the line. Before Ted could utter a word Kosmo said, "'Strive not to be of success, but rather to be of value.'"

And Ted had a very quick comeback, "'You will face many defeats in life, but never let yourself be defeated.'"

Then Kosmo said, "Touche'! OK, Ted, very nice. What's on your mind?"

"Well, Chief, I just got word that it might be possible that a personal friend of the Benchley's out in 'Sconset, Walter Cronkite, is staying with them. He has invited Henry Kissinger, our Secretary of State, to come to Nantucket on a friend's yacht. Also, there is a rumor that Mr. Kissinger might possibly be traveling with a Ms. Romanovska."

Kosmo asked, "A who?"

Ted repeated, "Ms. Romanovska. You don't know who she is?"

Kosmo admitted, "No, not really."

Ted revealed, "Just to get you up on the latest, Ms. Romanovska is from Latvia, that's way up near Russia.

She is, well, as they say, quite in vogue, meaning she's quite the popular model. Some of the Coast Guard guys found this out, and they are going nuts! She's evidently way up there in the fashion world. I think she will be traveling with her young daughter, Katherine, aka Kate Romanovska. I believe Ms. Romanovska is traveling with her own entourage as well. So, the point of my call is, I was wondering if maybe we could make some kind of official welcome to these famous folks, really roll out the red carpet?"

Kosmo rolled his eyes, knowing how much Ted liked to make a scene. "Well, Ted, here's the deal. If and when the State Department contacts me, and if Kissinger is arriving on a yacht, you will be the first one I contact. But as of now, nothing has come across my desk. If he's coming to the island I will be notified. But, until such time, let's keep a lid on it!" Kosmo knew that this was like asking a kid to not accept a free ice cream cone at the Pharmacy.

Ted replied, "Roger that. Over and out!"

Fifteen minutes later Mark walked into the station. Beth was manning the switchboard. He said, "Boy, do I have news! Harrry Kissinger, the Secretary of State, is arriving here next week on a huge yacht!"

"Really?" Beth retorted, all smiles and her eyes open wide.

"You betchya!" Mark exclaimed. "And that's not all! He might possibly be traveling with the super model, Inese Romanovska, you know the one that's in all those magazines? She's way up there, like Cheryl Tiegs! She's European, you know." Mark tried to sound nonchalant as if he was in the know about such things.

He continued, "I am going to go home later and pull out my dress uniform and shine my shoes. I've never met a Secretary of State before.

But in high school I studied a lot about political history. I can name every president in order."

Beth asked, "Can you really?"

Mark replied, "I sure can!"

Beth put him to the test. "OK, then," she asked, "who was our thirteenth president?"

Mark became flustered and quickly changed the subject of the conversation. "I can't wait to meet old Harry! I'll bet you he's a swell guy-just like one of us!

You need to make sure your camera is up to snuff. I can see it now-my picture on the front page of the *Inquirer & Mirror,* shaking hands with the one and only Harry Kissinger!"

"Sorry, Mark," Beth replied, "but it's *Henry* Kissinger."

"Oh, yeah, that's what I meant-Henry! This is big! We will need to buff up security. I am going to go into my office and make some notes and present them to Kosmo on what type of security protocol we need to put in place. I tell you, Kosmo will be mighty impressed with me taking this initiative without being asked."

Beth wondered, "How did you find this information out?"

"Oh, I just ran into Ted Hudgins. You know that dog of his, Bella, is such a cutie, always wearing the goggles in the side car of his motorcycle."

Kosmo overheard the entire conversation but just chuckled. It did not take Ted any time to start spreading the word.

That evening Kosmo had a very strange dream. The first part was he stepped on the back of a lady's dress as he was walking on Main Street, and as he did, it made quite a large tear in it. Not knowing how to respond to this, as the lady did not notice it when it happened, he just let it slide past the moment and decided not to mention anything about it. He figured the dress had to be rather expensive, and on his minimal salary, he thought it would take weeks of working to pay her for a new one.

He awoke, and trying to make sense of such a weird dream, he went to the kitchen and drank a cup of tea and ate a few biscotti.

He returned to bed, only to fall back into another weird scenario in his dreams. This time he was in the office and he snagged his shirt tail on a rough metal edge of the dispatch desk. First off, he did not even know the person on the switchboard. It was some unknown man. As he walked into his office, he decided that a cup of coffee would hit the spot. So, he went and made a fresh pot. As he was waiting, he walked towards the back of the station and out the back door. He returned to the office via the front entrance and noticed that the snag on his shirt tail was now numerous long strings that had managed to unravel everywhere as he had walked, making it almost into an unraveled cocoon! The old man was still on the dispatch desk, and he started to transform into a spider, almost catching Kosmo in the cocoon that had started from the string of his shirt tail. The more he turned around to untangle himself, the more he was being engulfed! The man, who was now a full-grown spider with pinchers, was coming closer and closer to him! Then he awoke with a jolt. He was sweating and trying to clear such a bad dream out of his thoughts.

AITOLIKO, GREECE: THE ISLAND OF SPIDERS

For some unknown reason, Aitoliko is covered with spider webs! "Behind the phenomenon," Greek biologist Fotis Pergantis said, "are the spiders' favorite snacks: gnats. The spiders rule this island and can be extremely dangerous if one is bitten or falls into one of their traps.

Small mosquito-like insects with a lifespan of two to three days, gnats use most of their existence to reproduce. They thrive in hot, humid temperatures and continue to reproduce during that time. And since temperatures in Aitoliko lately have been ideal for gnats," Pergantis said, "there has been a whole lot of reproduction going on.

When these temperatures last long enough, we can see a second, third and fourth generation of the gnats and end up with large amounts of their populations."

The next morning Kosmo still could not shake off the dreams. He tried reading any magazine he could find in the house. Then, as he was pouring out his coffee, of all things he spotted a spider making a web on a tree branch outside his kitchen window. He left the house, drove to town and stopped in at the Pharmacy lunch counter. A kid there with his mother was reading a *Spiderman* comic book. When the waitress asked what he would like, he just said, "I'll come back later. I forgot something in my car."

He went to Mignosa's Market where he sat at the counter and asked Les for a cup of coffee. "No, Les," he corrected himself. "Let's change that to a cup of tea." He thought that perhaps the caffeine from coffee might steer his thoughts into more spider related things. It felt a little creepy.

Nick and Professor Rolf met at ten a.m. in the hotel lobby. Nick felt much more refreshed. They enjoyed a pasty and a coffee.

"So, Professor," Nick asked, "any thoughts?"

"Here is the best I can come up with. I called a friend who is an avid hunter and asked if he knew anything about Golden boar. He told me he hunts boar, but to him a boar is a boar. He referred me to a fellow he knows that deals in farm livestock. So, I called him up. This guy was a wealth of information. Apparently, there are Golden boars. He has never seen one, but he has heard about them. They roam in the hills of Provence, France, and are sacred to some of the French peasants." He stopped to sip his coffee.

"I also asked about their pheromones. This he knew about, but not Golden Boar pheromones specifically. He said it's just pig sweat. Some perfume companies use pig pheromones mixed into their scents, which is supposed to bring out some amorous effects on people."

Nick made a bit of a face but didn't laugh. "OK, well now we know two things: that there is such a thing as a Golden Boar, and what their boar sweat is used for," he summarized. "But how do we find a gypsy that's one hundred and seventy odd years old?"

Rolf held up one index finger. "Ahh, that's the million-dollar question! As it is written in the *Wizard of Oz* one must start at the beginning of the road. It looks like our road starts in Rungis, France."

A large yacht arrived on Nantucket. Henry Kissinger was on board where he met with Constable Kosmo and Ted Hudgins. It was made clear to Mark and Beth that this was a private stay for the Secretary of State and his guests. They were going out to lunch at Mrs. Benchley's home in 'Sconset with Walter Cronkite, followed by a return to the yacht. Dinner that evening would be at the Chanticleer. The following day they would all enjoy lunch on the yacht, then depart around four p.m. Kosmo offered to have Mr. Kissinger and his guests driven out to 'Sconset and back with himself and his deputy. Mr. Kissinger readily accepted his offer.

Mark suggested, "We might need two cars as we don't want them all squished up together in the back seat." He volunteered, "I could drive Ms. Romanovska and her daughter."

Kosmo clarified the situation. "I believe her daughter will remain on the yacht and maybe have a chaperone take her around town if she wants to."

When Kosmo relayed this message to Mark, he was ready to run home and put on his finest dress uniform. Kosmo gently told him that Mr. Kissinger really would prefer to have this a very low-key affair.

Ted started to explain that his entire staff, which actually consisted of himself and his latest temporary employee, John Vega, who was a visiting friend of his, were at Mr. Kissinger's beck and call.

Mark had Beth's camera on the front seat of the squad car, ready for a photo opportunity with Mr. Kissinger and possibly Ms. Romanovska.

Mr. Kissinger was ever so grateful for the ride from Kosmo and Deputy Donato and was quite inquisitive about the island on the drive out to 'Sconset.

It was a very quiet gathering with Walter Cronkite, Mr. Kissinger, Inese Romanovska and the Benchleys.

On their last ride back to the yacht, Mark was itching for a photo with Mr. Kissinger and Ms. Romanovska. They seemed to sense it, as Mark had mentioned a few times that he just happened to have his camera handy if they wanted a photograph taken with Mr. Cronkite and the Benchleys. When they arrived at the yacht, Mr. Kissinger ever so gracefully asked Mark and Kosmo if they would be so kind to have his and Ms. Romanovska's picture taken with them. Then he would appreciate it if Deputy Donato would send an eight by ten copy to his office in Washington. Mark was thrilled when Mr. Kissinger offered his official Secretary of State card to him.

Mark had several eight-by-tens developed the very next day after he had told the captain of the yacht to snap several different angles. Mark sent the photo off, secured in cardboard so that it would not bend. Two weeks later he received, on official Secretary of State stationery, a hand-written letter from Mr. Kissinger thanking him personally for all the kindness he had shown him while visiting the island. It had an added note saying the door to his office was always open for the deputy to stop by and visit an old friend!

What Mark did not know was that Kosmo, when he escorted Mr. Kissinger from the front door of the Benchley's home to the car, explained to Mr. Kissinger how thrilled Mark was to meet him and asked if he would be OK with a photograph being taken. Mr. Kissinger said he and Inese would absolutely be happy to do that. To wrap it up and make his claim to fame, Mark had his photo taken for the newspaper holding the personal letter he had received from The United States Secretary of State. He was beaming!

AUSTRALIA'S MOST HAUNTED PLACE: THE STORY OF PORT ARTHUR

This site is about the disembodied laughter of children and other ghostly stories. Thousands of people tour the Port Arthur Historic Site every year, and many of them report creepily similar experiences.

Port Arthur has a long history. It began in 1830 as a timber station, and for the next twenty years it housed some of the most hardened criminals from England, along with petty convicts and repeat offenders from other prisons around Australia. Towards the end of the 1700's, Britain was unable to continue sending its convicts to the Americas, and Australia became the next best option. Countless prisoners were to arrive on Australia's shores as well as on Tasmania, with Port Arthur being a popular destination. Those sent to this new land endured a harsh life, with most never returning home. This seemed an unfair punishment for the petty crimes of minor theft necessary for survival which most convicts had committed.

Nick and Rolf made their plan for the very next day. They were going to take the ferry from Dover, England, to Calais, France. Then they made their list. They took the ferry, and upon arrival in France, they boarded the train to Paris. They checked into a very nice hotel in the heart of Paris that a hotel concierge in London had recommended to Nick. That evening they dined at a very small but wonderful bistro in the Latin Quarter. Rolf declared, "What a good fit! A Latin clue goes well with a Latin area, but not Latin wine!"

The next morning Rolf inquired about getting to the area of Rungis. The concierge was taken quite aback and was not sure he understood what Rolf was requesting. Rolf, thinking his French skills were not the best, wrote the town's name down on a piece of paper. The concierge then explained that Rolf must be mistaken as that was an area full of gypsies that would surely rob him blind.

But Rolf quickly responded that he was writing an article about gypsy life, and he would be extremely vigilant. He was not even wearing a watch or any jewelry, and he kept his few French francs totally unavailable to pickpockets no matter how hard they tried. He added he had visited several gypsy camps in the last several months for this article.

The concierge recommended that they should take a private driver. The distance was about a twenty-minute drive, and he would have the driver escort them to where they were going and act as a translator for them. When he booked the driver, the hotel concierge also requested that if they had a large stocky-type of personnel, he might come in handy if the gypsies were getting too pushy for the men. He noted the clients were willing to pay more for the service. The private car service, when it found out the location was Rungis, said it would take two employees, as one would have to stay with the car. Otherwise, there was a good chance that the car would be stripped clean if left unattended. The larger of the two men was an off-duty gendarme.

One hour later they were at the entrance of the Demon Pub. Their driver, who remained with the car, was shooing off beggars, as Rolf and Nick stood out like two sore thumbs. They entered and looked around the dark interior of the pub. It certainly was eerie. It took them a few moments to get their eyes adjusted to the dark interior which smelled like cheap stale beer and cigarettes. Rolf asked the driver if he could inquire if anyone ever knew of a man named Aberama who resided at the pub many years ago.

At a back table was an old gypsy woman and her dog. She looked to be a hundred years old. After the driver asked a few people in the bar, he was referred to her. She wasn't giving anything up to these three foreigners until Nick pulled out a ten franc note and asked the driver to see if that might persuade her to talk.

She saw the money and smiled, showing that she had about two teeth left in her mouth.

Her name was Valdoma, and when asked how old she was, she said she did not really know. She said she was born in a cave in the mountains of Provence.

Nick looked at Rolf upon hearing Provence, and he thought that this might turn out to be a good thing.

Valdoma asked them to sit, and she wanted a glass of wine which was quickly ordered. Then she asked for the money, but the driver said firmly, "Not a centime more until you answer some questions for these men."

Valdoma quickly smiled at the promise of the francs and said, "What do you want to know?"

Rolf told the driver, who translated the fact to the gypsy woman that there had been a man from many years ago who resided at the pub and had knowledge of where to obtain Golden Boar pheromones.

She thought for a moment then said, "Golden Boar can only be found in the area of Provence. If that is what you are seeking, you will have to go to the town of Les Saintes de la Mer. There you should seek out an old gypsy farmer named Draper, if he is still alive, and he could advise you." After telling the men that information, she held her hand out. Nick gave the driver ten more francs and they departed.

On the way back the driver asked, "Why would you be interested in pig pheromones?"

Rolf told him he was a professor at Oxford University in London, and they were doing an experiment that required pheromones from a specific breed of wild boar.

The driver looked at his colleague, shrugged his shoulders and said, "It takes all kinds!"

They returned to the hotel. Both took hot showers to wash the odor off their bodies. They changed their clothes that still smelled from the stench of the Demon Bar. They agreed to meet in the lobby in one hour. Nick opened up the windows of his room and draped his tee shirt and button-down shirt on the lamp in the warming fresh air.

Heading out they went to a very upscale restaurant near Montmartre and enjoyed a nice bottle of wine, fresh oysters and Coq au Vin. They discussed their new options and agreed that Provence was their next stop!

Back at the hotel, Nick called JoAnn and filled her in on the latest developments. He asked her to call Wendy and Nancy and give them the latest.

Wendy and Nancy were thrilled to get the update and said they would be at home daily at four p.m. if JoAnn had more to report. That afternoon the girls went back to town to do some more sleuthing. They scouted out three more inns. At the third one they hit paydirt after Nancy went through the whole spiel about her friend who sent her a present that was to be delivered to a male friend of hers and how Nancy lost the paper with the inn and the man's name. She once again explained how she was going inn to inn to find her friend's friend and deliver the gift.

The innkeeper, at her third stop, said that she indeed had a single gentleman by the name of Randy Sheehan spending a few days at the inn. But Nancy did not think to ask how long the man had been residing there. Nancy, trying to not show her emotion, asked the innkeeper what room Mr. Sheehan was staying in and told the innkeeper that she would stop back in later on with the package. Hopefully it was the correct gentleman to whom she was to deliver the gift.

She went out and met with Wendy who was about three stores away watching the comings and goings into the inn's front door which turned out to be nothing.

Nancy whispered to her, "We might have found our guy. There's a single male staying in room twelve. Now all we have to do is stake it out from the outside, watch for either lights being turned off or a single man exiting like he is headed out for dinner. It won't be a walk in the park as we are going to have to do some surveillance on the inn. But let's figure that most people head out between five and eight for dinner. So, we start off by getting a good parking spot to watch the front door. Then we need to find out where Room Twelve is located at the inn. I asked where Room Twelve was, and she told me - second floor all the way down on the left, and said only one other room is rented and the couple checks out tomorrow."

Wendy nodded, taking in all the next steps.

Nancy added, "I also managed to see where the room keys are kept on the back wall past the desk on separate hooks. I saw each one had at least two keys per room on the hooks. Now, if we can spot our guy leaving the inn, one of us will grab a spare key and go through the guy's room–in and out in five minutes!"

"The only thing," Wendy mentioned, "is either our stalker is out as his car is not around the area, or it's not our guy."

"Well, one step at a time," Nancy said. "But, Wendy, I really don't feel up to going into the guy's room. Can you do it?"

Wendy nodded, "I'll get that part done. Doesn't bother me in the least!"

Deputy Mark was walking around town every shift he was off from the station. He was wearing a different undercover outfit each time. He changed his clothes every hour or so at the station.

Mike DiFronzo was watching Mark enter the station in one outfit and depart wearing another. Mike asked him, "So what are you doing?"

Mark said, sitting on the edge of the dispatch desk, "You see, Mike, it's like this. Some of us have the true lawman approach to their work. For example," he explained, "it's plain as day that you just don't have it. What I am doing is real undercover surveillance, trying to catch the murderer of Bob Tonkin."

"Oh, I get it kind of like a store detective!"

"Well, exactly, in a matter of speaking. You see I am scouring the streets, trying to observe anyone out of character, out of place, someone who doesn't belong in the everyday normal life on the streets of Nantucket."

Mike then started rambling on about his aunt was a store detective for Woolworth's in some town in Ohio. He said she used to wear sunglasses and different wigs. Then he asked Mark if he had any wigs.

Mark just glared at him and said, "Wipe the crumbs off the desk, and throw away all those candy bar wrappers! Wigs!" he muttered, walking into his office. "I'll give you wigs!"

Mark told Kosmo of a story in one of his *True Crime* magazines about a private detective who wrote about undercover techniques. This guy lived in Chicago and did a lot of surveillance work, so Mark said he was honing up his skills and might send off an article himself. He related that if they published one's article, the writer received twenty-five dollars. Kosmo told Mark how impressed he was with his initiative and hoped his skills were good enough for the *True Crime* staff!

Kosmo reflected to himself how differently he had to handle his staff members; sometimes gently, sometimes to encourage them, sometimes to discourage them. It takes all kinds, he thought, and chuckled as he went to his office.

PLUCKLEY VILLAGE, KENT, ENGLAND: A HAUNTED VILLAGE IN WHERE 15 GHOSTS ROAM AND CHILLING SCREAMS CAN BE HEARD

The village is nestled in the Kent countryside, with just 1,000 residents who live in a mix of adorable cottages and picturesque country homes. But, in addition to the living residents, the village is said to be home to 15 ghosts, according to the villagers.

One of its many haunted sites is the Screaming Woods, which has attracted many brave tourists in recent times, with some people camping under the canopy of trees. There have been several reports of the sound of screaming men and women after dark. They are said to be the sounds of those who died while getting lost in the woods.

Elsewhere people claim to have spotted everything from ghostly horse-drawn coaches, to hanging bodies.

In the haunted graveyard people claim to have heard screams of agony from a dying man to a grieving mother.

It's quite spooky with unexplainable sightings from Pluckley.

Nick and Rolf headed out for lunch. The concierge recommended a place named Bistro Paul Bert which had classic French décor and a very flavorful menu with fresh ingredients from local butchers, fishermen, and farmers. Their leg of lamb was very well known by food lovers, and fresh asparagus was a staple on the menu.

They took a taxi, and Rolf asked the driver if he could take them slowly around the Joan of Arc statue, Place des Pyramides, knowing it was the one that was referred to in the Latin clue. Once they arrived at the restaurant, they ordered a bottle of Muscadet and split a dozen oysters. The wine and the oysters were consumed quite rapidly! They enjoyed the roast chicken and ordered a bottle of wine suggested by their server, a red lighter-style wine, Moulin-a-vent from Beaujolais. Their server suggested a platter of cheese from the cheese trolley, and they were loving life.

Rolf suggested to Nick, "We should take the train to Les Saintes de la Mer. The trip would take us directly though the town of Beaune where the famous wines of Burgundy are produced. Seeing how we are passing right through the town we should spend a night and explore." Rolf had been there twice before and said he thought Nick would truly enjoy it.

Their plan was made, and they walked back to the hotel after a stop at the Museum D'orsay for a view of some very fine French paintings.

They returned to the hotel and spoke with the concierge, asking if he could arrange two first class seats on the early morning train to Beaune, book them two rooms at Hotel Le Cep, and reserve dinner at L'Ecusson for nine p.m. that evening as well. The concierge bowed after receiving a handsome tip.

Soon after a note was delivered to both of their rooms, confirming their train time of seven a.m., arrival at twelve-thirty and that a driver would be there from the Hotel Le Cep to meet them. Nick and Rolf agreed that a light dinner would suffice after such a very fine lunch.

Meeting at the hotel's restaurant that evening, they both dined on some Burgundian escargot and filet of sole vapeur with a julienne of vegetables coated with a light lemon-infused oil.

Rolf told Nick that he called an old friend of his back in England and asked about some type of pork refinery in the Beaune area that he thought he had read about awhile back. His friend told him it was more like a college and a scientific academy all revolving on the study of pork, as France exported quite a lot to other areas of Europe. He told Nick, "If we are in the area maybe we can stop in and gather some information on the Golden boar if there actually is such a breed.

Nick smiled and asked for clarification. "A school for pork?"

Rolf replied knowingly, "They have tea schools in China, pasta schools in Italy, perfume schools in Switzerland, cheese schools all over Europe, wine schools in almost every county in Europe, hairdresser schools in the United States and a pork school in Beaune!" and he started laughing. They retired to their rooms for the evening. A new adventure was to await Nick in Burgundy - seeing some of the sights in France which was really quite exciting for him.

On Nantucket the girls scoped out the inn. Nancy had taken the side of the inn to keep an eye out for lights in Room Twelve. Wendy was watching the front door for a single person to exit. They waited from five-thirty until eight-fifteen and nothing, not one person exited the inn.

They went to Cy's Green Coffee Pot for a bite to eat.

That same day, Kosmo had something stirring in his mind but could not put his finger on it. It had something to do, he knew, with the dream about the spider forming a web, but how was that related to anything? Back at the office he was calling it a day. Nothing of any importance had happened on the island in almost a week, and he was hoping it would continue that way.

The next day all was well until an extremely loud booming explosion suddenly occurred. The station's phone started ringing immediately. A house had gone up in a blast, and a fire had started just a few blocks from the station! Dan Connor, the fire chief, had his hands full. This was one for the record books! The blast was so powerful that it did major damage to several of the surrounding homes which also caught on fire. The blast had taken the main house right off its foundation, and shattered windows as far as two blocks away. The flames were reaching fifty feet high, and the entire surrounding area was engulfed in very dense thick smoke.

Kosmo, Mark, Jimmy, and Rick Blair had already managed to block off streets as far as three blocks away to avoid congestion. They did not know if there possibly might be a secondary explosion. It took almost four hours to have the fires almost completely extinguished.

The entire neighborhood of the blast was in utter chaos. One fortunate thing was the first house was uninhabited at the time, as well were the adjoining houses due to it being off season. However, the serenity and orderliness of the neighborhood had unraveled extensively, and it would take quite a while for life to get back to normal on that street.

Nick and Rolf boarded the train and took their first-class seats. They were offered a reserved table in the dining car for breakfast. Nick was amazed at the dining car with its crisp linen draped on all the tables, fresh cut flowers, silver salt and pepper shakers, and a waiter in dress whites. He whistled softly and declared, "Rolf, this is like being at the Ritz Carlton in New York where JoAnn and I have stayed a few times!"

The menus were presented with quite the array of selections. Nick had some fresh squeezed orange juice, a freshly made omelette consisting of tasty sautéed onions, peppers, cherry tomatoes and spinach. It was served along with some sourdough toasted bread, and he finished with a bowl of fresh raspberries with a dollop of crème fraiche.

He and Rolf discussed the day's plans. Rolf suggested they check in first, then see if they can get a visitor's appointment to the Acadamie du Porc to see if they might find out information about the Golden Boar.

They arrived at the train station in Beaune where their driver was waiting, holding a sign that read 'Hotel Le Cep' and underneath was 'Mr. Casselli.' They were shown to the car, and in the back seat was a bottle of Puligny-Montrachet on ice and two glasses. The driver asked if they would like him to open the wine to which they said both replied a very quick "Oui!"

There were two hotel brochures on the seat, and Nick started reading the English version. He exclaimed, "Look at this place! I wish JoAnn was with us!" He read aloud, "Exceptional services at the Hotel Le Cep, in Burgundy!

History and tradition of Hotel Le Cep

Step over the threshold of the Hotel Le Cep and let yourself be transported through time. A unique welcome, a reception staff attentive to all your needs, a warm and cozy atmosphere, all this will make your stay in Beaune an unforgettable moment. We strive to create a unique relationship with our guests thanks to a family-run hotel that is open and friendly and where you will be the center of all the attention our staff dedicates to our guests!

Affiliated with the Small Luxury Hotels of the World, which include some of the best hotels in the world, the Hotel Le Cep owes its charm to the uniting of two private mansions and their historical 16th century courtyards.

The 62 rooms, including 32 suites, are all decorated with antiques collected throughout the years. Each room is named after a Burgundian village or a Grand Cru wine: Chablis, Clos Vougeot, Romanée Conti, Charmes Chambertin, etc.

Another essential element for us is our staff. Each staff member guarantees a unique service and will easily and passionately meet all your expectations!

We can easily begin a countdown: 30 years, 20 years, 15 years of service... over half of our staff has been with us for more than 10 years! Such loyalty is proof of the mutual respect between staff and management and helps create this wonderful and unique atmosphere at Le Cep. I can't wait to check this place out," Nick ended.

Upon check-in Rolf asked if they could be put in contact with the Acadamie du Porc. They were given an appointment at 1:30 in the afternoon and took a taxi through the vineyards to a rustic building on a hillside slope in a town named Cluny. Upon speaking with the receptionist, a gentleman by the name of Serge greeted them, asking if they might like a rather informal tour. They accepted, and Nick was quite impressed that they took the different strains and breeds of pigs in such a high account.

Rolf then asked politely if Serge had any knowledge of a species of boar referred to as a Golden boar.

Serge looked at Rolf with raised eyebrows and asked, "How have you heard of the Golden Boar? They are very rare and are mainly located further south in the mountains of Provence." Serge was quite impressed that Rolf knew something about the Golden Boar as was not much known outside of Provence.

Rolf asked some questions, explaining to Serge that he was only privy to a small amount of background of the Golden Boar's existence, and the only information he really knew was from a short conversation with a group of other professors at a dinner gathering.

Rolf then explained, "We are going to Provence so I am curious to know more about the breed. Then, when I attend the next dinner with the other professors, I may add some additional knowledge of the topic."

Serge nodded and had them follow him into the bibliotheque (library) where they had just about every published book or article on any type of animal in the porc family. Nick and Rolf were amazed looking at one entire wall dedicated to anything related to 'porc'.

Serge offered them coffee, and they accepted. Coffee was served along with some delicate biscuits, and Serge brought them a large older looking book titled *Wild Boar*. Serge scanned the index and found the page he desired to share. There was a large color photograph of a Golden Boar stating a few facts. One explained that there are only male boars, and they can weigh up to two hundred pounds and can be very aggressive if provoked. Their average lifespan is around eight to ten years if food is plentiful. The photo showed that they had almost a golden hue around their eyes, thus being referred to as Golden. They were considered very rare, and historically served as sacrificial animals. Lastly, it stated that the main area they are found in the world are Mongolia, areas of China, and in the Provence area of France, and that they prefer rugged mountain terrain.

"Well, gentlemen," concluded Serge, "that is about all I can offer for your quest for information. I hope I have been of help to you. It has been a pleasure having you visit our little academy. Enjoy your travels." Nick and Rolf thanked Serge politely and left the school.

They returned to the hotel and regrouped. The concierge recommended a restaurant for a late lunch. They arrived at La Tavola Calda, a restaurant with an Italian flair to it. Rolf had told Nick that some pigs were trained to sniff out truffles, but they could be quite aggressive and possibly uproot the truffles with their snouts, and damage the rare fungi. But perhaps they would find truffles on the menu, and indeed they did.

They each had an order of Carpaccio of beef with shaved truffles as an appetizer along with a bottle of Meursault wine. The next course they shared was a very rich creamy risotto with fresh mushrooms from a local forest, topped with a generous offering of truffles on top.

Then they split a platter of linguini with cracked pepper, aged shaved Parmesan and large sliced shaved truffles.

During their lunch they reviewed what they had learned from Serge. By this point in time, they knew that everything, or close to it, that was deciphered in the Latin clue actually made some sense. But they still had the elusive boar grease to obtain.

Nick had placed a call to JoAnn prior to going to lunch to tell her what a wonderful and informative trip this was turning out to be, and he assured her that Rolf was a very experienced tour guide!

JoAnn told Nick, "Well, don't rush it. It is not likely you are going to turn around and hop on a plane and fly back to France anytime soon. So, enjoy the good life!" She said everything in Boston was fine, cloudy but still warm for late fall. They would talk again in a couple of days.

Nick told Rolf that he would quite enjoy staying another night in the area if Rolf was up to it.

Rolf nodded and reassured Nick, "Not a problem at all!" They returned to the hotel and extended their stay for another day.

Nick inquired if it might be possible to get a private tour to a few of the vineyards. The concierge told Nick they had a very reputable and knowledgeable English- speaking person whom they have used for many years. She would inquire if the interpreter was free tomorrow and asked if they would prefer a morning or afternoon visit.

Nick suggested, "I would like to see some more of the countryside of Beaune, and I read that there is a Route des Vins. Perhaps our driver could take us along that route, and we could visit one or two vineyards for a tasting, followed by a lunch out in the countryside."

The concierge nodded and said she would deliver a note to his room once she confirmed this for the following day.

Nick and Rolf walked in the quaint town of Beaune, feeling the need for some exercise after such a flavorful lunch. They were both anticipating the next day's vineyards trip.

That night they arrived at a very upscale restaurant at which the hotel had booked them a table. It had high vaulted ceilings and had been an abbey some four hundred years ago. Nick was in heaven, as he was a man who enjoyed food and wine. They were seated near a crackling fireplace, and each man was perusing a wine list the size of a small novel.

The extra cost of another day in Beaune did not bother Nick at all, nor did the prices listed with the wine list. He and JoAnn were considered very well off financially in life. Nick had been acquiring rare stones, jewels and gold in all forms, from various pieces, coins, and Krugerrands from South Africa. He had enough gold that could be sold or melted down to last a couple hundred years, cash wise. JoAnn was always telling him, and he agreed, enjoy life and spend it now, unless one is running short of savings for retirement, which would never be the case with Nick and JoAnn.

When the wine steward approached the table, Nick asked if he could possibly select a nice bottle of red wine from the Burgundy region. Nothing was said about the price, except Nick, who had glanced at the list, quickly told the sommelier, "Something nice but not the price of a new Citroen!"

Rolf laughed and said, "Exactly! Something memorable but not the price of a mortgage payment."

The sommelier brough over a wonderful Clos du Vougeot wine that was so silky and smooth they indulged in a second bottle.

For the first course Nick had a persimmon soup with tiny herbed croutons. Rolf had riz de veau a la champignon crème. (Veal on rice with creamed mushrooms.) Both agreed they were excellent selections.

For the next course they each had caille grille (grilled quail) with a hint of Chardonnay reduction garnished with fresh grapes from a vineyard right out back of the abbey. The main entrée was carre d'agneau (rack of lamb) pour deux. Nick leaned back in his chair, patted his full stomach and declared that the night was in perfect harmony with the wine, the lamb, the ancient restaurant setting and the company he was in. Rolf toasted him with the remainder of his glass of wine.

Wendy and Nancy returned to the inn, and Nancy found Wendy out front when at six-ten the lights went out in Room Twelve. They watched from afar the front door of the inn, and soon a lone man exited the front entrance. Wendy then went quietly in the front door of the inn. The main desk was vacated with a note saying if anyone had a question. they were to dial the number from the phone located on the side table. Otherwise, the innkeeper would return by seven a.m. Wendy casually went behind the desk, easily located the key for Room Twelve and quickly walked down the hallway.

She was inside the room in a moment. Turning on the wall switch she saw a large box which contained wine bottles. Also on the writing desk in the room were several account pages for restaurants and liquor stores. She quickly exited the room and replaced the key.

She found Nancy where she had left her and said a bit disappointed, "Well, that's a no go."

"What do you mean?" Nancy responded.

"The person in that room is a wine salesman," Wendy explained. "Not likely to be our snooping guy."

"Was it hard to get into his room?"

"Nope, a piece of cake. These people here on the island just leave the keys right out in sight. I guess theft is not a common thing at inns here!"

Kosmo was walking through the mess of the aftermath of the explosion with Dan Connor. As they were exiting what was the remains of a damaged house Dan's pantleg was caught on a nail in a piece of door frame. Then it hit him! Kosmo told Dan to keep him updated on any inspection report on the cause of the fire and headed back to the station.

He pulled out the Tonkin file and photographs and found what he was looking for. He brought his flashlight with him and entered Tonkin's Antiques on Main Street through the back door which was now secured by a padlock. The sunlight was fading but he knew where he was headed. Turning on his flashlight he spotted it. There was a torn piece of fabric on the edge of a rough mantelpiece by where Bob Tonkin had taken his final breath.

THE HAUNTED CATACOMBS
OF PARIS, FRANCE

What better place to start off this chapter than the renowned "Empire of the Dead?" Paris may be known as the "City of Lights", but when you factor in the creepy dark tunnels winding underneath, it's more like "City of Fright!" The Catacombs of Paris are one of the eeriest and most haunted places in the world and is also considered the largest grave on record. Opened in the 18th century as part of the city's efforts to decongest its space (and move the occupants which are least likely to go on strike—i.e., the dead), this underground labyrinth with skeleton-lined walls and chambers filled with human bones is home to the remains of about six million people, some of whom may still be seen wandering around the dark pathways.

Nick and Rolf awoke to a beautiful clear crisp sunny day in Beaune. Their driver, Francoise, arrived precisely at ten-thirty and took them along the Route des Vin's.

The first stop was about ten miles to the north of Beaune to Clos de Tart. They were very well received as it is not open to the general public, but their driver and guide had a family connection with this vineyard. The property was described to them as being quite remarkable for, despite a long history stretching back hundreds of years, the Clos de Tart estate has never been broken up or divided. It is indeed the largest Grand Cru Monopole in Burgundy today. The vines, as well as the ageing and winemaking facilities, have always been on exactly the same site.

They toured the cellars after a short stroll though some of the vineyard.

As was often the case in Burgundy, and also other winemaking regions in Europe, it was the Church that discovered the best *terroirs* and worked to showcase them. Clos de Tart was founded in 1141 by Cistercian nuns of Tart Abbey, a dependent house of Cîteaux Abbey. Clos de Tart belonged to this order right up until the French Revolution. At the beginning of the twelfth century Clos de Tart was called Climat de la Forge. It was only after the Cistercian nuns of Tart Abbey acquired the land in 1141 that the estate became known as Clos de Tart.

After a lovely tour and tasting they were led back upstairs to the main reception area to enjoy some coffee and a light pastry. Nick was engaged in conversation with the director of the Chateau, Emile, and the subject of what Nick and Rolf's professions were. Emile was ever so interested when Nick told him he dealt in diamonds, but not just any type of diamonds as they had to be of very high-quality ratings. Emile was now holding Nick's elbow, and he told him his twenty-fifth wedding anniversary was coming up. He was starting to research a diamond to have mounted into a fitting any way his wife most preferred.

Nick told him that made perfect sense, as every woman has a preference to what feels correct on their finger. Nick then gave him his business card and said, "If you have any questions, feel free to call me. I would be glad to walk you through any information you need. Furthermore, I would be happy to search for the size that you are looking for, and I would sell you one at my wholesale cost."

Emile smiled and put Nick's business card in his coat pocket, patting it in place. Rolf and Nick were given three bottles of wine to take as a gift from the winery. Nick offered to pay for the wine, but he was assured that it was a pleasure from the winery's director, and, if Nick and Rolf were ever to return, they would be happy to arrange a lovely luncheon in the formal salon.

As they were stepping out of the entrance of the foyer Emile was ever so ecstatic that Nick had been so kind to offer him to locate a diamond at a wholesale price. He then asked, "Might you gentlemen be free for dinner?"

Rolf smiled and replied, "As of now our evening is wide open." Immediately plans were made for them to arrive at the Chateau at eight p.m. dine there.

Nick hesitated for a moment, then feeling slightly embarrassed, told Emile that he did not have a tie and sport coat on this trip.

Emile said reassuringly, "Oh, Monsieur, just come as you please! It will just be my wife, myself, you and Rolf along with Francoise and his wife if they are available."

Upon hearing the invitation, Francoise smiled and accepted the offer to have his wife and him join in the evening meal. He then drove them along the Route des Vin's, heading towards other vineyards. They stopped in a village named Echezeaux where they visited another winery. This establishment, Domaine Georges, offered them a private wine and cheese tasting. It was quite enjoyable both for Rolf and Nick.

They stopped at a restaurant for lunch that Francoise had selected and reserved them a table earlier on. They insisted that he join them, and he readily agreed.

The Clos Lenoir 1623 restaurant was in the village of Gevrey-Chambertin. Their server brought over a chalk board and set it on a chair next to their table. He read it to them word for word, and with some assistance from Francoise, they were set to order. But first they would have some wine which they asked Francoise to select.

They had a lovely Gevrey-Chambertin by Alex Gambal Vineyards.

Nick enjoyed his salad of walnuts, a hint of crumpled Roquefort, and some sliced dry-aged ham. Rolf and Francoise enjoyed buttery escargots. Nick ordered roasted confit of duck with grilled asparagus, Rolf had a pot au feu of duck, and Francoise had a simple chicken in a pearl onion and lardon red wine reduction. After a satisfying lunch, they returned to the hotel and rested.

Kosmo had inspected the torn piece of cloth before using a pair of tweezers to remove it and place it in an evidence bag that he had brought along. He noticed that the torn cloth did not seem to have been part of Bob Tonkin's apparel the evening of his murder. So, unless he was incorrect in his judgement, it could have been part of the killer's sweater or shirt.

Mark was still changing his clothes as he was still going undercover. At one point he had a pipe in his mouth, a hat and a long tweed coat while sitting in the lobby of the Jared Coffin Hotel.

After about thirty minutes, the front desk manager approached him asking, "Excuse me, Deputy, are you here to meet someone?"

Mark was trying to keep a low profile and responded very quietly, "Don't pay any attention to me. I am working under cover."

The manager, who could not hear him, replied loudly, "Deputy, do you have a cold? I can barely hear you. Would you like some tea? Of course, there's never a charge here for a member of our local law enforcement."

Mark snipped back, "Pipe down! I am working under cover!"

The manager, feeling a little uncertain as to what he was hearing agreed, "You're right, Deputy, you should be home under the covers. Now, do you want me to bring you a blanket for your legs and some tea?"

Right then Mrs. Frechette and her dog, Teddy, entered the lobby. Upon seeing Mark and the front desk manager, and always wanting to be known as a personal friend of the deputy or Kosmo, the police chief, she walked right up to him and greeted him with a loud, "Hi, Deputy! What are you doing this fine morning?"

Then Teddy got into the action by barking and jumping on Mark's legs. Mrs. Frechette continued by adding, "Oh, my dear Teddy, he's a huge fan of yours, Deputy!"

Now, with all this commotion the front desk manager told Mrs. Frechette that he was just about to get the deputy a blanket for his legs as he was feeling poorly.

At that same moment, walking out of the hotel's main dining room, Jareds, and carrying a to-go container was Mike DiFronzo. He saw Mrs. Frechette and Teddy, and then Deputy Donato.

Mrs. Frechette, seeing Mike said, "Oh, Mike, I am glad you're here! Deputy Donato is not feeling well and the front desk manager is going to get him a blanket."

Every time Mrs. Frechette said the word 'deputy', she emphasized it a little louder than needed, but she wanted people around her to know that she was a personal friend of his.

Mark put his newspaper down that was part of his disguise and was going to speak.

But Mrs. Frechette leaned towards him and started feeling his forehead, knocking his fedora to the floor. She commented in a worried voice, "Oh, my, you do feel quite warm!" She obviously did not notice that the fireplace was putting out some good heat which could be the reason Mark felt warm. And, to make matters worse, Teddy snatched up Mark's hat and trotted around their feet with it.

Mike now added to the conversation. "You know, Deputy, you should go into the dining room. They have a really good cream of potato soup special. I had it, and the server was really great! She brought me another bowl on the house! Then I had the chicken parmesan, and I have got to tell you, it was a huge serving, even for me!" He patted his belly and persisted with the food talk. "It was absolutely delicious! It also came with a side salad and garlic bread. I have a to-go container here with the leftovers. And I had a piece of carrot cake for dessert. Ot had all the right flavors. I don't know who their baker is, but I am going here to call tomorrow and see if she could bake one for me to take home-a whole cake! My mom *loves* carrot cake, and I think she would really enjoy the one that they make here. She does get them sometimes at the Farmer's Market, but they are not as good as the one I just had."

With all the patience he could muster, Mark was trying to remain calm and not draw any more attention to himself. But now Teddy, having abandoned the hat, jumped up on his lap and started licking Mark's face.

Mrs. Frechette reacted, "Oh, isn't that cute! Teddy is such a fan of yours, Deputy!" By then she was trying to place the blanket on his lap that the manager had located, but Teddy thought it was a fun game and was jumping all around. Now the newspaper was all wrinkled and the scene was quite noisy. Just what Mark had totally hoped to avoid.

The manager asked Mark again if he still might like the free cup of tea. Then he asked Mike, "Was the chicken parmesan was really that good? I get an employee discount."

Mike nodded emphatically, "Oh, yes, it was one of the best I can ever remember. But I had one at Bella Vita a few months back and that rated pretty high up on my Parmesan entree list."

Now a small crowd had formed a few feet away as people enjoyed the ambiance of the front living room fireplace. One lady inquired, "Did I hear they offer free tea and carrot cake?"

Her husband, noting the attention being given to Mark chimed in, "We might need to wait a moment, dear. It seems like this guy in the chair might be having a heart attack."

One other lady heard 'heart attack', and told her friend go to the front desk now and have them call for an ambulance. Another staff person who was coming out of the back office called the fire station, saying a man at the hotel was having a heart attack and they should respond quickly as he might not make it.

Every time Mark tried to speak, Teddy would start licking his face. Mark did *not* want to open his mouth for fear of Teddy's tongue coming in contact with his tongue.

Mark tried to slowly rise out to the over-stuffed chair, but with Teddy still wiggling around on his lap, he developed an intense leg cramp. Mark let out a loud yell which scared Teddy off his lap.

The lady who had returned from the front desk after telling them to call for aid said, "Don't move him! Help is on the way!"

Mike DiFronzo, oblivious to the chaos that was underway, asked the manager, "Do you know what tomorrow's lunch special will be? If it will be anything like today's lunch special, I might just come in for lunch." Then he asked the man, "Might you be hiring? I could possibly work a shift or two on the front desk. And would I also get the fifty-percent off by being an employee?"

Despite the scene that was unfolding, the front desk manager explained to Mike, "When the restaurant is down to just a few orders of the daily special, they stop offering it. That way customers are not upset if they sell out after they have placed their food order." He also told Mike, "They put out the extra lunch specials along with things like the carrot cake quite often. You are entitled to an employee meal for each shift you work at no charge.

You only have to pay if you order off the menu."

Mike was salivating at this and said enthusiastically, "I will fill out an application first thing tomorrow!"

Mark was now in agonizing pain. His leg was all knotted up. The lady who had them call for help said despairingly to her friend, "He's not going to make it! Look at his face! Oh, my, he's going for the big one!"

The other lady was still asking her husband to place their jackets on a couple of chairs, noting that, "If everyone shows up for free tea and carrot cake, we won't have a place to sit!"

The ambulance showed up the same time as the fire truck. Fire Chief Dan Connor saw Kosmo also arriving from down the street. Dan let the ambulance crew enter first, knowing that there was not a fire. He was used to just waiting around for the 'all-clear' signal.

Kosmo entered, and, not being able to see past the small crowd to where Mark was seated, asked Dan, "So what's the situation here?"

Dan explained, not having accessed the front of the crowd and wanting to leave it up to the EMT's, "Well, from what it sounds like, it is a possible heart attack."

Coincidentally, Doreen Burliss, the reporter from the *Inquirer & Mirror*, was in the Tap Room directly below the family room of the inn. She heard the commotion a few moments earlier but paid it no attention while eating her burger. But then she heard the words, 'heart attack' and ventured upstairs at the same time the emergency vehicles arrived. She saw all the commotion going on, but what she did not see was Deputy Donato.

Dan Connor told Kosmo, "You handle this. I will await your 'all clear' signal.

Kosmo nudged his way right behind the paramedics. When they approached the heart attack victim, he saw Mrs. Frechette, Deputy Donato with a wincing expression on his face, and Teddy prancing around at Mark's feet.

Dorleen Burliss finally got an angle to see who was seated in the chair. Mike DiFronzo, thrilled to see her, walked over and started talking to her. She looked at him and said, "Not now, Cocoa Puff!"

Mike replied, "Oh, no Cocoa Puffs today. I had waffles with melted butter and maple syrup and some bacon. But I do have to tell you . . ."

At this point Doreen had tuned Mike out of the conversation as he was telling her about the chicken parmesan he had for lunch and how he might be working part time there soon and if so, if she wanted to join him for lunch, he could most likely get her the employee discount. Mike's chit chat died away as he noticed his boss moving in on the scene.

Kosmo was quite surprised to see Mark sitting in the chair in front of the hotel's living room fireplace.

Mrs. Frechette, thrilled to see Kosmo, blurted out, "Hello, Chief!" like they were long lost friends.

Kosmo immediately asked, "*What* is going on here?" Mrs. Frechette blurted out, "Well, Deputy Donato was feeling under the weather. So, the manager brought him a blanket for his legs. I have no idea why all the commotion! I mean, it's only a cold, I figure."

Mark, finally seeing some relief in this whole situation said as best he could muster, "Mrs. Frechette, will you heel your dog! And please find my hat that he ran off with!"

Kosmo asked Mark, "What the dickens is going on here?"

Mark tried to explain, but then Mike DiFronzo chimed in, still totally ignoring the situation, "Chief, would you mind me picking up a few shifts on the desk here at the hotel? You see, Chief, if I work here, I get an employee discount on the food."

The front desk manager, seeing the chief of police, quickly added, "Oh, remember, Chief, that you are entitled to free coffee or tea any time you feel like it."

The lady whose husband had reserved the two chairs asked the manager if they could still get the free tea and carrot cake?"

Kosmo rolled his eyes while the paramedics sent out for the stretcher. What was it about Mark and these out-of-hand public scenes?

Mark tried to explain to Kosmo, "Well, Chief, I was just sitting in front of the fireplace minding my own business when old Mrs. Busybody here and her dog decided that I was sick with the flu or something. Next thing you know, old DiFronzo and the front desk guy are getting me blankets! Then Mrs. Busybody's dog hops on my lap and has his saliva drooling all over my face and mouth, not to mention taking off with my fedora and rumpling up my newspaper. Then I got a fierce cramp in my leg . . ." His hand went out to indicate all the crowd around him.

Doreen Burliss just rolled her eyes and said, "Does it ever end with this guy Donato? Lunatics, they're all a bunch of lunatics! I mean, who's running this insane asylum on this island?"

Mike, seeing how Doreen was going to turn around and leave said, "Oh, Doreen, I might even know the daily specials a few days in advance. So, if you prefer one day over another for lunch, I can see if I can change my schedule to accommodate you if we can have lunch sometime together."

Doreen waved him off and stated, "It will be a month of Sundays before that will ever happen, Cocoa Puff!" And she stomped back down to the Tap Room to have another drink.

Mike continued on, "Well, I am not sure what the specials will be all the time or on Sundays, but hopefully there is something you will like on the menu!"

Kosmo, as soon as all the excitement had settled, checked in with Mark to see if he was OK to head home, then returned to the station. Things sure could get to be a scene on this little island!

In his office with the door closed and a cup of coffee on his desk, Kosmo revamped his list of people to interview about the Tonkin murder. It was a very short list. He circled the words, 'Scepter' and 'Caselli', still not knowing at all what these odd words might imply in this stubborn story. He was at a loss, but now he had a fiber from a torn sweater or shirt that he knew had to be from the murderer. He had the fact that someone had re-entered Mr. Tonkin's home and business as well as his warehouse. How did this person know about the warehouse? He must be privy to the island's layout and businesses. So, he was leaning towards a local person, maybe a past employee? Someone who knew Mr. Tonkin had possibly come across a valuable artifact? Did this have something to do with a possible monthly 'royalty check'? His list was short, but it was all he had to go on.

He knew the answer would come soon. Shaking his head, he had to admit, well maybe not too soon as the clues were almost non-existent. His notes were still:

Caselli? Scepter? Monthly royalty check? Past employees? Dagobert is who? Another antique dealer's jealousy of his business? Why was Bob Tonkin murdered and by whom?

BEWARE OF THE HAUNTINGS
AT CHÂTEAU DES FOUGERET
QUEAUX, FRANCE

Château de Fougeret, a 14th century castle located in Queaux, western France, has been recognized as a paranormal hotspot by specialists who have investigated the location. The château has seen a lot of history, including the Hundred Years War. The current owners, Veronique and Francois-Joseph Geffroy, first began noticing strange activities when they purchased the château. Since that time, they have allowed paranormal investigators, psychics, and tourists to visit the château to document the haunting and to try and get some answers as to the reasons behind the ghostly activity.

The château has been featured on French television due to the activity, and the Geffroys have photos of the specters that have been captured by investigators displayed in the living room.

Some people who have visited the château claim to have encountered threatening spirits, while others state that they've heard disembodied voices screaming at visitors to leave the premises. Apparently, the Château de Fougeret spirits have no desire for publicity and wish to be left alone.

Nick was looking over what he had packed and was not sure if anything he had brought with him was quite dressy enough for being a guest at such a fancy château.

He went to the front desk and asked where he might be able to shop for some better clothes as he was invited unexpectedly to a fine château for dinner.

The man asked him which château, and when Nick said Clos de Tart, the man said knowingly, "Ooh, la, la you're mingling with royalty!"

Nick found the store without any problem. When he entered a male clerk said politely, "Bon jour, how may I help you?"

Nick explained his situation and added that, "You see, monsieur, this will most likely be a one-time event of attending a formal dinner other than dining at some nice restaurants as my friend and I continue our travels down through France for the next week."

The clerk stood back, looked Nick over briefly and said, "I think we can get you out fitted very well with what we have on our racks."

Thirty minutes later Nick was on his way back to the hotel. He was quite pleased at the outcome. The sales clerk had him suited up with a very nice cashmere pullover and pair of excellent black fine-wale corduroy dress pants along with a nice dress shirt that matched the sweater for a sophisticated look. He told Nick no belt would be needed as the pullover would cover his waist. Nick also purchased a very comfortable pair of black semi-formal dress shoes, along with a dark maroon silk scarf, and he was all set. The sales clerk, Jean Paul, told Nick he would fit right in at a casual restaurant as well as a three-star restaurant, unless a sport jacket was required.

Nick met Rolf in the lobby, and Rolf did a double take, saying, "Man, you clean up nicely! We could walk into any first-class restaurant here in France and they would probably think you are some famous American millionaire!" Rolf gave him a wink and a thumbs up.

Nick explained to him that he was looking through what he had brought with him for the trip and said he would feel terribly underdressed with the clothes he had in his suitcase. So, the front desk clerk sent him a few blocks past the main square and, "Voilà! Here I am!"

Francoise and his wife, Marie, arrived in a beautiful black stretch Mercedes and whisked them off to the château. They were both dressed 'to the nines', and Nick felt comfortable in his choice of attire as well. Professor Rolf always had a nice British outfit complete with a herringbone weave Scottish sport coat.

The evening began in the salon with a Cremant de Bourgogne served with a warm fragrant light cheese known as Gougeres. Emile's wife, Elisa De Corso, was as nice as she was pretty. Emile told them the chance story of how they met.

Elisa, who was from the border area between Italy and France, was in Paris for a fashion show. Emile had noticed her during the event but did not engage in any conversation with her. Later on, as it was the final day of the show, they had a small closing reception with about twenty people at the Hotel Costes. Emile had supplied the red wine for the gathering, and Elisa was quite impressed by it. At the end of the party, she just happened to be talking with a small group of four including Emile, and she mentioned that the red wine was exceptional. She commented that usually at these gatherings the wine is not of the best quality.

One of the ladies in the group said, "Elisa, you will have to thank Emile here, as he is the director of Clos de Tart in Beaune, a very old vineyard with a fine reputation." She nodded at Emile over her glass in hand.

It turned out, after a brief conversation, that both Elisa and Emile were staying at the Hotel George V. They ended up riding together back to the hotel, and thus dinner plans were made. Emile invited Elisa to be a guest at the Château anytime, and he presented his card to her after a very nice long dinner for which he selected the wines.

Elisa was quite vague about her back ground, but Emile could sense that she came from a wealthy family, part French, part Italian, by the way she shared in the conversation. It included places she had traveled to as a child with nannies and chauffeurs, along with references made to private boarding schools, a chef, kitchen staff and riding stable personnel. They parted quite cordially after the fine dinner, each musing on their dinner partner.

A few weeks later Emile was just returning from inspecting the vineyards when the houseman said there was a long distance call for him. He climbed the steps to the château and took the phone.

"Hello, Emile speaking."

"Hello, Emile it's Elisa. How are you these days?"

For a second Emile drew a blank, but then he quickly recalled her face after hearing her voice with its lovely blended accent. They enjoyed a very nice conversation. It turned out that Elisa and her friend, Inez, who was a runway model in Stockholm, were planning on a trip to France, beginning in Paris, and then they were traveling down to Monaco where a friend had a large estate.

Emile told her the train from Paris is direct to Beaune, and when she finalized the dates to visit, they would be picked up at the station by the chauffeur at the vineyard. He emphasized they would be most entirely welcome as guests at Clos de Tart. Elisa thanked him graciously, told him she would finalize their plans to include a visit to the château and would inform him nicely in advance of their trip. She then said "Au revoir," and hung up.

Emile took a moment to catch his breath, and the houseman looked at him asking if everything was all right. Emile told him yes, and he was most excited as the woman of his dreams was coming to stay at the château in a few weeks.

Elisa and Inez arrived, and the entire three days flew by quickly. Emile had managed to get the name of the estate in Monaco where they were to travel to, and before Elisa had arrived a case of Clos de Tart had been delivered with a dozen roses.

"The rest is history," Emile told them with a subtle smile.

Emile showed Nick, Rolf, Francoise and his wife, who was originally from Switzerland, to the dining salon.

Elisa was asked about Marie's family history. They learned that her family was in the glass bottle business. Nick and Rolf learned later that it was not just a small bottle business, but one of the largest in all of Europe! They supplied wine bottles to just about every winery in Italy, as well as other countries.

When they were all seated the formal dining room, both Nick and Rolf, who had not viewed it before, were taken back by its beauty. It was tastefully decorated but not too ornate as to be a distraction to the diners.

The first wine served was a Corton-Charlemagne, and Nick thought he was drinking the most beautiful white wine ever. This was followed by a Domaine Romanee-Conti, which was described to Nick and Rolf as one of the smallest vineyards in Burgundy. It was considered throughout the world as one of the greatest wines of all times.

Emile told Nick and Rolf, "Well, professionally speaking, in the area of Beaune we produce a very small amount of wine as is true throughout the whole region of Burgundy. We have a saying, 'Let them drink Bordeaux, as they produce a much larger of amount there then we do in Burgundy!'"

The first course they had was a sea scallop with the roe attached in a white wine buerre blanc. That was followed with a very thin slice of foie gras upon a crisp slice of toasted herbed bread. The entrée was a mammoth roast of standing prime rib, with Duchess potatoes, and crisp green beans. For dessert, they were served a mixed berry fruit tart.

After dinner they went to the salon off the main entrance hall where a crackling fire was burning in the fireplace. Conversations flowed, and so did the cognacs and other libations. Emile spoke with Nick asking him about the diamond business. He did not bring up the fact that he wanted to purchase one for his and Elisa's twenty-fifth anniversary.

Nick was able to share his professional expertise in detail by answering all of Emile's questions. He told Emile that he had been in the diamond business most of his life. He was following in the footsteps of his father who was a diamond merchant for fifty years. Nick emphasized that he only dealt with the most respectable dealers, explaining that many a diamond dealer, well, to put it mildly, is not necessarily the most honest merchant.

He went on to explain that the reason people fall for an inferior diamond is related to the lighting in which a stone is shown. Many stores treat unknowing customers as if they were herding cattle. They rustle you in, and they use special lights which makes the diamond look much more impressive than it really is.

He continued to describe that in the trade, one also has to look for the best clarity as well as possible flaws. Unfortunately, some lower-end diamond dealers also falsify the report on a diamond's quality by using a lower type of grading for their certificate on the diamond, thus making it seem like it gets a higher rating than it actually deserves.

Nick ended the conversation saying, "If one buys a cheap wine, it tastes cheap. If one buys a cheap pair of shoes they wear out in no time. If one buys a cheap diamond, the minute one gets home and is not under the jeweler's special lights, it will look cheap." He then summarized, "There is no substitution for a quality diamond! If one scrimps, one will most likely regret it down the road. And, not surprisingly, the resale price drops faster than a Volkswagen with one hundred thousand miles on it with a loud muffler!"

Nick then told Emile if he was ever in need of a diamond that he would be more than happy to get him one at his cost, plus shipping and insurance. He felt he owed Emile at least that much as it had been a memorable evening. The evening ended most amicably, and Rolf and Nick headed back to their hotel with Francoise at the wheel.

Kosmo decided that he needed to get more information to help him with the murder mystery. He went to the Atheneum and searched as best he could for information on scepters. He had a pad of paper with him. He did not find much. All he really knew was the word 'scepter', with a slight sketch next to the word that Bob Tonkin had done. He had three encyclopedias open and was not learning much.

He had his radio on low volume just in case a call came through. He was just about to turn one of the pages when his radio went off. A person had come to the station reporting a break in. Kosmo shut the encyclopedias, returned them to their proper places and headed to the station. What Kosmo did not know was that on one of the following pages was the history of 'The Scepter of Dagobert', one of the words he had copied from Bob's notebook.

Nancy and Wendy were getting ready to head into town. They were producing six of the reserve flower boxes a day, and every third day was dedicated to their regular models. They were still doing their sleuthing every other evening but were still having no luck.

Ted Hudgins was hoping for another storm. He was in contact with Sheila Lucey at the Coast Guard station every afternoon for one of her official weather updates. But, sadly for him, the seas were looking calm for the near future. His friend, John Vega, was still residing on his yacht in the harbor, even though many a boat had departed for the season.

Mike DiFronzo had filled out his application for the front desk part-time" position and was awaiting the next week's manager's meeting on hiring for hotel positions. He actually became a buddy with the front desk manager and was kept abreast daily of the lunch specials. He hoped with all his heart (and stomach) that he would be accepted for a position!

BRITTANY, FRANCE LE CHÂTEAU DE CHÂTEAUBRIANT AND THE POISONED WIFE

Located in Brittany and built in the 11th century, the Château de Châteaubriant has seen more than enough in the way of history and events to collect its fair share of ghosts. In 1252, the current lord of the château, Geoffroy IV of Châteaubriant, left his home to join The Crusades, leaving his wife Sybille behind. Approximately a year later, it was thought that Geoffroy had died, and his wife was stricken with grief, mourning his passing. However, Geoffroy had not died; he returned home several months later, causing Sybille such a shock that she died in his arms.

In the 16th century, another tragedy struck at the château. Jean de Laval traveled to the court of King Francis I, his wife Françoise de Foix accompanying him. While there, Françoise became the Queen's lady-in- waiting and she also became the mistress of the king. Infuriated, Jean locked his wife away at the château, where she later died under strange and mysterious circumstances on October 16th, 1537. There are legends that say that de Laval poisoned his wife, while other rumors state that she bled to death.

Regardless of how she died, it is said that at midnight on October 16th of each year, Françoise leads a spectral procession of monks and knights up the stairs of the Château de Châteaubriant before disappearing at the final stroke of midnight, making this one of the must-see haunted places in France.

Nick and Rolf boarded the first-class compartment and made the easy journey to Nice. Both men were in awe of the town's beauty. Rolf declared that the area from Nice to Monaco was breathtaking. Their driver from the hotel was waiting to take them to the Hotel Negresco, again in a sleek Mercedes with hotel brochures on the seat. This time occasioned a chilled bottle of rose and two glasses.

Nick read the brochure and asked Rolf, "Does it ever stop, the magnificent architecture of these buildings?"

Rolf shared an interesting story. "Henri Negresco, born Alexandru Negrescu, was the son of an innkeeper. He was educated and worked as a confectioner at the luxurious Casa Capşa in Bucharest, Romania. He left home at the age of 25 (earlier sources mentioned 15, but it is not really possible as he finished the military service in Romania. Rolf explained there is at least one photo with him in Bucharest at older age.) Henri went first to Paris and then to the French Riviera where he became very successful. As director of the Municipal Casino in Nice, he had the idea to build a sumptuous hotel of a quality that would attract the wealthiest of clients. After arranging the financing, he hired the great architect of the 'café society', Édouard-Jean Niermans, to design the hotel with its now famous pink dome."

Rolf went on to describe more of the building. "It contains 'The Royal Lounge' with its splendiferous chandelier and historically acclaimed stained-glass window. The spectacular Baccarat 16,309-crystal chandelier in the Negresco's Royal Lounge was commissioned by Czar Nicholas II, who due to the October revolution, was unable to take delivery.

Contrary to popular belief, the large window of the Royal Lounge – listed as an historical monument – is not the work of Gustave Eiffel. Eiffel never worked at the Negresco; instead, it is entirely the work of Edouard-Jean Niermans."

Rolf continued to share his knowledge of the hotel. "Henri Negresco faced a downturn in his affairs when World War I broke out two years after he opened for business. His hotel was converted to a hospital. By the end of the war, the number of wealthy visitors to the Riviera had dropped off to the point that the hotel was in severe financial difficulty. Seized by creditors, the Negresco was sold to a Belgian company. Henri Negresco died a few years later in Paris at the age of 52.

On February 28, 1948, Suzy Delair sang *C'est si bon* in this hotel during the first Nice Jazz Festival. Louis Armstrong was present and loved the song. On June 26, 1950, he recorded the American version of the song (English lyrics by Jerry Seelen) in New York City with Sy Oliver and his orchestra. When it was released, the song was a worldwide success, and the song was then performed by the greatest international singers.

Over the years, the hotel had its ups and downs, and in 1957, it was sold to the Augier family. Madame Jeanne Augier reinvigorated the hotel with luxurious decorations and furnishings, including an outstanding art collection and rooms with mink bedspreads. She also popularized it with celebrities; Elton John featured it in the video for his song, 'I'm Still Standing'.

Noted for its doormen dressed in the manner of the staff in 18th-century elite bourgeois households, complete with red-plumed postilion hats, the hotel also offers gourmet dining at the Regency-style *Le Chantecler* Restaurant. Le Chantecler has two stars in the Guide Michelin and 15/20 in Gault Millau. It has previously been under the leadership of famous chefs such as Bruno Turbot and Alain Llorca, who left to take over the equally fabled Moulin de Mougins. The restaurant interior is decorated with Gobelins and Rococo design in untraditional colorings such as pink, lime, lemon, and cerulean." He sat back and sipped some wine after sharing the long story. This detailed history gave Nick something amazing to anticipate!

They arrived after almost finishing the entire bottle of wine on the short ride to the hotel. When Nick arrived at his suite, he was in awe. A breathtaking view was out every window. He called JoAnn. After catching up on the happenings in Boston, he filled her in on all the wonderful things that took part in Beaune. He informed her that a diet might be in order upon his return as the food was extraordinary—almost every meal he had enjoyed.

They made small talk and he told JoAnn, "Let's see what tomorrow brings. We are headed to a town named Les Saintes Marie de la Mer which is supposedly where the gypsy, Draper, can be found residing. But who knows, all that I can say is that, so far, a lot of the pieces are falling into place. But, as one knows, it only takes one bad cog to stop the wheel from turning. I will give you an update tomorrow."

When Rolf and Nick asked for dinner suggestions, the hotel said they could recommend a host of places. What were they seeking?

Nick replied, "A simple dinner would work as we have been wining and dining quite richly for three days straight."

The concierge made couple of recommendations of nearby eateries. Rolf and Nick found a nice bistro named Hermitage down a very quiet street a few blocks from the hotel. the owner who seated them explained the specials of the day, and Nick asked for a nice bottle of rosé. They split a large salad tossed with goat cheese and warm lardons. Their entrée was a whole herb-roasted chicken for two, and the potatoes were cooked underneath the roasting bird with the juices of the chicken having dripped upon them the entire cooking process. The combination was ever so tasty!

The bottle of rosé did not last very long. Rolf asked for a dry white wine from the region. The owner brought over a white Bandol which they enjoyed with the roasted chicken.

They engaged the owner in conversation, and Rolf told him they were planning on a visit to Les Saintes Marie. The first thing the owner, Claude, said seriously, was, "Watch your wallet! That is a gypsy town, and they have their own rules." He continued, "But why go there?

Many fine villages are much closer by, and no gypsies to rob you. They will take the fillings out of your mouth, given the chance!"

Rolf explained that he was doing a study of different gypsy cultures around France.

Claude shook his head slightly and said, "Better you, Monsieur, than me!" They chatted awhile longer and Claude told them, "Do not bring or wear any type of jewelry. Even if you can't remove the ring off your finger, it will draw attention and they will find a way to remove it! And you won't have a clue!"

Rolf nodded and thanked him for his advice. They knew they would have to proceed with caution.

They enjoyed a cognac in the hotel grand lounge and agreed to meet at eight a.m. in the lobby. Rolf said he would arrange transportation and he let them know the destination just in case it was the same situation as in Paris.

The next morning at the police station, Beth alerted Kosmo, upon his arrival, that he had a phone message from a man named Tom Kendrick. It seemed that Mr. Kendrick had a concern about some suspicious activity in Surfside. Kosmo called him back, and Tom volunteered to come down to talk with him that morning.

Kosmo met Mr. Kendrick in the front waiting area of the police station. Mark had just arrived at the station, so Kosmo asked the deputy to take notes.

As it turned out, Tom said he often goes down through a very private dirt road off of Surfside Road once a month to do some fishing. He called it his 'secret spot' and revealed that all of his friends were still trying to discover it. He said enthusiastically, "It's a spot where I catch some really great stripers! But, getting back to the reason I am here-you see, there is a cabin hidden off the dirt road. I have hardly ever seen anyone at it, and if so, it is mainly in July or August when I am out there for a quick afternoon of fishing. Well, here it is, off-season, and I noticed that there were fresh tire marks in the soft dirt. I have got to tell you, no one is joy riding down in that area. The road is rough and there's no reason to be there." He surmised, "Unless the owners have a caretaker that might stop by one in a while, this is the first time I have ever noticed tire tracks, especially at this time of year."

Tom shrugged his shoulders and went on. "A few days later I saw a red pickup truck parked there. I only paid it a moment's notice and continued walking to my fishing spot. I didn't have much luck during the day, and then it was about dusk which you know comes early now. I was walking back to Surfside Road and I see two pickup trucks parked there. In all the years I've been going there, I have never seen so much as a seagull perched on the roof of that cottage after August. So, what I guess I am saying is, maybe someone should go and check it out?"

Mark had him draw a sketch of where this small dirt road was located. Then Mark stated, "Ah maybe it's some squatters. I will check it out first thing tomorrow. If you can give us your number, Mr. Kendrick, I will give you the update in a few days. We appreciate you checking with us about this activity. Good luck with your fishing."

After Tom left, Kosmo told Mark, "That's a good idea. You can head out tomorrow after our staff meeting. One never knows what might be going on, even on a small island like this one. Thanks, Mark, for taking notes."

Mark went to his desk feeling a very important that he had responded in such a helpful manner. And he would be all geared up for a 'secret investigation!'

Nancy and Wendy gave their sleuthing one more try but to no avail. "Well," Nancy said on the way home, "at least we get an 'A' for the old college try! Somehow, some way, we will smoke this stalker out."

Kosmo made a call to Michelle Volpe in the Commissioner's office in Boston.

"Hey, Kosmo! How is one of my favorite people in the world these days?" she asked cheerfully.

Kosmo smiled and answered, "Michelle, boy do I miss seeing you every day! But I have to admit, overall, things are pretty good down here."

Michelle inquired, "Any progress on your murder down there?"

Kosmo replied hesitantly, "Well, yes, things are moving along slowly, though I haven't nailed much on the situation. It's a very compelling case. It seems like it should be simple, and on this small island it should be easy to locate a suspect. But I have only a whisper of a clue, and any suspects seem almost non-existent. I'm pretty close to stumped!"

Michelle said encouragingly, "Well, Kosmo, if anyone can solve it, it's you! Go eat some red onions and sweat it out!" she added, laughingly.

Kosmo chuckled. "Yeah, you know it! If I can get a solid clue the red onions are on my list!"

"So, what can I do for you, Kosmo? Do you want to speak with the commissioner?"

Kosmo said, "Yes, in a bit, after I finish tapping your brain."

Michelle wondered, "OK, what do you need?"

Kosmo clued her in. "I know that you have more connections than anyone I have ever met in the Boston PD."

Michelle smiled to herself and said unabashedly, "Well, I can't argue with you on that point!"

Kosmo, feeling a little behind the eight ball on this request, asked Michelle, "Can you put out some feelers on the following names? One is Caselli and one is Dagobert."

Michelle repeated them. "Caselli and Dagobert?"

Kosmo confirmed them. "Yeah. Anywhere from New York to Maine."

Michelle questioned him again. "Caselli? Do you know how many Italians with that last name must reside in New England? Hmmm, and, Dagobert, well not so much. That is a more unusual name for this region."

Kosmo explained, "I know it's a long shot, but if I could get a printout faxed to me in the next few days, state-by-state, and you might as well add New Jersey to the list, it might impact something in my search."

Michelle was glad to help out her former colleague. "Consider it done! Let me patch you through to the commissioner. He is going to be thrilled to hear from you! Don't get a big head, but your name comes up all the time around here!"

After meeting with the chief and Tom Kendrick, Mark went into his office and shut the door. He quickly dialed up Beth at home. "Hey, Chickee-poo," he said when she answered, "old Marky boy here, your little red rooster!

What do you say to me coming over later on? I can bring some caramel popcorn, and we can snuggle up on the couch and toss it into each other's mouth. Every time one of us misses, we have to give the other one a kiss?"

Someone replied, "Well, I hate to disappoint you, but Chickee-poo Beth is not home yet. And I am trying to lay off the sugar so I don't think tonight's a good time.

Mark almost dropped the phone in surprise. He firmly asked, "Who is this, and what are you doing answering Beth's phone?"

"Well, Mr. Big Red Rooster, Chickee-poo Beth asked me over, and she's running late. She told me just to wait inside for her."

Feeling flustered and confused, Mark demanded, "Well, who the heck IS this?"

The voice replied teasingly, "I will give you a hint. If you guess wrong, well, you have to buy me lunch at the Pharmacy."

Mark, feeling annoyed and embarrassed, growled into the phone and hung up. "The nerve of her! Just wait until I get in touch with Beth!"

Mike DiFronzo had followed Mark to his office and was standing outside the partly closed door. He heard the word caramel and popcorn in the same sentence and started salivating. He nudged the deputy's door open and said, "Hey, Deputy, I overheard you talking about caramel popcorn! That's one of my all-time favorites! They used to carry it at the Dreamland Theater, but now they switched over to Cracker Jacks which are OK but not as good as the caramel popcorn they had before. But, hey, you have to remember-at least with the Cracker Jacks you get some peanuts and a prize! I usually save the prize and mail it off to my nephew. He really enjoys them!" Mike stood looking like an expectant puppy waiting for a pat on the head.

Mark looked up and glared at Mike. "What do you want? Why are you standing in my doorway? Do you have some official police business to discuss?"

Mike stood there without replying, dreaming about caramel popcorn.

Mark fired it up on two engines. "See, that's it! All you want to do is talk about food! Food this, and food that. Well, just to let you know, while you are sitting out there at the front desk you represent Nantucket and everything it stands for! What do people see when they walk into this department of law and order? A desk full of crumbs, candy wrappers, chocolate milk containers, sandwich wrappers, potato chips! I mean, this is how you represent this fine department?"

Mark took a quick breath and went on, trying to put Mike in his proper place. "Let me tell you something! I am headed out for some real police work, undercover, almost espionage stuff! Kosmo entrusted me to complete a task, and that's what I am going to do! Not like you who just wants to pick up the phone and order a pizza!"

Mike continued to stand there, actually while leaning on the door jamb, and acted like everything was just normal. He then asked Mark, "Speaking of pizza, who do you think makes the best pizza on the island?"

"Pizza, schmitza! Enough of your junk food talk. Go back to your desk, clean it up, and don't say another word to me. I've got more important things on my mind. And, if Beth calls here, just tell her I'm out." Mark glared at him and got ready to head out. Mike ambled back to his desk, thinking it was almost lunch time.

Mark went home to change. Even though Kosmo had said wait a day to investigate, he wanted to get some action going. This new information of an out-of-the-way cottage, and possible squatters, well, they were not going to sneak under the eyes of Deputy Donato! No way, no how!

Mark suited up. He put on his camouflage coveralls. He had his night vision goggles and his camouflage helmet adorned with pine tree trimmings which kept falling off. He laced up his combat boots and was headed out to catch the no-good squatters red-handed in the act!

Right as he shut his front door, he could hear the phone ringing. Back inside he went. He picked up the phone to a, "Hey, Marky, it's your Chickee-poo. I heard you called."

Mark barked into the phone, "I'll Chickee-poo you!" and hung the phone up abruptly.

At her house Beth had a puzzled look on her face when she replaced the receiver in its cradle.

Mark was fuming, turning all shades of red. First that dweeb DiFronzo and now this Chickee-poo woman, friend or no of Beth's, it didn't matter. Mark sped away fast from his apartment when he realized he had left his camouflage helmet and had to return to his apartment.

This time he was ready and started making his check list to himself. Mace, check. Billy club, check. Pistol, check.

Bullet proof vest, check. Walkie-talkie, check.

As he was on the way to Surfside Road he ran out of gas! Flustered as he was, he then realized he did not have any cash on him to refill the gallon can in the trunk. As he was pondering what to do, Duke from the hardware store pulled up. Seeing Mark all outfitted in camo clothes he advised him, "You know, son, hunting season is two weeks away."

Mark replied as confidently as he could, "Well, Duke, it's good to see you. I was just going to do some early scouting in this area. Say, I happened to have run out of gas. I have a can in my car. Wondering if you could run into town and get me a gallon? I'll stop by the store soon to repay you."

Duke agreed, and Mark waited for him to return. It gave him a chance to come up with a strategy or two in his surveillance work ahead.

MYSTERIOUS HAPPENINGS IN THE JARDIN DES TUILERIES, PARIS

There is a darker history hidden behind the beauty and attraction of this garden in France. Queen Catherine hired Jean L'écorcheur to assassinate political foes after the death of her husband, Henry II. Due to his unsavory line of work in her service, Jean was savvy to many of the Queen's secrets, a situation that Catherine wasn't comfortable with. She employed a man name Neuville to murder Jean, which he did – in the Jardin des Tuileries. Soon, the specter of Jean was seen in the garden, and he became known as the Red Man of the Tuileries. He was seen by numerous individuals, including Neuville, who some say witnessed Jean's ghost shortly after his death, covered in blood. Apparently, Jean delivered a final message to the Queen through Neuville, stating that he would haunt Queen Catherine for the rest of her life.

Other notables who have seen the 'Red Man of the Tuileries' include Marie Antoinette and Napoleon Bonaparte. It is believed that encountering this apparition is a portent of tragedy that shouldn't be taken lightly.

Kosmo pulled out his short list and kept thinking that something would get his mind to discover of some type of clue in this mysterious murder. But nothing, nothing at all. He reviewed his short summary of the topic of scepters that he had made in the library, but that was not really any help.

He drove out to visit Wendy and Nancy. One thought was bothering him. If nothing was stolen, or at least he still believed so, from Bob Tonkin's, home, warehouse and antiques store, and the prowler, who was twice at the girls' home where nothing was stolen, was there any connection?

The girls were in the barn working away. Kosmo admired their work and told them how Judy was thrilled with the window boxes they had put up at Hatch's.

They had a nice short conversation, and Kosmo wondered if possibly the intruder was looking to steal their expensive copper? Nancy told Kosmo that at the time of detecting the stalker and the break in, they had not started their 'reserve collection' using the copper linings, so that could not have been the reason.

Wendy and Nancy, between themselves, believed that the whole situation tied into the discovery of the

Scepter, but they were not going to put forth that information as of yet. they were still having a hard time trying to figure out how such a person ever found out that they had unearthed it, as no one but Nick, JoAnn, Bob Tonkin, and themselves knew about it. One thought they had tossed around was that possibly Bob mentioned something about it prior to finding out how rare the scepter was, and a person overheard it, but that was about as best of a guess as they could come up with.

They told Kosmo they hadn't had any suspicious activity around their house recently, and that they appreciated him coming out that way to touch base. They assured him they would contact the station if they saw anything else of concern.

Deputy Donato, as soon as his car was gassed up with the help of Duke. He parked about twenty yards past the dirt road turn off and suited up. He made his way slowly to the muddied dirt road. After about a minute's walk he slipped on his night-vision goggles. He did not have them adjusted quite correctly over his nose, and they started fogging up. He was about to readjust them so he could see where he was walking, but as he was not watching his footing he fell head over tea kettle into a large deep mud puddle, covering his goggles and the entire front side of his camouflage outfit! As he was trying to stand up his foot slipped again, and down he went, face first! He was covered in mud, and he did not have any rags to clean his goggles which were now smeared inside and out with mud. Mark was cursing the saints, saying to himself, Enemy camp, is going to have to wait. Abort mission, abort mission! He headed home, trying not to get the mud all over his car seat.

Nick and Rolf met the driver in the lobby at nine the next morning. He had another person with him due to the location to which they were headed.

The associate, Pascal, said, "Les Saintes Marie was not a dangerous area, but it's full of gypsies, and they are a strange bunch-almost kind of eerie, or spooky people. They train at an early age as children to learn the art of pickpocketing tourists, and if they succeed you have about a zero chance of seeing your belongings ever again.

They have the whole town mapped out with secret alleys they run off into. The thief usually dumps the wallet or watch or whatever they have managed to lift off one's person, quickly to another look-out. So, if the original person is apprehended, he has nothing on him. Therefore, it cannot be proven he is a thief. They are clever, very clever!"

Pascal said he would be with them the entire time and Jean would remain with the vehicle.

They arrived and Rolf told Pascal, that even though this could be like finding a needle in a haystack they were going to give it their best. They told Pascal that Rolf was doing a research paper on 'Gypsy life' and was referred to a man that goes by the name of 'Draper'.

Pascal recommended that they possibly find a bar, run by a gypsy, enter and ask the bartender if he might know of a man named 'Draper' in Saintes Marie. They first walked along a couple of streets, and the beggars were nonstop. One young boy, about twelve years old, would not give up asking for a few francs.

Nick said, "Hold up for a minute, Rolf." He then asked Pascal if he could tell this young gypsy kid he would give him two francs, which was about the equivalent of twenty cents, if he could locate a man by the name of 'Draper' then Nick would double that amount.

Pascal gave the young man the francs, and off he went. Pascal whistled for the kid to return, saying they would be in the bar across the street waiting.

Then Rolf said, "Let's try this," nodding across the street. "We go in there to that bar, Papillion, and spread the wealth very quietly with the bartender. Let's offer him twenty francs, which is about what, two American dollars, and see what happens."

They entered, and the dark smoky atmosphere reminded both of the travelers of the Demons Pub in Rungis. Pascal spoke with the bartender and gave him the twenty francs, asking that if he could spread the word about finding a man named 'Draper'.

The bartender took the money and said, "If I put out feelers, it might also take a donation of twenty francs to one or two of my assistants."

Pascal relayed that message to Nick and Rolf. Nick who was thinking that a bribe could run up to fifty dollars, nodded and said, "Let it roll." As of now they had two feelers out for a total outlay of two dollars and twenty cents!

The bartender, Motshan, was on the phone instantly putting out his feelers. He was also eying the trio and realizing there were definitely two well-heeled men in the party. He wondered why they were seeking a local man. But a little pay-off went a long way.

They ordered two bottles of beer, and Pascal had a bottle of water. After about thirty minutes a big burly man entered the bar and spoke with Motshan. He signaled for Pascal to approach the bar.

After a brief conversation, Pascal said to Nick and Rolf, "This guy at the bar knows a man named Draper who works at a small shop his family owns a few blocks from here. He wants twenty francs."

They agreed, settled up for the beers with Motshan and gave him the extra twenty francs.

Five minutes later, when they approached the shop, the man asked for his twenty francs. Pascal wisely said, "As soon as I confirm that this information is true, I will hand it over and not a moment sooner."

Pascal stepped into the store, then exited the shop and paid the man. This was the correct shop. Draper was on an errand but would return soon. The shopkeeper's assistant asked the men to come in, but not out of the kindness of her heart as she was hoping to make a sale.

However, the men remained outside, watching the pedestrians walking the cobblestone street. There was no shortage of gypsy beggars: some sitting on an old blanket, some with dirty children for more of an effect, some with a small cup for spare change. Pascal told Rolf and Nick that some of these beggars go home at the end of the day to a very nice apartment.

Ten minutes later after Rolf and Nick had strolled the quaint narrow street, Pascal signaled them to return. Draper had appeared back at the shop. Nick and Rolf entered along with their guide.

Deputy Donato went home to clean up and regroup. He wiped off his goggles, his helmet and binoculars. Using a damp cloth, he cleaned as much mud off his shoes and camouflage jump suit as he could, and he was back on his mission. This time he drove in slowly until he had the house in sight but parked where he thought his car would not be detected. He exited it quietly with his gear in hand or attached to his outfit.

There was a red pick-up truck parked out front. Mark snuck up ever so quietly and felt the hood which was warm. He approached slowly and cautiously, ducking low and went around the perimeter of the building.

The windows were all covered over with bed sheets, but one window off to the side had just enough of an opening where the sheet rested on the inside ledge to give him a view of the cottage interior.

As he was trying to get a better look, another car arrived. This time he peered around the corner and he saw a blue pick-up truck with a man bringing in some plastic garbage bags. Mark froze. He started shaking, thinking, "They have a body in there! Most likely after they tortured the poor soul they were going cut to him up!"

He started patting his chest: Bullet-proof vest, check; gun, check; mace, check; radio, check! He thought to himself should he call for back up. No, not this time! He was going to do this solo! He was not going to share this story with anyone else trying to get in on his spotlight. He envisioned the newspaper headlines:'Deputy Donato captures two of the most ruthless murderers Nantucket has ever encountered, single handedly!!'

Boy, wouldn't that make it into *True Crime* magazine! Maybe his picture would land on the magazine's cover! They would probably pay big dough for that story and, as an 'exclusive feature' they might add a few action photos of him and his trusty pistol, 'Old Betsy.'

Mark took a deep breath and sprang into action! He took a few paces back and started to charge at the front door. There was a slight miscalculation as the door was not fully shut, and when he hit it with the added weight of the bullet-proof vest and his momentum, he tripped as the door flew open! He went crashing on to the floor and knocked over a green

Hunter Laroche

five-gallon bucket that was full of fish heads and bones and general fish gut slop! The bucket actually tipped over sideways, completely covering him with the terrible smell of decaying fish guts.

The two men who owned the pickup trucks just stood there looking in total amazement at what had just happened. Mark was trying to untangle himself from all the fish bones and the stench, when one guy said, "What the heck do you think you are you doing here? What a mess you made, you stupid hunter! This is private property and hunting season has not even officially opened up for the season! You've got some explaining to do, not to mention cleaning up this mess!"

Mark had not a clue on how to respond. He was trying to think as fast as he could, but the stench of the fish guts all over his camouflage jump suit and his goggles all covered in the fish slime, caused him to mumble some excuse. He lamely said, "Well, um, I am really sorry but I knocked and you guys did not answer. The door was kind of wedged shut, and when I used my shoulder, the door gave way and, well, here I am. All I wanted was to ask for a drink of water."

The same man barked, "Get your tail off the floor and get that fish slime and yourself out of this cottage! This is my aunt's property, and now you went and mucked it all up!"

Mark rose off the floor and almost fainted with the odor of the fish guts. He stumbled outside, and once again found himself covered with disgusting material.

He made his way back to his car and knew that there was no way he could drive back wearing the camouflage outfit. He would never get the odor out of the cloth seats! He had to remove his outfit completely. He opened the trunk of the car and, standing off by the passenger's side, he removed his shoes to get out of the jumpsuit. He was looking for on-coming cars, as when he removed the jump suit, all he had on underneath were his boxers and a tee shirt and socks. He was going to have to drive home in just that.

Mark managed to get out of the jumpsuit almost completely, but when he put his sock foot down, he stepped into a pile of burrs! Now he was hopping around as they pricked his foot quite badly. He had one leg still in the jump suit but he was almost naked to the world! A car approached him driving down Surfside Road, and he had to duck behind the side of his car. In doing so he fell over and landed, as one would guess, into more burdocks. To make matters worse there were some ants crawling up his legs!

After doing his best to get the ants off his leg and trying not to step on the foot with the burrs in it, after a few minutes leaning on his car he managed to get his other leg free from the jumpsuit. He was still feeling rather nauseous from the stench of the fish guts that were now soaked into his camouflage outfit. He quickly tossed all the gear and his jumpsuit into the trunk. He was still in his stocking feet and was almost as naked as a jay-bird. He looked around and did not see any cars approaching. He feeling quite chilled from being undressed in the elements so close to the ocean. He ran around to the driver's side door, and then the terror entered his brain! The car was locked and so were his keys inside of the trunk in the jumpsuit!

He turned around, only to see a black pickup truck about twenty feet away, Mark was in direct line of the truck's high beams. He was trapped! He was frozen like a deer in the headlights! The truck pulled right up and Mark was lit up like being on stage. He could not move and he thought he was going to faint. He mumbled something like *'Mommy, make the bad people go away!'*

Sean Divine and Colin Keenan, two local young fellows who loved to tease and heckle the deputy, were bursting with laughter! They could not control themselves! Colin had tears rolling down his cheeks. They could not believe their luck! They could blackmail the deputy for years to come to get out of paying parking tickets or being stopped for drinking and driving above the speed limit - all sorts of stuff! It took them several minutes to stop laughing, and then they would roar right back into a hysterical fit.

They were just about to get Mark into the back of their pickup with an old blanket to cover him up, but at first Sean called out, "Well, Deputy Dawg, I don't think we can give you a lift. As you see, we have been drinking and we also have two open containers of beer in the car and you might arrest us!"

Mark was shivering and mumbled, "No arrest, no arrest! Just let me in the truck, you two characters."

They drove him home, but they would not release him until he promised that he would clear up any past parking tickets and stated if he stopped them for any reason, he was to let them go, and no traffic citation was to be written. Mark quietly agreed and managed to get into his apartment without anyone being the wiser.

Colin and Sean were hooting and hollering when they drove away.

Mark could not believe his bad luck that entire day. And, he realized, he would miss the staff meeting. The chief would be wondering where he had gone. Oh, well, he had a lot to face when he went out the next day.

THE HAUNTED BASTILLE OF FRANCE

As prison fortresses go, The Bastille was one of the more impressive ones. It had eight towers reaching as high as 80 feet as well as fortifications that included a bastion located to the east of the fortress and a surrounding moat. Construction began on the Bastille in 1357, and it was declared a state prison in 1417. The Bastille was home to a number of famous prisoners including Voltaire and the Marquis de Sade. The French Revolution saw the end of the Bastille. It was destroyed on July 14th, 1789, but some of the ruins can be found on Boulevard Henri IV while its original location hosts the Place de la Bastille. There are numerous reports of ghostly encounters at both locations, with visitors noting unusual smells, sensations of fright and unease, and the sighting of ghostly apparitions.

Mark awoke the next morning still shaking from the nights prior experience. He had terrible nightmares all through the night. In his first dream he was in the pinchers of a big red fire ant. Then, in the next dream, he was falling into a pit containing thousands of burrs piercing his skin from every angle. In the third dream, Mark was being chased on dry land by a huge catfish, whose jaw had a double row of upper and lower teeth.

In the final dream was he was laying on an old wooden table. Some old creepy dirty-bearded man with a big fat belly wearing a terrible smelling grungy tee shirt with holes in it was getting ready to filet him like a fish.

As he sat up, he was prayed that Colin and Sean would keep their promise that if he fixed their tickets, they would be true to their word and remain silent about the whole matter.

Kosmo entered Mignosa's Market right as Don and Rita were headed out with Daisy, saying they were taking the next boat and up to Boston for a few days. Kosmo sat at a booth at Les's Lunch Box and ordered a coffee and a corn muffin.

Les politely inquired, "Any new developments on the case?"

Kosmo said he was working on a few things and left it at that. Les brought him the muffin and coffee along with the *Boston Globe* that was three days old.

Two men entered and sat directly in back of Kosmo's booth. They ordered blueberry muffins and coffee.

One of them said, "What a bozo that hunter was, busting into my aunt's cottage knocking all that fish slime everywhere! Man, that clown, he was coated in it. I tell you, he is never going to get that stench out of his clothes. Serves him right!"

The other man mused, "Who was that jerk? And didn't he even know he was on private property?"

His friend replied, "My aunt's family has owned that cottage forever, and there are 'No trespassing' and 'No hunting' signs posted all over the place. If we knew who he was, we could even press charges. But I think he got his due, all right."

They continued their conversation. "And what was that clown wearing? He had a helmet with some kind of tree branches hanging off it, then the night vision goggles, and he had a camo jumpsuit on. You'd think this clown was in 'the special forces', except he could not even manage to stand up rolling and sloshing around in all that fish slime!"

His buddy joked, "He will most likely shoot himself easier than a deer! I hope he doesn't come around the cottage ever again!"

Kosmo heard the whole story and thought, another fun Nantucket adventure! His ears perked up when one of the guys said, "It's a great place, my aunt's cottage. A private five acres of land, and about a four-minute walk to Surfside Beach if you just stay on the dirt road. No one has been at the cottage since the end of August. And I don't think anyone will stay there until next July. It's the only time it's ever used."

Kosmo paid his tab and stopped over at the booth where the two men were talking.

He introduced himself and said, "Excuse me, but I overheard some of your conversation about the hunter bursting into their cottage. If you don't mind me asking, exactly where is it was located?" Then he asked, "Would you be willing to relay the story in more detail to me?" which they did happily, almost like it was written into a play.

He then knew the whole story, thanked the men and departed.

Mark took the extra set of car keys and rode his bike out to where his car was parked. The seagulls were circling it as they could smell the decaying fish guts that were all over his camouflage outfit.

He opened the trunk to place his bike inside when he was just about knocked over by the terrible odor. He felt ready to vomit. No way could he place his bike in that trunk, so he shut it quickly and rode back to town.

Mark entered the station to find Kosmo at his desk.

Kosmo asked him in so they could discuss the daily log from the night before. Kosmo then asked Mark if he wanted to stop by Souza's Seafood Market, and he started to turn green. Kosmo explained that Mrs. Sousa had some fish that she wanted to donate to the Island Home, and she had some really nice fresh filet of bluefish. She had said it was good stuff, but as we all know, bluefish doesn't keep too long, and the smell of it, raw or cooked, can leave an odor in your kitchen for days. Mark was now looking for a waste basket just in case his insides decided to blow out.

Mark kept his head and suggested, "You know, Chief, that might be a good job for Mike DiFronzo as he likes food." Mark really wanted to stay away from this little scenario. He still had his car and clothes to deal with, and any more fish situations would turn him off seafood for the rest of his life!

Kosmo shrugged and replied, "Well, unfortunately, one thing Mike does not enjoy is seafood. He says the stench of it makes his stomach turn."

Mark was not so far behind old Mike, thinking he could not ever eat it again. Then, after a few minutes, Mark's color started to come back to his face ever so slowly.

They finished the reading of the log, and Kosmo said, Hey, where were you at staff meeting time yesterday?"

Mark snapped to and explained that he wasn't feeling too well so went home and took a nap. By the time he woke up his shift was over. He apologized to Kosmo for not informing him.

Hunter Laroche

Kosmo kept up his joke, having put two and two together. "Oh, that's OK, Mark. Next time, just check out with someone. Say, do you want to join me for lunch at Faregrounds? Today's special is fish and chips, with free second helpings if you'd like. You know how good that place smells on 'Fish and Chips Day.' The whole place smells like fried fish!"

Mark almost lost it on that one, and he could not stand up fearing he might faint. But his boss persisted.

"Or," Kosmo added, "I could swing over to Chins and pick up some sushi. They have some great raw salmon sushi and some striped bass Hamachi. They might even have some raw eel sushi. That stuff is delicious!"

Mark ran out of the room and collapsed at his desk.

A few minutes later Beth arrived and said she was just down at the A&P and picked up dinner. She was going to bake some of Mrs. Paul's fish sticks for dinner. Mark started to turn pale.

Beth walked out and said, "See you at six for dinner."

Nick and Rolf stood next to Pascal when he was speaking with Draper. He was translating the fact that Rolf was doing a research paper on gypsy life, and they wanted to know if it was true that there was such a place in Provence where one could actually see a live Golden Boar. The man was quite hesitant in responding, thinking that these men might be possibly from the police and were setting him up in some kind of a trap. What kind of trap he was unsure of, but he started to clam up.

Rolf and Nick both sensed this, so Nick pulled Pascal aside and said, "Let the cash game begin. Start off with fifty francs which is a grand total of ten dollars."

Draper saw the fifty francs and seemed to ease up a little bit. Pascal said to him, "You know, there's nothing wrong about inquiring about seeing a wild boar in person."

Now Draper figured if these men were willing to offer fifty francs to see a wild boar, he did not want to lose the opportunity at hand. So, he explained to Pascal that Golden boar were very rare. He did not know if these men were from some carnival and planned to steal the wild boar from the owner and put the rare animal on display.

Pascal translated the message to Rolf and Nick, and Rolf removed his wallet which was under a sweater in a button-down pocket. He removed his college professor's identification card from Oxford University, England. Pascal showed it to Draper who seemed to become even more relaxed.

Nick whispered to Pascal, "Double the offer up to one hundred francs." Nick knew it was about twenty USD.

Draper realized two things: that if these guys were offering that amount, 1 they must not be police, and the fact that the one guy had a college professor's ID, that they might offer more money for the information

He also knew that they could most likely find the information on where to locate a Golden Boar with a little more searching, and he would be kissing that money goodbye.

Nick again whispered to Pascal, "Well, it's either put up or shut up time. Let's make like we are finished here and will try another avenue."

Pascal said to Draper, "Thank you for your time, but we will look someplace else."

Draper, seeing the men start to turn around, blurted out, "Add another fifty francs and I will tell you!"

Pascal shook his head and said, "I think we are done here. He then told Nick, "He is trying to squeeze you for another fifty francs."

Nick had no problem adding to the last quote or to even go much higher but figured, this is like a poker game let's see who bluffs first.

Draper was now starting to squirm a bit, for if he let fifty francs just walk out the door, he was a fool. The standoff remained for a few moments, and Nick said, "Tell him we are leaving. It is his last chance."

The men turned to walk away, and Draper now acted as though he was one of their best friends, telling Pascal that he was only joking, and of course he would give them the information they sought.

Pascal also stated that if the information he delivered to them was false, that his uncle was in code enforcement in Marseille, and Pascal could cause all sorts of problems for his shop and the surrounding shops, and furthermore, he would let it be known that it was Draper who brought all this heartache on them.

Draper said he was a man of honor. Pascal had to do his best to keep from laughing and keep a straight face.

Pascal nodded and nodded for him to proceed.

Draper took a piece of paper and a pen and told Pascal that they would have to travel to a very small village up in the mountains north of Nice named Peillon. It was about a one-hour drive or less. He advised that one will need to use caution as it's a medieval village with very rocky soil and the roads are almost unpassable unless you're a mountain goat. A four-wheel drive automobile is recommended.

He then gave them this information. "You are to seek out a local herdsman. His name is Silvanos. He's a very secretive man, so one will have to use caution. I will hand write you a note which will help to open the door for further discussions." He wrote the note, they paid Draper, thanked him and left.

Upon returning to the hotel, they both showered to get rid of the smell on their bodies from the Papillion pub they had visited earlier on. Then they regrouped in the lobby lounge for a quick snack consisting of a quiche jambon, and a salade verte.

Rolf chuckled at their negotiating process, and commended Nick on holding strong by not offering up another fifty francs, a whopping ten dollars!

Rolf then told Nick that the restaurant at the hotel, the 'Chantecler', was world renowned, and if Nick would like to split the cost of a dinner there, he would be up for it.

Nick quickly accepted under certain terms.

"What is that?" asked Rolf.

"That I sponsor the dinner," was his reply.

Rolf started to protest, but Nick said, "Look, did you see me negotiate the deal with Draper? There is no way you are going to beat me in this negotiation!"

Reservations were made. They further discussed the route on which this supposed clue would lead them. But it truly seemed that they just might be onto something.

Dinner was booked at eight p.m. Nick wore the same outfit he had at Clos de Tart minus the pullover and scarf.

As jacket and ties were required the manager said that they would send a cleaned pressed sport coat and tie up to Nick's room within the hour.

Even though it would be late in Boston, Nick placed a call to JoAnn. A phone was by their bed, and she never minded getting a late call from him. He detailed the entire day's events around finding and meeting with

Draper and how he was now a top negotiator. He laughed, and she said it didn't surprise her one bit.

He then said the plan for the next day was either sink or swim: to find the pheromone oil from a Golden Boar. He finished the phone call saying he and Rolf, who had offered to pay his own way, were dining at the Chantecler Restaurant which was located at the hotel and was one of the most highly regarded restaurants in the world.

JoAnn, knowing Nick's gentlemanly ways, asked "You did not accept his offer to split the cost of the meal, I hope."

Nick only offered to describe the meal in full detail the next time he called. He asked how business was going and told her how much he missed her. He was hoping to return in a reasonable length of time.

The fellow travelers met at the entrance of the restaurant precisely at eight p.m. They were seated a few tables back from the large fireplace which lent a nice ambiance to the restaurant. The maître d' explained to them that if they were too close, he would happily reseat them as the temperature could get quite hot. However, for the time of year, they were content with its comfort.

They started with Rolf's suggestion of white wine kirs, made properly with the Aligote wine, not Chardonnay as many a place incorrectly makes it. The wine list was massive, to say the least. Nick wanted to look but felt it might take him a good hour to select a wine.

The wine steward returned to their table, and Nick told him they would like a nice red Burgundy, and if they possibly might have a Clos de Tart as friends of theirs were the owners. They relaxed and wanted to take their time. The ceiling must have been thirty feet high, and the ambiance was breathtaking. Rolf described more of the history of the hotel dating back to 1751.

Their meal courses began. They each started with escargot, then they relished a sliced breast of duck with a mild plum sauce. The entrée was a châteaubriand of tenderloin with a bounty of fresh grilled vegetables. It came with a selection of bearnaise and marchand de vin sauces. They managed a small assortment of local cheeses, and for dessert a warm tarte Tatin served with some crème fraiche. Rolf commented that the dessert was named for the Tatin sisters who created it at their hotel in the Loire Valley. Despite their fine repast, dessert disappeared as quickly as the wine!

Hunter Laroche

ONE OF THE MOST HAUNTED CITIES IN THE WORLD: SIGHISOARA, ROMANIA

Few the of most haunted cities in the world have a history quite like this Romanian town. Sighisoara's claim to fame centers around one individual: Vlad the Impaler, the real-life inspiration for Dracula. This city was his birthplace, and visitors can now go on tours of his childhood home which features a nearby torture museum. Some say you can hear the pained screams of some of Vlad's victims piercing the dead of night.

Mark needed a way to get back to his car. Kosmo had already driven out to the dirt road on Surfside and saw his car sitting there. He was puzzled at this. Why would Mark's car be parked on the side of the road? He went back to town and, entering the station, he knocked on Marks door.

He said, "Hey, Mark, maybe we should take a drive out to 'Sconset and check things out. We have not been out there for a while."

Mark shrugged and said, "Sure, good idea."

Kosmo drove out the Polpis route. They made the loop through Codfish Park and headed back into town using Milestone Road. At that time of year, things tended to be very quiet, but it never hurt to just cover some of their less traveled territory from time to time. When they got to the Rotary, instead of heading into town, Kosmo went out to Fareground Road.

Mark asked, "So where are we going, Chief?" He was beginning to wonder if something was up.

Kosmo waited until they were just short of the turn onto Surfside Road. He told Mark, "I thought now that we are close by, we could check out the potential squatters at the cottage near Surfside Beach.

Mark quickly countered, "Oh, there's no need for that, Chief! It's on my list of things to do later on today." He started to sweat a bit, hoping he could deter his boss's plans.

But it was too late. Kosmo turned left, and a few minutes later with Mark sinking ever so low in the passenger's seat Kosmo said, "Hmm, that must be the dirt road that Mr. Kendrick described to us." Then he said, craning his neck a bit, "Hey! Isn't that your car parked there on the side of the road? What the heck?"

Mark sheepishly answered, "Well, you're right, Chief. It is." Mark gulped and got ready for a fast explanation. Kosmo, confirming his own suspicions after his time at the Lunch Box, asked, "Why is it parked there?"

"Well," Mark said, "I had put my bike in the trunk and rode all around the area. And I just got so carried away that I ended up riding home on my bike. I mean, I was really in the groove casing out the place. So, I figured that I could just pick up the car today or tomorrow. I tell you, nothing beats a great bike ride! I need to do it more often."

Kosmo then asked, "Why didn't you just ride your bike from your apartment if you were just going to do some initial surveillance?"

Mark stuttered a bit. He quickly countered, "Well, one time I was riding out here and I got a flat tire. It took me forever to walk the bike all the way home. I also never know if a call is going to come in to which I'll need to respond."

Mark did not realize that Kosmo had stopped and stood next to Mark's car. The chief could smell the rotting fish odor from ten feet away.

Kosmo then asked, "Do you have the keys? If so, you can drive it home now."

Mark agreed, "Yup, I have them."

So, wanting to get to the bottom of this smelly kettle of fish, Kosmo suggested, "While we're here, let's do this. We go knock on the door of the cabin and roust the squatters out if they happen to be there. You can take the lead, and I will just hang back. Then we can double back if we don't have any trouble, and you can pick up your car."

Mark hemmed and hawed a bit. "I am not ready to tackle the squatters just yet. I wanted to check out any comings and goings first. You know, get my bearings on the case."

Kosmo saw Mark squirming and said, "I guess that's a good way to approach the situation. OK, let's go get your car turned around in the Surfside parking lot." Then he asked Mark, "Why did you park here on the side of the road? It's only a quarter of a mile to the parking lot, a much better place to load and unload your bike." Kosmo was having a barrel of fun teasing Mark who hadn't a clue that he was onto the situation.

Mark was at a loss for words and said, "You can just drop me here and I can walk to the car. It's such a nice day."

Kosmo wrinkled up his face and said, "Nice day? It's misting a cold rain."

Once again Mark tried to think fast. "I know, but I have been reading a lot about Ireland, and, well, this weather makes me feel like I am out on the Irish moors."

Kosmo kept stringing him along and gently demanded, "No, I will take you to your car. And, oh, by the way, I have some safety flares I have been meaning to give you to put in the trunk of your car. We had an overabundance of them in the back storage area, and you never know when you might come upon the scene of an accident when you're in your personal vehicle. So, you pop the trunk, and I will load the box in there for you."

Mark was now starting to squirm again. He told Kosmo, "Thanks for the thought, Chief, but that is going to have to wait. You see, a few days ago I was fishing, and my waders and other stuff are still in the trunk, along with some seaweed tangled up in my rods. So, it needs to be cleaned and wiped out with some disinfectant. They're rather stinky."

Kosmo figured he had tortured Mark enough and said, "OK." But wanting to put in one more jab he said, "Hey, why don't you just stop over my house? It's right down the road. We can clean it out as I have lots of cleaning supplies."

Mark looked at his watch and replied quickly, "Wow! Look at the time! I have got to get moving! I told Beth I would pick her up and it's going to be cutting it quite close. She's probably already waiting for me."

"That's fine," Kosmo replied. "You don't want to get into any hot water with Ms. English!"

Nick and Rolf had arranged with Pascal to secure a more rugged vehicle for the mountain journey and to meet them at the hotel at nine a.m. the following morning.

He was waiting for them along with Jean who was with them on the previous day's adventure. They headed out for the village of Peillon.

Pascal alerted them that it would be slow going due to the narrow winding roads they would encounter the entire trip. But he guessed they should make it within an hour. They were climbing higher and higher, and during the climb they went higher than the low-lying fog. The region around Nice was cloudy when they left, but up in the higher elevation the sky was clear and the sun was shining brightly.

They arrived on the outskirts of Peillon and parked the car. Jean remained behind and Pascal said, "We are not allowed to drive into the village. So, they proceeded on foot. Rolf told Nick the night before to wear comfortable walking clothes as where they would be going was a medieval village, not like the streets of Beaune.

They walked into the quaint rustic village, and definitely no tourists were rushing about there.

They stood out from the local gypsy crowd, but not nearly as many beggars were on the small lanes in the town. They mainly received many quiet stares.

Soon they were inside the pub, yet again ordering a beer they really did not want. The pub was named Le Chevreau, and they put Pascal to the task of locating the goat farmer, Silvanos. The bartender gave them a look like he had no intention of offering up any information. Then he saw the twenty francs in Pascal's hand, which he was not waving around but held out just enough for the bartender to think maybe it was meant for him.

The bartender balked at the question, almost like he did not hear it correctly. But then, looking down at the twenty francs, asked, "For what reason are you inquiring about one of our people?"

Pascal told the barman, "We were referred to him by a friend of his, Draper, from the town of Les Saintes Marie." He then explained, "The gentleman with the beard sitting at the table is a professor who is doing a paper at the college of Oxford, England, on mountain sheep herders. He had six mountainous villages on his list in the Provence region to visit, and he wanted to interview this man, Silvanos. It would be just a short interview, and I will give the you twenty francs for your time." Pascal raised one eyebrow as if to say that's the deal.

The bartender said gruffly, "Make it thirty francs and I will tell you." Thirty francs exchanged hands, he provided some directions, and they headed out.

Nick said, "Well, he drove a hard bargain-an extra two dollars!" and started laughing.

According to the bartender's directions, they were to continue up the narrow lane to the top of the hill, about a quarter of a mile. Then the lane would split at the old schoolhouse with the lane going on either side of the schoolhouse. They were to take the right side and follow that a short distance to the small abandoned church which would be on their right. A very small passage would be directly past the church, and they were to take it to the very end. They would see a field on a grassy and somewhat rocky slope. Down to the left side they would see a small house, most likely with smoke coming out of the chimney. That is where Silvanos lives. It was his farm and land. The team headed out immediately.

Once they came within view of the house, Pascal said it might be best if he went there alone, first, so as not to spook the old gypsy, as the bartender stated that Silvanos was in his late seventies and lived alone.

Rolf said, "Please tell him that I am doing a research paper on the sheep herders of Provence, and I am allowed to compensate any interviews with thirty francs."

Pascal nodded and headed down the rocky path to the house.

Mark walked into the station with all sorts of real estate brochures and listings in his hand. Beth was at the dispatch desk, and she asked him what he had.

"Well, Sugar Pie, you're looking at the newest part-time employee of Kendrick's Real Estate Office!"

"Really? What's the scoop?" Beth asked

Mark nodded with bravado. "You got that right, Babe. You see I have been watching the real estate market for the last couple of months, and I keep abreast of the trends of buying and selling. I have been writing down the latest recorded sales for a few months. Yup, got it all in check. So, when

I told Mr. Kendrick the trend was moving up, he was quite impressed and asked me to keep an eye out for any possible listings. If I ever found someone in the market who is looking to purchase a home that I would get a referral fee." He brushed his knuckles on his shirt as if he had hit the lottery.

Beth looked up adoringly. "That's great! All you have to do is find a seller or a buyer and you get a referral fee?"

"Yup, easy as pie!"

Beth continued encouragingly, "I would love to see your notes on the real estate trends. You showed them all to Mr. Kendrick? And, by the way, wasn't he the fellow who came here the other day wondering about the squatters out by Surfside? Whatever happened to that situation?"

Mark was now fidgeting when Beth said, "Let me see them. Are they in that stack of papers you have? So, what is the biggest margin between the actual sales price and the asking price? Also, I would like to see the margins you have for how much one paid for the property they are selling. I think that is fascinating that you did all those calculations! Can you show them to me? I have plenty of time now to look them over." And she put out her hand.

Mark was now all wide-eyed, not thinking that Beth was going to actually want to see solid figures. And it just so happened that Kosmo was standing behind Mark and listening to the entire conversation. He walked over to the desk and sat down next to it. "This is pretty interesting stuff you're working on. I had no idea you were such a mathematical whiz. If you follow the uptick in prices closely, you will make a pretty nice little nest egg to retire on!" He looked over at Beth and back again at Mark, wondering how this would all play out with his somewhat entrepreneurial deputy.

Kosmo continued. "Now, show us the spread sheets and your margin numbers. I might have you do an estimated value of my house. Do you use your own formula or a pre-existing one for the margins on selling and buying? And do you mark the percentages in red for plus and black for minus, as they do in the stock market?"

Beth chimed in, "This is so way advanced! I am proud of you, Mark! I'll bet you can become the number one real estate agent on the island with your formula. I read somewhere that a lady also did some sort of formula. I forget what it was used for. I think it actually was in commodities, but I am not sure. But she sold it for big money to a company in the agriculture field. Wouldn't that be exciting if you could sell you formula to some big real estate firm?"

Mark had no idea that all this was going to develop into such a deep conversation. Luckily for him, right then the station's front door opened, and Mike DiFronzo walked in carrying a bag of doughnuts from the Downyflake.

"Hey, everybody! What perfect timing! I just picked up some doughnuts! I got some glazed, blueberry and cream-filled ones." He set the bag down on the counter and asked Beth if she could clear off the table to make room for coffee and doughnuts.

Mark, seeing this as a perfect diversion, said, "Well, Mike, that's great! Perfect timing as we are all here, and I could sure use a doughnut. I'll bet Beth is going to take one of the blueberry ones. You know, Mike, she loves them. Let me just get rid of all these papers, and we can make a little coffee party out of this!" Mark hurried into his office and placed all the real estate listings in his top desk drawer.

Mike spread out the doughnuts on the platter that was next to the coffee maker. Then he asked, "What were you all talking about?"

Kosmo nodded at Mark. "You are looking at the newest real estate baron of Nantucket!"

Mike, already biting into a glazed doughnut and getting the frosting all down his shirt, asked, "Really, Mark, you're moving into real estate? Are you going to do development?"

Mark wanted to change the subject, so he said, "I just started a fresh pot of coffee to go with these doughnuts. Who wants a cup?"

Mike confessed, "Well, these are a day old, but I tell ya, I can never tell the difference. My mom says 'a penny saved is a penny earned.'"

Mike then rambled on that last year he was thinking of taking the real estate classes at the Cape Cod Community College. He was going to take the boat over twice a week, but his mom did not like all the travel time involved. Furthermore, he would have to stay all alone at a motel, he would have to eat all his meals out and his mom would be at home by herself." He brushed a few crumbs off his shirt and concluded, "So, as of now, those plans are on hold."

Mike then asked Mark, "What are your big real estate plans? Are you going to open your own office?"

Beth stepped in to say that Mark had developed some new type of margin spread-sheets and he has been monitoring the ups and downs of the market trends. Apparently, Mr. Kendrick was really impressed by it.

Mark, again wanting to change the subject, said, "Coffee's ready."

However, Kosmo, having seen Mark undertake a variety of such ventures, and, not wanting this fun little game to end, said, "Well, I'll tell you what. I've also done some spread sheets regarding different crime spikes in Boston. But I was very fortunate as my secretary back then was quite brilliant with spread sheets, so I really could not take all the credit when it came time to present the data."

Kosmo turned to Mike. "Mark was just about ready to give us an official presentation of his new formula."

Mike offered, in an unusual gesture, "That's nice. Let me clear off the desk so you have some room to use."

Mark jumped into the conversation with some hesitation. "Well, it's not one hundred percent perfected yet, so let's just wait until I have it totally done and tested!" And, instead of hanging around for the coffee break, he said, "Enough of this chit-chat. I have got to go make my rounds." He put on his jacket and exited the station.

THE GHOSTS OF CANBERRA, AUSTRALIA

Way 'down under' in Australia, you may be surprised to find one of the most haunted cities in the world. Canberra, Australia's capital city, is full of terrifying ghost stories sure to thrill any supernatural enthusiast. For example, visitors to Canberra's Blundell's Cottage may want to leave their jewelry at home. Teenager Flora Blundell died in a fire in this cottage. As she was wearing a necklace at the time of her death, wearing a necklace seems to attract her spirit.

One of the most interesting of Canberra's haunted sites is the Hotel Kurrajong. In 1951, former Prime Minister Ben Chiffley was working in a room at the hotel when he died suddenly of a heart attack. According to numerous staff and visitors, the room where Chiffley's life ended has retained the former statesman's spirit.

Nick and Rolf watched Pascal from up top of the rocky path that led down to the small stone cottage. They saw him knock on the door and then walk around back side of the house. They figured that since no one answered the door that he might possibly be working out back. A few minutes later, Pascal gave them a wave to come down to the property.

Pascal explained to them that the note was presented to Silvanos, and Pascal had a quick glimpse of it. It seemed to be written in some Gypsy gibberish but told them it most likely said, 'Ask for more than they are offering.' He also said that Silvanos' face lit up slightly when the offer of thirty francs was presented to him.

Rolf spoke with Pascal and had him translate the fact that he had been doing research on the goat herders of Provence. After one such interview he learned that a Golden breed of wild boar could be found in the area of Peillon. Rolf wanted Pascal to please let him know that after a little more searching he was interested in talking with Silvanos as it was rumored that he might either raise them or know where Rolf could actually see one in person.

Rolf added to tell him that they would never reveal the fact to others if he could steer them in the right direction to actually observe such a creature. Rolf described what they supposedly looked like, with the yellow or golden hue around their eyes.

Rolf also said that he had thirty francs for the man for meeting with him, and Rolf offered to add some additional francs if they were able to take a photo of one. Again, Rolf repeated that they would never reveal the location of where the rare Golden Boar was located.

Silvanos thought for a moment and asked, "How many more francs?" which Pascal translated.

Nick and Rolf were ready for that question, but they did not want to seem overly anxious. They quietly talked amongst themselves and wanted to make Silvanos wait.

After a short time, Rolf spoke with Pascal who understood the whole negotiating scene that was transpiring.

Then Rolf spoke to Pascal and said, "Let's make him sweat a moment, then offer him twenty francs in addition." The total amount they had now offered was around ten US dollars.

Silvanos, also savvy to the game and not wanting to show his cards yet said, "It costs a lot to keep wild boar here, as the rocky terrain does not provide too much food for them. If a poor farmer was to raise one, it can be costly."

Rolf countered, "If you have a friend who might be raising one, we would be ever indebted if Silvanos could get arrange a meeting with him."

Silvanos figured he should take the total of fifty francs and get this show moving. He held still for a moment and said, "Make it sixty francs total, and I will make this happen."

Rolf responded, "We are not paying you yet if this involves another farmer as this bargaining could go on all week."

Silvanos shook his head. "No, I am asking a total of sixty francs, and the deal will be done with payment up front."

Rolf now knew that the boar was most likely on the premises, and added "To close the deal it must be completed today as we are headed to yet another area where a farmer was supposed to have a Golden Boar."

As Rolf was starting to look around Silvanos caught his roaming eyes. He quickly said "Yes, you will see one today, but before that you must come into my house. I wish to offer you some hospitality."

The three of them sat in a dingy small room with a wood burning stove with a pot of water sitting on top.

Silvanos left the room and brought back a pig's bladder filled with some sort of liquid. He poured Nick and Rolf each a small glass and told them they would have to drink it.

Rolf looked at Nick and shrugged, "We have gone this far, I guess we go along with the local customs." He asked Pascal to find out what the dark liquid was.

Silvanos quickly and firmly stated to Pascal, "It is a gypsy serum, and if red welts or spots appeared on either of the men's faces it would reveal that they had evil in their bodies! Thus, the deal would not proceed, but he would still be entitled to his original thirty francs."

Again, Rolf shrugged. "I have done a lot of crazy things in my life but drinking gypsy serum in the medieval village of Peillon is a first!"

"Ditto that!" Nick replied and said, "Now or never!"

They both drank the serum and waited. It tasted of burnt molasses and mushrooms, and it had some type of fern and fresh herbs that must have been stewing in the serum. Silvanos then left the room taking the glasses and the pig's bladder of serum with him. He returned and sat across from them, not saying a word.

Luckily, Nick and Rolf felt nothing happening to their bodies. Silvanos grinned, held out his hand and said, "Now pay me the rest of the francs!"

Nick laughed. "That was the easiest test I have ever passed, and I just hope I don't grow a third eye as finding reading glasses would be a problem!" Rolf smiled, also.

Silvanos indicated that they needed to follow him. They went through the kitchen to another room that looked like it was his larder for the winter months supply of food. At the back of that was a locked door. Silvanos removed a key chain from his pocket and unlocked the door. This led them down a narrow hall with uninsulated wooden walls. At the end of that hallway was another locked door.

Rolf commented, "Who knew a small country house could have so many locked doors? And, behind door number three is. . .?"

Pascal was directly behind them. Silvanos slowly used another key to unlock this door which opened to a large pen. It was totally enclosed with old wood but you could see the elements of the outdoors through a lightly thatched roof. The pen was about twenty feet deep by ten feet wide. Inside the pen were four large boars. Silvanos then told Pascal proudly, "These are prime Golden Boars. Each one is about four years old, and they are my prized possessions!"

The visitors stood in awe. Nick quietly commented, "It's amazing how all of this has transacted. I can hardly believe it!"

Rolf had been rehearsing this possible moment in his head for a few days. He pulled out a small note pad and pen. He asked Pascal some random questions to translate to Silvanos. Then he asked, "What actually makes the Golden Boar so priceless?"

Silvanos took the bait and replied, "The liquid they excrete through certain glands, naturally, is supposed to hold mystical healing powers. It is an oily excretion.

The price can go for as much as one hundred francs a milliliter!"

Rolf quickly figured out how much a half an ounce would cost and wrote the down the amount-around three hundred dollars.

Rolf then had Pasqual ask, "How much might a person usually buy?"

Silvanos held up his thumb and forefinger. "It's always a very small amount, just under a milliliter."

Rolf continued his questioning. "How does a person extract it from a boar, and how does one store it?"

Silvanos, gesturing, explained, "The boar is led into this very tight and strong slot. Two large bands of leather strapping are lowered and placed under the front and back area of the boar. Then the boar is hoisted up and swung over to the side. One has to milk it out of their glands. It is a slow and rather tricky process as the boar is strong and not happy to be so confined."

Again, Rolf asked, "How is the oil stored, and how long would it have as a shelf life?"

Silvanos told Pascal, "It has a very long shelf life due to the fact it is an oil. As long as the secretions are kept air-tight and not able to evaporate, then it retains its mystical strength."

Rolf inquired, "What is the best storage temperature for the secretions?"

Silvanos clarified, "It is fine to keep it cool or at room temperature, but not hot."

Rolf turned and spoke with Nick. He confided, "Here's the moment of truth. We need about a half an ounce or three hundred-dollars worth of the product. I want to handle this very gently. I am thinking we have gone this far, and, if we add a few more dollars to the offer for the half ounce he might take it. I was thinking that we go up to two thousand francs-that's about four hundred US dollars. What do you think?"

Nick nodded. "I think we need to secure it no matter what the cost is, as this is the end of the line. And, if the outcome is what we figure, for the one hundred units that old Joan of Arc is guarding, then that is a mere pittance to obtain the reward."

Rolf asked Nick even more quietly, "Do you have enough on you to cover the cost?"

Nick winked, "Despite being in gypsy territory, I could fund a small bank with the amount I am carrying."

Rolf nodded to Pascal and asked him to convey an offer. "Tell him we are quite interested in purchasing fifteen milliliters of the oil. We realize the time and effort that it will take Silvanos to milk the boar's glands. For that they will give him two thousand francs. However, he needs to know they will be departing from Provence very soon. We have the cash with us, and we will never reveal where we acquired the oil."

Silvanos eyes opened widely. He relayed, "That is a large amount of oil! But it is what it is, and it's your decision on how much you wish to purchase. I do have that much available, but it will pretty much wipe out my supply for the next few weeks."

Rolf thanked him heartily and shook his hand. "So, what is the next step?"

Silvanos told them that he wanted the francs in his hand. Then he would take them back to the living room, go to his supply cabinet and return bringing them the oil.

GHOST OF VERLATENBOSCH, CAPE TOWN SOUTH AFRICA

Cape Town is the oldest city in South Africa and one of the most haunted cities in the world. Visitors to Cape Town's Table Mountain should be wary of encountering the Ghost of Verlatenbosch. This spirit is said to be that of a man who angered the governor and was forced into exile on the mountain. Visitors can still hear the mournful sounds of his flute echoing through the air.

In addition, visitors to the coast might spot the ghostly image of the doomed 'Flying Dutchman' sailing the waters. This ship sank during a terrible storm off the coast and allegedly continues to sail the waters searching for safety.

Kosmo called Michele Volpe back at the Police Commissioner's office in Boston.

"Michelle Volpe, how may I assist you?"

"Hey, Michelle, it's Kosmo."

"Hey, there, Kosmo! Two calls in one week! We are going to have to be careful or people are going to start to talk!"

Kosmo laughed and responded, "You think they talk in Boston! Try this little island! You sneeze, and by the time it gets to town, they are saying you've died!"

"So, what can I do for you, Kosmo?"

"Well, I know your direct channels can probably get me a faxed list quicker than I can get one here. Can you get me a printout of the phone numbers called in the last month from these two numbers?" He read them off to Michelle.

"Sure, can do, give me a couple hours. I have your fax number and will send all of my findings of the two numbers you requested printed out. I will send them later on today. I hope it's helpful."

Kosmo replied, "So do I. Appreciate your work!"

He then retuned once again to Bob Tonkin's home. This time he was searching for Bob's personal address book. He found it, and started to look up names and addresses. He first started looking for 'Dagobert' but to no avail. Then he turned the pages to the letter 'C' for Caselli, but before he managed to open that section his radio went off.

"Base to Chief, over."

"Kosmo here, over."

"Chief, we have a report of a boat accident in the harbor from Ted Hudgins, over."

"OK, so what is the reason for the call? Over."

"Well, it turns out that the guy who caused the accident is being detained by Ted. He states the guy is being resistant and thinks he is under the influence. Over."

"OK, I am on my way. Over and out." Kosmo picked up the address book and took it with him.

Nick and Rolf received the thick small glass vile containing the pheromone oil and departed. They agreed they were carrying some 'liquid gold.' They thanked Pascal and his assistant for their fine work in the translating and transportation needs.

Back at the hotel it was just around one p.m. They reread the original clue. Rolf thought the best way to coat the oil on the hide would be to use a clean cloth, but it would be important to use one that did not have any cleaning additives in it. Thus, a hotel towel might not be the best option.

Nick offered to go down to the hotel lobby and check out the small gift shop. There he found a set of three white cotton handkerchiefs. He also purchased a small package of tissues.

Back in the room Rolf reminded Nick, "The skin needs at least twenty-four hours to lay flat and undisturbed in a dry warm setting. "OK," he asked, "who wants to do the honors?"

Nick graciously put out his palm and pointed, "It's all yours!"

Rolf unsealed the vile with the pheromone oil.

He chuckled. "I have heard of snake-oil salesmen, but this is the first pig pheromone-oil salesman dealing ever!"

Slowly he dampened the cloth and rubbed it ever so gently upon the animal hide. The hide absorbed the oil rather quickly. The hide was about eight inches by six inches. He figured with the way oil was being quickly absorbed, he had best use it sparingly. After completely covering the hide, he repeated it. That left them with just about enough to make a third covering of the hide, if needed.

Nick suggested, "Let's use it all. If it doesn't work, then we are done. However, you have to admit, it's been a strange and unusual ride!"

Rolf placed it on the desk which received some natural light, and he guessed it should dry the oil evenly.

Nick and Rolf regrouped thirty minutes later in the lobby to go out and find some lunch. Rolf hung the "Do Not Disturb" sign on his door as they did not want anyone coming close to their last effort to uncover the final clue and possibly destroying it.

When they returned from their casual lunch, no change had taken place yet on the hide.

Nick said, "There's the old proverb: a watched pot will not boil. Let's give it some more time."

From Boston, Michelle Volpe faxed five pages to the Nantucket Police Department.

Kosmo had finished up writing out a report with Ted Hudgins on the boater, who calmed right down when he saw Kosmo arrive.

Kosmo called Judy and asked her if she wanted to 'slum it' with him and meet him for a pizza. They met at Foood's, to the delight of the owner and chef, Johnny Acton. They ordered a large Caesar salad, and a sausage and mushroom pizza, which John said would be made personally by himself. Judy brought along a very nice bottle of La Breccesca Montepulciano which John enjoyed with them while they had the pizza.

John inquired about any updates on Bob Tonkin's murder. All Kosmo would say was that he was working on it, slowly but surely, and left it at that. John said he had to get back to the kitchen and thanked them for the wine.

Then Kosmo's thoughts switched channels, recalling something he noticed that morning. He bounced his thoughts off Judy

"I noticed Hunter, Eelskin and Krebs were down on the docks earlier in the day. When I was upstairs in Ted's office, I could see them coming off a fishing trawler. I thought to myself, 'What are these guys up to?'" He took another bite of pizza, wiped his mouth, and tapped his fingers on the table.

"Of course, I know a few things about that interesting trio. They are almost always together, and they never have once had caused any trouble except the altercation at the Rose & Crown when everyone was singing their praises for coming to the rescue of a 'damsel in distress.'"

Judy nodded as she munched on the tasty salad. "Yeah, they are a funny little group of guys, that's for sure."

"Well, I certainly keep an eye on them, and I have my suspicions, but why make unnecessary waves until the proper time calls for such action. The three of them seem to enjoy going to charity auctions and placing high bids for useful causes. And everyone who ever does business with them-auctioneers, restaurants, shop keepers including you, Judy-all have nice things to say about them as does the service industry staff. I just wonder what they really are up to, sometimes!"

Later in the evening, as Rolf and Nick enjoyed a glass of port by the large fireplace in the hotel's main lobby, they discussed their plans for heading back to Paris.

They both agreed that by one p.m. the following day it would be the end of the twenty-four hour time frame. If the clue was not revealed then, it most likely would never come forth. It was ten p.m. when they returned to Rolf's room and the hide was still blank.

Nick did have his heavy-duty magnifying glass on the desk and gave it a once over under the glow of the desk lamp. He told Rolf, "There's one small little black line that was not there this morning."

Rolf took a look and said, "Well, if that's our clue we are out of luck. It looks more like a cat hair has fallen upon the hide! We'll look at it again in the morning. We have done enough sleuthing for today, Sherlock!"

Kosmo and Judy were just finishing up when, lo and behold, the trio of men they had been discussing walked into Foood's. John Acton quickly greeted them like long lost friends. They were seated at the back round table in the corner. They saw Kosmo and Judy and gave a friendly wave.

Hunter pulled out two bottles of a French Bordeaux and said to Judy, "I bought these babies last week, and if we like them, I will have you order us a case!"

Judy said quietly to Kosmo, "I sure hope so! That's pretty pricey juice!"

Kosmo, almost not wanting to know, asked, "How much is a case?"

"About twelve hundred dollars total for both cases."

"Wow," Kosmo said, "too rich for my blood."

Judy continued, "Well, you know, Eelskin wanted to buy the two bottles of the Massetto wine I have in the cellar. I told him that was private stock and not for sale. He asked me if I could order him some, and I said it was on strict allotment but I would try. I am still waiting to hear back from my salesperson, and I might want to remind him it's been three weeks now. You and I had a bottle at the Languedoc a while back. I was turned on to it by Tracy at Cioppino's.

Kosmo nodded. "I remember! Great stuff, costly as well."

Judy nodded and added, "But if Eelskin is buying, I am in the business of selling!"

John returned to their table with two glasses of a red wine he said was from his personal stash. "It's quite different from what you just drank, but it's a nice Côtes du Rhone."

Judy nodded. "Ahh, one of my all-time favorites to fall back on, delicious stuff!"

Then he said, nodding towards the corner table, "You got to love those guys! The staff loves it when they come in to eat. They pay the corkage fee on each bottle, never squabble over the check and tip like it was their last meal. Even if they do take-out, they always leave at least a fiver if not more. Two weeks ago, they called in an order for ten pizzas to go and said it was for the Boys and Girls Club. They asked if I could have one of my staff drop it off, which I did. They came in the next day, paid the bill, per usual in cash and tipped the kid twenty dollars for dropping the order off. On top of that they told me to not say who it was from, just an anonymous donor. Now isn't that something?"

Kosmo chimed in. "I know, no one has a bad thing to say about them. I run into them at so many different places. I have known them since the day I arrived on Nantucket. They happened to be on the same ferry I was on with my car. They were seated close by the table I was sitting at, and Hunter, looked over and said 'Hello.' I said 'Hi' back, and we started up a conversation. One thing led to another, and they asked me what was bringing me to the island. I told them that I was moving down from Boston as I had accepted a job with the town. Krebs said 'Well, there are worse places in life to land. Eelskin asked me what position was it that I accepted, and Hunter said 'I bet I know!' So the conversation really got focused on what I was doing there, which of course, I now know is a classic discussion on this island."

Kosmo sipped some of the classy wine John had served them. "I then asked, 'What makes you say that?'

Hunter then nailed it which surprised me. 'Well, the new police chief arrives this week and is supposedly from Boston. And, well, you fit the type. I mean you don't look like a pencil pusher, and I doubt that you were hired for the town maintenance crew! Or, you could be the animal control officer, chasing dogs and horses all over the island, removing cats stuck up in trees!' and he started laughing. 'So, how did I do?' Hunter asked. 'Bravo!' I replied. 'Very good deducing skills. Maybe I should hire you as a detective.' Then Hunter, Eelskin, and Krebs all introduced themselves. At that point the announcement came over the loudspeaker that drivers were to return to their cars. So, I bid them goodbye and headed across the ferry ramp to my new home, the island of Nantucket, the Grey Lady!"

MORE ON THE HAUNTINGS OF CAPE TOWN, SOUTH AFRICA

The oldest building in Cape Town, the Castle of Good Hope, also has a variety of ghosts to tempt tourists interested in the supernatural A ghostly black dog is said to walk the grounds along with the spirit of Lady Anne Barnard, a noblewoman who still appears when important dignitaries visit. In addition, visitors often hear the sound of the bell in the castle's tower being rung, even though the tower was walled off centuries ago when a soldier hanged himself with the bell rope.

The next morning, Rolf dialed Nick's room at the hotel just as Nick was about to call him. Every so faintly the words of the clue seemed to be getting darker on the animal hide. It was still too faint to read, but, then again, two things were evident. First, the pheromone oil was working as it stated in the original clue! Secondly, if it was true to form as stated, they still had at least six hours to go until the proper time arrived for the clue to emerge.

They made arrangements for a late check-out and to board the two o'clock afternoon train to Paris. It would be about a seven-hour journey. They acted like two school kids in anticipation of Christmas morning. This was absolutely fascinating to them both!

Rolf said, "Can you imagine the fact that one: you are in the ownership of such a clue, the original one, and, secondly, you had the foresight to try and uncover the second clue? And how many years has it been hidden— 70 or so? If it actually transpires that the clue is revealed, this will be one for the history books! But, then again, you will not want to advertise the fact as all sorts of people will be coming out of the shadows, claiming that it rightfully belongs to their country! That's just one of the headaches that will begin. More likely than not, some state department head will get wind of it, and the tax man will as well! You had best be very low key on this."

Nick agreed. "If we pull out something worth selling, I will see to it that you get your percentage that we agreed on. It might take a while to sell whatever we uncover, but that's the next step."

Rolf suggested, "When and if this clue surfaces, I will take several non-flash photos of it, just in case it fades after a few minutes. I can develop the film in Paris."

Nick nodded and gave him the thumbs up. They went to the lobby and enjoyed breakfast. Yet both of them were excited and nervous, wondering if anything was going to happen. They agreed to go back upstairs, pack and keep a watchful eye on the animal hide.

Shortly, Nick was fully packed and left his luggage in his room. He joined Rolf, who was also packed, in his room. When Nick entered, Rolf was using the magnifying glass to read the light transformation on the hide. He dared not to touch the skin.

Nick was pacing the room, trying not to keep going over to decipher the faded clue.

Rolf calmly recommended, "Let's not make ourselves crazy by staring at it every few minutes." He handed Nick a magazine which was titled *Monte Carlo* and said, "Suffer through the million-dollar views in this magazine. It will help pass the time." Nick settled in a comfortable chair and tried to get focused on the magazine.

The time was approaching eleven when Rolf said, "The person who created this riddle - how could they know the timing for the pheromone oil to develop the clue unless it had been used in the past? Maybe an army wrote secrets in this manner so that, if agents were captured, they would not know anything about how to reveal them?"

Rolf laughed. He admitted, "Here I am trying to keep you calm, and yet this is killing me!" He went over to the hide. He exclaimed in a whisper, "Nick, come look! It's starting to appear, and I think I might be able to decipher it!" Holding up the magnifying glass he squinted and read softly, "Vos qui instar sicco bene tradendi non intelligimus sub ratione finalis clue nunc autem necesse est sequi ex originali clue et incipiens a catacomb ion es ambulare sex longe gradientem et lapis non altius quam quattuor ex censeo inferioribus locis constiterat, per Bethelem 'o' est in inferiore parte anguli recti. Supra et infra centrum removere lapis, et revelaverit turpitudinem ejus, et qui ad C condita est arca I aurum minuunt."

He stood still a moment, thinking about the words in front of him. He set down the magnifying lens and picked up his camera case. "Remember what I said about the words possibly fading? We have to capture this now!"

Rolf snapped a few photos then set down his camera. Continuing in a soft voice he shared with Nick, "Even though it's quite faint, it translates, to the best of my ability: 'You hath figured out the correct translation to understand the final clue. Now one must follow the original clue. Starting at the catacomb which you are in, you are to walk six long strides. On a stone to the left, not higher than a hand's width off the ground, one will see an 'O' in the lower right-side corner. Remove the stone above the center, and below you shall hath uncovered and found the hundred gold coin box."

The script remained ever so faint and was quite hard to read just as the case in the original faded clue. They were not really sure what to expect other than the intensity of the script would increase.

Nick exclaimed, "This is unbelievable! I can't for the life of me believe that we did it! Now we need to get to Paris and find out how to get into the catacomb area!"

He then wondered out loud, "One hundred ancient minted gold coins - what would the value be?"

Rolf ventured a guess. "Possibly a thousand dollars or more per coin, if it's a proper weight. That could possibly add up to $125,000. Not bad, not bad at all!"

Rolf was calculating a bonus of $2,500 in his head, and Nick knew he might realize a payment of $20,000, leaving the girls with roughly $100,000." He let out a low whistle. "Now, are the coins still there? That is the million-dollar question!"

Wendy and Nancy were at the kitchen table when Marshmallow jumped up on the kitchen counter and let out a loud meow! They looked up, smiled, and Nancy asked, "You want to answer it?" Right then the phone rang.

JoAnn spoke to Wendy, "Here's the latest update." She told her what Nick had told her just a few minutes ago. JoAnn said the men were checking out of the hotel soon.

Nancy was standing there sharing the phone receiver with Wendy. Then she asked, "What is the value of something like that?"

JoAnn explained, "After Professor Rolf receives his $2,500 bonus, and Nick gets his cut of about $20,000, you should net about $95,000, as Nick also would receive a smaller commission for selling the coins."

The girls, after they thanked JoAnn and hung up the phone, were ecstatic! They had a possible steady monthly income check for the traveling scepter for years to come, and now a possible windfall of close to $100,000 should all play out according to plan.

"Wow!" is all they kept saying over and over as they held each other's arms and danced around the room.

Kosmo gave the printouts to Beth of all the telephone numbers that had been placed in the last thirty days from Bob Tonkin's home and the antique store. He asked Beth to start calling each number and asking if there was either a Dagobert, or a Caselli residing at any of those numbers. He did tell her she could take her time, making a few calls here, a few calls there, as it seemed like quite a long list.

Allen Bourgeois, the photographer of the 'Nantucket Calendar' was once again up on the roof top above Bosun's Locker on Main Street. He had been trying to get perfect shots of the street from early morning to mid-afternoon, then into the twilight hours and late evenings for the next season's calendar. Kosmo had seen him around town a few times, and Judy gave him one of the calendars every January. Allen he was a perfectionist. He would take photo after photo, still shots and rapid-fire shots until he thought he had the perfect shot for each month's page.

Nick and Rolf arrived in Paris and checked into a different hotel, the Hotel Regina which was located right by the Joan of Arc statue in Place des Pyramides. It was also very close to the Louvre. They had had dinner in the first-class dining car on the train, and Nick was still amazed at the experience.

They checked into the hotel, taking a very upscale two- bedroom suite with a living area and dining room. It had a great view of the Joan of Arc statue right outside their window. The Louvre was past that, and the River Seine flowed just beyond it.

Now they needed a plan. They went to the concierge. Rolf introduced himself as a professor from Oxford. He explained that he was there to write a paper on the Catacombs of Paris, which he knew must be located directly below the hotel and the Joan of Arc statue.

The concierge said that was correct. He told them there was an historian who specialized in private tours of the catacombs, as there was a direct entrance below the lobby on the main floor. It was actually in one of their small 'caves' where they often hosted private dinners and wine tastings.

Rolf asked the concierge if he could arrange a private tour for them the following morning. The concierge nodded and confirmed their appointment soon after.

"Bingo!" he told Nick gleefully. "This is perfect! We might be able to gain entrance to the catacombs after the tour as we should see exactly how to enter them."

Nick smiled and held up one finger, indicating a need to pause. "We are going to need a few things if this transpires. Our list will include a flashlight, a satchel for the box of gold coins, and some sort of chisel to break the cemented blocks free."

Rolf nodded. "OK, let's do the tour, and we will pay close attention to where we enter the catacombs and see if it's a locked door. If so, we are going to have to plan how to open it. So, we add 'locksmith' to the list. Hmm, how we are going to convince him to unlock the door if need be?"

Nick shrugged. "I am sure we can think of something. Perhaps we can pretend to be managers of the hotel and explain that we want to update the door lock."

They went into the exquisite lounge bar and were seated by a host wearing a tuxedo. Nick just could not get over how elegant things were in Paris. They each enjoyed a 1959 Calvados, called it a night and retired to their suite.

BEIJING, CHINA: "THE HAUNTED CITY"

Beijing ranks high as one of the most haunted places in China. One of the more haunted locations is Gongwangfu, or Prince Gong's Mansion. The prince was well-known for his dishonesty and was said to keep at least 80 concubines. The mansion is now haunted by the spirit of his wife.

In addition, the Huguang Huiguan is said to be home to several ghosts. It was built as a house for the poor, but unfortunately was set atop an old graveyard. Apparently, anyone who throws a stone in the courtyard will get a lecture from a ghostly voice.

In the heart of Beijing lies the Forbidden City, the former Imperial Palace. The city was once home to the Emperor and his family and hundreds of concubines, guards, servants, and soldiers. Visitors to the Forbidden City frequently report ghostly animals running about, crying women in the concubine quarters and other melancholy women roaming the grounds. As the site of frequent murders and executions, it is unsurprising that the Forbidden City would be rife with ghosts.

Kosmo slept but not very restfully. He had a reoccurring dream that he was up on a widow's walk with a telescope watching the stars. It was clear crisp night. All of a sudden, he saw a mugging on the street below! He switched the direction of the telescope to the incident. The mugger had a face that looked like a short whitish-grey owl. When Kosmo attempted to get a closer look to be sure of what he was seeing, he wanted to rush down from the widow's walk to assist and aid the poor victim. But no matter how hard he tried, his legs would not move! He was stuck in place!

As his dream continued, he leaned over the railing of the widow's walk and suddenly, it gave way! Kosmo fell towards the ground below! He awoke just before landing on the hard ground. He was covered in sweat and tried to make sense of it all. Yet the same thing recurred in his sleep pattern two more times.

He awoke in the morning trying to remember if he had any onions the day before as they always gave him nightmares. He shook his head, mystified by his dreams. He realized he was still in one piece and slowed his breathing.

At the station that morning Beth English was slowly but surely making the calls from Kosmo's list. As of yet, nothing had surfaced but the locations of other art dealers, a plumber and the veterinarian's office who said that orphaned Daisy had an upcoming appointment. One number was for Cioppino's Restaurant and others for places in town.

At nine a.m. sharp Nick and Rolf were greeted in the lobby by Antoine, who was an aspiring historian in his mid-twenties. He had been studying the French catacombs and giving tours of them for the last four years. The three men enjoyed a coffee before heading down to the catacombs.

Rolf told him of his professor's degree and how he had always wanted to get a tour. He added, "This just might work out perfectly. By the way, we both brought flashlights for better viewing of the catacombs."

They took the back hall stairway down to the lower level. Then they walked to another stairway that led them to an old stone-arched wine cellar. At this time it was empty.

Antoine explained, "During the summer months the hotel offers a few wine tastings and small cocktail parties in the cave. However, at this time of year it is hardly ever used."

The door leading to the catacombs was off to the side at the end of the cave. As they got closer to the door, they saw the deadbolt lock and a large thick wooden frame around the entire door. Antoine reached above the door frame, felt for the key, unlocked the door and replaced the key above the frame. Nick and Rolf looked at each other with subtle smiles and they both winked.

The door opened slowly and with a creak. Antoine alerted them to watch their step as they entered. They had to descend down a narrow rounding metal staircase another ten feet or so. Once they landed on the dirt floor below, they needed to let their eyes adjust for a few minutes.

They all turned on their flashlights, and Antoine also wore a headlamp. He started walking towards a four-way intersection, saying "Follow me." At the intersection he pointed out the four cardinal directions: north, south, east, and west. Then he looked up and said that twelve meters straight up was the statue of Joan of Arc directly out front of the Regina Hotel.

Rolf made a mental note of the east facing pathway. Antoine took them along the south-facing walkway. He pointed out historical elements of the catacombs and shared some stories related to them. The tour lasted about forty-five minutes, after which they reversed their steps and ascended back to the hotel above. Nick and Rolf thanked Antoine for the very informative tour. They concluded with some conversation in the main salon.

After Antoine departed, Nick said, "Well, there's no time like the present! Shall we?"

They casually headed back to the far stairway and made their way back down to the cave. Nick reached up feeling around for the key, removed it and unlocked the door and replaced the key. They retraced their steps to the four corners and went east to the fifth section, remembering the directions from the animal hide. They took six long strides, shined their lights to the left on the well darkened stones, and saw that there was indeed an 'O' inscribed in a rock.

Nick exclaimed, "You have got to be kidding me! We actually found it!"

Rolf nodded, "It sure looks that way! Now let's see what we are going to need. We will have to get a hammer and a chisel, possibly a long sturdy screwdriver and pliers. Maybe some work gloves as well. That should cover it. We also should find a sturdy satchel as it should weigh about sixteen to twenty pounds. And I don't think we are going to want to walk through the lobby with some old rusty box in our hands. However, at some point it might be nice to have the original box for a keepsake. We can figure that part out later. Let's get moving on this task!"

They returned to the lobby and asked where they could find a store that carried all sorts of household items. Fifteen minutes later they were in a 'Galleries' store which sold everything from washers and dryers to toilets and picnic tables. They easily found everything they needed, including a nice small-sized canvas bag.

Beth English called another number on her list with a Boston local code. A woman answered, "This is JoAnn Caselli. How may I help you?"

Beth, thinking quickly, said "Oh, I'm sorry. I was just following up on a number that was on my phone bill and must have misdialed. My apologies." Then she hung up.

She wrote the phone number down, the time the call was placed, and who answered. She left a note to Kosmo explaining she told the woman she must have misdialed but thought that the Caselli name was right on track. Beth left that information on Kosmos desk and departed for the day.

Mike DiFronzo took over the shift on the dispatcher's desk. A short while later Ted Hudgins stopped into the station and had a magazine with him. He said that Kosmo might enjoy reading the article about a top cop in New York City who had a certain knack for solving crimes and that he had found it quite interesting.

Mike took the magazine into Kosmo's office, but in doing so he knocked a pile of manila folders onto the ground. He quickly picked them up and placed them on the desk after replacing some of the pages that had fallen out. One was the note from Beth.

On his way to work Kosmo decided to look in at Tonkin's Antique Shop which still had the yellow tape around it. While he was walking up Main Street a huge gust of wind came from the harbor, and it whispered in his ear, "You're getting closer to the answer." He continued towards the shop and planned another walk through it to see if he missed anything in the past few visits. Later on in the day he would return once again to the warehouse. He felt there just had to be another clue, another connection towards solving this riddle of who killed Bob Tonkin and why.

Kosmo returned to the station. Beth knocked on his office door frame and asked him if anything had panned out with the information he now had, meaning the note about a Ms. Caselli answering one of her calls. But before she could finish her conversation, the Chief's radio went off.

"Harbor Master Hudgins to Station Chief, over."

"Kosmo here, over."

"'The only impossible journey is the one you never begin,'" Ted said. "Over."

"Very nice, Ted, but what can I do for you? Over."

"Well, Chief, just checking in. All is quiet here. Did you get the magazine I dropped off? Over."

"Yes, I did, thanks. I will read it this week. Over and out."

Kosmo got ready to head to the warehouse for another walk through. He still was not sure what he was actually looking for, but he knew it would come to him, hopefully sooner than later.

Nick and Rolf separately headed down to the wine cave area of the hotel. The tools were in the satchel along with the flashlights, and they both had headlamps in the canvas bag. They found the stone with the 'O'.

Taking a deep breath, Nick said, "OK, here we go!"

They put on the work gloves and set out the tools within reach. Working slowly and steadily, they tapped around the stone block and, after a bit of work, removed it as well as the one below it and the one sitting directly on the dirt ground. Each stone weighed about twenty pounds, and they worked together to set each one down carefully.

Nick shined the flashlight inside. Rolf had his head- lamp on and was also shining his flashlight. Clear as day they both could see a rusted metal box, but it looked larger than what they had expected.

Nick declared, "Lo and behold! We just might have actually found something! I hope there are no snakes or spiders hidden inside the wall." He went to pull the rusted box out from its tight quarters but it was much heavier than sixteen pounds. He needed a better grip, but the opening was way too small for both of them to reach in.

Nick said, "Wait a minute!" He removed his belt and wrapped it around the back of the box. Hoping not to snap his belt, he leaned back a bit with his knees up against the wall. He started slowly pulling the box which made a gritty scraping sound in the cave-like opening. He told Rolf that he might need to use his belt as well. Rolf handed it to him, and Nick reached back in to wrap it around the box. He now had a stronger leverage on the box. Grunting a bit, he was able to move the box closer to the opening.

He told Rolf, "I don't know what the heck is in there but its heavy, really heavy!" After a few more minutes of concerted effort, the box was out of its enclosure in the wall. Nick set it down quickly but gently on the floor.

He stood back and told Rolf, "That treasure box weighs about as much as five of those stones! Grab the pliers and see if you can break the lock free."

Kosmo went back to the warehouse. Entering through the front door he looked around. The small piece of paper from the window he had left as a trap to see if it had been opened was now on the ground. His suspect had returned once again!

He took his time walking through the maze of paintings and antiques, not really knowing what he was looking for. It made it seem like an impossible task.

He kept thinking, "Caselli, Dagobert, Scepter." What did they mean, if anything?

After about twenty minutes he replaced the paper in the window jamb and exited the warehouse. He went home and called Duke at the hardware store. He asked him if he might like to join Judy and for a simple grilled steak dinner at his house?

Duke said, "Let me do this. I have to go see a friend at the meat market. He owes me a few favors. He gets some really top-notch New York strip steak. They are like cutting through butter! they are so tender, and the flavor is amazing!"

Kosmo objected mildly. "But I am inviting you!"

"Don't sweat it, Kosmo! Once you taste these babies you will be hooked for life! I'll be over at 6:30. Thanks!"

He then called Judy and told her the time to be at his house. He sat down to read Ted's magazine which he found quite interesting. It felt good to take a short break.

It was a lovely evening despite the cool late fall weather. After his two good friends departed, Kosmo sat in front of the fireplace with a glass of wine. A while later he awoke at midnight, the glass still half full and the fireplace just a very soft glow from a few embers

NEW ORLEANS, LOUISIANA:
THE HAUNTED CITY

New Orleans, in the southern United States, is known as one of the most haunted cities in the world primarily because of its history of voodoo. For example, tourists are likely to spot the ghost of the former voodoo mistress at Marie Laveau's home. However, the infamous Queen of Voodoo is not always keen on having visitors. Some have felt vicious scratches on their arms, felt their clothing being tugged and have even been pushed by a mysterious unseen force.

The Lady of Guadalupe Church is another haunted locale. Here, victims of the yellow fever epidemic were held while they awaited burial, and it's said that many of their spirits still linger inside the church's walls.

Rolf bent down and took a closer look at the rusted padlock sealing the lid on the metal box.

Nick pondered, "Why would it take such a large box to store one hundred coins? I don't know what they used to weigh the box down with, but the two of us will have a hard time lifting it back up again."

After a short time of probing the lid with the screwdriver, Rolf freed the lock and opened the lid. They both just stood there, amazed at what reflected back from their lights.

Kosmo had another restless night's sleep, if one could even call it sleep. The dream took place on a high perch of a tree branch. When he turned around a small owl spooked him, and he was falling directly down onto the cobblestone street below him! He awoke just before crashing onto the hard surface. He found himself falling out of the bed and almost crashing onto the wooden floor. What was with these dreams of him falling from various heights?

Kosmo arrived at the station, pre-occupied with his thoughts. Something was coming, some type of answer, but he could not quite grasp it.

Beth arrived at ten a.m. and resumed calling more of the numbers. She was now down to the final twenty numbers.

She stopped in and spoke with Kosmo. She inquired, "So, Chief, who did that lady turn out to be? The Ms. Caselli I left the note about?"

Kosmo looked up sharply. "Note? What note?"

Beth pointed to his desk top. "I left you a detailed note with the number, the time and who answered. I placed the note on your desk. Then yesterday I asked you if there were any updates, and you said not really."

"Oh, now I know," Kosmo explained. "I thought you were referring to the search at Tonkin's warehouse."

Beth countered, "So, where did that note disappear to?"

Kosmo assured her, "I am sure it will show up." He reached over for the manila folders and noticed that some of the pages that were for different folders were now mixed up. Beth stood there, and Kosmo pondered, "Hmm, I wonder if this has something to do with Mike?

He placed a magazine from Ted on my desk the other day. I think it was the same day that I went to Tonkin's warehouse."

Noticing all the papers were not one hundred percent in order in each folder, he put two and two together. "Beth, I'll bet this is what happened. Mike brought the magazine in here and placed it on my desk. He might have knocked some of the folders onto the floor. In his haste the note you left for me went over as well. He picked everything up, and now the note is in one of these folders!"

Beth said, "OK, let me have a look." Two minutes later Kosmo was dialing the number. He got the answering machine recording saying, "Caselli Fine Antiques. We are out of the office. Please leave your name and number and we will return your call promptly."

Kosmo left a message and disengaged the call.

Rolf and Nick were still gazing at the contents of the box. Nick said in a soft whisper, "I have a feeling we missed a faded zero on the number of coins! There has to be over a thousand coins here!"

Rolf picked one up, studied it in the glare of his headlamp and declared, "These are amazing, truly amazing!"

They removed about twenty pounds of the gold coins, put the box back into the wall, remounted the large stones and made it look as undisturbed as possible.

They did this three times in a row as they wanted to be cautious, figuring they would begin again the next day. A rough calculation was that they would need to make at least four more trips in total to claim all the coins. To move the coins more efficiently, they returned to the Galleries store and purchased two more canvas bags. They were very cautious when walking through the lobby time after time so as not to raise suspicion. Luckily the hotel was relatively quiet. The hard job so far got done without any interference! They figured they were about halfway through garnering their historic haul.

Up in Nick's room, they placed the coins in stacks of ten. Nick did a quick mathematical count and reported, "Well, Rolf, it seems to me that the total value of these coins is closer to one million and two hundred thousand dollars!" His calculations moved everyone's slice of the pie up tenfold!

He made a call to JoAnn at home, telling her the entire journey from the tour to locating the correct stones in the wall to remove. Then he said, "You might want to sit down for this part."

JoAnn, now thinking something terrible had happened, sat down. "What's up, Nick?"

Nick explained, "We misinterpreted the first clue and the second very faded clue. The number of coins is not one hundred, and, no, not lower than that amount. JoAnn, it's possibly ten times higher! We are guessing one thousand coins, give or take a small amount! A whopping one thousand coins!"

He told her the estimated value. He also told her the estimated weight was around one hundred and sixty pounds, and it was going to take a few trips back down to the catacombs. He told her they purchased another canvas bag to shorten up the trips, but they had to be careful walking through the lobby every thirty minutes carrying the canvas bags. He let her know they hoped to finish up the next day and then they would plan their return trip which would be challenging in of itself.

Marshmallow hopped up on the office desk and let out a loud "meow!" Nancy looked at Wendy and said, "I'll get it." A moment later the phone rang.

JoAnn said, "Hi Nancy. Another update. You might want to put Wendy on your other phone and sit down for this one."

Wendy went into the kitchen, picked up the phone and said, "I am here."

Nancy worriedly said, "Oh, my god! Did something bad happen?"

JoAnn laughed. "That was my first reaction when Nick told _me_ to sit down." She then relayed the story just as Nick had explained it to her.

Neither one of them spoke, as their breath was taken away. Finally, Wendy stammered, "How much?"

They talked seriously with JoAnn a few more minutes as the news was rather stupendous. JoAnn said that she would give them an update the next day when she learned more.

JoAnn retuned Kosmos' phone call the next day. He inquired if she was a friend of Bob Tonkin's as he made a call a few weeks back from his antiques shop on Nantucket. JoAnn informed him that they had some dealings with Bob and had known him for several years. They were devasted when they learned of his death. She then asked if they had made an arrest yet.

Kosmo wrote down some notes as they were talking. JoAnn said that Nick, her husband, and Bob had some business dealings in the past with some antique paintings, but she avoided telling him anything about the scepter. JoAnn then told Kosmo that Nick was in Europe traveling with a professor friend, and that he would be back in the states within a week or so. She would have Nick call him straight away upon his arrival back in Boston.

The next morning Nick and Rolf both headed down to the wine cave five minutes apart from each other. Rolf went first, but soon met Nick on his way and said, "No go. There are some people meeting down there, almost seems like they are planning an event. So, we need to regroup."

They both headed upstairs at different times. Rolf was stopped by the concierge in the lobby who wanted to know how they enjoyed the tour of the catacombs. Rolf chatted with him for a moment, and Nick, spotting them, remained around the corner.

Back upstairs in their suite they discussed how to get the coins back to England and to the United States. Rolf's suggestion was to try for a trans-Atlantic cruise. Due to the weight they needed to get one-hundred-sixty pounds of gold coins smuggled past customs into the States.

Nick suggested that they make stacks of ten coins rolled tight in some clear plastic wrap. They would use a few layers of the wrapping so they would not break apart. Then they should use a good clear packing tape around each coin roll, sealing them quite well.

Nick calculated, "Now, with each stack weighing about a pound and a half, we will have one hundred of them. If in each carry-on luggage we have fifteen or sixteen rolls of ten coins, that's roughly twenty-five pounds per bag. We can each have three bags. That leaves us with about seventy pounds more to pack. Then we can have three more checked bags. We get a porter to take the bags on and off the ship. We land in New York, rent a car and drive to Boston."

He looked at Rolf. "I hope you're feeling strong enough for this venture! Now, all we need to do is find a trans-Atlantic ship sailing for America from England. And we use the same system traveling to England, but we must travel separately, as if one gets caught the other does as well!"

A couple of hours passed, and they figured that the event planners were probably done in the cellar. They each went separately back down to the wine cellar, went through the extraction process again and brought up the remaining coins. It was not easy work, but they both realized the incredible value of what they were handling.

After all was said and done, they ordered room service, not wanting the gold out of their sight. A fine bottle of wine would certainly help their muscles relax!

Their next move was to get proper luggage. They could not just waltz out of the hotel with two eighty-pound bags of gold coins.

Then Rolf made a call to his travel agent in England, inquiring about trans-Atlantic sailings to America.

She placed him on hold and returned back on the line a few minutes later. She said that in six days the Queen Elizabeth Two would be sailing from Southampton to New York. Rolf now asked if there was space available on it, possibly two very nice suites. She said she would have to call him back in about thirty minutes. Rolf told her he would call her back it as it would be easier for him.

He gave Nick the dates, and Nick called JoAnn giving her the latest updates and travel plans. He asked her to call their travel agent and see what was available for the Queen Elizabeth Two as he and Rolf would travel separately.

Rolf called his travel agent and she said there were still a few suites available, but they were quite costly. Rolf said the price was not an issue and to secure him a very fine suite. Nick called JoAnn back as well and repeated the same booking request. Nick also told Rolf that this was covered under the expenses for the trip. Rolf smiled at his good fortune to have been included in this most amazing venture.

Marshmallow let out a large "meow", and Nancy picked up the phone. JoAnn gave them the latest information, and with everyone's fingers crossed, they hoped for smooth sailing!

Kosmo dialed up Johnny Acton and said, "Johnny, old boy, I need a sausage pizza to be picked up at seven o'clock and give me a double dose of red onions!"

"Really?" John asked. "You know what they do to you! You're going to have some bad nightmares!"

"Load it up!" Kosmo confirmed.

Kosmo headed out and met Judy at Fareground's for a drink and gave her his latest thoughts on the Tonkin murder. He then told her about the pizza, and she said,

"You must be close, if it's the red onion deal. Call me in the morning. I want to be sure you're OK." He picked up the pizza only after enjoying a small glass of wine with John and Judy.

The dreams that he had that evening were not as bad as he predicted. He was soaring like an eagle above Main Street. He saw the mugger once again who still resembled a short haired grey-white owl. But by the time he had soared back, the mugger had killed his prey and the man lay face down on the brick sidewalk, with blood running down onto the cobble-stoned street. Kosmo actually awoke in the morning fairly refreshed.

He went to the station and Deputy Donato was waiting for him. Mark said, "You know, Chief, I have been working over different scenarios on the Tonkin murder, and I might have an answer."

Kosmo invited Mark to come into his office. He closed the door most of the way. "OK, fire away!" Kosmo said. He figured it might help to have another perspective on the whole situation.

Mark looked at his notes and said, "Well, the way I see it, there are three of them involved, most likely. One is the lookout, one is the driver, and the third one is the mastermind and thief. You see, the lookout, well, he was to intervene if old man Tonkin was to arrive back at the store after the closing of business hours. They knew his schedule like clockwork. He always leaves Daisy in the car, and comes back to the car after his dinner at the Ships Inn like he does all the time. The driver was not watching at all. He was ready to do was peel out if they had to run. Perhaps the lookout did not see Mr. Tonkin arrive back at the store. Maybe he must have walked into the Pharmacy for a cup of coffee. Anyways, the guy inside the store hears the front door open and thinks he's got to hide. But he's not quick enough, and Bob Tonkin spots him, and that's when the trouble started. And now they are still casing the joint looking for whatever valuable antique that Tonkin evidently has or had in his possession. My thoughts are that maybe we should put an all-points-bulletin out to the Cape and up and down the coast as well at the airport and ferry here. There just has to be some suspicious looking characters somewhere in the vicinity! And we want to catch them, red-handed!"

Kosmo listened and told Mark, "Well, I think you have made some good points here, and you might not be too far off the reason for his death. But we now need to get more solid background information, facts, hard facts.

You keep working your thoughts on this, and we should regroup tomorrow on updates. I have a few ideas I am tossing around as well."

Mark exited Kosmo's office feeling like a true detective and giving himself credit for really being onto something that would really pay off! He could see the headlines now – 'Deputy Tracks down Murderers and Thieves through Clever Detection Techniques!'

GETTYSBURG, PENNSYLVANIA: A GHOST HUNTER'S PARADISE

The Battle of Gettysburg during the United States Civil War was one of the bloodiest battles in history. This carnage makes it unsurprising that the city is now a supernatural hotspot. Ghost hunters are often drawn to the Doubleday Inn, which was built on the site of Iverson's Pit: the location of a brutal massacre of hundreds of soldiers whose spirits still roam the area. Visitors also see ghosts at Devil's Den, the site of another brutal massacre. Here, a Texan soldier is regularly seen wandering the battlefield in full Civil War regalia.

However, one of the most haunted locations in Gettysburg is the Sachs Covered Bridge. Here, numerous Confederate soldiers were killed as they attempted to desert the battle. Visitors frequently feel cold spots and photograph orbs at the bridge. Many who visit after dark are terrified to hear the sounds of a raging battle and see the bloodied spirits of the soldiers who died there.

Rolf and Nick's trip went smoothly and uneventfully back to London. Gold coins safe at hand, Nick checked into Claridge's Hotel in Mayfair. He took one gold coin to an antiques dealer in Mayfair. The owner of the shop was trying to figure out exactly where this gentleman who entered his shop had acquired such an exquisite and flawless gold coin. Nick just told him that he uncovered ten of the coins while clearing out his uncle's attic back in the States. When he took this trip to London, he thought he might bring them and see what the value might be, as where he resided there were only small regional antique stores. He wasn't even sure from where the coins might have originated.

The man asked if he knew the value of the coin. Nick replied, "Not really, but I was referred to you by a friend in Oxford who said you had been in business for a good number of years and that you had a very honest reputation. So, I thought I would start with you, then go from there. It's easy for me to get another assessment if I go to Oxford as my professor friend knows a coin dealer there. But the man is traveling in Spain for the next few days. I could leave the coin with my friend and get a fair value price if you are interested in doing business over the next few days."

The man in the antique store did not want this coin to leave his shop, so he told Nick, "I will give you what I truly think is the highest value of the coin. If it turns out that my offer is lower than the offer in Oxford, I will match it, no questions asked. But what I would like to do is give you a documented paper stating what I have just mentioned. As you see, here in London if one is caught cheating a prospective client, we can lose our business license and be fined. We have been in business for seventy-five years and do not have one blemish on our records."

He then gave Nick the offer of nine hundred British pounds for the coin. Nick did some quick calculating and it equaled just about eleven hundred US dollars. He told Nick that he would be willing to take all ten of them for cash or check, whatever Nick might prefer.

Nick had already calculated the value of the coins, and it was almost spot on the price. Nick figured if he could sell some for cash while in London, he could pay Rolf, making the final payout less cumbersome once he was back in Boston.

The agreement was made, and Nick started scouting out a few different antique shops in the surrounding areas. He called Rolf and gave him the latest update. Nick had the hotel set him up with a driver after asking the hotels concierge for a list of reputable coin dealers.

In under four hours Nick had sold off fifty coins, all for cash at the exact same amount, a total of fifty-five thousand dollars. Nick did not disclose any information regarding his name or where he was staying, and no one pressed the matter.

Now, only nine-hundred and fifty more to go! He let Rolf know the amount he had taken in and said, "Well, we have several days. Why don't you make a list of towns, and let's see how many coins we can move for cash?"

By the time they set sail, boarding the Queen Elizabeth Two, they had moved another one hundred coins in sets of five or ten. No offers for fewer coins were accepted. Nick gave Rolf what he figured he would owe him by the end of all the coin sales. Yes, it was an advance payment, but Rolf trusted him implicitly.

Nick would keep the remainder with the promise of a full accounting soon after his arrival in the States.

Before setting sail, he called JoAnn and gave her the latest update. JoAnn mentioned to Nick that she had received a call from the chief of police on Nantucket Island asking what their connection was with Mr. Tonkin. He had said was going through phone records from Bob's business and his home. She said she remained very vague and said that Nick just dealt with him on a business level.

The men boarded the ship separately without an issue.

Kosmo asked Beth to contact Steve Turrentine and Allen Bourgeois, the newspaper photographers, and ask them to stop down at the station, if possible, the next day around ten a.m. At the appointed time, both Steve and Allen arrived simultaneously at the station. They were shown into Kosmos' office, and Deputy Donato joined them.

Kosmo asked the men about recent photos they might have taken in the vicinity of Main Street, and most importantly, any of that might include Tonkin's Antique Store on the day Bob was murdered. He extended the timeframe to include just a few days leading up to the day of the murder.

Steve said he had taken some from the top of Main Street. He also said that he had taken several photos with the fire truck, ambulance, and the crowd of people. Kosmo made a note on his pad sitting on the desk.

Then he asked Allen, "I have seen you up on the roofs by Mignosa Market taking pictures, isn't that correct?"

Allen said, "Well, yes, but I have permission from Mr. Mignosa."

"That's fine," Kosmo replied. "What I am getting at is, can you get me all of the photos that you have taken of the area around Tonkin's shop in the last couple of weeks or so?"

Both men said yes, and with no problem. It might take a couple of days to get them all developed.

Two days later, as promised, Allen arrived in the morning with a large collection of photos. Kosmo looked at them, made a few piles, thanked him and told Allen that he would return the photos to him after he was finished.

Just after lunch time, Steve arrived with a few photos of Main Street he had taken from upper Main looking down towards the wharf. He also had shots from lower Main looking up towards the bank. He told Kosmo that at different times of the day he enjoyed using various filters catching different lighting. He had some taken as early as six a.m. and as late as ten p.m. Then he had another folder of his photos from the day Bob Tonkin was found murdered.

Kosmo also put them into separate piles and thanked Steve, saying he would return them soon. He had just pulled out his magnifying glass when Deputy Donato knocked on his door frame.

Mark saw the photos and asked, "Do you think our culprit is in one of these photos?"

Kosmo shrugged. "Only time will tell, but one thing is sure, many a murder or an arsonist likes to report back to the scene of the crime. With our culprit, well, we know he's been back to the warehouse and the shop as well as to Mr. Tonkin's home."

Mark reminded him, "Well, we might want to look for a group of three culprits if my hunch is correct." Mark added, "I'm off to Pastrami Day at Les's Lunch Box, and after you're done was done reviewing the photos, Chief, I'd like a crack at them."

As Mark was leaving the station Mike DiFronzo was finishing his shift. He asked Mark, "Say, did I hear you say you're headed over to Les's?"

Mark was about to say, "Just mind your own business, you busybody, but he thought differently and said, yes."

Mike eagerly responded, "Hold on a minute! I will join you!"

Mark rolled his eyes as he did not see that coming. But he acquiesced and quietly said, "OK."

When they entered the place, it was packed with people, some waiting for to-go orders, others waiting to be seated. Les, on Pastrami Day, kept one booth roped off as he had so many friends who could never manage to get a seat as it was such a popular day.

Mark tried to catch Les's eye and at the same time told Mike, "Watch this. I am pretty tight with Les. Let me see what I can do to get us moved up in the waiting line."

Mark finally managed a little wave to Les, who just rolled his eyes and said, "Sorry, Deputy, it's going to be awhile."

Then Les saw Mike. He came right out from the counter, gave Mike a pat on the shoulder and asked, "How's my bowling partner?"

Mark looked bewilderedly at Mike, then at Les who declared, "Man, you should see this guy bowl! We clean up at all the games! And don't even ask about his dart skills-they are off the charts!" Les took them to his private booth, set them up with two Cokes, two overly- stacked pastrami sandwiches and smiled. "Compliments of the house!" He dashed back to the counter to attend to the next hungry customer.

Mark just remained quiet while they both gobbled up their meal. They left a tip, and Mark was back at the station smelling of pastrami. "Oh, well, that was a good connection to make. Who would believe it?"

Rick Blair was manning the dispatch desk. Kosmo asked him into his office. He said to Rick, "Would you take a good look at these and tell me if you see anything that jars your thoughts?"

Rick asked, "Are you looking for anything in particular?"

Kosmo explained, "Just tell me anything that pops into your head. I will write it down in my notes."

Rick first looked at Steve Turrentine's photos of Main Street, then of the day at the crime scene. He looked at all of the photos and told Kosmo exactly what he wanted to hear. Then he had him look at Allen Bourgeois' photos, and there it was again, the same consensus. He thanked Rick for his input, and Rick went back to his desk.

Kosmo called Mark into his office and asked him to take a look at all the photos. Mark was studying them but only came up with different lighting on different days. Allen's were taken with a zoom lens, and some were just nice clear stills while others were rapid-fire shots taken every few seconds.

Kosmo spent the next two days reviewing the photos. His thoughts were closing in. He recalled his dreams, and he thought he almost knew what they meant.

He asked Beth, "Did anything ever transpire with the calls on the name 'Dagobert'?"

Beth shook her head. "No, sorry, Chief. Out of every call not even a hint of a 'Dagobert'."

He still needed to get more information on the word, 'scepter.' He had notched one off his list of three-Caselli-but nothing really on the scepter and Dagobert. Yet they were all on the same page of notes. The next day he returned to the library where he took the three books off the shelves that he was looking through a few days before. The answers had to be hidden somewhere!

Nick and Rolf disembarked from the Queen Elizabeth Two in New York. Instead of driving, they took the train to Boston. They had quite a haul to move with them!

THE QUEEN MARY IS ONE OF THE MOST HAUNTED GHOST SHIPS!

A ghost ship, also known as a phantom ship, is a vessel with no living crew aboard. It may be a ghostly vessel in folklore or fiction, such as the Flying Dutchman, or a real derelict found adrift with its crew missing or dead, like on the Mary Celeste. The term is sometimes used for ships that have been decommissioned but not yet scrapped, as well as drifting boats that have been found after breaking loose of their ropes and becoming carried away. Such ships were once marked by Time *magazine as the most haunted places in the world. The* Queen Mary *has once again opened its most popular room that is widely known for its hauntings, Room B340.*

Kosmo was rereading everything he had on 'scepters' from his previous visit to the Atheneum. He turned the page, and there it was, staring him right in the face: 'The Scepter of Dagobert!'

"Now here," he breathed with a big sigh, "are the two last pieces of the puzzle."

He went to the librarian on duty and asked if she could make a copy of a few pages. While he waited, he stopped in Bob Rully's office as he was the town's unofficial historian. He asked Bob if he knew anything about 'scepters'. That led Bob on a rambling discussion. After fifteen minutes, Kosmo was now more confused about what Mr. Rully was talking about. He spoke about everything else but nothing that had to do with the topic of 'scepters'. He thanked Bob and went back to the front desk.

The librarian handed Kosmo a few of the copied pages. He thanked her, filed the copies in a folder and went back to the station. Now things were falling into place. He had information about the names Caselli and Dagobert as well as facts about scepters. Toss in the photos from Allen and Steve, and it was all starting to add up.

He called Mike DiFronzo into his office and asked him to look at Steve's photos and to see if he observed anything as a common denominator. He gave him the same directions with Allen's photos. Mike gave him some observations similar to Rick Blair's thoughts.

As he was reviewing the latest notes Nick Caselli called the station. His call was put through to Kosmo.

Kosmo made small talk with him about Bob Tonkin and asked how long they had known each other. Then he asked Mr. Caselli point-blank, "Do you why anyone might have killed Mr. Tonkin for any reason?"

Nick hesitated and said, "To tell you the truth, Chief Kosmo, he called me about a discovery he made a few weeks back. At first it was a mystery as he described a particular object. Bob thought that the item in question was most likely a replica. He could not believe that it could actually be the original."

Kosmo laid his cards out. "Are you referring to the 'Scepter of Dagobert?'"

Nick was stunned and shocked, as, supposedly, no one knew about that discovery. Nick was silent for a moment, wondering how he knew about the 'Scepter of Dagobert.'

Nick cautiously proceeded. "Chief Kosmo, before we go on, and if this possibly has something to do with Bob's murder, I would like to know how you possibly arrived at this line of questioning? In total respect to your work, I am not going to hold anything back, but I would like to know why you are asking such a question."

Kosmo felt like he was dealing with responsible person so he explained, "First off, the information that I am going to share with you is possibly evidence for a court case. Therefore, I would like you to keep it confidential. In going through his office after the murder, I discovered some notes on a pad of paper in the bottom of a drawer in Mr. Tonkin's desk. There were three things written on it along with a sketch of an item which I now know is a scepter. One was the word 'Caselli', from which I located you through records of Mr. Tonkin's phone calls. If I had not been interrupted while searching through his desk, I would have found your phone number in Mr. Tonkin's address book. However, right before I was about to look in it, I was called away."

Nick nodded to himself and realized that Chief Kosmo was certainly doing his job.

Kosmo continued his tale. "The next was the word 'Dagobert' about which I had zero knowledge. Lastly, the word 'scepter' was also written on the page." Kosmo took a breath, and he hoped he was drawing Mr. Caselli into helping him with the mystery.

He continued his explanation. "I wanted to see exactly what a scepter was, so I went to the library. I was reading about scepters. I was one page away from learning about the 'Scepter of Dagobert' when I got a call on my radio. A short time later I returned and finished reading about scepters, and there was the story about Dagobert. So, the three things on that notepaper have now come full circle." Kosmo paused, hoping he hadn't revealed too much of his professional work.

Nick said, "Thank you, Chief Kosmo. This has become very interesting. To tell you the truth, I would feel best discussing this matter in person and laying out all the details of how I relate to Mr. Tonkins' business. I will say that I do know something about a scepter that relates to Nantucket from some clients of mine. However, like you, my clients want to keep the 'scepter' part confidential for now, if you don't mind. I know how small island gossip can spread like wild fire." Nick felt he had not revealed too much, but if his work would help in solving the crime, he felt obligated to pursue his conversation with Chief Kosmo.

Kosmo began to feel a small sense of relief and hope that a solution was about to emerge. "I totally understand as well. At this point in the investigation, I have not connected all the dots. But keeping this private at this point in time in the investigation is also crucial to me as well," Kosmo said. He added, "Do you think you could make a trip to the island sooner than later? It would be very helpful to see if we can move this case along. I would very much appreciate your cooperation."

Nick replied, "Certainly. My wife and I can be there tomorrow. We will book a room at Martin's Guest House. I will also notify my clients of our arrival and the reason for our visit. As of now, they are still in a state of confusion as to the fact that this mysterious scepter came into their possession. But I believe the four of us, my two clients, my wife and I can meet with you. And here is a suggestion-we should meet where perhaps some answers lie which is at their residence. And we need to make doubly sure that no one is eavesdropping on our conversation."

Kosmo was amazed that some critical information might be forthcoming so quickly. He agreed, saying, "OK, that sounds logical. Why don't you give me a call tomorrow regarding your expected time of arrival on the island? I will clear my calendar and bring all my notes to the designated meeting spot. And, thank you. I will appreciate any help you can offer. This has been a difficult case to resolve up until now. See you soon."

Nick had JoAnn get the ferry schedule and book a room at Martin's Guest House.

Marshmallow jumped up on the kitchen counter, and started batting a pencil around but only after letting out a big meow. The phone rang. It was Nick Caselli calling to update them on this enormous venture. They were thrilled to be able to talk to Nick directly.

He explained to the women how the trip on the Queen Elizabeth Two proceeded, the train trip to Boston, and most importantly, that all the coins that remained were locked securely away. He explained that Professor Achilles was returning to London later on the following day from Boston.

He then said, "We have a lot to discuss. So, my wife and I will be coming to Nantucket tomorrow after we take the professor to the airport." He told them all about his conversation with Constable Kosmo. Then he said that Kosmo might just have a few more things figured out about how to find Mr. Tonkin's murderer, but he might need some background information from them. Nick went on to say that at this time Kosmo did not know anything about them being involved in the complicated situation.

At that, Wendy and Nancy both took a big breath and let it out. They thanked Nick for contacting them and said they would be very happy to see him back safe and sound from the incredible undertaking he risked for everyone's sake.

The next day Nick called Kosmo at the station and said that they should be on island by noon. Nick would call him at two p.m. or thereabouts and set the meeting time.

Early the next morning, JoAnn and Nick said their goodbyes to Rolf at the airport, declaring that it had been one incredible adventure! They drove to Hyannis to catch the ferry. Upon their arrival to the island, they checked into Martin's Guest House. Wendy drove into town and picked them up.

Once they were out in Quaise, the four of them sat at the kitchen table and discussed how the whole adventure began. Nancy chimed in, "I believe Nick mentioned that none of us has done anything wrong. But we need to get what we know so far, all the information about this discovery, to the constable."

She drummed her fingers on the table. "The thing is, how did the killer figure out about the scepter, as we all assume that is what he is after?"

Nick made the call to Kosmo and relayed the address to him.

Kosmo told Nick, "Hmm, I know that address. I was there a while back, first hearing about a prowler, then a break in. I'll be there in 20 minutes. It's time we got to the bottom of all this mystery."

Kosmo arrived and had his files with him. He asked if they could start from the very beginning. Wendy was the designated spokesperson for the two friends. She told Kosmo how they found the "bomb" box buried under the barn in a cellar that had been closed off for who knows how long. Then Wendy had taken detailed photographs of the scepter in a step-by-step manner, not having a clue as to what it was. Next, they had made a sketch and showed it to Mr. Tonkin. They had not said anything to him except that the sketch was from a friend who had told them about her scepter. She explained that they wanted to keep the location of the artifact a secret.

Wendy went on to say that Mr. Tonkin told them about Mr. Caselli in Boston if 'their friend' wanted more information about such an item. But he had shared that it was most likely just a knock-off, something purchased in a souvenir shop, as many of them sell replicas.

She continued the tale explaining how they went to Boston. She mentioned they had a man at the Rexall Drug Store develop their photos into eight by tens.

Next, they took the photos to Nick's antiques store. They didn't provide him too much information, departed after a chat with him, and they returned to Nantucket.

After that, they waited a few days and finally returned to Mr. Tonkin's store. They told him the entire story about the wax seal, the metal tie closure and how the item just appeared to be something old, real and unusual. Thus, Bob and Wendy ended going back to Mr. Caselli's store.

Nick then said, "So, Chief, after Bob and I did some more research, we were almost certain that it was the original 'Scepter of Dagobert.' Of course, if this was true, this would be one of the most incredible antiques discoveries of the century if not longer!"

He continued, "I came to the island and met with Mr. Rully, the town's historian, (at which Kosmo nodded) and dug up some information on the original owner of the home. Apparently, it was a man named Gerard Dubois whom it was rumored to be an escaped jewel thief from France."

Wendy chimed in at this point. "We found an old diary after the break-in of the house about which you know, Chief. It up in our attic, and there was a reference to Mr. Dubois who was supposed to sell his treasure in Newport Rhode Island, but he died prior to that meeting or so it seems."

Kosmo interrupted saying, "Pardon me, but what is the latest on this scepter and where is it? I want to be sure it is not where this crook can get at it."

Nick reassured him. "That's fine, Chief. It's securely locked in our vault at the store. We are planning on having it put on loan to different museums around the country as well as Europe. The amazing thing is that we have agreed that every one of us will get a share of the royalty check every month. It's far too valuable and historic to just keep it under lock and key on my property!"

"That makes sense," Kosmo replied. "Though I wouldn't have a clue as to how to go about doing such a project nor how to insure a valuable antiquity! I'm glad that's in your bailiwick, not mine!"

Kosmo refocused on the murder. "A local restauranteur, Bob Moulder, said that Bob Tonkin had briefly mentioned on the night he was murdered something about an object that might bring him a royalty check every month for many years to come. So, we're getting closer to matching up all the facts." He paused for a breath, also to calm his eagerness to wrap everything up.

"But here's the question, Nick - who else knew about this scepter besides you and your wife, Wendy and Nancy and Bob Tonkin? That was everyone, correct?"

Nancy nodded. "As far as we know, all of us were sworn to secrecy. We haven't let on to anyone anywhere!"

Kosmo asked another question for clarity of the situation. "What is the value of the scepter, Nick? This is certainly in your line of work."

Nick tilted one of his palms back and forth to indicate some uncertainty. "It's hard to say, but possibly over a million dollars."

Kosmo summarized his understanding to this point. "OK, this scepter definitely ties in with the prowler and the break in at the house. It's the only common denominator. It seems to me that our suspect is still snooping around for it. As of two days ago, I left a few small traps on my own, which let me know that someone has returned to Bob's warehouse and his home. Now that I know what I am looking for, I have some thoughts on how to proceed."

He turned to Wendy and Nancy. "This person might become more desperate as time moves on. So, Wendy and Nancy, be extra cautious and keep your doors and windows locked. Have your friend Rusty stay in the main house with you both. Is there anything else that can be added to this insight?"

"Only one thing we can add," Wendy replied, "is the fact that I thought a couple times I might have been followed after leaving the house here driving into town. I managed, after making a bank deposit, to casually stroll down Main Street and get a look at the guy. But he was wearing a large kind of floppy hat, so I could not get a good look at him. But then Nancy and I discussed it, and we figured maybe the guy was just driving into town to pick up his wife at Miller's Hair Salon. Who knows?"

With a serious demeanor, as perhaps they had actually seen the suspect, Kosmo inquired, "Did you get the license plate by any chance?"

Wendy offered, "No, but it was a brownish rust- colored four-door Falcon. We thought we would do some sleuthing ourselves by asking around at different inns to see if there was a single man staying at any.

But, no, we had zero luck. We tried eight different inns, and we still keep our eyes open trying to spot the car."

Kosmo wrote on his pad, 'Car - Ford Falcon, four-door, rust-brownish color and circled it. "Hmm, I wish you had checked in with me sometime along the way. But I can have my crew keep their eyes out for that car. There aren't too many vehicles on the island at this time of year compared with the summertime. Thanks for agreeing to meet up with me. I think we've got some solid leads, and I do hope that we'll nail this culprit sooner than later. All of you, take a little extra pre-caution in your comings and goings, and do let me know if anything else crops up, no matter how inconsequential it may seem. And I'll keep you posted on my progress when we land something substantial. See you around."

STURDIVANT HALL, SELMA, ALABAMA

Built in 1856 in the Greek Revival style, this beautiful antebellum mansion was bought in 1864 by John McGee Parkman. In the years after the Civil War, Parkman was arrested and imprisoned for cotton speculation. While in prison, Parkman attempted to escape but was shot and killed in the process. When his wife was forced to sell their house a few years after his death, his ghost began to appear regularly throughout the house and grounds, where it is still seen to this day. People often report hearing windows and doors being opened and shut when no one else is in this real haunted house, as well as doors that close behind people and lock on their own. The apparitions of two little girls are also frequently seen, though their identities remain unknown.

Kosmo returned to the station and called Steve and Allen, asking them for a few things. He explained he would be quite grateful if he could have them by the end of the day or early the next morning. They both were able to comply with his requests. He made a few more notes.

Just then, Judy called him and asked, "So, Kos, what are your dinner plans tonight?"

He explained, "Well, Judy, I'm actually at a critical turning point in the Tonkin murder case. So, I will have to defer a date for a few days. I hate to tell you but a trip to see Johnny Acton again is my next stop."

She asked, "Ho, another date with the red onions?"

"Yes," he admitted. "What I've recently found out just might be what I have been searching for. All I need is an interesting nap to nudge it along! I'll call you when things fall into place."

"You've got my number, Chief. Good luck!"

Kosmo hung up, then redialed. "Foood's, how may I help you?"

"Kosmo here. Hey, Johnny boy, I need a meatball sub, no cheese but load it up with red onions, and don't hold back! Onto a situation, and I need to work it out!"

"OK, you got it! See you in fifteen, it'll be ready."

Kosmo left the station telling Beth, "I am headed home to see if I can get the final clue all sorted out. I have my radio on Channel Two. Don't let anyone know that, and only contact me it the President of the United States decides to fly in for a quick lunch at the pharmacy!

I will be off the grid until around two this afternoon."

Kosmo picked up the sub sandwich and headed home. He enjoyed every bite. Then he went to his bedroom, put on a pair of comfortable sweatpants and his 'shirt to come home to.' He lit a fire in the fireplace, sat in his recliner, kicked it back so his feet were raised and he drifted off to a deep sleep.

The dream came slowly. It was teasing him. It would drift in, then fade away. This happened three times. The images in the first three scenarios were very faint and foggy, but in the fourth round, it was clear as day.

He was sitting in a car, a brown car. On the back seat was a box wrapped up in a torn sweater which was covered in blood. He was eating something in a waxed paper wrapper. Just then a knock on the driver's side window startled him. A man asked, "Are you from Cusco?"

Kosmo was confused. The man asked again, "Are you from Cusco?" Then, "What are you eating?"

Kosmo rolled down the car window. "No, I'm not from Cusco. Why do you ask? And I just picked this up at the pharmacy lunch counter. It's the special of the day."

The man said, "Well, Señor, I can see you're eating cuy!"

Kosmo then asked, "What the heck is cuy?"

The man answered, "It's one of our delicacies in Peru. It's fried guinea pig."

Kosmo now looked at the man who was smiling away. His hair was salt and pepper grey and short clipped. He looked like a baby owl!

Then the man reached inside and took a piece of the cuy! Kosmo noticed blood on the man's torn sweater.

He awoke with a start! Immediately he went into the bathroom and gargled with mouth wash. He was glad his meatball sub wasn't fried guinea pig or whatever!

He refreshed himself, got dressed and radioed into the station to say he was coming in but had some serious work to tackle and would not want to be interrupted. Upon his arrival, Kosmo hung the '*Do Not Disturb*' sign on his office door. Beth gave him the 'AOK' sign.

When he got settled in at his desk, he began reviewing the photos that both photographers had dropped off in sealed manila envelopes. He started to review the photos requested. First, he opened the envelope of photos from Steve Turrentine. He looked them over carefully using a magnifying glass which almost wasn't necessary as the photo enlargements showed him exactly what he wanted to see.

He then did the same with Allen's photos. The second clue he expected to see was clear as day.

He spent a few minutes looking at each and every one of the photos. He made just a few short notes and opened his office door.

He asked Beth to get on the radio and have Rick Blair, Jimmy Jaksic and Deputy Donato meet him at the station. He added, "Beth, I'll want you in on this job, too."

As soon as they were all in the station, Kosmo explained to each of them to casually keep an eye out for a Ford Falcon four-door sedan, rust-brownish in color. He then showed each of them the enlarged photo of the car taken by Allen Bourgeois from on top of Mignosa's Market. The next thing was to keep their eyes on the lookout for a man about five foot six, short-cropped silver-grey hair. He wanted each of them to take an area and walk the streets to see if they could spot anyone fitting that description. He then showed them the photograph that Steve had taken the evening at the crime scene of Mr. Tonkin's death which clearly showed a man fitting that description. He told them he believed that the man shown in the photo could possibly be the murderer, and if they spotted the suspect, they were not to approach him. They were to just quietly call it into the station using Channel Six.

Mark jumped into the conversation saying, "Now don't try to apprehend the suspect! Just do what the chief is requesting. We don't want anyone getting 'trigger happy.'" Mark then realized that none of them wore guns.

Kosmo gave them their daily area to concentrate on. "Just walk the street like any other day, saying hi to the storekeepers, and people on the street. Do not look out of place, act just like the everyday life we lead here."

Again, Mark jumped in. "You heard the chief! No sudden movements. If you spot the subject, call it in when he's out of hearing range. You can 'tail him' but don't spook him as he's liable to make run for it. He might even take someone hostage if he's desperate enough." Mark was feeling as if he was very experienced in nabbing criminals at this point!

"One thought I have," Kosmo added, "is that you can do this wearing civilian clothes, but keep your radios on low and wear a jacket to cover the radio."

Mark chimed in, "If you need some tips on surveillance work, stop in my office. I have studied a lot about this topic in my home schooling courses."

Kosmo urged them, "OK, let's break this up and get this party started!"

After changing in their offices, everyone went to their designated areas in the core and along the outskirts of the town. Rick and Jimmy radioed in every thirty minutes at the top and half-past the hour. Mark and Beth checked in at quarter-after or three-quarters of the hour.

Mark and was given the area of Broad Street to Main and Federal Street, then onto Orange Street and then he would loop around back to Union Street. Beth decided she could do the same route only in reverse. Nothing was reported right off of any sightings. Mark was wearing his long trench coat and his fedora hat. He was walking up Main Street past the Pacific Bank when Mrs. Frechette was walking her dog down Main Street.

She saw the deputy and became all smiles. She said, "Look, Teddy! There's your friend Deputy Donato!" Teddy started barking and pulling on his leash, trying to get closer to the deputy.

Mrs. Frechette called out, "Oh, Deputy, you know how much Teddy likes you!" Teddy started jumping up and down, nudging his head into Mark's trench coat. He then ran in circles around Mark's legs, getting him all tangled up in his leash. Mark just about tripped and fell to the ground when he spotted a brown car driving right past him! It was a four-door brownish-colored Ford Falcon!

Mark tried to get untangled and his eyes were as wide open as they would go! He said gruffly, "Heel your dog, heel your dog!"

He reached for his radio, but between Teddy having Marks legs all tangled up, and the fact that he had his trench coat buttoned, it was not working out so well.

When he managed to get the radio out from underneath his coat, he pressed down on the transmit button yelling, "Deputy Donato to base!"

Mike DiFronzo was keeping Channel Six open. He radioed back, "Come in, Deputy. Over."

Mark exclaimed, "I just saw him!" and then added, "Heel, heel!" Teddy was still jumping up on Mark.

Mike cocked his head wondering, "Heel? What does that mean?"

Mark continued excitedly, "I just saw him-Mr. Brown! I mean, Mr. Falcon! I mean, get off of me, you stupid mutt!"

Mike was still tilting his head when Kosmo came live on the radio saying, "Calm down, Deputy. Where are you?"

Mark chattered into his radio, "Upper Main Street, but this silly woman, Mrs. Frechette, has her dog all tangled around my legs! Yikes!" Then he fell over onto the sidewalk, and his radio sailed out of his hands a good three feet away!

Kosmo, not being able to see the situation, waited then asked, "Did you see who was driving? Over."

Right then Mrs. Frechette scolded Mark. "You should learn some manners and respect the elderly!" She walked away with Teddy who was looking back at Mark like he had just lost his best friend.

Kosmo asked again, "Did you get a description of the driver or a license plate number? Over."

Mark grumbled into his hand-held radio, "Negative. That Mrs. Frechette's dog had me all tangled up! We ought to bring the both of them in for assaulting a police officer and interfering with an ongoing police investigation. Over." Mark sat up then got to his feet, brushing off his coat and adjusting his hat.

Kosmo told Mark, "Just take your time. Keep walking up in the direction the car went. I will be there in my own car in a few minutes. Over." Then he rebroadcast, "Base to all on Channel Six. Everyone meet at Pacific Bank, not in a group but in close proximity. I will be there in less than ten minutes with instructions to follow. Over and out."

Kosmo parked his car a few doors down on Main Street. He radioed everyone monitoring Channel Six, "First off, it seems that our suspect is still on island, and it might likely even be an island resident. Secondly, I do not think that this person has any idea that we might be onto the description of his car and himself. So, what I want to do now is for everyone fan out, two on each side of the street. The first team split up and wait five minutes so that the second officer is behind the first officer." Kosmo paused a few minutes. "Now, Rick, you go as Deputy Donato has a few minutes lead time. What we are searching for is the car. I hardly doubt that our suspect will be sitting out on a chair on a front porch waiting for us to find him."

Kosmo then said he was going to do a street-by-street grid. "I'll be driving in my personal car. Everyone remain calm and collected. Remember, if you see something, move a good distance away before taking out your radio as the suspect might just happen to be looking out a window and spot you."

The two teams were slowly but surely strolling along Main Street, acting calm, just like everyday tourists enjoying the old captains' houses. Kosmo drove up to Pleasant Street and started his street grid search.

BEAU-SEJOUR PALACE, LISBON, PORTUGAL

A list of the most haunted places in Europe wouldn't be complete without the beautiful Beau-Sejour Palace. Even though it looks like an idyllic place, the Beau-Sejour Palace isn't one of the places to stay. You would want to be cautious if you chose to stay there.

It's actually one of the creepiest places in Portugal after the sun goes down. The palace is supposedly haunted by the Baron of Gloria, whose ghost has been seen walking around the corridors and gardens of the castle by multiple witnesses. Employees at the palace also claim that objects in the castle move on their own and doors and windows close suddenly. Some visitors also claim to have heard bells ringing, despite the fact that there aren't any on the property.

Mark reached the monument at the top of Main Street. He was about to turn around when he saw the sign for the Petit Maison Guest House. He figured after scouting a few more yards he would turn around. He was at the front of the guest house, and he walked up the walkway and entered the inn. He saw a lady wearing a name tag that read 'Holly', and underneath it read 'Innkeeper.' Mark did not know Holly but had heard a few stories from people said she was a little nutty.

She greeted Mark saying, "What could I do for you, sir?"

Mark replied, "Oh, some friends of mine are planning a three-day weekend to the island, and somcone recommended your guest house. What can you tell me about your accommodations?"

Holly then started on a non-stop, one-sided conversation including, "A homemade breakfast is served to all and is included in the room price, and that coffee and tea is available also from six a.m. until six p.m., free of charge."

Mark then asked, "Do you offer parking, as my friends will bring a car with them?"

She said, "Well, they can park out front with no worry about a ticket this time of year." She went on to remark how greedy the town was writing tickets way up there on upper Main Street. She added she did not have much free parking out back, and that it is a bit of a nuisance to her business. She felt the police department should spend more time catching the crooks that invade this island in the summertime as well as all the beach partiers at night.

Holly gave another example of folks who annoyed her. "This past summer I had two teenagers rent a room, and they snuck in four others! They ran up her electric hot water bill, and they left beer cans all over the room when they departed along with several pizza boxes and soda cans. I called the police station but was told that as I have a lodging license, that I would have to call the lodging association to file a formal complaint. Anyways, we have four very nice rooms-two with a private bath, and two with a shared bath. And, as seeing it is now what we innkeeper's call 'off-season', I am sure I can get them a really good rate."

Then Mark said, "So, it's off season? Well, that's good to know. Business really slows down this time of year?"

"Yes," she shrugged. "In the summer I am booked two months straight."

Mark was reeling her in. "Putty in my hands," he thought. He would have her giving him whatever he asked for! This one was a talker! Mark picked up a brochure and asked her, "Might I be able to see the different rooms you have to offer?"

She nodded, "Sure thing! I have three of them open right now, but next weekend two are booked."

Mark felt as if he was holding all the cards in a poker game. He replied, "Really? Well, that's good, for off- season. How many are booked now?"

"Only one," she responded, "but it's a good one. The man has been here for a pretty long stretch. He is very quiet, comes and goes at different times of the night. He said he enjoys bird watching at sundown and star gazing.

He's from South America, Peru to be exact. He has told me a few nice stories about his homeland."

Mark raised his eyebrows in interest. "You don't say! Why, that's fantastic, very interesting! I thought there was a poster placed on the Hub bulletin board, with a man giving a lecture this week at the Atheneum on a talk about the different species of birds of South America.

I wonder if it's the same person? Wouldn't that be a coincidence?"

Holly asked, "Coincidence?"

"Yes," Mark explained. "I think so as I just happen to be asking for some room information, and then I mentioned about the poster I saw and the upcoming lecture at the Atheneum, and it's a coincidence I tell ya, coincidence. It's probably not the same person, though, as the one I saw on the poster was a man about thirty, with salt and pepper hair." He hoped he was onto a big clue right then and there!

Right then the phone rang on the desk. Holly excused herself, and picked up the receiver. She spoke into the phone, "Hold on one second," and put her hand over the mouthpiece. She then gestured to Mark, "You can go upstairs and see the rooms. One is labeled 'Basil.' The other two are 'Jasmine' and 'Rosemary'. They are unlocked. 'Chrysanthemum' is occupied by the single gentleman."

Mark said thanks and headed up the stairs. He glanced out the window overlooking the back driveway and saw two cars-one rusted black Jeep and a rusty brownish four-door car, but could not make out the make or model from his angle. He was <u>sure</u> it was the suspect's car, and as he turned around in the narrow hallway, he found himself face with the man in person! At least to Mark, he seemed to fit Kosmos' description!

Mark was in shock! He was stunned, not able to move. He was actually facing the killer! He tried to speak but couldn't. His legs were frozen still. He mumbled something to himself like, "Mommy, make the bad people go away!"

Despite Mark's sudden apprehension at whom he was facing, the man smiled at Mark and said, "Hello!" with a pleasant smile on his face. "There aren't many guests here right now, so it's nice to meet another person up here."

Mark was at a loss for words and just stood there. The man asked if Mark was all right, when the faintest word, 'mommy', came out of Mark's mouth.

The man looked at him puzzled and said, "Excuse me, I'm just heading out for a walk."

Mark just stood there like a deer frozen in the headlights.

Right then Holly called up the stairs, "Did you like any of the rooms?"

Mark snapped to, regrouped a bit and called back down, "Yes, everything looks fine!" He let the man pass.

He waited until the man departed and went out the front door.

He hustled downstairs, telling Holly he would be in touch soon, and exited the guest house.

Holly called after him, "I will get them a great deal!" as he closed the door behind him.

Mark noticed the man walking down Main Street towards town. Mark stepped a few feet away out of sight of the Petit Maison's windows. He got on the radio and said, "Attention Channel Six! I found our package. I repeat, I found our package! He is heading down Main Street from upper Main past the monument. He's on the east side of the street wearing a dark brown waist-length zip up coat." He released the talk button and took a breath.

Kosmo came on and said, "All units, please act natural. If you spot the suspect, do not engage. Just follow at a very safe distance."

Kosmo then radioed to Deputy Donato. "Please give me your ten-twenty."

Mark relayed that information and the fact that the suspect was staying in the room labeled 'Chrysanthemum' upstairs to the right at the Petit Maison Guest House.

Kosmo asked Jimmy and Beth to see if they could act like a couple, possibly walking arm in arm and follow the suspect.

They immediately said they had him in their sight and would do so.

Kosmo drove the longer route so that he was headed down Main Street towards the monument. He spotted Mark and pulled over to the curb. Mark hopped into the front seat. He told Kosmo how the whole story played out, that he had the innkeeper eating right out of his hands.

Mark said excitedly, "She gave up all the dirt! Our guy is from Peru, that's in South America, ya know."

Kosmo raised his eyebrows and responded, "That is one more nail in the coffin as Mr. Tonkin told Bob Moulder at the Ships Inn that he had a man in his store from Peru the day before his murder. So, what are those odds?"

Mark informed Kosmo, "The owner of the Petit Maison is named Holly. She was in the lobby of the inn when I went in, and this guy is the only one staying there at the present time."

Mark continued on, saying how he pretended he had friends who wanted to book a long weekend there, and told Kosmo the brown car is parked out back in the driveway.

Kosmo cut him off saying, "Excellent work! Now, let's go check this guy's room out."

Kosmo radioed Beth and Jimmy and said, "I need an update, especially if this guy starts heading back this way. Mark and I are at the top of Main Street. We're going to check out the Petit Maison Guest House. Jimmy, I want you to sit on the bench near Main Street and the monument. If he starts heading up towards the inn, give me four clicks on the radio button. That's all, I will get the meaning."

Beth then radioed that their suspect had entered the Tap Room. She explained to Kosmo, "Rick is stationed in the lobby at top of the stairs reading a magazine. I'm outside across the street leaning against the wall of the Languedoc, so there is no way he can slip through our net. Will keep you posted! Over and out."

THE WHALEY HOUSE, SAN DIEGO, CALIFORNIA

A private residence, this mid-19ᵗʰ century house is now a museum dedicated to its former owners and the history they created here. Part of the house was once rented out to the County of San Diego for use as a courtroom which may explain the appearance of several unidentified ghosts within the house. Apart from these unnamed apparitions, the original owner, Thomas Whaley, his wife, one of their children-a little girl, and a convict are repeatedly seen within the house. The house was apparently haunted as soon as it was built, as the spirit of a man who had been convicted and hanged on the site took up residence in the house upon its completion. The Whaley apparitions are often seen engaged in the normal activities of their former day-to-day lives. Doors have been known to close and lock on their own, and footsteps are often heard throughout the house, along with music and the crying of a baby.

Kosmo said to Mark, "Ok, let's go in."

They walked from where the car was parked, and entered the inn. Holly was delighted that Mark had brought a friend with him. She started on a one-sided nonstop conversation again, but Kosmo pulled out his badge and presented it to her. She promptly said, "Well, Chief, business was very quiet and slow this summer so I cannot contribute to the police benevolent fund this year."

Mark just rolled his eyes, recalling she had just told him that she was booked all summer.

Kosmo told her that they were not there for a donation, but he wanted information on a guest they had residing at the inn.

Holly started by saying, "Well, we don't give out private information on our guests. Their business is their business, not anyone else's."

Kosmo tried to reason with her but she was adamant. He then said, "OK, well, Holly, here is how this is going to play out. Right now, in plain sight, I can see your innkeeper's license has expired. Also, I'll bet that if I do a quick walk through that I will find your fire extinguishers are also expired and out of date for inspection. And, if you can't cooperate a bit with me, I can call the Fire Chief, Dan Connor, and have him here in, let's say, fifteen minutes. I can have the health department inspector here, also, in a very short time to see if your kitchen meets all health regulations. And then it will just go on from there. Hmm, your fines, well, they might be quite hefty. So, Holly, it's your call." Kosmo tapped on the check-in counter.

Holly, very wisely, did an about face and said, "The only guest I have registered is a man named Auriello LaValencia. His address is right here, and he has a car parked in the back."

Kosmo turned to Mark and said, "Take down his license plate number, and while you are at it, see if the car is unlocked. If so, take a look and see if the car is registered to him and if the address matches what is written here on the reservation sheet."

Holly felt puzzled and asked, "Why do you want to know about this man?"

Kosmo knew he had to keep the information under wraps. He deviated from the truth. "It has something to do with a dog that was hit, and his car matches the description. Just a routine check, that's all."

Holly asked, "Is the dog OK?"

Kosmo nodded without looking her directly in the eye. "He's fine, we just need to check this out at the owner's request. Now, if you'll please excuse me, I need to check in with my staff as there is another situation to which they are attending right now."

Kosmo placed a call out on his portable radio. "Update, Rick. Over."

"All clear."

"Update, Beth. Over."

"All clear."

"Update, Jimmy. Over."

"All clear."

He turned back to Holly. "It seems that everything is under control for the time being. Now, I need the key to his room if you don't mind."

Holly did not flinch and handed it right over to Kosmo.

Mark retuned to the front desk and told Kosmo the car is his, same address in Cambridge.

Kosmo told Mark, "Why don't you stay right here and keep Holly company. I'm going to go upstairs and look around a bit." Mark gave him the AOK sign.

When Kosmo went upstairs, Holly asked, "Now what are the dates your friends are thinking of coming? You said it was a three-day weekend?" asked Holly.

Mark put his hands up as if to say 'hold it right there.' He said, "I will get back to you on the dates."

Then she asked Mark if he might like some coffee or tea. She said, "Even though you're was not a guest, any member of the police force is a friend of mine."

Upstairs, Kosmo entered the guest room, which was neat and orderly. He opened the bureaus drawers. All the clothing was folded and neat, but underneath some tee shirts he found one photocopy sheet referring to a scepter. He murmured to himself, "Aha! We're headed in the right direction, that's for sure!" Then he searched the closet which was all in order: things neatly hung up, shoes in place. He checked the bathroom and all was in order there.

He took a set of keys which were laying on the desk and he returned downstairs to the lobby. He told Mark he would be right back. He went and searched the car under the seats and the center console. Nothing. He opened the trunk to find a paper bag. He opened it up to find some bloody rags and a bloodied sweater that had a tear in it! Kosmo was almost one hundred percent certain that the sweater matched the torn piece of cloth he had removed from Tonkin's. However, Kosmo left it where it was, returned the room key to Holly and told her, "I think you're all set here. No violations as far as I can see. Just be sure to renew your innkeeper's license soon."

Holly felt relieved and said, "Well, I hope you found everything you were looking for."

Kosmo nodded. "We are just about finished here." Suddenly Beth came on the radio. "Our package is on the move. Looks like he's heading towards Main Street. Over."

"Roger that. Over," said Kosmo. Mark started looking out the front window.

Kosmo turned to the innkeeper. "OK, Holly, you're done for the next hour or so. Why don't you go home or to your lodging if that's it out back?"

Feeling a little scared, Holly asked, "What do you mean? I'm on duty here."

Kosmo, in a polite but insistent voice said, "Well, Holly, we need to speak with this gentleman in private. So, give us an hour, and then we will knock on your door and you can come back inside the inn. We'll make sure everything is safe and sound. Don't worry."

She started to protest, but Kosmo reminded her, "We don't want those violations to come back into play, do we?"

Holly headed to a back hallway, turning to look back at the lobby. "Whatever you say, Chief."

Kosmo then radioed to Beth.

"Beth here. Over."

"Do not follow package. Return to base. Over."

"Roger that. Over and out."

Kosmo to Rick, "Chief to Rick. Over."

"Rick here. Over."

"Rick, give me three clicks on the radio if subject is heading back towards the inn. Then head back to base. Over."

"Roger that. Over and out."

About five minutes later Kosmo heard the three clicks. Mark was in chair in the lobby reading a magazine at the inn. Kosmo was in another one facing the front door, but his face was covered by a newspaper. The front door opened, and the man entered and shut the door.

Kosmo waited until the man was inside a good six feet or so to lower his paper and say, "Good afternoon, Mr. LaValencia."

Mr. LaValencia knew the minute he saw Kosmo's face who he was. He recognized him from seeing him when he had returned to the crime scene out front with the crowd that had gathered on Main Street. Trouble had arrived.

Kosmo offered in a firm voice, "Why don't you have a seat here so my deputy and I can have a chat with you."

The relaxed look on Mr. LaValencia's face faded away. Auriello hesitated for a minute and said, "No, I don't think I'll sit and chat. Not really, but do I need a lawyer?"

Kosmo asserted, "That is within your rights, but then we are going to have to detain you from this moment on at the station." He paused to let the criminal think about his words. "However, we could do this, and if you play well with us, we will play well with you."

Kosmo put up two fingers. "Now, Mr. LaValencia, in regard to a couple things: first, a dog was injured, and the car we are searching for is one that resembles yours which is parked out back. We are requesting information from all drivers of similar automobiles. And, more critically, we are interviewing people who were at the crime scene on Main Street to see if anyone has anything they might add to help us in our investigation of the death of Mr. Bob Tonkin. He was a very good man and an important member of the community here, so anything you might have seen or remember if you happened to be in the area of the crime the day it occurred."

Mr. LaValencia remained standing. He shrugged his shoulders. "I don't know who you are talking about from any crime scene."

"It just so happens we recognize you from some photos taken on the day we discovered the body of Mr. Tonkins who was killed in his antique store. What's it going to be? You play nice, we play nice."

Both Kosmo and Mark stood up, and Kosmo was a good head and shoulders taller than the suspect. Mark waited patiently, thinking to himself, "I can have this guy spilling the beans in no time! Let him try the 'lawyer stall tactic.' He won't last an hour!"

Kosmo asked quite firmly again, "How do you want to play this out? If you give us any information that we are requesting, then you can enjoy the rest of the day."

Auriello shook his head as if he didn't know anything about the situation. "I'm sorry, sir, but I don't want to get involved. I just like to keep to myself."

Mark was waiting patiently, quietly tapping his foot. He respected Kosmo way too much to interrupt.

Mr. LaValencia said, "I have to tell you, I was nowhere in the area of the murder. I don't know to what you are referring. Additionally, I have not had any parking tickets since I have been here. I am just a visiting tourist. I do not know what you are seeking from me, but I have just been walking the nice lanes of Nantucket and enjoying the peaceful surroundings." He was looking down at the floor as he gave some excuses.

Kosmo then took the situation firmly in hand. "Well, Mr. LaValencia, no matter what you assert, we have a few more questions and we do not want to do it here in a public place. We need a detailed statement from all parties we contact, and we are almost finished interviewing everyone who might have some information for us. So, if you would please come with us and let us make a report, then you will be on your way to stroll some more quiet lanes in no time should you be as innocent as you declare." Kosmo nodded to Mark to indicate his next task.

Mark escorted Mr. LaValencia to Kosmo's car. He jingled his handcuffs on his belt, though his boss had not said anything about using them.

Kosmo went and notified Holly that she could return to the lobby of the inn.

She queried, "Is everything OK? No trouble here, I hope!"

Kosmo nodded and said, "It'll all be fine. Thank you for your cooperation. We'll let you know if there is any fallout from this visit."

They placed Mr. LaValencia in the holding cell at the station. "We just want to be sure you will stay around long enough to talk with us. Let us know if there is anything you need as we have not yet made any charges against you," Kosmo informed him as he locked the door.

Mark knocked on Kosmo's office door frame. "Bad cop? Good cop?"

Kosmo already knew this was coming. "Let's let Mr. LaValencia cool it for a while. I appreciate your help. Why don't you take a break and perhaps update the others, though don't say anything that you haven't already observed. Innocent until proven guilty."

Kosmo needed time to collect his thoughts as not everything was black and white. There were still some undermining questions for which he wanted answers.

Deputy Donato was chomping at the bit and knocked again on Kosmo's door. "Hey, Chief, let's fire this interview up. I can have him chirping like a canary in no time. And, if he has two other accomplices, they might be heading south as we speak."

Kosmo knew that Mark could go off on a tangent, not thinking the whole process through. He had Mark go back into his own office to prepare for the interrogation.

While Mark was writing his questions, Mike DiFronzo walked into his office. He had just finished his shift on the dispatcher's desk. Mark looked up and said nothing.

Mike said, "Hey, Deputy, nice 'collar' on the suspect! I monitored the whole thing on Channel Six!" Mike gave Mark a thumbs up. He continued, "Now comes the interrogation process. You know, if I were you, I would sit back and think. Maybe you should approach this like a game of bowling or chess."

Mark looking up with a quizzical expression. "Really, like bowling or chess? What does that have to do with a murder investigation?"

Mike explained, "Just saying - you want to outsmart your opponent, right? So, you study how they move, like you would either in darts, bowling or chess."

Mark was about to tell Mike, "Gee whiz, thanks, but we're not playing games here."

Mike continued, "If you want to out-think them silently, watch their moves and watch their facial expressions. You can really tell a lot from a person's actions and facial expressions." He finished up saying, "Well, Mark, I have got to go. I need to hit the grocery store. Mom wants to make a lasagna for dinner and she gave me five dollars to get the ingredients. You know it takes a few hours to make, so I'd better get moving. Yeah, you guys did a good job this afternoon. Good luck."

THE HAUNTING SCREAMS OF CHATEAU MIRANDA CELLES, BELGIUM

In its prime, Chateau Miranda was one of the most beautiful castles in Belgium. However, after the 1950s it was used for housing mentally ill patients and an orphanage, and today it no longer exists due to lack of use and neglect. Many people claim to have heard screams coming from the castle despite the fact that no one lived there for years. That's why the castle got the nickname, 'Chateau de Noisy.'

Mark started to think about what Mike had mentioned, so he made more notes. He added a few more questions and thought about how a chess player would move in this line of questioning.

Still in his office considering the whole situation at hand, Kosmo made a call to Wendy and Nancy. He gave them the latest update on locating the car and the owner. He told them the man was now in a holding cell. He asked them if they could go to the Petit Maison Guest House and look to see if the car in the back parking area was the one that followed Wendy into town. Then he asked if they would come to the station and possibly identify the man that Wendy thought she saw sitting in the car when it was parked on Main Street. They agreed.

Kosmo did not want Mr. LaValencia to see the girls though, at least not at this point. So, he planned to have the shade pulled down in the interrogation room. It was quite easy for someone to see in, but if you were being interviewed you could not really see the person looking in at you through the shade.

Wendy and Nancy headed to town, feeling someone nervous and relieved at the same time. They were so ready to have this whole murder situation resolved, and they had so much on their minds with the discoveries that Nick and the professor had accomplished.

They stopped by the inn and looked for the car out back. Wendy knew it at once! Then they went to the station, and Kosmo had Wendy take a look through the screen. As she was standing there with Nancy she exclaimed, "Oh, my, that's the guy!"

Kosmo wanted clarification. "Is it the man who was driving the car you think followed you?"

Wendy had to admit, "Well, I am not one hundred percent sure, as the guy in the car had a floppy hat on, so I did not get a good look at him. But the car behind the inn is definitely the car!"

Then Nancy dropped a bombshell. "Kosmo, he's the guy who developed the photos of the scepter in Boston at the drug store! When we picked up the photos, he was very intrigued about them. He asked if we worked for a museum as it was a beautiful piece and the photos were very fine. I could tell he was quite interested in the object, but we didn't share any information about it or our photos. We just paid for them and left. Then we went to Nick's store to see what he thought about the scepter."

Kosmo quickly put two and two together. "Well, ladies, that's how he got your information! He got it off the ticket you filled out for the film. He had your address, so all he had to do was drive on down, bring his car over and locate the scepter! He probably figured Nantucket is an easy place to find something like that as no one locks their doors, that type of thing. He located your house, scouted it out, and he also followed you to get to know your moves." The girls nodded somberly in full understanding.

Kosmo went on, filling out the scenario to the best of his ability. "What he did not figure into the equation was that you might leave the scepter at an antique store to have an evaluation done on it. Thus, he had to monitor both your movements and Bob Tonkin's. He entered Bob's store and had brief talk with him. Bob asked where his accent was from, and he told Bob, 'Peru.' Luckily Bob mentioned to Bob Moulder while having dinner at the Ships Inn that he had a customer from Peru. He commented that was about the most exciting thing that happened at his store in the last few days. And I believe that this gentleman is also from Peru. I'm quite convinced we have our suspect, but we do need to let the situation play out according to the law." He gave them a thumbs up, and they both took a deep breath and relaxed.

"Why don't you two go have a drink, and you should definitely feel a lot safer tonight. Be sure to let Rusty know that we've got the situation well in hand. I'll keep you updated, and we'll get in touch with Nick and JoAnn along the way. It sure has been one trying mystery to me."

THE HAUNTING OF THE HELL FIRE CLUB DUBLIN, IRELAND

The Hell Fire in Dublin was built as a hunting lodge where Dublin elites used to gather in the 1700's. The ruins of the club are located on the top of Montpellier Hill, overlooking the adjacent Massy Woods. There have been numerous stories about black masses, animals, and even human sacrifice rituals happening in the Hell Fire Club, but that's not all. Multiple witnesses claim to have seen a satanic-like creature with a human appearance and cloven feet. Another common visitor is the ghost of a young lady who is believed to have been burned inside a barrel and rolled down the hill.

Mark went back to his desk and rechecked his notes and felt he was ready to go! Kosmo met with Mark in his office and gave him the latest update from the gals and how it was now all falling into place.

They entered the interrogation room. Mark had his official pad of paper with his notes, as did Kosmo. Mark had brought his interrogation lamp into the room. He plugged it in and shined the bright light directly on Mr. LaValencia's face.

Kosmo nodded to Mark, letting him start.

Mark sat up straight in his chair opposite the suspect at the table. "OK, Mr. LaValencia, I am Deputy Donato and I need to inform you of your rights. First, I also need to let you know that the entire session will be tape recorded for use at a later time."

Auriello LaValencia agreed to everything, waiving his rights for an attorney until such time if he changed his mind at which point the interview would cease until a lawyer was procured.

Mark started and asked Mr. LaValencia, "Would you mind if we call you Al? Your first name is a little difficult for me to pronounce." The man nodded in agreement.

Mark continued. "We are all acquaintances here now, and this will be just a little discussion to clear up a few things related to why you're here on Nantucket. Then, if everything is above board as we say, then you can go home." Mark had his pad of paper and turned it over. "OK, Al, can I get you some water or anything?"

Al shook his head. "No, I am fine." He then asked a little nervously, "How long do you think I will be here, as I was planning on checking out. I have done enough sightseeing, and it's time to head back to Boston."

Mark tapped his pencil on his notepad. "Well, Al, that depends on what you might be able to tell us. We have brought you in to see if you might be able to give us some assistance on obtaining some more facts to a murder that took place a short time back."

Al play-acted a new role. "Oh, I know, what a shame! I heard about it from the innkeeper, Holly, at the inn where I am staying. A real tragedy. But I really don't know what that has to do with me."

Mark nodded. "That's correct, Al. The man was a very well-liked person here on the island, a pillar of the community. We are very sensitive when we lose someone on this island as you may have realized, it's not very populated. Not like Boston where you indicate you now live. And, to make matters worse, his poor dog, Daisy, was left over night in the front seat of his car. Do you like dogs, Al?"

Al thought to himself, "What is this guy rambling on about? If this is how the interrogation is going to go, maybe I'll be out in no time."

Out loud to Mark he said, "Yes, I like dogs," and left it at that.

Mark asked, "So what do you do for work? Are you married or do you live alone?"

Al kept thinking, "What's the deal with the lamp shining in my eyes? Are we in some 1930's detective film?"

After Al gave all the answers to the simple questions, Mark broached, "So what brought you to the island?"

Al explained that he had some free time, knew that it was a good time to visit as things were less crowded, and he went on to say that, at first, he did not know if he would go to Martha's Vineyard or Nantucket. However, next thing he knew he had checked into the Petit Maison.

Mark then asked more pointedly, "Did you happen to be at the crime scene the day of the murder at Tonkin's store?"

Al hesitated for a moment and said, "Yes, I think I was walking by and happened to see a crowd gathering there."

"Al," Mark pursued the question, "it's either yes, you were or, no, you were not there. So, what is it, Al?"

Kosmo thought to himself, "Mark is really zeroing in on the situation. Good for him."

Al shrugged his shoulders. "Yes, I was, but only for a moment. I was walking up Main Street and saw all the commotion, so I was curious."

Mark nodded. "Great, as that's the reason we happen to have you here. We are trying to locate witnesses to this terrible event."

Al took a breath, hoping that he might actually get off the hook rather easily with these small-town cops.

"Oh, I see. Well, that's about all I can tell you. I did not witness anything. I was just walking by."

Mark shared what proof they had to corroborate his statement. "We have photos from two different photographers, and we noticed you at different times with your car on Main Street. That's how we tracked you down."

Mark was silent for a few minutes. Kosmo let him do his magic.

Al thought, again rather hopefully, "This is a piece of cake." He was ready to run back to the inn, pack his stuff and head for the hills as they were known to say in America.

Al went to stand up. "So, if that's all of it, may I be on my way?"

Mark persisted with more lightweight questions. He indicated to Al to stay seated. "We are almost done here. I'm curious. Did you visit many places on the island?"

Al stated, "Well a few. I toured the Whaling Museum and drove out to the Sankaty Lighthouse."

Mark looking and inquired, "Did you enjoy it?"

"Enjoy what?" Al asked, wondering to himself what this so-called deputy was driving at.

Mark clarified his question. "The Whaling Museum."

"Oh, very much so," answered Al, trying to play along with whatever the deputy really wanted to know.

Mark dallied along. "Really? That's nice. I understand they have a few new exhibits, and they sound very interesting. You know, my girlfriend and I tried to go there two days ago, but the funny thing is, they have been closed for the last several days. So can you explain to me how you managed to get inside?"

Al little squirmed in his seat and said, "Perhaps it was some other museum. Although sight-seeing here isn't quite like it is in Boston, heh, heh."

Mark waved his hand to brush the question aside. "We can get back to that later. Next question, have you ever been to Quaise?"

Al tried to look puzzled. "Quaise? What is a Quaise?"

"So, what you're saying is you have never been to Quaise?"

Al nodded in agreement. "Not that I know of. That's correct."

Mark said encouragingly, "Just gathering some information here. You're doing great, Al, really great.

Oh, did you happen to know Mr. Tonkin, the deceased, had another entire showroom out by the airport?" Mark was doing his utmost to stick with the 'good cop' angle to this interrogation.

Again, Al put on his puzzled expression to maintain a look of innocence. "No, why would I know that? I didn't even go into his store on Main Street. We have plenty of antique shops in Boston, and they really aren't my taste in furniture."

"No reason. Just moving along here."

Mike DiFronzo knocked on the interrogation room door. "Chief, you have a call."

Kosmo excused himself and told Mark, "Please wait until I return before asking any more questions."

Bob Moulder was on the phone. "Excuse me, Chief, and this might be nothing of any importance. I just recalled that one of my servers, the night before Bob Tonkin was killed, made a remark to me. We were talking about some of the foreigners not leaving very good tips when they visit the island. She said, 'Just a short time ago I had this customer. He kind of looked like an owl. He had short greyish-black hair, and a round face. He was sitting at a table in the lounge. He said was from Peru when she asked him where his accent was from.' Perhaps I didn't mention it to you, but Bob Tonkin told me a day or two later that he had a guy in his shop from Peru. I'm not sure it means anything but thought I would put it out there to you. If he was trying to get any information from Mr. Tonkin, the man, well, he could have followed him here, sat down close by and maybe overheard Mr. Tonkin mention something? Just my thoughts, perhaps they don't connect in any way."

Kosmo thanked him and went back into the interrogation room.

Mark picked up on a new line of questioning. "Thinking about the animal that got hit by a car that reportedly looked like the one you were seen in from the photos, would you mind if we borrowed your keys and took a gander at your car?"

Al looked over at Kosmo who was motionless.

Mark explained, "You see, Al, one other thing that witnesses said was there was a reddish car, or perhaps it was brown in color. We are asking all owners of similar colored cars in town to take a look at their car. A dog was injured the other evening. The dog is OK, but it has a broken paw. The person who did it is responsible for the veterinarian bill. On this island, with the fog that rolls in, sometimes a driver has no idea if they hit something or if it was a pot hole."

Al, starting to get a bit impatient with the zig-zag nature of all the questions, snapped back, "Well, I never hit any dog, if that's what you're asking."

Mark retorted, "See, there's the answer, so you have nothing to worry about. We will give your car a once over and then you are on your way."

Al hesitated. "I don't have my keys on me. I had been out walking when you met up with me at the inn."

Mark said, "No problem. Please tell us where to find your keys and we will bring it down here. Once we're done inspecting it, you drive away!"

Kosmo thought, "I'm very pleased that we have that nasty evidence in the trunk. Now we're getting somewhere."

Al figured to himself, "They are not going to find any broken lights or damage to the front of the car, nor any dents or dog hair." He explained where his keys should be located at the inn.

Kosmo said, "This has been a bit of a long sit. Al, why don't we just have you go back to the cell for a stretch. We'll give you something to eat and drink, and we'll resume our questioning when the car is delivered here."

Having the keys in his pocket, Kosmo gave them to Jimmy Jaksic who went up to the inn, drove the car to the station and parked it out front.

Kosmo and Mark walked out, and Kosmo said, "When we go back in, ask him if he's ever been to the Ship's Inn."

Kosmo searched the trunk again, this time a little more thoroughly. Under the spare tire he found a thin bladed hacksaw, along with the bag containing the bloodied torn sweater.

Kosmo and Mark came back inside, had Al rejoin them in the questioning room, and Kosmo said "Hmm, that's not the car that was reported to have struck the dog. All is good in that department."

Mark chimed in. "I have another question. While you were here on the island did you go to the Ship's Inn for a drink or some food?"

Al patiently replied, "No, never heard of it."

Kosmo then told Mark, "Let's wind this up and let Mr. LaValencia get back to the inn so he can pack up and make the ferry. Mark, bring your notes out front. Mr. LaValencia, we will have this report typed up. I'm sorry you'll have to continue to wait in the cell. We will be right back, and if all seems set, then you'll be free to go."

Mark paused and turned to Al. "I almost forgot, Al. One more teeny thing. Do you know either a lady by the name of Wendy Dow or one named Nancy Eblen?"

Again, Al shook his head. "No, I can't say that I do."

Mark turned to go out to the front office, stopped and gently hit the heel of his hand on his forehead. "You know what? I am not sure where my head is today. I forgot *one* more question. Do you know happen to know what a scepter is?"

Al stopped behind Mark. "Oh my, things are getting a little warm for my comfort level," he thought to himself. "Maybe these guys aren't quite as provincial as I've been hoping." Responding to Mark he replied, "Pardon me, but a what?"

Mark attempted to enlighten him. "A scepter. It's like a baton with jewels embedded in it."

Al played along as he had been all the time. "No, not really. I can't say that I've ever heard of such a thing."

"Well, OK. I do need to ask you to wait in the cell again. Let me go out with Kosmo. We will get this report typed up, and if you'd like, you may have a copy. We will be with you shortly. Oh, and your keys are with Mike at the dispatch desk."

Al waived his hand so indicate that they needn't bother with the report. "I don't need a copy. I just hope I was able to help." He crossed his fingers in his pockets.

Kosmo closed and locked the cell. "We will be right back. We need you to read over the report then sign and date it, stating that it's as truthful as you know to have us believe, and then you're free to go."

THE HOUSE OF NO RETURN
CA'DARIO, ITALY

This architectural masterpiece is known among locals as the 'house of no return'. This is a worthy nickname, considering the bad things that happened to anyone who ever owned this building. The first owner and original designer lost both of his children (murder and suicide) while they lived in the house. After that, 13 successive owners died under mysterious circumstances. Needless to say, this house is abandoned today and doesn't have an owner.

Kosmo and Mark went into Kosmo's office. Kosmo said "So, Mark, I am quite surprised at the method you used in there. You remained very calm and collected. Good job so far. Now we just need to get him to confess."

Mark countered, pleased with praise from his boss, "I decided to use one of the tactics from my home-study courses that I was brushing up on a few weeks ago. It was called 'Interrogations' and had a lot of good stuff in there. I sent my summary in the self-mailer and got an 'A' and a note from them saying I was excelling in my studies. You see, I was using what they refer to as the 'chess method.' Slowly but surely you study your opponent's movements."

Beth typed up the report given to her from Kosmo's dictation. He then reviewed it with Mark and said, "I am giving you the lead on this, Deputy."

Beth was grinning ear to ear. She was proud of Mark's efforts on the job. She gave him a wink.

Mark and Kosmo returned to the interrogation room along with Mr. LaValencia. Mark read the report out line- for-line with the responses that Mr. LaValencia had given them. Mark said, "I need you to sign here stating that this is as truthful as you can confirm on the questions that were presented to you. As stated, this will be filed away if we should have any other questions at a later date."

Mark then asked in his most serious voice and while looking firmly at the suspect. "One more time, this is what you swear to us as the best of your knowledge? And, you know that it is against the law to lie to a police officer?"

Mr. LaValencia said, "Yes," and signed it. As he rose out of his chair, he was all smiles. He thought to himself, "Well, this weasel is going to get away!"

Mark commented, "So, Al, this was a lot of help to us to start solving this murder case. We don't get very many here on the island. But why don't you take a seat for a few more moments? You see, I have a few things that need to be cleared up."

Al, looking puzzled, slowly retook his seat.

Mark took his notepad and tapped on it. "You see, Al, I am going to give you my theory on how Mr. Tonkin was murdered. I am sure you would want to know the inside scoop, wouldn't you?"

Al shook his head vehemently. "No, not really! What I really would like is to go back to the inn, pack up and get my car on the ferry. I'm a little tired of what feels like a 'cat and mouse game' to me. If you don't mind, I'd really like to leave."

Mark nodded and gave him an understanding smile. "Well, Al, all in due time. You know, we have a saying on Nantucket, 'There's always the next ferry!' Kind of catchy, isn't it? Why rush off when you are in such a lovely place in the world! So, Al, let me explain it to you."

Mark settled back a bit in his chair, and Kosmo did the same, putting all his fingers together in front of himself. He was eager to see how Mark would proceed.

Mark started in. "So, there are these two women, Wendy and Nancy, who live here on the island. They are the two ladies I asked if you might know them, and your answer was 'no'. However, Al, they took some very nice photos of a scepter they had discovered, but you told us you did not know what a scepter was. It turns out that they took the film to the Rexall Drug Store in Boston, the one of which you happen to be the photo department manager. It seems they returned the next morning and picked up the eight-by-tens, and then they went on their merry way." He paused to let the image set in with Al.

Mark pointed his pencil at Al. "What they did <u>not</u> know is that you made a set of copies, and you also had their name and address that you copied off their process form. The next thing, according to my thinking, is that you realized they had something possibly quite valuable in their possession, and it would be a 'piece of cake' to head down to Nantucket and steal the item. I'm wondering if any of this might be ringing true in your mind, Al?"

Al just sat there, stone-faced.

Mark picked up his thread of discussion. "But the situation becomes a little more difficult, as they ended up meeting with Mr. Tonkin, who now adds another element to as where the scepter is actually stored. Are you following me?"

Al nodded slightly.

"So, you then headed out to Quaise, a place you stated you had never been to. But their cat happened to spot you in the brush one day. The first time you staked out the property, but they paid it no mind. These women just thought it might be a deer that the cat was looking at. However, they had an eerie feeling about it. The next time you were at their property, it was quite late at night-the early morning hours to be exact. Wendy just happened to be in the kitchen with no lights on, and she spots you roaming the property. She started to feel suspicious but couldn't pin down any criminal act at this point." Mark stopped for a drink of water and a quick glance at his boss, who gave a subtle nod.

"Then a few days later, Wendy drove into town and headed for the bank. Yet she had a feeling she was being watched or followed. She parked on Main Street, heads into the bank, and when she comes out, she crosses the street and walks down the sidewalk behind your car. She spotted you sitting your car on lower Main Street wearing a floppy hat. But she was at a loss as to what to do. So, these gals just blew that off, thinking you are in town picking up your wife at the hair salon or from shopping. Not enough criminal activity to confirm any suspicions yet. However, a day later, while these two someone worried women are out and about, they return to find their cat, who was outside when they left, now inside the home. How do you think the cat got inside, Al? Do you think this super cat opened a window and climbed in?"

Al just shrugged.

Mark moved right along. "The next thing, lo and behold, they discovered that someone had broken in through the basement entrance. Any of this sound familiar, Al?"

He did not respond, just looked at the desktop.

"Also, Al, you stated to us that you had never been to the Ships Inn. Well, you know the waitress who served you while you were at the restaurant there? She remembers you quite well as you told her you were from Peru when she inquired about your accent. It turns out that Bob Tonkin, the innocent shopkeeper, also told Mr. Moulder, the manager at the Ship's Inn, that he had a customer from Peru in his store as well one day, right around that time."

Mark leaned in towards Al and pointed his pencil at him again. He spoke more firmly and loudly. "I have got to tell you, Al, we are one hundred percent sure the waitress will pick you out in a line up if requested. And, another thing, Al, the constable and myself, well, we think that the that the odds are very low of two different men from Peru visiting this island at the same time. You've seen that it's a very small island. And that has helped us do our job very well." Mark tapped his pencil on his pad three times.

Al thought to himself, "Yeah, you aren't quite the dummies I had you pegged for. You've been on my tail longer than I would have guessed."

Mark went on. "Another thing is that Mr. Tonkin never reported any break-ins at his warehouse in the past. But oddly enough, someone has been entering it recently, since his death. We've done our homework on that front. We might also add that it seems that someone, and not the cleaning lady, has also entered his home. We were going to do a canvass search with all the neighbors, as we understand Mr. Tonkin had two very nosy neighbors that have nothing better to do than see who's coming and going on his street. If we had performed that door-to-door canvass, what do you think we would find out? Any guesses, Al?"

Al once again shrugged his shoulders.

Marked picked up the pace. "Our hunch was that one or both of those two busy-bodies would remember seeing a car that resembles the one you drive, and when we asked them first to describe it, then if we showed them the photos of your car, what do you think they would say? Remember, I told you this is a small island."

Mark sat up straight and held up his notepad. "Now, as we add up all these inconsistencies with your interview, they are stacking up pretty fast. Is there anything you might want to correct on your statement that you signed? Now's your chance. Remember, we offered to play 'nice' if you played 'nice.'"

Mr. LaValencia did not move.

Mark chuckled a little bit. "And just remember, Al, only a few hours ago you stated that you were here doing all sorts of sightseeing, and you said that you enjoyed the Whaling Museum which has been closed for several days. That was a little odd, wouldn't you agree?"

Mark held up a large manila envelope with the photos they had gathered. "Then we have photo documentation of you at the crime scene. In our realm, one known fact is people love to return to the scene of the crime in which they were involved. And the types of crime that stand out for repeat visits by the suspect are -can you guess, Al? Let me tell you - they are arson and murder scenes. Hmm, is this starting to hit home, Mr. LaValencia?"

Al wiggled slightly in his chair, but he knew enough to keep his mouth shut.

Mark was in his element as he knew he had plenty of substantiated evidence to nail this guy. "Moving onto the next step that has developed: in your car we discovered a few things. You gave us permission to look at your car, so we did. Kosmo looked inside the car and discovered nothing of any importance in the seats. But he did notice something that was partially hanging outside the closed trunk lid. So, he opened it to tuck the object back inside correctly. Do you know what he found Al?"

Al shrugged as if to say, "Yeah, I know."

Mark looked over at Kosmo, then leaned in, as he knew this was the nail to put in the coffin lid. "He found several things. One was an envelope containing the exact same photos the girls had developed. Then there was a hack saw, one that seems to be possibly the tool that was used to cut through the dead bolt of the back French doors of Mr. Tonkin's Antique Shop."

Mark then made an expression as if to say he was sorry and couldn't do anything about the deal. "And here's the key part, Al. Kosmo found, a few days after the murder, a torn piece of fabric at the murder scene. It was something that, upon our first search of the crime scene at Tonkin's store, was overlooked. There was a torn piece of fabric on a chair frame, and we have a feeling that it just might be a perfect match to the bloodied sweater that is in a paper bag inside your trunk. What do you say to that?"

Mr. LaValencia did not respond except to say, "I want a lawyer."

Kosmo said, "Yes, you have that right and one will be requested. But let me add one thing. You know your goose is cooked here, and to save a lot of time and hassle and expense, if you will write out a full confession, I can make that go a long way in your favor. If not, we will play hard ball. This is a small island with a close-knit community. We all work together, and it could have a tremendous effect on your sentencing if we have to prove all the things that we have found out already. I mean, a huge effect. This has been and will be a lot of work, and it will be very obvious to a jury what has transpired on your behalf. It's your choice."

Mr. LaValencia said, "OK, bring me a pad of paper and a pen."

THE MANY GHOSTS ON NANTUCKET ISLAND

The Nantucket Historical Association's '1800 House' on Mill Street seems benign enough these days. To look at the recently renovated two-story house from outside, one simply sees a restored building, home to many of the NHA's workshops, but otherwise, not too much else. Its restored interior, though representatively true to its historic origins, may also manifest nothing out of the norm, but this has not always been so. The '1800 House' is just one of many buildings on Nantucket that have reportedly been haunted by the ghosts of the long-departed.

Additionally, the old Wood Box Inn on Fair Street has the ghost of a little girl who sits by the main fireplace.

And in the well-known Jared Coffin Hotel people report hearing screams and voices during the night in the upper hallways. Along with that one, 19 Broad Street is reported to have the ghosts of the original Three Sisters Inn, up in the cupola.

The 'Oldest House' is believed to be haunted by the original farmer who resided there and is upset at all the people taking photos of the property

In the building at 20 Broad Street, to this day, there are reports that a little girl who died in the home is full of mischief and locks the upstairs bathroom door. She has been known to issue giggles, and it is reported that she knocks things over from time to time while people are dining in the small dining room on the second floor.

With the murder case wrapped up, things were buzzing all over the town. Mark was talking to anyone who would listen to him tell how he cracked the case wide open. He informed them that Kosmo had given him full reign on the interrogation process. He also let it be known that this elusive and supposedly brilliant man from Peru had many tricks up his sleeve as he was a past operative for the secret police in Lima. Thus, Mark had his work cut out for him!

But, in sharing his prowess, Mark pointed out he cautiously had studied the suspect's eye movements during the interrogation process and knew when he had him trapped in a lie. Mark described how he had him squirming at times and he thought the guy was going to fall out of his chair!

The police department, with the help of some of Kosmo's former colleagues in Boston, learned that the guy had a nick name of the 'Avenger', as he liked to squash his prey while they were in jail in South America, forcing his suspects to confess in Lima.

But Mark 'out-foxed the fox,' as he liked to say!

The paper did a front-page story, and Kosmo authorized them to have Mark be the feature in the article, just as long as Kosmo could proofread it for any corrections that might be needed in the story before having it go to press.

People were stopping Mark on the street after it hit the stands! He felt like a hero, and perhaps he really was!

Kosmo went to the Languedoc and made a reservation for the entire staff, and, of course, Judy was always included. He went over the menu ahead of time with Neil, the chef, and Allan, the front-of-the-house supervisor. They were to start with a platter of bacon- wrapped fresh Nantucket Bay scallops, followed by a platter of clams steamed in 'Rainwater Madeira.'

The next course was to be individual lobster soufflés. The entrée would be a platter of chicken thighs braised in red wine with pearl onions, peas and Portobello mushrooms. Dessert was planned as individual bowls of caramel-crunch ice cream with butterscotch cookies.

For the night of the actual dinner, everyone arrived dressed in their best outfits. The wines were served in this order: a French Meursault, followed by a French Chablis, 'Premier cru', Sancerre from the Loire Valley, and a red Burgundy. The dessert wine was from Inniskilin, Canada.

The slush fund at the station had grown to a large amount which Kosmo was allowed to use any way he saw fit. Sitting back before the final treat, he told everyone at the table, "We are going to do this more often!"

A large cake was brought out along with the ice cream, decorated with a large frosted badge reading: *'Congratulations, Deputy Donato!'*, which Judy had arranged to be made at the bakery for the dinner party!

EPILOGUE

Jimmy Jaksic remained gainfully employed with the Nantucket Police Department but was still working a few nights a week at the Languedoc as a server.

Rick Blair and his dog, Madaket, continued doing the "'Sconset Whisperer" tours in the village.

Steve Turrentine and Allen Bourgeois were presented with a certificate of thanks from the Nantucket Police department.

Rusty Riddelberger kept on with project after project at the property in Quaise. His apartment that he built above the barn was an envy to all his friends with the sweeping views of the moors.

Bob Moulder told people that his staff and he were a big help in the solving of the murder.

Robert Romanos stopped by his old property in Quaise that he sold to the girls, as he loved seeing the transformation it had taken on

All of the guys from the men's club formed a handy man group simple called "The Men's Club." They spent more time at the VFW hall talking about prospective jobs than working on any.

George Williams teamed up with Tom Kendrick and Don Mignosa. They were on a roll, purchasing homes, mainly in 'Sconset, and remodeling them and selling them almost as soon as the last coat of paint was dry. Tom Kendrick was also in search of other rundown properties at the request of Don Mignosa.

Duke was a standard guest every Sunday at the dinner table in Quaise, never missing a dinner. He always brought fresh flowers and a jug or two of wine.

Susanna Groskowsky, Sylvia Lussier and the Contessa, Mariangela Biagiotti, all had plans to meet in Tuscany at one of the Contessa's vineyards for a week-long get together.

Marie Lafrontiere was still bartending at numerous restaurants all over the island. She had a very large group following her to every bar when she worked. Some were now touting themselves as her personal bodyguard if anyone disrespected her.

Elisa De Corso received the most beautiful six-carat diamond on her twenty-fifth wedding anniversary that was selected personally by Nick Caselli and sent via private carrier to 'Clos De Tart.'

Don Mignosa kept finding real estate project after real estate project to keep himself busy. Don and Rita met with Kosmo every Monday for coffee and a Danish.

Carol McGarvey was now the new owner of Daisy and could not be happier.

Marshmallow still let out a loud 'meow' moments before the phone rang at Nancy and Wendy's house.

Mrs. Frechette would bake cookies every few weeks and drop them off at the police station where she was best friends with everyone in the department. Mike DiFronzo asked her for some of the recipes and wanted to know if she could make some brownies - the chocolate fudge ones.

June Hutton kept a private table off to the side on the nights that Mark called in advance at the Tap Room. He also asked the owners of the hotel if they might possibly have a small plaque mounted on the wall above the table, stating that it was the 'Official Birthplace of Spy Nights.'

Mike DiFronzo began taking some cooking classes at the high school. His real estate classes were still on hold for now. He made the cover of *Bowling Magazine* as one of the top ten bowlers in Massachusetts. He still lives with his mom.

Nick Caselli received a letter from Professor Achilles who gave Nick a lead on a person named 'Richard' who resided in Chicago. Richard, as it seemed, was a collector of rare coins and other antiques as well as vintage cars.

Richard, too, it turned out, had great wealth. A photo, along with a letter, was sent to Richard. Then Nick was asked if he could bring some of the coins to Chicago. They had a very productive meeting. Richard said he would take every coin in the lot and added a twenty- percent mark-up to secure them all.

Nick and JoAnn made all the arrangements for the 'Scepter of Dagobert' to be on loan to numerous museums. The figure that he quoted the girls for the monthly royalty check was actually much higher than first estimated.

Doreen Burliss never missed a deadline at the *Inquirer and Mirror* newspaper. She still figured that one day she would be covering a story on how Deputy Donato and Mike DiFronzo ended up shooting each other by accident! The only problem with that scenario was Mike's mom would never let him own a gun.

Nancy and Wendy's business grew at an impressive rate: they now were averaging a four-month backlog on their window boxes. The check arrived like clockwork on the first of every month from the traveling scepter. They contacted a man in Boston that Don and Rita recommended by the name of Ken Zises who managed their newfound fortune from the gold coins along with the monthly check from the traveling scepter. Upon his advice they added to the original investment amount slowly, as not to raise suspicions. Mr. Zises sent them into 'the stratosphere', financially, on all the investments, and advised these now wealthy women to let the dividends be reinvested.

Kosmo did not consume a red onion for quite a while. Judy, Duke and he enjoyed many a great cookout on his newly upgraded patio, much improved with the help of Wendy, Nancy, Judy, Rita, and Don as the designers. Of course, Duke a managed a special deep discount for the materials.

Ted Hudgins and Sheila Lucey talked every day. Ted asked Sheila what she thought of mine-sweeping equipment for the harbor, as one never knows when a Russian sub might slip in. She told him, "Well, I can request it, but I do not think it is on the Coast Guard's 'high priority' list. Ted's most recent quote was at the lady's club luncheon where he was seated at the head table. He ended the talk with, 'The thrill of victory, the agony of defeat.'

The super model, Inese Romanovska, with whom Mark had a photo taken while she was on the island with Henry Kissinger, wrote Mark a personal letter after he sent her two letters. She enclosed a color eight-by-ten photo of herself, personally signed, with a red lipstick kiss, and "*XOXO.*"

John Acton kept a red onion always fresh at hand just in case Kosmo made the call. John, Kosmo and Judy tried to get together at the Faregrounds Restaurant every week or so to enjoy a cold beverage together.

Krebs, Marty McGowen, Eelskin Joe, and Hunter LaRoche were seen loading several duffle bags onto an eighty-five foot sailboat by Ted Hudgins. He thought how nice it was that the three men were going for a long sail upon such a beautiful sail boat. He bid them good luck and smooth sailing as he watched them heading out of the harbor. The four of them arrived back on the island in the quiet darkness at two in the morning two weeks later, pulling up to the Wauwinet Hotel dock, where a waiting truck driven by Jeffery Cook, aka 'Cooker,' was backed up at the dock.

Mark and Beth were still quite the talk of the town on 'Spy' nights. The list grew longer and longer each week with people wanting to dress up and join them on the progressive dinners.

Mark sent in a very detailed typed letter to *True Detective* magazine where he was featured for his arrest of the murderer, Auriello LaValencia, a ruthless criminal from Lima, Peru. He received fifty dollars for his submission. He also included numerous action photos taken by Mike DiFronzo. One was selected for a full-page blow-up on page twenty! Mark bought several copies and mailed them to friends and family.

Eileen Berg was becoming ever so popular, both as a well- trusted lawyer and advisor on financial matters and as a first-class defense attorney in DUI cases on Nantucket and Martha's Vineyard.

FINALE

Kosmo and Judy were having dinner with Don and Rita at Cioppinos. Kosmo looked across the dining room and saw Hunter LaRoche and his cronies at a table in the corner. Eelskin Joe had a large briefcase under the table. Kosmo nudged Don and nodded over to the corner table. Kosmo shrugged his shoulders as if to say, "Hmm, I wonder what they're up to?"

Kosmo said, "Out of sight, out of mind."

Don smiled and said, "You know, I always used to carry a briefcase. But now the funds I have, well, they won't fit inside one anymore!"

Kosmo chuckled. "Well, I can only imagine where the rest of the personal files of that briefcase are at, but I'll bet it's a large file cabinet!"

When Don requested the dinner bill, Tracy, the owner came over and said that their tab was all set, paid for by an anonymous donor: tab, tax and tip, the whole shebang. Then Tracy crooked his index finger and hinted, "You all have a *leetle* surprise waiting for you at the bar!"

They got up and walked over to the polished granite-topped bar. Placed on top of the bar was a magnum of Krug Rose Champagne and a note saying, 'To my good friends-enjoy! Signed, Billy C.'

The following week, Judy and Kosmo checked into the Chatham Inn on the Cape using the gift certificate that Judy had won. The Inn was extraordinary! Each of their rooms had a working well-stocked fireplace, a Jacuzzi tub and a separate shower. Judy's room was stocked with three bottles of wine; a selection of red, white and rose, with a note saying they could be exchanged for any wine of the same price if requested.

They enjoyed fabulous lunches and dinners, cheese and appetizers in the lobby nightly, saunas, steam-baths and massages. Every night they would toast each other saying how good it was to be such close friends.

And, folks, that's the end of this story, I sincerely hope you enjoyed this fun adventure...

Hunter Laroche

The *next* adventure in the Hunter LaRoche Murder Mystery Series, Book number seven, is: *Murder at the Three Sisters Inn.* Ahh, the plot thickens!!!

CPSIA information can be obtained
at www.ICGtesting.com
Printed in the USA
BVHW041831270622
640757BV00004B/18

9 781665 563550